Having a lovely time

JENNY ECLAIR

TIME WARNER
BOOKS

TIME WARNER BOOKS

First published in Great Britain in January 2005 by Time Warner Books
This paperback edition published in July 2005 by Time Warner Books

ISBN 0 7515 3605 9

Typeset in Palatino by
Palimpsest Book Production Limited, Polmont, Stirlingshire
Printed and bound in Great Britain by Clays Ltd, St Ives plc

Time Warner Books
An imprint of
Time Warner Book Group UK
Brettenham House
Lancaster Place
London WC2E 7EN

www.twbg.co.uk

For Geof and Phoebe
and 'The House on the Hill'

1

In the Beginning at the End of the Day

Guy Jamieson is on his way home from work. His wife, Alice, thinks he uses public transport, getting off at the bus stop round the corner on the main road. He doesn't. Guy can't stand rush-hour buses; they smell of poor people, of sweat and despair.

Five minutes ago he got a black cab to drop him at the local off-licence, where he bought a bottle of blood-red Shiraz from a man behind a metal grille. A grey-furred Alsatian lurked in the corner, one eye gone milky.

I live in a dump, thinks Guy. There are bones on my street. They could be Kentucky cast-offs but they look like babies' knees, gristle and sinew. I am thirty-nine years old, I am a married man, I am a father.

The blue plastic bag twists round his wrist. He bought a litre bottle; the normal-sized ones are never enough. On the corner stands a girl of fifteen or so, an inhaler in one hand and a cigarette in the other. She is pregnant, with skinny arms, skinny legs and a Humpty-Dumpty belly. She shouts up at an open window, 'Come outside, Bernice, you slag.'

'Fuck off,' comes the reply.

Oh the joys of south London, Guy thinks, sidestepping a shiny orb of fresh phlegm. Gob, dog shit and up-the-duff schoolgirls.

As he crosses the road, his pride and joy Timothy Little lace-ups

(£130 per shoe) crunch on ruby shards of broken tail-light. Nearly home.

Guy casts a critical eye over Number 3 Derrington Road, as if he were a prospective buyer viewing the property for the first time. Victorian, single bay, end of terrace, three bedrooms – four if you went up into the loft. It's nothing special – there are millions of them. His just happens to have a navy-blue front door.

The paintwork needs doing and the clematis is dead. Boredom washes through his veins and his head feels granite heavy. 'I can't be bothered. I don't want to live here any more.'

The gate is rusty and he almost has to lift it off its hinges to open it. Ten years ago he and Alice first walked up this path – Max in a buggy, Alice fretting about being late, the tell-tale pink nerve rash creeping like poison ivy above her collar. 'The estate agent said eleven. It's ten past, Guy.'

She could have saved her breath. The estate agent wasn't there. What with this being a Saturday morning in 1994 he was under the duvet worrying about possible Ecstasy-induced brain damage.

We were so young, reflects Guy. I had optimism and Alice had fluffy golden curls and smooth freckled cheeks. These days, grey frizzes through her hair and her cheeks have become jowls. A reel of old memories plays pictures in his head: he and Alice standing on the threshold of their future. 'Well, go on then,' Alice had urged, 'ring the bell.'

A woman had answered the door in a towelling dressing gown. 'Oh,' she muttered, 'I suppose you've come to have a sniff around the place, have you? Come in, I'm not going to apologise about the mess because to be quite honest I couldn't give a flying fuck.'

Alice gave a small cough, scratched her neck and nodded her head at Max as if to say: Actually, we don't swear in front of our child.

The woman gave Max a cursory glance. 'Boy, is it? You poor cow. I've two of them and a girl, more fool me.'

The hall was full of packing cases; a guitar with its strings adrift poked out of one of them. The three of them did an awkward dance around the boxes.

'I'm Alice,' tittered Alice, as if her name was a really good punchline. 'This is Guy, my husband,' she added, her wedding band still shiny and new, 'and this little fellow is Max.'

'I'm Sonia.' The woman threw her name over her shoulder. 'Coffee?'

'That would be lovely, thank you,' replied Alice, and they followed the woman down a narrow corridor.

The entire kitchen seemed to be hanging off its hinges. All the cupboard doors were open and a packet of rice had erupted over the floor. They ground their way in. 'Kitchen, obviously,' sneered Sonia. 'French windows.'

There was a crack in the left-hand pane of glass; beyond the grimy windows, a garden drooped listlessly.

A baby sat in a high chair with what looked like a badly cut face. 'Bloody hell, Hugo,' the woman snapped, picking a filthy rag out of the sink and wiping the child's jam-smeared chops. She chucked the rag back into the sink, opened the fridge and sniffed a pint of milk. 'Have to be black, unless I can tempt you to anything stronger.' She laughed but her eyes filled with tears. 'Sorry.'

A girl with matted hair sidled through the door. Alice guessed she might be about eight. She was still in her nightie. Pouring herself a bowl of cereal, she got a spoon out of a drawer and walked off.

'Verity's eight,' explained Sonia. 'I've a thirteen-year-old goes by the name of Harry, and this one, the mistake, is Hugo.'

'Hello,' said Alice, who prided herself at being good with children now that she had one of her own. Hugo arched backwards in the chair. 'I think you've missed a bit of jam on his cheek,' ventured Alice. One side of the baby's face was still dark red.

'It's a birthmark,' snapped Sonia, sitting down. Guy suddenly realised she was naked under the robe. If she leant a little more to the left he might catch a glimpse of nipple. Suddenly the woman hauled herself up. 'Oh just help yourselves. I've a shitty headache, I'm going back to bed.' And with that she exited, leaving the baby with his mouth open and a battery in his hand. Quick as a flash Alice removed the Duracell AAA from Hugo's soggy fist.

'He could have swallowed it,' she gasped.

When Alice had been in the top class at primary school all the children had been given photocopied black-and-white pictures of a kitchen to colour in. Once they had done this (without going over the lines), they were meant to circle a number of health and safety hazards featured in the picture. A pan (with its handle turned out), a sharp knife (not put safely away in a drawer), a bottle of bleach (lid off), a toaster (with a frayed flex), a box of matches that should have been 'out of reach of children'. Eleven-year-old Alice had dutifully drawn big red rings around all the danger zones. She always was a sensible girl.

Once upon a time, Guy had needed this. Alice was his port in a storm, a metaphorical Rennie of a woman who had calmed his queasy heart. She could drive, assemble a flatpack of IKEA shelves, sort the bills, dress a wound, use a compass. Alice could do anything, apart from make pastry.

Rather than leave Max in 'this death trap of a kitchen', Alice lifted him from the buggy and, making sure that Sonia's cigarettes and lighter were out of 'poor little Hugo's' reach, the three of them tiptoed through the house.

'It's within our budget,' murmured Guy. There was a half-eaten Chinese takeaway on the sitting-room floor alongside an empty bottle of wine and a full ashtray. 'Hazarding a guess,' he added, 'I'd say divorce.'

Alice agreed. 'Very sad,' she tutted, hugging Max a bit more tightly.

Still, the rooms were a decent size and the original fireplaces were still in situ. They climbed the stairs. A couple of the banister rails were loose and there was scribble on the walls.

In the back bedroom Verity was playing with a pile of Barbies. They looked like they'd been in a motorway pile-up, naked and limbless. 'Hello, darling,' Alice said brightly. The girl ignored her. 'Disturbed,' whispered Alice. 'Nice light room, mind,' she added, a bit louder.

They peered into the bathroom next. 'Lino needs replacing,' said Guy, and Alice nodded: 'So does the toilet roll.'

A quarter landing led up to another bedroom on the left. 'Smells like teenager,' ventured Guy. The curtains were shut and the walls were smothered in Heavy Metal posters sellotaped at odd angles right up to a purple ceiling.

'Just a lick of paint, maybe a nice cheery yellow,' Alice whispered, genuinely feeling sorry for this house, all scribbled on and smelly.

The master bedroom was at the front of the house. Sonia lay under limp sheets; on the table next to her lay another brimming ashtray, another packet of cigarettes, a jar of paracetamol and a bottle of Diet Coke. She pulled herself up on her elbows. The pillows behind her were grubby with make-up, smears of orange foundation, streaks of black mascara. 'So what do you think?'

'It's really nice,' replied Alice, a bit lamely.

'Well, it's got to go, now that the shit's done a runner.' Sonia lit a cigarette. 'We were going to have an extension but his cuntiness has decided that he'd rather go and live with a twenty-seven-year-old Portuguese lap-dancer, arsehole! Seventeen years of marriage down the khasi. You never think it's going to happen to you' – Alice passed her the ashtray – 'so here I am, forty, three kids and I'm going home to Mother. Fucking joke, that's what it is.'

No one laughed. Alice noticed a dent in the wall. Sonia's eyes followed hers: 'Typewriter,' she coughed. 'Chucked it at his fucking head.'

Well really, thought Alice, there's no need for 'language'. She instinctively covered Max's ears. He'd now heard more swearing in thirty minutes than he'd ever heard in his life. She backed out of the door. Guy followed her. A red lace bra got tangled on his shoe. 'We'll be in touch,' he said. And they were.

The day the estate agent told them their offer had been accepted, Alice was so thrilled she bought a bottle of sparkling white wine and allowed Guy to have sex with her on the sofa during *Have I Got News for You*. Some months later they worked out that was the night Alice got pregnant again.

Hoorah, a new house and a new baby on the way! What's more, the surveyor found a damp patch and managed to knock another £6,000 off the asking price! 'How lucky we are,' gloated Alice, rubbing her belly in glee. Poor old Sonia. Alice felt a good deal of pity for her. But surely she must have been partly to blame?

Ten years ago – a different decade, a different millennium, when Alice was still the right side of fat and bothered to wear her contact lenses. She has let herself go, thinks Guy sourly, and I haven't. I am trim and well dressed; on a good day I look like Clark Kent. I have a good head of dark auburn hair and all my own teeth.

Guy feels oddly disconnected. He can feel his keys in his pocket: a Chubb and a Yale hang from a chunky silver ring (Conran), but rather than reach for them, he rings the bell. The words 'Hi, honey, I'm home' dance silently at the back of his brain. If he were to verbalise them, he has a horrible feeling he'd sound like Jack Nicholson in *The Shining*.

Alice opens the door. She is carrying a bin-liner of old clothes. 'Oh, it's you. I thought you were from Cancer Relief. Have you lost your keys?'

'No.'

Guy follows his wife down the hall. She drops the bin-liner at the foot of the newel post; the hessian stair runner is frayed at the edges. Everything is worn out, thinks Guy, everything has come to the end of its life. He brushes past various anoraks and school blazers, sidesteps a rollerblade.

'Cup of tea?' puffs Alice. 'Di and I are just having a lemon and ginger.'

Guy has an almost uncontrollable urge to hide in the cupboard under the stairs. He swallows a groan. Di Clements – chief witch of the coven with her bulging, overactive thyroid eyes and her gruel-coloured clothes. He can see her over Alice's milkmaid-fat shoulder, thin as string. As Alice parks herself on to a chair, Guy realises that his wife and her friend look like Laurel and Hardy in drag.

'Hello, Guy.'

Di Clements is Welsh. So is Catherine Zeta Jones – it is the only thing they have in common. Catherine Zeta Jones has breasts that heave in red satin gowns; Di Clements has tits that droop down her chicken-bone ribcage. Guy knows this for a fact: he has seen them. She is forever flipping them out. Di Clements is still breast-feeding her three-year-old.

Guy surveys the kitchen. Subconsciously he is searching for the bottle opener. It could be anywhere – under today's *Guardian*, behind the bread-making machine. 'Jesus, Alice, it's a pigsty in here.'

Di bristles; she is of the feminist old-school brigade. Her husband

6

Michael is very supportive. He teaches children with learning difficulties, plays the acoustic guitar and practises tai chi in the local park. He has a thick beard, obviously, and Guy loathes his guts. 'How's Michael?'

Alice shoots him a look. He did say 'Michael' and not 'that moronic arsehole', didn't he?

'His sinuses are playing up but apart from that he's fine,' sings Di. 'Anyway, Alice, must be off. Silas has got his cranial massage at the crack of dawn, so I need to wash his hair.' Silas Clements has behavioural problems. Di thinks this is because he had a tricky passage into the world; Guy thinks it's because Di and Michael are the poor little sod's parents.

Di exits looking like she's on her way to a dress-like-your-favourite-cereal party. She is half woman, half Weetabix. Alice sees her out.

Guy finds the bottle opener – it's in the drawer with the take-away menus. Everything is in the wrong place, everything is spilling out. The washing machine gapes open, twisted laundry hanging from its mouth, Alice's vast knickers clinging to Guy's pyjama legs, the boys' T-shirts a strangled heap of navy and grey. What a mess, thinks Guy, what a fucking mess. It never used to be this bad.

Once upon a time he was proud of this house, determined to make something of it – a house, not a flat, with a garden and stairs, these bricks and mortar, his blood and sweat, a place to put down roots, grow plants, dig a pond, light a bonfire. Sometimes it seems to Guy that the house conspires against them: bright yellow paint turns to a dingy ochre, water refuses to go down plugholes, there is always a funny smell on the landing and, on top of everything, it seems to be shrinking.

When did it get so small? It's Alice's fault: she cannot throw anything away. Crap vies for space on every surface, the fridge is grubby with magnets, the corkboard thick with yellowing invites from people they never see any more. Alice marks her territory with avocado stones growing in margarine tubs, hideous clay pots made by nursery-school fingers, jars of home-made chutney gone grey with mould in the cupboard.

What does she do all day? It's not like she's off down the gym or shopping for new clothes – Alice is a domestic Buddha, fat and content, smelling of biscuits, happy to be at home.

The wine glass is smeared. Guy fills it with red liquid to the brim. Once upon a time he found his wife's presence comforting. Having a wife had been a bit like having a really good dog. But things have changed. Alice is still faithful; she's just not so eager to roll over and beg any more.

Alice reappears. She looks like a mother, thinks Guy. She looks like being a mother is her fulltime job.

The evidence speaks for itself. Alice's legs are unshaven, her skirt is merely some fabric attached round her waist, her shoes are brownish and she is wearing one of his old Aertex shirts – it used to be white but it went in with the coloureds.

Hello fat wife I no longer want to fuck, says the voice in Guy's head.

'Drinking already?' tuts Alice, sounding even more like a Sunday-school teacher than she intended, and as she clears the table she absent-mindedly picks up a piece of left-over breakfast toast, glazed scarlet with jam, and eats it. 'Damn.' She was only meant to nibble fruit between meals; a brown-spotted banana lies forlornly next to a mouldy plum in the wicker bowl on the table.

'Where are the boys?' Guy's mind is drifting. Alice says something but he's not listening, he's looking into the back garden at the plants he never bought and the pond he never dug. 'Someone could get drowned,' Alice had said, and somehow the years went by.

Everything is closing down around my ears – there's got to be more to life than this. And Guy thinks for the seventy-sixth time about the girl. The girl is called Peanut. Stupid name for a girl who looks neither dry roasted nor salty. Peony, yes, Petunia, hmmm, Persephone? 'Just call me Peanut,' she'd said. How old? Twenty-five, maybe younger. This makes Guy gulp. It is conceivable that there might be a bigger age gap between himself and Peanut than Peanut and his eldest son.

His glass is empty. He turns round. Alice has put the cork firmly back in the bottle, quite possibly the only bit of tidying she's done all day. As Guy pulls the cork out of the bottle's skinny green neck, a joke hiccups into his memory – how does it go? Something about a husband and wife sitting at the breakfast table. The husband says to his wife: 'I hate you, you've ruined my life.'

'Pardon?' says the wife.

'Sorry,' says the husband, 'I meant pass the sugar.'

Guy burps. Alice looks disappointed.

We're in a play, thinks Guy, some godawful play. Any moment now the phone will ring.

The phone rings.

Alice answers it. 'It's for you-hoo.' (She always says this.)

The receiver is greasy. 'Hi, Guy, it's Peanut, remember me?'

Remember her! He's already had a wank on her behalf!

'Ah yes, um, this afternoon – if I didn't remember you I'd have Alzheimer's,' jokes Guy. Oh God, maybe he shouldn't have said that, maybe her mother is in the grip of dementia . . . No, of course she won't be. Her mother is probably only in her forties and quite possibly a very attractive woman. 'How can I help?'

'I've got your diary – it's the same as mine. I must have put it in my bag by accident.'

Somebody once said 'there is no such thing as an accident'. Was it that Nietzsche bloke? While Guy ponders the source of the quote, Peanut says, 'Sorry,' in the silence.

'No worries, I'll pop by and pick it up tomorrow. You will be at work, won't you?'

'Sure, see you then.'

'Oh, listen, maybe I should take your mobile number just in case?'

Good thinking, Batman! Guy congratulates himself on his cunning.

The girl reels off a string of numbers and Guy shouts 'Pen, pen' at Alice's backside, as she picks the washing up off the floor. Suddenly Guy remembers he has a Mont Blanc in his pocket precisely for these occasions. He whips the lid off with his teeth and scribbles the number on the back of a gas bill, resisting the temptation to draw a heart around the digits. I'm thirty-nine, I'm a married father of two, he reminds himself.

'See you.'

'Thanks, bye.'

Alice holds the washing in her arms. A pair of Sam's Harry Potter underpants escapes her grasp.

'Who was that?'

'A girl called Peanut,' replies Guy, blushing for the first time in years.

'What a stupid name.'

'I think I'll have a shower,' Guy mumbles, wishing not for the first time that Alice would agree to having a lock put on the bathroom door.

Alice picks her youngest son's knickers up off the grubby lino.

On reflection, it's already too late to put the clock back. Let's face it, it always is.

2
When is a Home not a Home?
When it Belongs to
your Ex-wife

Joe Dobson no longer has a key to his house. His house isn't strictly his any more – once the paperwork is done it will be Hils's house. He lives somewhere else now. Life goes on, things change; his old front door is a newly painted lilac but the stained-glass panels are the same as they always have been: leaded squares of green and purple. It all feels so familiar, like coming home, only it's not.

Joe rings the bell and braces himself. It's always difficult to know how to greet his ex-wife. 'Darling' is too extravagant, and only bank managers shake hands. Unfortunately divorce doesn't come with an instruction manual. It should, then Joe would know whether pinging Hils's bra straps (not that she ever wears one) would be a suitable salutation.

Occasionally they kiss, accidental clumsy pecks on the cheek, like myopic maiden aunts. But it leaves them both uncomfortable, especially when it happens in front of the kids, who immediately swap glances loaded with false optimism. Apparently all children dream of their estranged parents getting back together. Dreaming is one thing, thinks Joe, making it so bleedin' obvious is embarrassing.

A shadow appears – good, it's his daughter. The door opens and Joe flings wide his arms. 'Hello, gorgeous!' he bellows in a stupid Ed Grundy voice. But it isn't Tabitha, it's his wife – correction, ex-wife.

11

'Well hello yourself,' sniggers Hils in an equally ridiculous cod country accent, raising an eyebrow towards her bleached hairline. 'Go blonde before you go grey' has always been her battle cry, but Joe knows her pubes are hamster-brown.

She turns her back and shouts 'Kids!' up the stairs. Joe lowers his arms. She's looking good for her age. At forty-one, in her trademark baggy Levi's, Hils still has the arse of a teenage boy. Her feet are bare, they always are. 'They get claustrophobic,' she used to say. Hils has incredibly dextrous toes. Her party piece is removing a cigarette from its packet, putting it into her mouth and lighting it – with her hands behind her back.

Joe can't forget the things he knows about his ex-wife. They are ingrained in his memory, harder to shift than the mould that gallops along the grouting in the bathroom above their heads. A few 'facts about Hils' leap into his brain: her birthday, 16 March; Hils is a Pisces, he is a Scorpio. Her inability to differentiate left from right, always a tense one on long car journeys: 'Left, Joe, left, oh you idiot, you know I mean right.' Her short-sightedness: 'Joe, do you know where my glasses are?' and his customary reply, 'On the mantelpiece, Helen Keller.'

Distinguishing features? Hils has a mole under one of her breasts. Joe hasn't seen it for a couple of years, but if there was ever a party game called pin the mole on the ex-wife, he'd be in with a good chance of winning. Mole under left breast, size 34A (that's breast, not mole).

By contrast there are things about his girlfriend Nina that he can never remember. Is she twenty-four or twenty-five? One of her little fingers is crooked: left or right? That mate of hers, the one with the pink hair, what's her name?

Saul comes crashing down the stairs. He reaches the halfway mark and jumps, commando style, over the banister rail. He lands heavily. Age ten, Saul is very clumsy. 'I've broken my leg,' he announces, jumping up and down on it. His cheeks are balloon-red and he is still as blond as a Scandinavian new-born baby.

Tabitha descends in new suede boots that her skinny legs refuse to fill. She hugs her father, smelling of teenage girl, of shampoo, deodorant and strawberry lip-gloss. Bamboo thin and just thirteen, she smiles through a mouthful of metal.

Well, I truly fucked this up, thinks Joe. He always does when he sees his children, but the feeling wears off; it has to, otherwise he'd have driven himself mad with guilt by now.

Hils watches them leave and congratulates herself on how much easier it is now than it used to be. There was a time when just seeing him, with his Jeremy Clarkson legs and his craggy cowboy face, was like putting razor blades in her mouth. I can do what I like, she reminds herself. I don't have to cook – I can have a sandwich and call a girlfriend. I could go out, I could go for a swim. But before she does anything she pours herself a stiff gin and smokes a cigarette on the back step.

How did it happen? How come after fifteen years, three hamsters, any number of goldfish, two Saabs, one Golf, two kids, numerous birthdays and barbecues, jellies and cakes, holidays and Christmases, how come he left? Because she threw him out, she supposes, and lights another Silk Cut.

Once upon a time there was a paddling pool in this garden and Joe sprayed the children with the hose and a weird clown came to entertain Tabitha on her fourth birthday and all the children were so frightened they hid behind the shed. Mr Winky, that was his name, possibly because he had a facial tic. Hils remembers having to tempt the kids out from behind the shed with Smarties, Tabitha in a white dress with a big Ribena stain down the front, and Mr Winky launching into his act. 'Pissed as a fart,' Joe had muttered, a prophecy confirmed when the magician referred to himself as 'Mr Wanky' and all the grown-ups laughed.

Saul was just a baby then, crawling and forever putting things up his nose. 'Blow, Saul, blow.' And Saul would sniff even harder and the berry or the button or whatever it was would become lodged even further up his nostril and it was back to Casualty again. 'Hello, Saul,' the nurses would say, 'we've missed you.'

Hils steps back into the kitchen. It wasn't an entirely bad marriage – some of the wedding presents still work, and she shoves a couple of pieces of bread into an ancient Morphy Richards that was a present from Joe's cousin Stella. They'll be eating pizza now, thinks Hils, smearing Marmite thickly on her toast. That's what they do every other Wednesday. That's what the children of divorced parents eat, it's on the menu – parents split up, pizza or burger? Meanwhile, she is the one who tries to ram broccoli down Saul's throat.

They go to the Pizza Express on the High Street. Joe will drink a Peroni and his fingers will itch for a cigarette. She can see him now, patting his jacket pockets before remembering that he always keeps his tobacco in the back pocket of his jeans, Tabitha and Saul casually ordering dough balls and Margarita pizzas.

When I was their age, she reminisces, going out for a meal was a massive treat. Sometimes her grandfather would take the whole family – cousins, aunties and uncles – to a hotel where Hils had gammon and pineapple and the grapefruit starter came with a clown's nose of a glacé cherry. They all dressed up, Nanna in a hat and the enamel brooch of a cockerel with its real ruby eye on her lapel, her mother and the aunts in paisley shirt-waisters, Uncle Ray with his cravat, and afterwards the men smoked cigars and the ladies really did go and powder their noses. I mustn't drink any more gin, she realises. I'm getting maudlin.

She takes a coffee upstairs and turns on the television. There is an advert for a product that fills holes wherever you might have them in the house; it appears to be a foam substance that can be squirted via a nozzle into any gap that needs plugging. There are holes all over this house, thinks Hils, who is frankly a little bit pissed – holes where Joe's things used to be, his stereo and his Apple Mac. There was a time when the shock of him leaving had turned her heart to chopped liver, when she'd walk into the house and her first impression was that she'd been burgled. So much seemed to be missing – his coats and size eleven shoes, his collection of art books, his espresso machine.

And it wasn't just the big things she noticed, it was the small things. The piles of loose change, the Rizla papers, this week's *Exchange and Mart* with the biro stars marked against E-type Jags he could never afford.

Some things he took, some things she threw away, some things she threw away and then changed her mind, rummaging at midnight in leaking bin-liners, up to her elbows in takeaway leftovers and tea bags. 'Come back, please come back.'

Gradually, over time, her things and the kids' stuff have replaced these missing items – a vase here, a stack of homework there – and suddenly Hils comes to the conclusion that it's not the things he took that bother her but the things he consciously left behind. It's as if she has been left to play caretaker to the memorabilia their marriage collected along the way: the collection of novelty seaside rock, the silver box containing umbilical stumps and baby teeth, the sheep's skull found on a walk in the Lake District, the boxes and boxes of photographs.

That's the trouble with being married – correction – having been married to a photographer, there is so much bloody evidence. Instinctively Hils looks up at the mantelpiece where once upon a time there sat a big silver-framed photo of herself and Joe on their wedding day. Not that Joe had taken it – not even Joe could play groom and photographer at his own wedding, more's the pity; they'd have been much better if he had.

The photograph is tucked away now, in the cupboard of her bedside table, next to the box with the conch shells stuck all over, the glue gone brown with age. In this box is a withered rose from a fifteen-year-old bridal bouquet, a chocolate pig, a thin gold ring there's no longer any point wearing, and a bill from a restaurant that no longer exists: Bewleys Wine Bar. It comes to £4.50. The receipt is dated 2 September 1985, the first day she ever set eyes on Joe.

A long time ago when we were young and throwing snowballs at each other, my husband fell and cut his left knee on a broken bottle. The scar is twisted and purple, and for a long time after he left this is how I imagined my heart looked.
Diary of Divorcee

3

Life Swapping

Joe is patting his jacket pockets. Tabitha sighs and rolls her marble-green eyes. 'They're in the back of your jeans.' She is very like her mother sometimes. 'Anyway, you can't smoke in this bit,' she adds smugly. 'I wish you'd both give up. It's bad enough being victims of a broken home without being orphaned, thank you very much.'

'Yes, thank you very much,' repeats Saul. He always does this whenever Tabitha has made a point he wishes he'd thought of first. Saul is blowing bubbles into his Coke glass.

'D'you want another?'

'Actually, Dad' – Tabitha is looking at the watch Joe's parents bought her for getting into her secondary school – 'I've got to get back, I've got a project to finish. Geography.' She tuts. 'Blinking volcanoes.'

'Actually,' sniggers Saul, 'volcanoes don't blink, they erupt!' He convulses with laughter; it's his instinctive reaction to most things.

Saul is jolly, that's the only word for him. Anything that involves swearing or bodily functions turns him into a one-man sitcom audience. He lives his life with gusto – he likes practical jokes, fake flies in plastic ice-cubes, whoopee cushions and people falling into lakes. Enthusiastic and greedy, he still gets tummy ache from eating too much. Big and blond and charming, Saul is just like Joe when he was that age.

16

Sometimes Joe looks at him and remembers what it was like before he knew the meaning of the word cynicism. When just riding a bike and not holding on to the handlebars was excitement enough, and there wasn't a problem in the world that couldn't be solved with a really big ice cream.

'Remember the wattle and daub house, Dad?' Tabitha is checking her braces in the back of her spoon, licking her train tracks with her tongue.

Joe nods. Years ago, when Tabitha was still at primary school, he and Hils helped her make a house out of wattle and daub for a history project. They were up all night and still only got seven out of ten. Hils had been outraged. 'I'll have that cow Mrs Benson know I studied theatre design at Wimbledon.' Tabitha has a habit of remembering the 'good old days'.

'So, the volcano thing,' he enquires, gently leading her away from the past, 'how's it going?'

'Fine,' she answers. 'I've got to do it all on the computer.'

'Do you need me to come back and help?' Joe is what they call in the trade a Mac monkey: he can scan, photoshop, do fancy borders and all sorts.

'Actually, Dad, Mum's quite good on the computer now. Ever since she wrote the book, really.'

Ooh that hurts, thinks Joe. Hils had told him all about 'the book'. He hadn't minded – he'd thought it was a good idea, therapeutic if you like – he just hadn't expected anyone to want to publish it.

'Yeah,' echoes Saul, 'Mum's quite good on the computer now. Mind you, she's still bollocks at PlayStation.' Saul honks at his own wit.

Joe laughs and signals for the bill. 'Hello, my name is Wendy' trots over. They see her every other week but she still introduces herself. She's about nineteen and has a tendency to blush at everything Joe says, even when it's 'Just the bill please, Wendy.' Wendy instantly turns beetroot.

'What is wrong with that woman?' sighs Saul.

'She fancies Dad,' replies Tabitha.

It's probably true, Joe reflects to himself. He's not being arrogant but he's always had a way with the ladies, as his mother would say. He leaves Wendy a large tip, and the three of them, Saul with his usual ice-cream moustache, leave the restaurant.

I could turn round, thinks Joe, and give Wendy a wink. I could come back later. I could, but I won't. I have learnt my lesson.

They walk back to the house in Englestone Avenue where Joe has left the car. Freya's baby seat is strapped in the back, along with a beanie baby squirrel and a half-eaten biscuit.

'Bye, Dad, see you next week.'

Joe doesn't want tears, but there is something rather too casual about the way Tabitha and Saul disappear through the lilac-coloured door and back to their mother, who is 'now really good with computers'.

'Maybe she can change a light bulb as well these days,' huffs Joe, digging his tobacco out of his back pocket and unlocking the Saab. Back to my other life, he thinks, but he's got time for a quick pint first – just the one, mind, he's driving and anyway Nina will be waiting.

Nina *is* waiting. She is waiting to go to bed – it's only eight-thirty but all she wants to do is sleep. Shelley and Carmen are round; they are still her best friends but they haven't got a clue. They arrived earlier in a cab, waving bottles of vodka and endless packets of Marlboro Lights, marvelling at the contents of her fridge. 'Nina, you've got, like, food in this thing. I've only got amyl nitrate in mine!' Helping themselves to hummus and baby Freya's mashed avocado, Shelley and Carmen spill orange juice and flick ash wherever they go, while Nina swallows back a hundred yawns and tries not to feel left out.

Shelley is a make-up artist, she does a lot of pop videos. Carmen sources original seventies material which she turns into cushions and sells at Camden Lock. Floral corduroy is apparently big this season. Nina would buy one but Joe won't have anything in the apartment that isn't black, white, grey or beige; he says he's done colour. Not with me, thinks Nina, and sometimes she feels like getting a big tin of purple paint and sloshing it all over the flat.

Nina's friends are Hoxton hip. They wear their Maharishi trousers halfway down their backsides, all the better to show off

18

their tattoos (Maori mostly). They have rings through their eyebrows, noses and belly buttons. Shelley has pink and white dreadlocks sewn on to her scalp and Carmen has gone bald in preparation for the summer.

By comparison Nina feels as dull as a black-and-white television. She stopped dyeing her hair when she was pregnant because someone said it was dangerous, and her once platinum curls are now dormouse brown. All of a sudden she feels like Marilyn Monroe in reverse: she's looking very Norma Jean.

I'm a mum, thinks Nina. I'm a stay-at-home mum. I used to have a job, I used to be a stylist, I used to smear Vaseline and brown eyeshadow on pork chops to make them look appetising, I used to squirt shaving foam on apple pies. And then I met Joe, got pregnant, gave up work, had a baby, and here I am, two years on, my tits have gone and I'm knackered.

Shelley and Carmen are talking about going to the Glastonbury Festival. 'Why don't you come, Nina, it'll be really cool.'

'Um, because I've got a baby,' Nina replies.

'So,' demands Shelley, 'loads of people take kids, it's good for them.'

'I'll think about it,' says Nina, knowing full well that she can't think of anything worse. It's bad enough dealing with a toddler in a state-of-the-art warehouse conversion, never mind a stinking tent.

She wishes she could relax more, she wishes she didn't care that her friends have eaten the last of the pitta bread and are playing The Vines at a billion decibels. Nina blushes when she remembers how they'd laughed at Joe's CD collection. 'Nina girl, you've got to, like, educate this man, like, Johnny Cash!'

'Actually he's really good, you should listen to "Live at Folsom Prison", it's fantastic,' Nina had insisted, but Shelley and Carmen were too busy sniggering over Joe's back catalogue of Fleetwood Mac to listen.

Meanwhile, Joe is in what he likes to call (ironically, of course) his local boozer. There aren't many real pubs left, he muses, knowing full well that it's people like him who brought about their demise. The Lord Alfred still has a jukebox, a pool table and little bags of pork scratchings. On the bar stands a jar of pickled eggs, and in the toilet someone has graffitied: 'However much you fancy her, someone out there is sick to death of her.'

All of a sudden he feels tired and depressed. He doesn't want to be one of those men who'd rather have another pint than face going home. One of those granite-faced, nicotine-fingered blokes who talk of being taken to the cleaners by 'that bitch' and of children slipping from touch – 'Access every other Sunday, for fuck's sake' – turning the air acrid with their conversation, thick with smoke and bitterness. I'm not one of them, Joe decides, and leaves half a pint sitting on the table.

Ten minutes later, he's home. 'Hi, babes,' he calls, and then, 'Oh Jesus' under his breath. Carmen and Whatsername are here, he can smell them. It's not that Joe doesn't like the girls, it's just that they make him feel like a geography teacher in his own home. He can feel himself sprouting leather elbow pads as he walks into the living area.

'I'll just turn this down, should I?' he hears himself saying, striding over to the CD player. For fuck's sake, Joe, you'll be saying 'Right, atlases out' next.

Nina is on one of the sofas. Joe is very proud of his sofas. They are twin black leather three-seaters, mirror-imaging each other from either side of a low glass-on-driftwood coffee table. He kisses his girlfriend's head, glad that she hasn't decided to copy Carmen and shave her skull. Be weird being in bed with a baldy – like sleeping with your grandad.

When he's alone with Nina he forgets how young she is, but her girlfriends serve as a reminder. They're a bit – how can he put it? – a bit silly really.

'Ladies,' he announces, 'good to see you.' He is trying to be friendly but he sounds like a creepy uncle.

'Hi, Joe,' they chorus, as if answering a register.

Suddenly they are rearranging their limbs into standing positions, Whatsername flicking her dreadlocks. 'Um, time we were making a move,' she says, pulling on a pair of lime-green trainers.

'Yes, sorry, gang,' apologises Carmen, 'that vodka bar in Clerkenwell calls.'

'Oh, you mean Olav's,' ventures Joe, finger firmly on the pulse.

'No, Olav's closed down last year,' replies the pink-haired one.

She looks like Looby Loo, realises Joe, but wisely keeps his trap shut. Andy Pandy and friends mean nothing to this lot.

'It's called Three Sisters and a Samovar, actually,' Carmen says, giving her pate an idle scratch.

'How very Chekhovian,' and Joe does something he has never done before in his life – he chortles.

Nina, Carmen and Whatsername react with barely disguised horror. Chortling! He'll be growing hair out of his ears and sucking Werther's Originals next.

Joe sinks down on to his sofa. They just need time to wear in, he admits to himself. In a few years they'll be as comfortable as the one at his old house.

4

Mince and Manners

Alice has made a shepherd's pie. She's a big fan of mince, it's so versatile. This is despite the fact that every mince dish Alice makes always manages to taste exactly the same – vaguely school dinner-ish.

Shepherd's pie is the last thing Guy wants. He had 'fishcakes in sorrel sauce at Sheekeys for lunch'.

'Well, bully for you, I had cheese and Ryvitas,' snapped Alice, and, for once suitably chastened, he set the table.

Alice believes in 'the family' sitting down together at the end of the day and sharing a meal. It's 'what civilised people do'. After all, 'we're not savages'. Alice believes in 'elbows off the table' and 'may I get down please'.

'I haven't been a very civilised boy today,' reflects Guy, getting a bottle of tomato sauce out of the cupboard, 'all things considered.'

He doubts very much if fucking girls in a disabled toilet would rate very highly on Alice's list of 'what civilised people do'. To be honest, Guy doesn't know which would incense Alice more – the act of carnal unfaithfulness, or the fact that it was done in a cubicle designated for wheelchair users only.

'Really, Guy, there's no excuse, it's just selfish.'

Naughty Peanut, it's her fault really. This morning, when he'd walked into the reception area of Lexington Sound, she'd been perched on the desk eating a banana, if you please.

As if that wasn't enough, the foxy little minx was wearing a T-shirt that basically spelt out Guy's mission (should he choose to accept it) for the morning. The message was clear, in white letters on a pink background: 'Fcuk me till I frat!'

So he had – not that she'd farted, that wouldn't have been very romantic on a first date. Not that it had been a date as such. What would you call it? muses Guy, placing forks on the left and knives on the right (Alice is a stickler for tradition) – an 'encounter' whereby the swapping of bodily fluids had taken place?

Obviously he'd used a condom. Peanut is a gorgeous thing, a Kylie-sized Venus with the face of a kewpie doll, but then again, who knows where she's been? Around the block and then some judging by her arsenal of tricks. Her eyes might be baby blue but her smile is gently mocking.

Some women, Guy conjectures, seem to have gone to sex school. It's all in the arch of the back, the lick of a glossy lip, a low moan before a high-pitched squeal, followed by a whimper and the drawing of salon nails across a sweaty torso. Must check that actually, make sure she left no marks. This is practical Guy, running through a check-list of what exactly happened, of who did what to whom.

A banana-flavoured first kiss, followed by a finger in her knickers, an undone fly, hot breath on his cock. Practical Guy can put in chrono-logical order the events leading up to penetration, but after that he is lost. Physical Guy took possession of his senses somewhere around 11 am, his brain dissolving in a mighty orgasm, during which he'd almost dislodged the handrail from the wall. Afterwards she'd adjusted her skirt, picked a tiny scrap of pink lace up off the floor and said, 'Well, Mr Jamieson, that was very nice.'

Nice! It had been the best ten minutes of his life. As he'd floated out, his balls feeling deliciously light, the alibi diary safely in his briefcase, she'd blown him a kiss. Pathetically (on reflection), he'd mimed catching it. Only when he got back to his office did he discover the tiny scrap of pink lace in his jacket pocket. It took him a second to realise that it was a thong!

Alice doesn't wear thongs. 'Dental floss of the buttocks,' she says, preferring to harness her buttocks in stout ladies' pants.

Peanut's thong is now hidden in a drawer in Guy's desk. He'd texted her immediately: 'Can I c u, lunch t'morro – gx'. The reply came seconds later: 'Cum and get me 1pm px'.

Later, when Penny, his PA, had been going through his appointments for the week, he'd seen Peanut's pencilled memo, barely visible against the pale blue paper of his Smythson 2004 personal organiser. She'd written: 'Fuck Peanut'.

'Ah.' Guy reacted as a father would to a child's first painting, and rather than erase it he ripped the whole page from his diary and hid it with her knickers. The rest of the day he'd been on automatic pilot, handling calls, attending meetings, eating fishcakes, working on a pitch for a car commercial, sending Peanut a bunch of flowers.

'Any message on the card, sir?'

'Um, er, just love will do.'

'No name?'

'No, no name. She'll know who they're from.'

'Thank you, sir, and while you're at it would you like to order a bunch for your wife?'

Obviously she didn't say that, there was just something implicit in the tone of her voice that made him feel uncomfortable.

'I am having an affair,' he whispers silently to himself. I have a size-ten mistress with unblemished skin and pouting lips.

'Boys!' Alice is summoning the children to the table. 'Wash your hands, supper time.'

Guy pours himself a glass of red wine. He's got to pull himself together. 'Act normal, think about what you're doing,' he tells himself. 'Focus, you're having supper with your family, your wife and your sons.'

My sons, thinks Guy. I have two sons. I watched them being born. Max first, one dark February night in 1992, a little purple beetroot that erupted rather than arrived, and then Sam, three years later on a blistering August afternoon.

Guy remembers the sudden drama, his son's unborn goblin head caught in some internal bend of female plumbing, the falling heart rate and the sudden blur of activity, chubby nurses running, the black midwife skeetering along with the drip. He remembers looking outside and seeing people flopping around on benches, licking ice-lollies.

They put a little screen up, but he could still smell the blood, the heady scent of an old-fashioned butcher's; he was surprised not to see sawdust on the floor. There were noises, too – the renting of Alice's drum-tight belly followed by a blancmange squelching sound.

Seconds later they held the baby up like a floppy grey puppet. 'A boy, Mrs Jamieson, another little boy.'

Alice had been depressed for a while, hormones running riot. Still, she got over it. Women like Alice do. Alice is capable – what does she need him for these days? She's got the children, she's got her friends, ugly *Guardian* reading witches with hairs on their chins, her book club and her biscuit tin. Guy is so distracted he can barely remember his sons' middle names.

'Can I have some red wine, Dad?'

'Don't be silly, Max,' Alice snaps. It might be the done thing in France, but not in her house.

Max is twelve. His white school shirt is covered in blue ink, he talks fast and slightly incoherently, his elbows are sharp, and soft brown hair flops over his grey eyes. His middle name (Guy's mind is racing) is Thomas. Maxwell Thomas Jamieson. Not too small, not too tall, not too bright, not too thick, Max is just Max, one of life's round pegs in a round hole. Sam, on the other hand, is a trapezoid. It's Alice's fault – she babies him, she is much harder on Max.

As if on cue, Alice snaps at her eldest son. 'Hold your knife properly, Max, and don't shovel, we're not savages.'

Max is telling a long and rather involved story about a boy who's been suspended from his school. Words tumble out of his mouth as he reaches for the ketchup and squirts big red zig-zags over his meal.

'Max, you don't need tomato sauce. That really is revolting. Tell him, Guy.'

Guy doesn't know what to say. The shepherd's pie is as dry and tasteless as a nun's crotch. It's all right for him, he can swill it down with big swigs of Rioja.

Suddenly there is a long sigh from Samuel (William) Jamieson,

25

who hangs his head on his chest and drops his knife and fork theatrically on to the table.

'I can't eat it,' he whimpers.

Alice is immediately distracted. Sam has always been a faddy eater; as a toddler he had to be coaxed into eating every mouthful with elaborate games of chuff-chuff trains.

'Come on, darling,' she coos, 'it's your favourite. Why don't you sit on my knee?'

Sam is nine – he's too old to be climbing on to his mother's knee. Alice clutches him to her, feels his wide forehead and pulls up his T-shirt to check for rashes. Sam's skin is as pale as a church candle. 'Here, poppet,' says Alice, and making no apology for hypocrisy she reaches for the Heinz bottle and squirts a large blob on the side of his plate. Sam opens his mouth like a baby bird and Alice, mixing ketchup into the grey mince, feeds him. 'There's a good boy.'

Max looks at his father. I should say something, realises Guy, but instead he just nudges his glass closer to Max and winks at his older son as the boy takes a large gulp. She's driving us both to drink, he concludes.

Later, when Guy and Max have stacked the dishwasher and Guy has finished the bottle of red wine and hence become confused during an episode of *The West Wing*, he follows his wife up to bed. She is reading, her discarded knickers lying deflated on the bedroom floor like a small parachute. Guy steps over them. Alice puts her book down. 'I've been thinking about the holidays,' she says.

Fuck, thinks Guy, his shirt half off, I forgot to check for claw marks. Just in case, he gives himself a good scratch and climbs quickly into his pyjamas. May Peanut forgive me for having pyjamas, he pleads silently, sliding swiftly into the narrow corridor that constitutes his side of the bed.

'It's just the Clementses are thinking of going camping in France and I thought it might be rather fun to join them.'

I'd rather poke forks into my eyes, thinks Guy, stunned at the mere suggestion that he, Guy Jamieson, chief creative director of the award-winning advertising agency Shelby, Jamieson and Mott, might entertain for a second the very idea of going on holiday with that bunch of freaks. Tit-less Di, her wanker husband and their ridiculous children, smelly Solomon, fat Aphrodite and educationally subnormal Silas – you have to be joking.

He swallows hard. 'Actually, Alice, I've got something up my sleeve holiday-wise.' This is a lie, he hasn't even thought about it.

'Oh,' responds Alice, 'and pray what might that be?'

'Surprise,' bluffs Guy.

Alice rolls on to her side to read and in doing so releases a mighty shepherd's pie emission. Guy can almost feel the heat of it against his cotton-clad leg. 'Fcuk me till I frat' he remembers, and closing his eyes he conjures up Peanut, but the image is spoilt somewhat by the foul meaty aroma emanating from Alice's backside.

Guy opens his eyes. Alice is a shapeless lump next to him, a vast mound of duvet and flesh. She never used to be this big – she was pleasantly plump once upon a time.

When Guy first met Alice she was just his girlfriend's flatmate. He'd barely noticed her. She might as well have been Virginia's pet guinea pig, her funny little freckle-faced mate who tagged along with Ginny to watch him play rugby on Saturday afternoons. In the end Sloaney Virginia had got bored of shivering on the sidelines. She had better things to do than stand around getting her boots muddy, and Alice didn't. Guy got used to seeing her out of the corner of his eye, endlessly cheering him on, good old Alice. At half time she offered him hot tomato soup from a Thermos flask.

One particularly wet afternoon, he'd gone back to the flat she shared with Virginia to dry his socks over their little electric bar fire. He was hoping to see Virginia. She was in bed with a cold, according to Alice – only she wasn't, she was in bed with a bloke called Rupert. The ensuing scene had been rather ugly. Initially he'd blamed Alice, but to this day she swears blind she didn't know.

After Guy had slammed out of the flat he'd lost touch with both of the girls, but a year or so later, when the accident happened and he fell to pieces, Alice appeared out of nowhere and began to glue him back together. Somehow gratitude led to marriage and mortgage and babies, only not necessarily in that order. Alice had made a spectacularly smug, if slightly bulging registry-office bride. It had been a very small wedding – Guy's parents couldn't be there and Alice's weren't invited.

These days, Guy is embarrassed by his wife. They don't look right together any more – if you put them in a crowded room no one would guess that they were husband and wife. Guy knows this for a fact. He's seen the look of surprise on colleagues' faces when he's had to introduce her at business dinners, award ceremonies and Christmas parties.

Once, to his shame, he overheard one of his copywriters bitching about her in the toilets at the Dorchester. 'Old Jamieson pulled the short straw, seen the state of his Mrs?' Someone flushed a toilet at that moment and Guy couldn't catch the rest of the exchange, but whatever it was had obviously been hilarious, judging by the ensuing guffaws.

If I was playing 'me' in an advert, reflects Guy, and I had to cast someone to play my wife, I wouldn't pick Alice. People watching would think, 'Why's that fit-looking bloke got such an old boiler for a Mrs?' I'd go for Kelly Brook or a younger Amanda Holden.

Guy knows the value of good casting. It's one of the most important parts of his job, sitting in on the final say, this blonde or that brunette, the cheeky Irish fellow or the chirpy Cockney chappie, decisions, decisions. He's got a big one coming up – if only he could stop thinking about Peanut's breasts and concentrate. Obviously, the client, in this case a well-known make of lager, will wield some influence, but they tend to trust an expert opinion, which is where Guy comes in.

Nine times out of ten he'll have a gut instinct; an actor or comedian will have a certain gesture or an expression that makes them 'the face that fits'. With women it's often their legs, tits or arse that constitute the deciding factor.

I need a man who says 'I'm cool, I'm funny, but I'm vulnerable and I love my mum' Guy frets, sleep finally taking his eyelids hostage.

During the night he dreams of taking Alice down to the charity shop in a big black bin-liner. In his dream he says to the woman behind the counter, 'There are a couple of jackets, bit frayed round the edges, and this old wife, I don't really use her any more and she takes up an awful lot of space.'

Beside him, Alice dreams too.

5

Alice in the DOLL'S HOUSE

Alice has a recurring dream. She has it regardless of whether she's been eating cheese, blue or otherwise, goat's or cow's, full fat or cottage. It comes without warning after chicken casserole or tuna bake, sometimes twice a week, sometimes just once a month. It worms into her subconscious and plays out a scene that tilts her from sleep, leaving her clutching at her throat, knowing that she must check her sons, make sure they are still breathing.

In Alice's dream she is standing on the ground floor of a doll's house in a kitchen where miniature copper pans hang from tiny little hooks and a plastic ham squats on a scaled-down pine table. This kitchen has become horribly familiar to Alice, with its Welsh dresser, gingham curtains and three-legged stool.

Alice never had a doll's house as a child. She wanted one very badly. She had a friend called Sheona Davey who got one for her eighth birthday, but Alice wasn't allowed to touch it, she was only allowed to look. Once, when Sheona Davey went to the toilet – 'Remember, Alice, no touching' – Alice touched the little piano complete with its sheet music and was both taken aback and disappointed when the keys didn't work. Sheona Davey was a very bossy girl; years later (according to Friends Reunited) she joined the army, which came as no great surprise to Alice.

The Alice in the doll's-house dream wears a blue floral dress with a ruffle around the neck and a white pinafore – it could be Victorian but it could just as easily be Laura Ashley circa 1974. Under the dress Alice's legs are made of porcelain. This makes walking very tricky. In fact, to move at all 'doll Alice' has to fall over and crawl on her elbows. It's very slow-going but she keeps trying – she has to, she can hear the baby crying.

Alice knows where the baby is because although her doll self is inside the house, normal human-sized Alice is on the outside of the house looking in. Her face is clearly visible, even though she's fast asleep. Alice can see her eyes, nose and cheeks pressed up against the wall, but she can only look, not touch.

Big Alice on the outside can see into all the rooms. She can see her miniature alter ego in the kitchen, the grandfather clock in the parlour, and the Victorian bathroom with the roll-top bath. Most importantly, she can see into the attic room at the top of the house, with its sloped ceiling and the rocking horse in the corner next to the crib. The crying is coming from the crib, that's why little porcelain-legged Alice is trying to get to it. Big Alice would like to help little Alice, but she's not allowed to lift her up.

Little Alice crawls across the kitchen but she cannot open the door because her hands are lumpy stocking stumps and she is trapped again, face down by the closed door, hearing the baby cry even though she has no ears.

The dream always ends with big Alice breaking the rules and poking a finger through the window into the baby's crib, only to find that it's empty. Sometimes there might be a button under the cover, or a dried pea, once an earring Alice lost long ago, but never a flesh-and-blood baby.

This is why, when Alice wakes up, her heart drumming, she has to swing her legs out of the bed and convince herself that, although they are fat and wobbly, they are good working legs. Legs that can get her out of the room she shares with her husband and down the corridor to where her sons sleep.

She visits Sam first, her youngest and therefore most vulnerable. Sam sleeps so deeply she sometimes has to prod him for reassurance. When he was a baby she was forever holding a mirror to his lips, waiting for a patch of mist to form to prove his lungs were still operating. Max, her oldest, in the bedroom at the back of the house, sleeps much more fitfully. Usually she only has to put her head round the door to see him twitch, hear him mumble.

Alice hasn't told Guy about the dream. What's the point? He doesn't listen. Once she made the mistake of telling Di, who analysed it at great length as if Alice was too stupid to work out for herself what it meant.

What a pity, thinks Alice. I would love to have had a little girl, a little girl with a doll's house all of her own. I am, she reminds herself, a good mother. I would sew little curtains and make sausages out of plasticine.

When Alice has woken from the dream and checked the children, she is usually very hungry. All that crawling along on my elbows, she guesses, and she tiptoes downstairs to make herself a sandwich. It's the dream that makes me fat, she concludes, sloshing milk into a glass.

Once, a few months ago, standing right here in this real-life kitchen at three o'clock in the morning, slathering peanut butter on brown bread, she heard the cry for real. For a moment her legs froze as if they truly were made of porcelain and she stood rooted to the spot. 'Pull yourself together – it's a cat, Alice, just a silly old cat. There is no baby in this house.'

Had a burglar broken in at that moment, he would have found Alice sitting on the floor, crying, with her mouth full of half-chewed peanut-butter sandwich.

6

A Job for Joe

Joe has got a job, which is a relief. This year hasn't been great so far and there's a tax bill looming. It's a lingerie shoot for Asda. Ten years ago he'd have turned it down – these days he can't afford to pick and choose. He's a family man with two families; his Mario Testino days are over.

Once upon a time in the eighties he'd been the Royal College's golden boy. A glittering career beckoned, everyone said so, and for a while they were right. There were a few awards, ugly chunks of Perspex mostly, drunken acceptance speeches in Park Lane hotels, looking artily dishevelled in a tux, all designer stubble and skewed bow tie. Peppering his thanks with the F word. One year there had even been talk of the Turner Prize shortlist, but he lost out to a girl who made collages out of sanitary towels.

Had he got lazy or just plain greedy?

As his name got about, it seemed that integrity and art got in the way of making money, and he chose money. He was married; there was a baby on the way.

For a few years fat cheques rolled in. He, Joe Dobson, was the magazine editors' flavour of the early nineties. He lived up to the hype, grew his hair long, rode a motorbike and drank a lot of espresso. Even the broadsheets adopted him, their token rock-and-roll photographer. Then, overnight, it seemed as if everyone got bored with him: he'd open the Sunday supplements and see other photographers' names attached to shoots that just a month ago would have been his.

It had been a shock at first. Joe took to sniffing his own armpits in case he'd suddenly developed an appalling body odour. Occasionally he fancied he smelt a staleness, the stench of the has-been about himself, and he started to drink – a lot, which gave him a paunch.

One day he caught sight of himself: his jeans were too tight, his hair was too long and he was wearing cowboy boots, for fuck's sake. No wonder no one wanted him. He'd sorted himself out, cut back on the booze, touched his toes a few times, got rid of the cowboy boots and gradually the phone started ringing.

He had to accept the fact that the offers were different. He was no longer Linda Evangelista's pet photographer – tough. Pride, thinks Joe, is harder to swallow than roll-mop herring. Even now, all these years later, he doesn't feel he missed the boat. On the contrary, he was on it, but somehow he fell off.

These days it's just work, a little bit of fashion, but mostly food. Christmas dinners for *Good Housekeeping* magazine shot in September; step-by-step guides to making marzipan the Delia way for Sainsbury's; 101 ways with pomegranates and limes. Joe yawns so hard he feels his jaw crack.

'Tired?' the make-up girl asks. Actually, she's more of a woman – one of those well-preserved forty-pluses who can still get away with combats and a sleeveless vest. She is applying foundation to the back of one of the model's legs, covering up bruises. 'Fucking on the stairs again, were we, darling?'

'Knackered,' responds Joe, idly thinking how much more attractive she is than the five agency totty, who, despite being decades younger, are slumped yawning on plastic chairs.

'I'm Gina,' she says. 'I think we might have worked together ages ago, some Levi thing, years back.'

'I've been around a long time,' chuckles Joe (he's got to watch this chortling and chuckling thing).

'Me too,' responds Gina, and she slaps the girl with the bruised legs on the backside. 'You're done, I need Gayle now.'

A voluptuous brunette totters forward on toothpick-thin heels. 'Sit down, love, before you fall over.'

Joe's equipment is all set up. His agency has provided him with an assistant, a nice soppy Welsh boy with sweaty hands. Gina is scraping orange foundation off Gayle's face. 'Let's leave the make-up to the experts, darling.'

'Are we doing thongs?' queries Gayle. 'Only I've a massive boil on my arse.'

Oh the glamour, thinks Joe, remembering the glory days of top-league models with blemish-free arses. Kate, Naomi, Linda, the racehorses of the profession, long-limbed thoroughbred fillies. By comparison, this lot look like a bunch of pit ponies.

He knows he's being unfair. Any one of these girls could doubt-less cop off with a footballer in an Essex nightclub, they're just not his type. It may be his imagination but there's a definite whiff of silicone in the air.

The girls are sprawling around in dressing gowns. Joe knows that beneath their silky wraps they are naked. Underwear needs to be removed several hours before a shoot like this so that any elastic marks have time to fade. But despite this insider knowl-edge, Joe's penis lies dormant in his pants.

Two blondes, two brunettes (one Asian) and a redhead. Four out of the five are smoking, tapping ash with acrylic nails into empty Diet Coke cans. The one with the boil on her arse is flicking through *Bride* magazine. 'I'm getting married, me,' she announces, and suddenly they're off, talking of wedding cakes and bridesmaids and vodka ice luges, yak, yak, yak.

Joe feels a headache coming on. The stylist and the art director arrive and shoo the girls into a back room where a rail of bras and knickers, suspender belts and basques is waiting to be allocated. Joe can still hear them. 'Are you having a chimney sweep?' 'My friend done it in Antigua.' 'So what, I done it round the back of a Chinese.' 'Haaaaaaaaa,' they shriek, wriggling sunbed-baked bodies into satin and lace.

'Have you got any Nurofen?' he asks Gina, and she ferrets around in a pink leather bag, eventually holding up a foil package in triumph. Somehow Joe gets through the shoot on a couple of

Junior Disprin. The girls have to be reminded not to pout too much – it's Asda, not *Playboy*. 'Think George,' he instructs, 'not Hugh Hefner.'

For some of them it seems that adopting the pose of a lesbian porn star is like a nervous tic. As soon as Joe points the camera, they either assume pseudo-innocent schoolgirl expressions or clench their teeth like snarling sex sirens.

At one point Gayle is on all fours with the redhead on her back. 'Me and her done a *Loaded* shoot last month. D'you want her to feel my tits?'

'Um, I don't think so,' shouts Joe, 'just standing will do.'

Joe shoots roll after roll. 'Relax,' he yells eventually, and immediately they resume their talk of weddings, huddled together giggling and telling Gayle how she should have her hair on her big day. Surreptitiously Joe reloads his camera and takes his last film: this is more like it, a bunch of girls just mucking about in their skimpies. The redhead is laughing at something one of the blondes said, the other blonde has her hands over her mouth as if aghast at the joke, Gayle is pulling a stupid face, and the Asian girl for reasons best known to herself is standing on her head. That's the shot, thinks Joe, and for a second a rush of adrenalin hammers his heart. This is followed by an almost instant comedown. They won't choose it, it's too quirky; oh fuck it, who cares?

'That's a wrap, girls,' and they swoop off like parrots. 'Tiaras are nice.' 'What about the honeymoon?' And, 'Last wedding I went to, I got food poisoning, shat myself in the back of a minicab.'

Gina is clearing up. Joe offers her a cup of tea while the Welsh boy packs away his equipment.

'Well, that's me done till after Easter,' she tells Joe. 'Black no sugar, ta. I'm off on my hols, and before you turn into a hairdresser and say anywhere nice – yes, actually, Italy,' and she hums 'Just One Cornetto' hopelessly out of tune.

Instantly, Joe is reminded of Hils. She can't sing either. Hils can't even sing 'Happy Birthday' – she's not allowed, the children won't let her. Even when they were very small, she had to mime at their birthday parties. Easter, did she say? Of course, Hils is taking

Tabitha and Saul up north to see their grandparents. His parents. Why isn't he going?

Because I'm not invited.

'Nice hotel?' Joe suddenly remembers that he's having a conversation and that it's his turn to say something.

'Not really. Self-catering apartment in a palace thing – brochure's in my bag, actually. Here, have a look. I was going to show my sister on the way home. Kids and hotels don't really go.'

'You're not kidding.' Joe almost chuckles but stops himself. The brochure falls open at a page of primary colours – sunshine and sea and fishing boats. Palazzo Gardenia, he reads.

'Have you got kids?' she asks, reloading electric curlers on to their metal prongs.

'Thirteen-year-old girl, ten-year-old boy,' Joe replies, scanning the information in the brochure. Located on a glorious stretch of golden coastline . . .

'Oh,' she grins, 'same as me, only the other way round, thirteen-year-old boy, ten-year-old girl.'

Unique charm and relaxed atmosphere, the perfect family getaway . . . 'Oh, and I've got a two-year-old as well,' adds Joe. Blimey, he'd nearly forgotten Freya!

Secluded, yet within easy walking distance of the enchanting fishing village of Santa Helena del Castellabate, with its colourful weekly market, bars and restaurants . . .

'Big gap,' muses Gina, 'does it work? See, thing is, I keep getting really broody. I see a little sweet dribbly baby and I think I want one, then I think, nah, I'll have a new pair of shoes instead.'

Joe laughs, a proper laugh. He likes this woman. He tears his eyes away from the brochure. Large landscaped pool surrounded by bougainvillea, fragrant honeysuckle, private beach . . .

'Course, I'll have to get a move on, before the old eggs rot completely.'

'Actually,' admits Joe, 'the baby's with another woman, my girlfriend. I mean, I, er, my wife and I split up.' He can feel himself blush.

'You mean you left her because your girlfriend was pregnant?' Gina suddenly becomes very efficient. She is almost hurling brushes and hairdryers into a large canvas holdall. 'You blokes are such a fucking cliché.'

She doesn't like me any more, realises Joe, and he is so genuinely taken aback that Gina almost feels sorry for him.

'Oh, it's not you, it's just so boring. It keeps happening and when it happens to someone you love, you think, fucking hell, why do some men have to be such pricks? Sorry, what can I say? I can be a bitch.' A taxi toots. 'That's my cab, I'm out of here. Bye, girls,' she yells.

'Byeeee,' the parrots chorus.

'Bye,' says Joe, but she doesn't even turn round. 'You forgot your brochure,' he adds, but very quietly so that she doesn't hear.

She wouldn't listen anyway, she's decided he's full of crap.

Gina directs the minicab to Kennington where her sister is living in a basement flat with three kids under seven, having been dumped by her husband for a twenty-two-year-old croupier. Even the nice ones can be pillocks, she decides.

Italy, thinks Joe. He could take the kids, all of them – all he has to do is ask Hils. It doesn't occur to him to ask Nina. As Gina says, even the nice ones can be pillocks.

7

Hearts and Knickers

Guy has been fucking Peanut for exactly six weeks. It's their month-and-a-half anniversary. Guy buys her a silver heart-shaped key ring from Tiffany and some black-lace Agent Provocateur knickers. He'd have bought the matching bra but he got confused over sizes, and miming the shape of her breasts had turned him into Benny Hill.

In exchange, Peanut gives Guy an extra special blow job. She does it on her knees under his desk while he makes important business calls. It's possibly the most romantic gift he's ever received. The last present Alice gave him was a special glove for washing the car with.

Guy loves spoiling Peanut, watching her face light up as she tears into tissue paper packages. Treating Alice, on the other hand, is pointless. Once he bought her a satin dressing gown, just after she'd had Sam. But she took it back to Selfridges and swapped it for a breadmaker and a non-stick pan.

Peanut leaves Guy's office with her T-shirt on inside out and back to front, a detail that doesn't go unnoticed by Guy's PA, Penny Cheetham.

Penny Cheetham is fifty-four and has been employed by Shelby, Jamieson and Mott since before Jamieson or Mott were a twinkle in a head-hunter's eye. Guy inherited her, against his will, when old man Shelby retired, and she sits outside his office like a spectacularly ugly piece of furniture.

Bow-legged and bearded, Miss Cheetham is at odds with the rest of the premises, with its Scandinavian-style blond-wood floors, mandatory black leather sofas and swooping metal and glass fittings. The offices of S J & M are a homage to cutting-edge design. Note the Gaggia espresso machine and this season's big orange bird of paradise arrangement pecking away in the corner. Orchids are so over.

Unfortunately, Penny is by far the most efficient person in the company, and even though the sight of her makes Guy flinch, he has a horrible feeling that the business would collapse without her toad-like presence.

Miss Cheetham, despite suffering from agonising fibroids, has never taken a single day off sick. She doesn't even leave the office for lunch, preferring to eat hard-boiled eggs and pork pies out of a Tupperware box on her knee.

Guy despairs. 'Why can't she just be normal and eat sushi like everyone else in advertising?'

Penny lives in South Norwood with her mother, and you can tell by looking at her that she has never married or had children.

Toby Mott, Guy's partner, has had a succession of PAs that are forever going AWOL, crying over abortions or being caught stealing. Lucky bloody Toby. If only Penny would have the decency to choke to death on a Melton Mowbray.

Once Guy tried to lose Penny to Toby in a game of cards, but Toby lost every hand. 'Sorry, mate, looks like you're stuck with her.'

Penny is livid with Guy for 'carrying on with that girl'. Not that she has told him so – after all, it's not her place – but internally her soul rages at the injustice of it. It's Alice she feels sorry for, such a nice woman, and those two little boys – he wants castrating.

Alice has always been very pleasant to Penny. Occasionally she pops into the office with the children, when they've been on an educational visit to a museum in town, for example. 'Hello, Penny,' she says brightly, 'how's your mother?' She even has the grace to listen, without looking bored, to the ongoing saga of 'Mother's cataracts' and the stresses of her diabetes.

Thanks to Alice, Penny has someone to stand next to at the office Christmas party. They always have a lovely chat, even if Alice does tend to spit bits of crisp when she's talking. Penny always compliments Alice on the dress she's worn three years running, and Alice always marvels at the fact that Penny made her frock herself!

Last year Alice sent her a potted plant and a jar of home-made chutney for Christmas. I mean, Guy may have ordered Harvey Nicks hampers for all the staff, which was very nice, but it's the personal touches that really count. Even if Mother couldn't eat the chutney because of her diabetes.

Penny gives Peanut the evil eye every time she comes swanning in, 'the flibbertigibbet'. She's not sure who she despises more, Peanut for her pierced navel and constant hair flicking (she'll give herself whiplash if she's not careful, thinks Penny darkly), or Guy for mooning over the trollop like a lovesick seventeen-year-old.

He's taking the Michael, seethes Penny, who doesn't swear, and on top of everything else, this morning he casually threw a holiday brochure on to her desk and asked her to book a family holiday. It had been on the tip of her tongue to ask whether he wanted to include Peanut in the arrangements. Still, it does look a lovely place, Penny sighs. Every year she takes her mother to the same bed and breakfast in Weston-super-Mare, where breakfast consists of tinned grapefruit segments and they spend a lot of time doing jigsaw puzzles, usually of Weston-super-Mare.

Palazzo Gardenia, she reads. Imagine walking through a mellow stone portico into a beautiful flower-filled courtyard with the afternoon sun slanting through the archways and the scent of geranium and lemon trees filling the air . . .

Imagine, she thinks, walking into Marie Langdale's B&B, with its mustard-coloured anaglypta walls, the rain lashing down and the heady stench of boiled beef and cabbage filling the air. Imagine stopping in to watch *Coronation Street* and then having a walk along the front in a plastic mac. Imagine nylon sheets and a broken Teasmade. Imagine Mother's bandaged legs and gangrenous little toe. Imagine changing dressings every day and the constant cicada click of false teeth.

'He really is a cunt,' spits Penny, feeling the word for the first time through gritted teeth.

Guy has been goaded into action by Alice bleating on about 'lovely camping in lovely France'. She's even got the boys on her side. 'Mum says I can have a fishing net and catch a fish for tea,' enthuses Sam.

For weeks now Guy has been meaning to get on to the Internet and find something in a search engine under 'anything rather than camping in France with the Clementses'. In the end he'd had lunch with his accountant who'd recommended some palazzo place in Italy and he'd phoned for a brochure.

The rest is up to Penny. Guy hasn't got time to book flights and accommodation, not with work and Peanut *and* growing a goatee!

Guy's goatee is a source of much amusement to Alice. 'I can't imagine what he thinks he looks like,' she confides to Di Clements.

'A pimp,' responds Di, and the two of them hoot into their apple and ginger tea.

'Seriously, Alice,' titters Di. 'You've got to come to some decision on this holiday. Michael's booking the ferry next week. We've been saving money-off vouchers from the *Guardian*; there's only a few more to collect. Two cars for the price of one,' she adds.

'Ooh,' responds Alice, who loves a bargain and has a selection of dented tinned goods in the cupboard to prove it. 'I'll work on him tonight.'

Guy is late home. He often is, legitimately or otherwise. This evening he met Peanut for a 'quickie'.

'Have you got time for a drink as well?' she'd sniggered, unzipping his flies.

'Not really,' Guy answered truthfully, but he found himself phoning Alice and lying about his computer crashing, and he and Peanut shared a bottle of Pinot Grigio in a little wine bar tucked away in a courtyard off St Martin's Lane.

In the end it had been Peanut who'd looked at her watch and

leapt up. 'Fucking hell, Guy. I'm seeing The White Stripes at Brixton Academy in fifteen minutes.'

Guy made a mental note to buy a copy of The White Stripes' latest CD and watched her bottom disappear off to the tube. Waiting for the bill, he sucked Polo mints and checked out his goatee in the mirror. Very Johnny Depp.

At 8.30 he walks through the door.

'Hello love, bad day?' shouts Alice. 'I'm just getting Sam off to bed.'

Alice still reads Sam a bedtime story. This is despite the fact that according to her he has the reading ability of a thirteen-year-old.

'Dinner's in the oven on a low light,' she adds.

It's chilli con carne. Guy sits at the table poking at his dinner. It tastes exactly the same as Alice's shepherd's pie only with a sprinkling of chilli powder and rice rather than potato. It definitely requires a lager.

Three-quarters of the way through the can and about two mouthfuls into his meal, Alice appears. She has brushed her hair and put on a bit of lipstick.

'Are you going out?'

'Ha, ha,' trills Alice, picking kidney beans out of Guy's dinner and swallowing them like Smarties. Guy resists the temptation to stab her hand with his fork.

'Actually, Guy, I thought we might have a talk.'

A skewer of guilt stabs Guy's loins.

'About the holiday,' she continues. 'It's just Michael's booking the ferry next week.'

'Actually, Alice,' interrupts Guy, 'we're not going to France. We're going to Italy. We're not camping because I'd rather knock a rusty tent peg into my skull with a mallet than spend one night under canvas. We're staying in a fabulous old palace with a swimming pool and a private beach. We shall have daily maid service and chilled cocktails and I certainly won't be rinsing my smalls in a plastic washing-up bowl. We may go out on occasional day trips to places of historical interest, if you insist. However, we shall not be spending any time singing "Kumbaya My Lord" round a campfire with the fucking Clementses. I take it Michael intends to take his acoustic guitar to France?'

Alice nods.

'Well then, it's a good job we shan't be joining them, as I would find it very difficult not to set fire to him in his sleeping bag.'

Alice refuses to speak to Guy for the rest of the evening. At 10.00 she retires to bed, furious. At least she's got friends. Who has Guy got apart from herself and the boys?

Downstairs Guy drinks whisky and whispers sloppy declarations of adoration and sexual intent to Peanut on his mobile. It would have been nice to have spoken to her in person, but he supposes she must still be at the concert, and makes do with leaving three long messages while masturbating on the sofa.

8

These Things that are Sent to Try Us

Nina is having a bad day. So far, Freya has bitten a chunk of glass out of a Heals tumbler, smeared a fuchsia-coloured lipstick along the snow-coloured sitting-room wall, hidden the remote control and put her shoes down the toilet. Nina glances at the clock on the kitchen wall. It's so minimal it doesn't have any numbers on it, but she knows it's trying to say 9 am. No, she gasps – surely it must be lunchtime?

Nina has been up with her daughter since five. Unwisely, she decides to dry Freya's Start-Rite sandals in the microwave. Within seconds their rubber soles have melted.

'I hate you,' she tells her daughter. 'I fucking hate your guts, you're a horrible ugly little shit.'

It's true that Freya is not looking her best. She has thick green snot plugging each nostril, a gummy eye and a good deal of mashed banana in her hair. She looks like an advert for the RSPCC. Surely motherhood was never meant to be this boring.

Freya is so frightened by her mother's screwed-up face that she takes flight, tripping over the vegetable stand and somersaulting on to her head. For a second she is silent.

Good, thinks Nina. If she's unconscious, at least I might be able to have a shit in peace.

She doesn't mean it, not really, it's just that sometimes murderous thoughts creep uninvited into her head. Freya staggers to her feet, a small purple lump visibly swelling above her eye. She is almost too shocked to cry, but not quite.

'WAAAAghhhhhhhhhh,' she screams, and Nina can do nothing but sit on the floor and hold her until she stops. By the time she has rocked her daughter into thumb-sucking silence, it's 9.10 am. The day stretches ahead of her like a long string of grey chewing gum. This is bad. Bad days keep happening. Sometimes it's a toss-up as to who cries most, Nina or Freya.

I have to get out of this place, thinks Nina. Ideally she'd like to leave Freya home alone, but two-year-olds are so stupid they can't be trusted not to fall out of windows, drown themselves or burn to death in an accident involving 'playing with matches'. Toddlers have to be on twenty-four-hour suicide watch, decides Nina, shoving Freya's feet into her wellington boots and strapping her into her buggy. She puts a denim hat on the child to disguise the lump and heads for the bus stop.

I must learn to drive, she thinks. Joe has taken her out a couple of times in the Saab but it's always been a disaster. 'Maybe you need an automatic?' he suggests, which is basically a euphemism for maybe you've got learning difficulties.

'I wish I had a dad,' seethes Nina, waiting for the number 73.

Actually Nina does have a dad, but unfortunately Ray Bentham, otherwise known as 'Benny the Boy' to his mates and 'Vincent Clark' to the police, went out for a metaphorical packet of fags in 1980 and has never been seen since. Twenty-four years on, Nina's mum is still religiously recording *Crimewatch*, just in case.

'And why is my mum so crap?' queries Nina, still waiting for the number 73. 'Crap' isn't the right word really. Maxine Bentham loves Nina and she thinks Freya is a 'poppet', but, what with working six nights a week on the door of a gay club in Soho, her schedule is wholly incompatible with grandmotherly babysitting duties.

Maxine is a hopeless old fag hag. It's not normal, concludes Nina, struggling on to the bus. Her mother has spent so much time in the company of transvestites and drag queens she's beginning to look like one.

45

'Upper Street, please.'

Nina has set out with the intention of buying Freya a new pair of shoes. It should be simple, but unfortunately the only shoes Freya is remotely interested in are a pair of strappy alligator slip-ons with a six-inch heel. If she's inherited my mother's taste, I shall die, despairs Nina, paying thirty quid for four square inches of pink leather sandals.

There's just time for a quick latte, a chocolate muffin and two massive tantrums (one each) before Nina and Freya head for a mother and toddler group round the back of Highbury. Nina hasn't been to this one before, but the flyer promises music, games, soft play and fun. Nina wheels the buggy over a used condom. The Nissen hut of a church hall smells of damp, sweat and soggy nappies.

'Hellooo, are we new?' bellows a woman dressed in what looks like a pair of clown's yellow and black chequered trousers.

'Yes,' mutters Nina.

'Mummy or Nanny?'

'Mummy.'

'Hello, Mummy, and who have we brought along today?'

'This is Freya.'

'Everybody say hello to Freya and her mummy.'

A few people do.

Nina doesn't know where to sit. Freya has fallen asleep, and even the woman in the ridiculous trousers screaming at everyone to 'get ready for singing circle' doesn't wake her. Nina finds herself squashed between 'Jed's mummy' and 'Rhiannon's nanny'. Each of them have the aforementioned toddlers on their lap. Nina feels a bit stupid, what with Freya crashed out behind her in her buggy.

'Everyone join in, come on Freya's mummy, don't forget the actions.'

Nina finds herself doing 'The Wheels on the Bus' (circling movements of the arms), 'How Much is that Doggie in the Window?' (barking), 'Twinkle Twinkle Little Star' (hand actions and pointing) and 'Ring-a-Ring-a-Roses' (falling down). Whenever she forgets the words or misses an action, the mummy on her left gives her a 'look'. By the time they've all been given instruments for 'a few minutes of free musical expression' (Nina gets a triangle), she is on the verge of fainting with embarrassment. Imagine if Shelley and Carmen could see her now!

'Break time,' yells Checked Trousers.

Freya snores on. Nina puts 10p in a tin for a polystyrene cup of weak Ribena.

The nanny who'd been sitting on her right has congregated with all the other nannies at one end of the hall, while all the mummies are in the opposite corner. Nina dithers.

'Would you like to come to a chickenpox party?' asks a red-haired woman in glasses. 'I'd love to,' Nina hears herself saying, moving away. I'm so bored, she thinks. I could die of boredom.

'Hard work, isn't it?' suggests a very tall woman breast-feeding a baby while simultaneously fixing a rubber tyre on to a toy car.

'Yes, really hard,' says Nina. 'No one tells you just how hard.'

'How many have you got?'

'Um, just the one. You?'

'Four, actually. My husband was an only child and he felt he'd missed out on the fullness of real family life, and . . . well, we had a big house, only we haven't any more because he got made redundant. So then of course I had to sell the car, which makes life quite tricky with this little chap.'

The baby pulls away from the woman's breast and to her horror Nina realises it has Down's syndrome. I'm so selfish, she thinks, letting myself get all het up and ridiculous when this poor woman's got a redundant husband and a Down's kid.

Tall smiles beatifically. 'Oh well, the Lord will provide.'

Suddenly Clown Trousers is standing in the middle of the hall with a tambourine.

'Time to thank Jesus,' whispers Tall.

Time to fuck off out of here, thinks Nina, and she attempts to make her exit on tiptoe. She is almost over the threshold when Freya comes round. 'Hello, Mummy,' she says brightly and clearly. 'I fucking hate your guts.'

Joe doesn't stop laughing when she tells him. Mind you, he hadn't found the fuchsia lipstick all that hilarious. 'Really, Nina, you've got to keep an eye on her.' But now, Peroni in hand, he's chuckling away like some old grandad.

'Actually, Joe, it wasn't funny. I've had a pig of a day.'

'Well then, porky, catch,' and he throws a brochure into her lap. 'Page thirty,' he instructs.

'Oh, Joe,' squeals Nina, 'a holiday. God I can't wait. When?'

'Last week in July,' answers Joe a tad smugly.

Nina throws herself on to his lap, undoes his flies, hikes up her skirt, pulls down her knickers and plonks herself on his penis.

Whatever happened to foreplay? thinks Joe. He is slightly uncomfortable. The remote control seems to have wedged itself up his backside. He could do himself a mischief.

Nina bounces up and down enthusiastically.

'Oh, Joe, this will be our first holiday, me, you and baby Freya.'

'Hold your horses,' splutters Joe. 'Actually, it's me, you, Freya, Tabitha and Saul.'

Nina instantly assumes rising trot mode. Joe's penis falls out in a rather undignified manner.

'Tabitha and Saul?'

'My children,' he reminds her.

Nina dismounts. 'Where the hell's the remote control? I want to watch *EastEnders*.'

Ooh, she knows how to twist the knife in. Nina is fully aware that Joe's favourite programme, *Scrapheap Challenge*, is on the other side.

Joe hands Nina the remote control and tucks his penis back into his trousers. Well, he thinks, that went well.

9

Past, Present and Passports

Hils cannot imagine why she said yes.

A. Because I don't want to be needy.

B. Because one day they will leave me anyway.

C. Because he might have let me down as a husband but he's always been a good dad.

Even so, she wishes the situation had never arisen. He'd caught her off guard, unpacking the shopping on the kitchen table, oranges rolling from a split bag. She'd grabbed the phone and it had clattered to the floor. 'Hello, hello . . .'

There's always a moment these days when she thinks it might be bad news and her mouth goes dry. When you are young, a phone call is always a good thing: a party, a boy, dinner, a movie. Youth and beauty aren't the only things that are difficult to hold on to, thinks Hils. The older you get, the harder it is to be optimistic.

Anyway, she'd opened her mouth and 'yes' had fallen out. She can't go back on her word. The kids wanted to go, they danced on the sofa chanting 'Italy, Italy' to the tune of that 'Vindaloo' World Cup song. Watching them, Hils suddenly remembered when she was a Brownie, being taught that 'if you can't smile, grin'. So she'd grinned until Tabitha said, 'What's wrong with your face?'

Catching sight of herself in the mirror it occurred to Hils that maybe the wind had changed and she would be stuck endlessly grinning for ever. A divorcee with the face of a simpleton. Great.

Later, when Saul has collapsed into bed, face down and bottom in the air, Tabitha summons her mother to the bathroom.

Hils sits on the toilet seat while her daughter shampoos and conditions her cashmere blonde hair. She looks like a mermaid, thinks Hils, until Tabitha flicks a long leg out of the water and turns the hot tap on with her peculiarly long toes. Hils is mesmerised. I used to be perfect like that, once upon a time. I had those legs and that belly. Now I have blue veins behind my clicky knees and silver stretch marks all over.

'You don't really mind, do you, Mum?'

Mind about what: breasts drooping, thighs withering, gums receding? Years ago both her children would have been in this tub together, roly-poly Saul with his boats and plastic dinosaurs and knobbly-kneed Tabitha making up songs about babies and gypsies and unicorns.

'No, of course not, I think it's great,' lies Hils. 'Joe is your father, he loves you and he wants to spend time with you. Can't think why.'

Tabitha flicks water at her mother. 'I love you.'

Hils finds herself grinning again. It's the only thing she can do to stop herself crying.

'Oh, and Mum, will you go and get my pyjamas for me?'

Hils blinks her way out of the bathroom and into Tabitha's candy-striped bedroom. Over the last couple of years all her daughter's 'little girl' things have gradually been submerged under a tide of teenage ephemera. On the walls, posters of a band called The Strokes vie with framed prints of flower fairies. Feather boas, a sequinned bag and a collection of fluorescent belts hang from the bedpost, and her bedside table is crammed with tarot cards, hair bobbles and glitter nail varnish.

Although Tabitha is quite neat by nature, and her geography project sits in a file on her desk, her pens and pencils zipped away in a plastic Miffy pencil case, one long stripy sock hangs out of a drawer like a tongue. Hils tucks it back in. On top of the chest sits a jewellery box, a sixth-birthday present. Hils knows that when you open it music plays and a tiny ballerina twirls. Around it sit Tabitha's deodorant, spot concealer, lip gloss, tweezers and special magnifying mirror, all the better to spot blackheads in. She is growing up; I can't stop it.

But Bill the bear is where he always is, prostrate on Tabitha's pillow, an amber eye lolling on his cheek. Hils reaches under the pillow for Tabitha's Hello Kitty pyjamas, and before she can stop herself she lifts the bundle to her face and inhales her daughter's scent, wiping her eyes as she does.

'What the fuck is wrong with me? I'm getting soppy in my old age.'

Hils gets a grip on herself and throws the pyjamas through the bathroom door. 'There you go, you idle toad.'

Tabitha is sitting on the edge of the bath, drying her feet. When she was little, Tabitha would sit in a towel on her mother's lap and they'd play the feet game. Hils would pick up Tabitha's right foot and say, 'What does this one smell of?' And Tabitha would say, 'Potatoes.' Then Hils would pick up Tabitha's left foot and say, 'What does this one smell of?' And Tabitha would reply, 'Honey.'

Saul's feet, on the other hand, always smelt of Dairylea triangles. They still do. Hils glances into his room, ankle-deep in Lego, socks and dismantled radios. Saul is a slob.

Later, when the house is quiet and there's bugger all on the telly, Hils has a sudden panic about passports and she sits in front of the cupboard in the dining-room pulling out shoeboxes. They're mostly full of receipts for electrical goods long since broken and gutted by Saul, but she finds what she wants right at the back – a box file labelled 'documents'. In this file are all the important pieces of paper: deeds to the house, her driving licence, the children's birth certificates.

These should be made out to me, thinks Hils. I did all the work. I deserve a gold medal for delivering Tabitha. Her mind leapfrogs backwards: twelve hours in labour, a split perineum and seventeen stitches, no epidural and only the merest whiff of gas and air. Thirteen years ago, Joe at her side, looking faintly ridiculous in a pair of bulging swimming trunks.

Whose idea was it to have a home water birth? The living-room covered in plastic sheeting, the blow-up paddling pool with its slow puncture. I must have been mad, she reckons. Tabitha had made her appearance thirty seconds before midnight. For a couple of minutes they'd seriously considered calling her Cinderella, but she'd looked at them with such feline disdain that it had to be Tabitha. Tabitha Rose, 29 January 1991, seven pounds three ounces.

Saul had been much bigger. After seeing the size of him at her twenty-week scan, she'd insisted on having him in hospital. Thank God she had. He'd weighed in at nine pounds four, with the biggest head the midwife had ever seen. Big bald Saul, so cheerful that even when he cried it looked like he was laughing. Saul Valentine Dobson, 14 February 1994, hence the middle name, something Saul prefers to keep very quiet about.

The passports are all present and correct, apart from Joe's, of course. He'd had to collect it one night on the way to the airport; he was taking the pregnant Nina to Paris. 'Hurry, Hils.' For a second she'd pretended that she couldn't find it, just to see the look on his face.

The kids, being under eighteen, will need their passports renewing next year, she notices, and with any luck Saul will try to look normal. She remembers hovering outside the Photo-Me! booth in Woolworths, telling him not to pull a stupid face, and even though he hadn't, there is still an element of gurning in his expression.

Hils flicks through her own passport. Under 'Contacts in Case of Emergency' she has written her father's name. But my father is dead, she tells herself, and therefore not much use in an emergency. Hils chews her bottom lip. I can't get weepy again – but she can't help remembering.

A month after my husband left, my father keeled over in the street. My mother saw the ambulance when she went to buy wet fish from the van that parks every Friday morning just around the corner from the library. My father had been changing his books. When he died, he had Simon Schama's History of Britain *tucked under his arm and an Ed McBain.*

My mother says bridge is a great comfort. I say Southern Comfort is a great comfort.

Two of the most important men in my life are gone. One is in an urn, the other is fucking a twenty-five-year-old and bouncing her baby on his knee.

My mother says she would give anything to see 'your father' one more time. She feels guilty because that morning he said he didn't feel like fish and what he really fancied was a shepherd's pie. Her last words to him were: 'Tough, we're having cod.'

When my mother realised that the man lying on the pavement was my father, she fought her way through the small crowd. 'I'm here, Alan, it's all right, my love, I'm here,' and she got into the ambulance. Later, when it was obvious that nothing could be done, she came home alone and realised that she had two pounds of cod fillet in her shopping bag. She put them in the freezer. My mother doesn't like waste. Some weeks later the library sent a reminder for the books my father had taken out on the day he died. When she went in to pay the fine and explained the circumstances, the librarian had waived the fee. This was the first time my mother cried. Wailing in the public library until the librarian had no choice but to remind her of the notices on the wall: 'Quiet Please'.

I still see my husband, sometimes when I'm least expecting it – I'm on a bus coming back from town and there he is! Coming out of Gap on Regent Street, and I'm banging on the window before I remember that the bag he is carrying contains clothes for a child that has nothing to do with me.

Diary of a Divorcee

When Hils has finished remembering, she finds she is still sitting in front of the cupboard and the sky outside the windows is navy blue. She's almost too exhausted and sad to move but the phone rings and her heart leaps again.

'Hello, hello . . .' Let my mother be well, let my brother be safe. I don't want anything bad to happen for a very long time.

But 'It's only me'. This is how Hils's friend Sally always announces herself: 'it's only me', as if she were some unassuming mousy apologetic type, when in fact Sally Thorpe, wife of Joe's best friend Nick, is a big brunette with a terrifying cleavage and a mouth to match.

'Now listen, Hils, and I don't want you to get hold of the wrong end of the stick, but I have to tell you that my retarded husband has invited Joe and Nina for supper next week.'

There is a pause.

'Well, say something.'

'What can I say? Nick is Joe's oldest friend.'

'Yes, but I'm *your* friend.'

'Sally, we're not in the playground now, really it doesn't matter.'

'Well it matters to me. I've got to cook for the soppy little tart. Any idea if she's allergic to anything? Ha!' Sally always laughs at her own jokes, even if they're not very good.

'Really, don't even think about it, because I certainly won't.'

'Well, thank fuck for that. I've been miserable all day. I had to drink a bottle of red wine and eat a whole bar of cooking chocolate before I could pluck up courage to call, so if I get a migraine it's your fault.'

'Life's too short, Sal, but you won't . . .'

'What?'

'Make the you-know-what.'

'The sweet chestnut meringue? Will I, bollocks. That's just for you, princess.'

'Night, Sal.'

'Night, gorgeous.'

Hils hangs up. It's been ages since she's been to Sally and Nick's. It's been ages since she went anywhere. Actually, that's not strictly true. Only last week she'd been invited on a girls' night out to a comedy club in King's Cross. One of Saul's friends' mothers was celebrating her thirtieth – ha, thirty! Still, she'd had a nice time. One of the acts had been really good, some Irish boy. 'God, I'd give him one,' one of the mums had breathed, and Hils, three bottles of German lager into the evening, had found herself agreeing.

See, my libido hasn't quite withered away; I'm not dead from the waist down yet, she reminds herself. Though it has been a long time. I'll end up getting rusty round my big end, like an old Ford Capri. I'm going to need WD40 down there if I'm not careful.

Rather than get up, Hils decides to phone her mother. She's not in. Brenda's doing a lot of gadding about at the moment, thinks Hils jealously.

She's been sitting on the floor for so long that her legs have gone to sleep and she is suddenly filled with panic at the prospect of growing old alone. What if something happens to the children in Italy? What if there is a fire and Joe only has time to save two people – who would he choose, Tabitha and Saul or Nina and Freya?

10

The Domestic Dumpling

Alice is at home. I really should clean out the fridge, she thinks. Only this morning she pulled out a tub of hummus for the boys' packed lunches and it was covered in a thick pelt of furry spores. Alice hates to throw anything away and refuses to obey sell-by dates, hence the contents of the salad tray: cucumbers turned to green sludge, gnarled mushrooms and withered carrots resembling a small compost heap.

Alice puts 'leftovers' into Tupperware boxes and then forgets about them until only a forensics expert could identify their origins. Cheese rinds are saved for grating, vinegar is added to that last millimetre of ketchup, and surface mould is scraped off jam. Alice doesn't think she's mean, just careful. Guy, on the other hand, is madly extravagant, chucking stale slices of bread straight into the bin. 'I could use that for breadcrumbs!' screeches Alice.

These days she doesn't let him go to the supermarket. He gets silly in Sainsbury's, buying 'gourmet this' and 'oven-ready' that. Pickled onions in balsamic vinegar, Duchy of Cornwall celery biscuits. Once he came home with quilted toilet paper! Guy is the sort of man who buys his vegetables pre-washed and sliced. Alice would rather save twenty pence and spend forty-five minutes splicing leeks and rinsing out great clods of soil.

Alice likes to imagine herself podding fresh garden peas from a trug while listening to Mahler. It's a pity her idea for a vegetable plot never took off. In fact the only thing they've got in abundance in the garden is cat shit and punctured footballs.

Neither of them has green fingers. It's a shame, be nice for Guy to have a hobby. After all, what does he do? He drinks and watches the television, once in a blue moon he'll read a book, and recently he's been going to the gym. Alice shudders. At least thanks to an old knee injury he can no longer play rugby. She put up with that for long enough.

Alice likes to think of herself as cerebral rather than sporty. Occasionally she goes to a women-only keep-fit group at the local leisure centre, but even as a girl she could never really touch her toes. As for jigging up and down on the spot, there isn't a sports bra in the world that can make that a pleasurable experience.

Even so, I should get into shape for this holiday, she thinks. Cut down on Jaffa Cakes for a start. Of course, it doesn't help having a sluggish metabolism. Some people can eat what they like – look at Di, just burns it off, it's really not fair.

Alice has put on two stone in the past three years – somehow the pounds just crept up. Not that she weighs herself, it was her doctor who made her get on the scales last time she went for a smear. Dumpling Alice in her tatty underwear weighing in at twelve stone three. She blushes at the memory, the ensuing lecture: 'cholesterol, furred arteries, massive strain on the heart', as if she didn't know. She'd nearly said, 'Excuse me, Dr Malpass, I'm a highly intelligent, middle-class, university-educated woman! Please don't speak to me as if I was one of those pie-and-chip-eating fat women you see on *Trisha*.' But of course she hadn't, it would have been rude.

Still, it's a shock sometimes, absent-mindedly dragging something out of the wardrobe and then not being able to get it past her knees, struggling with zips and resorting to safety pins. These days she wears a lot of clothes she bought when she was pregnant with Sam.

Alice feels a surge of temper. It's ridiculous, this obsession with looks. She blames the media – body fascism, that's what it is, and before she knows it two Jaffa Cakes and a broken custard cream have flown down her neck. She is still licking crumbs off her lips when the phone rings. She hopes it's not the baby.

The baby calls now and again. Heavy breathing followed by gurgles and, in the background, the clatter of a kitchen, a mother's voice in the distance, 'What are you doing?' Then the phone goes dead. Alice supposes their number must be on some automatic redial and sometimes this unknown baby presses a button and abracadabra she gets a nuisance call from a two-year-old. Alice always rings 1471 but the number is withheld. It's silly to get upset about it. After all, it's just a coincidence.

It isn't the baby, it's Joe's PA, Penny.

'Hello, Penny, how's your mother?'

Penny tells Alice she's 'as well as can be expected and thank you for your kind concern'.

Alice preens a little. Yes, she thinks, I am kind, I am concerned. I might have legs like blancmange but I'm actually a very nice person.

'Anyway,' Penny goes on to say, 'it's about Italy . . .'

The gist of it is that the travel company have called to say that due to overbooking, none of the apartments in the old part of the palace are available, but they can offer very nice accommodation in the modern annexe, the added bonus being that it's much cheaper. Apologies, etc.

'Well, that sounds just fine,' decides Alice. 'Go ahead, Penny. No need to bother Guy, I'm sure it will be lovely. Let's face it, we'll only be using it to sleep in. We'll be off having exciting adventures during the day.'

Penny is relieved that Alice is so accommodating. Guy would have gone all stroppy and demanded she speak to the manager. Penny has a hot flush at the thought. This keeps happening, her face clashing violently with her favourite mauve blouse.

They chat for a while, about the boys ('very well') and Weston-super-Mare ('I'm sure it'll be super'), until Alice decides that even though she is 'a very nice person', she's now rather bored with Penny and wishes she'd get off the phone. Fortunately the door-bell rings and she has a valid excuse to terminate this really rather tedious conversation. 'Goodbye, Penny.'

It's Di. She's not stopping, she's just dropping off the subject for this month's book club. It's Naomi Wolf's *Misconceptions*.

'Coffee?' pleads Alice. Di's been a bit funny with her since she broke the news about Italy. But Di is adamant, she really is far too busy to stop, she's taking Silas to meet his little friend Eddie at the swings. 'Shall I come with you?' offers Alice.

Di looks slightly uncomfortable. 'Sorry, Alice, Eddie's mum, well, you don't know her and she's asked me for lunch. Bye, Alice.'

'Bye, Di, see you soon—' but Di is already halfway down the street, hurrying to meet her new best friend.

Oh well, she'll see her at the school fête. She and Di are running the bric-à-brac stall, so that's something to look forward to.

The Naomi Wolf looks a bit hard going, but then again the book club isn't just about reading for fun, anyone can do that. It's about broadening horizons and thought sharing and stimulating conversation, and, if they're very lucky, a big wodge of Janet Robinson's superbly moist carrot cake.

Alice feels uncomfortable when she remembers the last book club soirée. It had been her turn to play host and she'd made a very nice cheesy pasta bake. Guy had scarpered as soon as he could, making a stupid joke as he exited: 'Book club, my foot. I bet as soon as I turn my back you'll all be in that front room watching a video of the Chippendales.'

An unfamiliar hoot of laughter greeted Guy's supposed wit. Janet had brought along a new member and she'd forgotten to tell her that it was customary to bring a dish, just something simple, a couscous salad or some home-made guacamole. But the new girl wasn't exactly empty-handed – no, she'd turned up with an enormous bottle of red wine and then proceeded to light a cigarette without even asking!

'Actually, we don't really smoke in this house,' Alice had chirped.

The woman had merely lifted an eyebrow. 'What about the garden?'

'Well, if you're really desperate I suppose we could open the French windows and you can pop out whenever you feel the urge.'

She'd popped out ten times. Alice had counted the stubs in the morning.

59

As they'd been leaving the woman had said, 'Your husband's ever so good-looking.'

'Yes, I suppose so, if you like that sort of thing,' Alice had replied. She didn't really like this new member of the book club, this Rosy.

'I'd give him one.'

'Would you now?' and Alice had closed the door very firmly indeed.

Alice has always read. As a child, living in a house with very few books, she visited the mobile library – Agatha Christie was a particular favourite.

Alice doesn't like remembering her childhood – it wasn't very happy. That's why it's vital that her boys grow up in a secure and loving environment. That's why there are always crayons and paper and books and educational games in the house. That's why she takes them to puppet shows and junior piano concerts and Saturday morning tae kwon do. That's why she bakes fairy cakes, makes sure they brush their teeth and that they always have clean pyjamas. Alice believes in encouraging her children, in praise where praise is due, in extracurricular activities, in fairness and sharing and treats for special occasions.

I am a good mother, she tells herself. My children attend dental appointments, their shoes are polished, I keep plasters handy, I am careful about what they watch on television, I help with their homework and loofah their necks.

Being a mother is the most important thing in the world to Alice. She doesn't want them to grow any older. She is jealous of Di, even if Silas has got behavioural problems. She misses the world of the toddler – the high chair and the buggy, the nursery-school paintings and feeding the ducks.

Why does time have to go so fast, why do things have to change, why do the boys have to grow up?

Already Max is answering back and slamming his bedroom door. He no longer allows her into the bathroom when he's showering and she has a horrible feeling it may be because he's got pubic hair. All of a sudden there is a poster of someone called Buffy on his bedroom wall and his socks have started to smell. Alice suspects there are more horrors to come. She has read articles. There will be wet dreams and masturbation, his voice breaking, facial hair and the dropping of testicles – it's too gruesome for words.

At least Sam is still a baby, still happy to hold her hand when crossing the road, and not wiping his bottom properly. Alice thinks fondly of his skid-marked pants.

Next year Max will be a teenager and Sam will be in his last year of primary – which is a good thing really (when one considers the problems). But that's not the point. One day she will have no one to make pastry men with, no shoelaces to tie and no one to help with the colouring in.

I think I might be a little bit depressed, decides Alice, reaching for the biscuit tin. Oh well, she's got the holiday to look forward to, maybe they can go camping next year, unless of course . . . 'There's nothing physically wrong with you, Mrs Jamieson, everything seems to be in good working order, although you might find that your age and of course your weight affect your chances of conception. If I were you I'd cut down on saturated fats and relax.'

It might help, of course, if she and Guy had a bit more sex.

11

Mind the Age Gap

Nina and Joe are in the bathroom. Joe is tweezering the ever-advancing hairs out of his ears: it is very painful. Bikini waxes have nothing on this, he's sure of it. Nina is chewing the skin around her fingers.

'Do we have to go?'

'Yes. Ouch!'

'Why?'

'Because Nick is one of my oldest friends and Sally is the best cook since Fanny Cradock!'

'Who?'

Jesus, despairs Joe. This keeps happening. Their cultural reference points are decades apart: different Dr Whos, *Blue Peter* presenters, Radio 1 DJs, and now telly chefs.

Joe tries to describe Fanny Cradock: 'Orange lipstick, had a sidekick, her husband Johnnie, frightful old bitch, very funny.'

'Sounds just like Sally,' mutters Nina.

Nina is frightened of Sally. She's like a proper grown-up woman with her Rigby and Peller bras and her clickety-clack high-heeled shoes. Sally mixes lethal martinis, never wears trousers (probably because her arse is too big, thinks Nina meanly) and paints her fingernails scarlet to match her mouth.

When Nina was a little girl she was very scared of Cruella DeVil.

All Sally needs is a big white streak in her hair and a few dead animals round her neck and she'd be her double.

Nick, on the other hand, is very nice, but he deals in books about military history and has a tendency to talk about battleships.

Sally and Nick argue a lot and Sally is always throwing things at him, like knives. Their daughter, seven-year-old Esme, is very quiet and mostly stays in her bedroom reading, although Sally, when she gets drunk, drags her downstairs to play the clarinet in her nightie.

'I don't suppose you've heard of the Galloping Gourmet either?' says Joe. 'Now he had class.'

Sometimes living with Joe is like being stuck in one of those *I Love the Seventies* programmes.

Shelley and Carmen are babysitting. It was Joe's idea, but even he looked worried when they arrived. Carmen has brought her electric razor so that Shelley can shave the stubble off the top of her head.

'You won't let Freya anywhere near that thing, will you?'

'Nah,' replied the Looby Loo lookalike, casually chucking a lighter on the sofa and getting a can of lager out of her bag.

'And you will call, if anything goes wrong?'

Both Nina and Joe are silent as they get in the cab. 'Vaughan Terrace, please,' Joe instructs the driver. The Thorpes live in a very big house in Islington. Sally comes from money – apparently her grandfather invented packet soup.

The house is Georgian and there are real paintings on the walls. 'Fabulous collection of Pipers,' Joe told Nina reverently the first time they visited, 'and look out for the little Hockney in the upstairs bathroom.'

Joe can be such a snob at times, thinks Nina, conjuring up her mother's flat in the Elephant and Castle, crammed from orange nylon carpet to wood-chip ceiling with fifties paraphernalia.

Nina is wearing jeans because she knows Sally can't. The world of women's bodies is divided into those who can get away with Diesel hipsters and those who look like a burst sofa if they try. It's a small act of spite but it makes her feel more confident for the moment.

Sally answers the door all curves and cleavage in a black dress with huge pink roses all over it and vertiginous heels.

'Nick's on e-bay tracking down a replica of HMS *Vanguard*, the twat. Hi, Joe,' and she presses her breasts against him in greeting, 'and little Nina.' She seizes Nina by the cheeks and squeezes them, just that bit too hard. Nina's eyes water. 'Come in, we're eating downstairs,' and she clatters down to the basement, hips swinging like a metronome.

'I got you a bottle of ween.' For some reason Nina can't speak properly.

'Oh, lovely, ween,' repeats Sally. 'I do love a drop of ween. Chardonnay,' she adds, 'how very Bridget Jones.' Sally discards the 'ween' and pulls a magnum of Veuve Clicquot out of a pink fridge the size of a Cadillac. 'Bubbles,' she commands, and thrusts the bottle at Joe, who opens it without flinching.

Nina ducks, even though Joe has the cork in his hand. 'I always think it's going to take my eye out,' she stutters.

'Really,' says Sally arching an eyebrow. 'I didn't have you down as the nervous type.'

For some reason this makes Nina feel really nervous. I wish I smoked, she thinks, as Sally lights up a skinny white menthol and Joe rolls his own. She used to, but she gave up when she was pregnant.

'Can I have a cig, please, Joe?' It's Joe's turn to raise an eyebrow, but he rolls her one anyway and, feeling better with a prop in her hand, Nina sits down.

'Not there!' yells Sally, too late.

Nina has squashed a puppet lady that Esme made out of a toilet roll.

'Let's just hope to fuck she doesn't ask where it is,' snaps Sally, chucking it in the bin.

'It was only a bit squashed,' protests Nina. 'I could have fixed it.'

'I don't think so,' states Sally icily. 'Oh for heaven's sake, it's not the end of the world. She can make another one. She's like Tabitha – remember, Joe – forever making little houses and stuff.'

She always does this, sulks Nina – brings Tabitha and Saul into the conversation. Never asks about Freya.

'Oh, and how's little Fi-Fi?'

Bloody hell, the woman's a witch. 'Freya,' corrects Nina, 'she's fine. She had a nasty cold last week and a bit of conjunctivitis.'

Sally yawns. 'Niiiick,' she yells. 'Oh Niiiick!'

Two hours later Nina is very drunk. She has chain-smoked all night and for the last thirty minutes she's been mistaking the butter dish for an ashtray.

'Oh don't worry, it's only an old Royal Doulton,' Sally waves dismissively.

'For God's sake, Nina,' Joe hisses.

Now she's got hiccups – it was Sally's fault, mentioning Hils's book.

'She really is clever, Joe, you know. God I wish I had half her brain. And the thing I admire most is that she just made up her mind to do it and she did. I mean, that takes guts. Do you remember?'

And she's off again, 'Hils this, Hils that', and all the time some old bird by the name of Ella Fitzgerald is caterwauling in the background and Nick's got out his collection of miniature battleships and is talking to Joe about double funnels.

I want to be with – hic – my friends, fumes Nina. I want to talk about fake tan and the cute one from The Coral and Carmen's new bloke and – hic – what's hot in Topshop. The last thing she wants to talk about is the fact that Joe's ex-wife has written an about-to-be-published novel about the meltdown of a marriage.

'Apparently it's called *Diary of a Divorcee*,' Sally slurs sweetly. 'Can't imagine where she got that idea from. Have some cheese, Nina,' and she wafts a plate of what smells like dried vomit under Nina's nose.

'No, thanks.'

She hadn't enjoyed her dinner. Artichokes, well, they're a waste of time, and roast sea bass with vile fennel? I'd rather have fish fingers. Nina's head feels like a medicine ball.

'Nina' – Joe is prodding her – 'sorry, gang, I think she's a bit tired, Freya's not been sleeping too well.'

'Poor thing,' sympathises Sally, but there is an edge to her voice, 'and it must be so boring listening to us old farts droning on.'

Joe then tells Sally and Nick about Nina not knowing who Fanny Cradock or the Galloping Gourmet were!

'How hilarious,' shrieks Sally. 'Right, Nina, hand up when you know who or what I'm talking about.' And out of her mouth comes a stream of names Nina has never heard in her life.

'Peter Noone, *The Singing Ringing Tree*, *Follyfoot Farm*, Sally James, Mary Hopkins?'

'Sorry,' slurs Nina, 'I don't know what you're talking about.'

It's like they're playing a game, Baiting Nina. Even Nick joins in: '*Double Deckers*?'

'Something to do with – hic – chocolate?' she hazards.

'No, children's sitcom set on a large red London bus!'

Nina doesn't know quite how it happens, but Sally and Nick are suddenly having a stand-up fight in the kitchen over whether the fat one in *Double Deckers* was called Doughnut or Roly.

'Hils will know,' yells Sally. 'Hils is the cleverest person in the world. If I was on *Who Wants to be a Millionaire?* then I'd want Hils to be my phone-a-friend. Phone Hils now!' she demands. 'Come on, Joe. You know the number – you lived there for fucking fifteen years. Phone Hils!'

Joe gets out his mobile. 'I'll just call a cab,' he says very quietly.

Nina feels she hasn't breathed for a very long time. At least her hiccups have gone.

'I think we could do with some coffee,' sighs Nick.

There is a terrible silence . . .

'Hic.' Shit.

Fortunately Esme makes an appearance. 'I could hear you two shouting, you woke me up.'

'Sorry, darling,' they mumble, instantly contrite. Esme has been the grown-up in this house ever since she was born.

'Where's my puppet lady?'

'I'm afraid Nina sat on her and killed her.'

At this point there is a toot from a minicab and Joe and Nina stumble into the night. Nina falls asleep in the back of the Mondeo.

Back at the flat Shelley and Carmen have had a Chinese takeaway.

'I don't think Freya liked it very much. Maybe the deep-fried prawns were a bit rich?'

Why does Shelley sound like she's apologising? Neither of them can wait to get out of the door.

'Anyway, see you, 'bye.' And they are gone, Carmen's bald head glinting in the moonlight.

'I'll just – hic – check Freya.' Nina is having difficulty walking. She ricochets off the wall and into her daughter's bedroom. The smell hits her before she gets to the bed. Freya is still in nappies at night, only this nappy has burst open and there is green poo all over the bed and all down Freya's legs. Nina leans forward to pick up the sleeping child and the full force of the stench streams up her nostrils. She can't help it: Nina opens her mouth and is violently sick all over Freya.

As the evening's artichoke and sea bass reappear in a swill of red wine, white wine, champagne and Cointreau, Nina is struck by the conviction that she has been poisoned. That Sally and Hils plotted this and are no doubt cackling to themselves this very minute, 'This'll teach her, the marriage-breaking floozy.'

Nina remembers stealing sweets from the corner shop and making herself ill devouring the evidence. This is justice, this is what she deserves, she has done a bad thing and she will be punished. One day the truth will come out and Joe won't love her any more.

12

All Jumbled Up

Hils is trying clothes on Tabitha and Saul. Last year's shorts and T-shirts are heaped on the floor like jumble. Whatever happened to jumble sales?

Hils remembers her student days, when she and her friends would spend Saturdays visiting church halls, burrowing for dead ladies' nightdresses that smelt of mothballs and embrocation, outsize men's shirts and children's school blazers, making up fashion statements as they went along. Lace gloves and green stilettos, silk ties and cricket jumpers.

Once upon a time I was colourful and adventurous. I wore plastic flowers in my hair and frosted my eyelids purple and gold. When did I become so dull?

When Joe sucked away my personality and I retired into his shadow, or was it that I just got bogged down by motherhood? Maybe I should have a tattoo, just a little one, a butterfly perhaps.

Tabitha has grown four inches since last summer. Everything is indecent on her. As for Saul, he has grown as plump as a fully inflated dinghy.

Is he too fat, is it my fault, does he comfort-eat because his father left home, should I stop him eating biscuits?

'Oh leave him be,' says her mother's voice in her head. 'He's just what I'd call well covered.'

'I think I might need new trunks,' gasps Saul, and Hils has to resist blowing raspberries on his puppy-fat bare belly.

She remembers going on holiday when she was Tabitha's age and her brother James was ten, just like Saul, and she conjures up a black-and-white photo of the two of them. They are on a beach in Wales wearing matching knitted zip-up cardigans, standing over a dead jellyfish. 'Smile for the birdy.' Her father's camera was kept in a brown leather case, chunky as a gas mask; it hung behind the kitchen door.

Funny how she has accidentally recreated her own sibling set-up, the older-sister, younger-brother scenario. 'Look after your little brother.' Her own voice an echo of her mother's. At least I don't knit them matching cardies, she thinks, and her neck itches at the memory.

When Hils was a little girl she always presumed she'd get married and have three children, a boy followed by twin girls. When you are eight you think that life can be ordered as if off a menu: 'Handsome husband, please, not too hairy, sweet children preferably with freckles, and a dog and a cat and a pony, thank you.'

Childhood is so different now. A wave of seventies nostalgia crashes through her brain: tea on the table, paper doilies and home-made cake.

Hils is the first person in her family to get divorced. It's a horrible word, she decides, a combination of divide and force. Whenever she tells anyone she and her husband have split up, she can almost hear wood splintering in the background, taste blood from a cut lip.

It's not my fault, she reminds herself. He was the one who spoilt it all, he was dishonourable, he was unfaithful. Why? Not all men are – my father wasn't. I don't think he ever looked at another woman. Instantly she corrects herself – apart from the sisters who ran the post office, of course. What were their names? Two curiously glamorous brunettes her father referred to as a 'right pair of Bobby Dazzlers'. Her mother teased him every time he posted a letter: 'Been to see your girlfriends, Alan?' Marcia and Gwen, that was it! Fancy as Fabergé eggs in a small town where women wore headscarves, sensible shoes and a great deal of drip-dry polyester.

If my father had lived, my parents would have been married for forty-five years. 'You have to adapt,' her mother says, polishing silver with her dead husband's underpants. 'You can't sit around moping for the rest of your life.'

'Mum, I think we might have to go shopping,' says Tabitha.

But Hils is miles away. Her hands are folding shorts that are too tight and skirts that are too short but her brain is spinning on memories that are almost thirty years old.

My mother made my summer dresses on an electric sewing machine that could embroider edges and finish off buttonholes; she bought plain biscuits and we drank a lot of orange squash.

'Mum, I'm starving.'

We ate picnics from a wicker hamper, hard-boiled eggs and soggy cheese and tomato sandwiches on a tartan rug, and I was happy, everything was normal, a mum and a dad and a brother. A proper family that filled two easy chairs and a sofa. In the garage was a rabbit with the same red eyes as my grandmother's cockerel brooch.

Hils picks up a T-shirt. 'That's Dad's,' says Saul.

Instinctively Hils sniffs it. Once upon a time she slept with it under her pillow, when he first left, before he moved in with Nina and was sleeping in the spare room at Sally and Nick's. Those were the limbo weeks, when Hils couldn't remember how to function, unable to trust her voice or her legs, never knowing if she would fall down and cry on the floor, wondering what they'd say to each other the next time they met, wondering if he'd ever come back.

But of course he did eventually, he had to. He couldn't keep wearing Nick's underpants, they were too tight. He'd phoned to ask if it would be convenient and they both decided it would be better if he came round when the children were at school. 'Shall we say eleven, then?'

For the first time ever, it seemed, he was on time, catching her unprepared and awkward on her own doorstep. It had been weeks since she'd seen him – all communication since the night he'd left had been via Sally and Nick, the children spending weekends over at the Thorpes'.

'Hello.' Hils was as red-eyed as her old rabbit, stiff from not sleeping, brittle and polite. Joe was embarrassed. Armed with bin-liners, he began to remove himself from his own house. She had helped him! Why? Why hadn't she just taken all his stuff and burned it on a bonfire? Because she enjoyed his guilt – he was as uncomfortable as a fat man trapped in a turnstile, but it had been a useless victory.

That was the day he told her about the baby, the day she knew that they could never go back. The day before her father died.

'Darling, I'm so sorry.' Her mother's late-afternoon phone call, Hils jumping to the wrong conclusion, thinking that her mother had rung to offer sympathy when it was she who needed it most. Her mother weeping, the worst sound in the world. 'It's your father.'

Nina's baby and Alan's death are so tightly bound that in those raw early months Hils would dream of Nina's unborn baby looking like a tiny version of her dad. She doesn't, of course, she doesn't even look like Joe, and to some extent that's always been a comfort, the fact that Joe's genes, so evident in her own children, particu-larly in Saul, have bypassed Freya. It would be unbearable if a little Saul lookalike was growing up on someone else's knee. Freya's dark auburn curls are a stark contrast to Saul and Tabitha's infant blonde wisps.

'Who are Big Audio Dynamite anyway?' interrupts Saul, and Hils unfolds her stiff legs and staggers into the kitchen to make pasta. On her way she throws the T-shirt on to the charity shop pile. Her mother, she knows, keeps one special drawer full of 'Alan': a couple of sweaters, his glasses and slippers, a penknife and a red-and-white spotted handkerchief.

'I don't know why I bother,' Brenda says. 'He's everywhere in the house.'

She's right: every painting is hung from a nail he knocked into the wall, every tile in the bathroom he hand-grouted. In the utility room are the brushes he used to polish shoes with, properly, on laid-out newspaper; in the garage is the stick he stirred paint with, the jam jars full of nails. 'Your father was a doer,' her mother says, as birds swoop on to a feeder he made out of wood and tied to the apple tree.

71

'What did we do before pesto?' Hils is reaching into the cupboard. Everything changes, everything moves on, men leave their wives, fathers die, and in a post office over a hundred miles away, two little grey-haired old ladies sort mail with long geranium-coloured fingernails.

In the days leading up to her father's funeral, her mother prepared a buffet. 'I had to do something, darling,' so she poached salmon and stuffed vol-au-vents and garnished everything with frilly radish lilies. Spread out on the dining-room table with cutlery wrapped in scarlet paper napkins it looked like a wedding breakfast, and for a moment, with all the aunts, uncles and cousins packed into every corner, it felt like a celebration.

Only Joe didn't stay, he drove back to London, back to his pregnant girlfriend, and she and the kids caught a train home a few days later.

At least he came, shamefaced in his best suit, although, as Brenda said, 'He couldn't look me in the eye, Hilary, that daft ape of a husband of yours. If your father was here, he'd have a thing or two to say to him.'

They slept together that night, two women without their men, two sets of tear-stained pillowcases.

That's what I'll do, thinks Hils. When the kids are in Italy, I shall go and stay with my mother.

Tabitha has written a list. 'These are the things we need, Mum. I suggest we have a day out in town, possibly lunch. We can ask Dad for some money.'

'You don't need to.' Money is about the only thing Hils doesn't have to worry about.

Hils rings her mother.

'Sorry, darling, last week in July I'll be in the Lake District. A gang of us have hired some caravans.'

A gang? My mother is sixty-eight, thinks Hils. What's she doing in a gang? She'll be wearing a baseball cap next and referring to her bridge club cronies as 'my homies' next.

'And who exactly is going on this caravanning jaunt?'

'Oh, the Elliotts, Morag Stewart and her sister, the one in the wheelchair – poor thing – and Basil, of course. He and Tommy Elliott will be doing the driving.'

Hmmm, Basil: this name keeps cropping up. Bowling with Basil, bridge with Basil, now caravanning with bloody Basil. Sometimes it seems to Hils that widows have a better social life than divorcees.

Her mother laughs girlishly. 'Sorry, darling, Basil's at the back door, we're off to a flower and produce show, I've entered the chutney competition. Basil says if my green tomato and raisin doesn't win, then heads will roll.'

Not fair, sulks Hils, putting the phone down. Her father's face swims before her eyes – he is winking. Winking and whistling, the two things her father did better than any other man. Better than bloody Basil, she's sure of that.

Many things can bind a relationship, and I'm not just talking about a joint fascination with sadomasochism. Some couples enjoy rambling and it's in everyone's best interest that these types marry each other, thus sparing the rest of us the tedium of 'nice healthy walks'. Others share a mutual love of a certain football club and are equally happy to live in a house painted the pale blue and burgundy stripes of Aston Villa.

My parents' relationship was bound by food, his favourites and hers; they knew each other's tastes inside out, down to who should have which Liquorice Allsort.

As my father got older his tooth got progressively sweeter and he took to buying paper bags of sugary treats from the newsagent's on the corner. In the evening, while they watched The Bill, *he would occasionally throw my mother a jellybaby. Instinctively, she would catch it, without taking her eyes off the screen.*

Later, at bedtime, she would make him a mug of hot milk, removing the skin with a teaspoon and, if he had a cold, she would add a drop of whisky, some honey and a squeeze of lemon. In return, every Saturday morning, when my father got up early to play golf, he would take my mother breakfast in bed. A bowl of cereal and a piece of buttery toast. Carrying it through on the tray with the picture of a woodpecker on it and the wicker handles, he would say, 'I spoil you, Brenda.' And my mother would always respond with,

'Oh, Alan, you've not booked another cruise, have you?'

Death robbed my mother of my father. It crept up unannounced and took him away, just like the thief who stole my husband.

Diary of a Divorcee

13

Hangover Hell at the PTA

The Saturday of the school fête dawns to cooked-liver skies. 'It's a crying shame,' says Alice. 'I've really been looking forward to it.'

She pulls open the curtains and even the sulky graphite grey light makes Guy wince. He is appallingly hungover.

'What time did you get in last night?' Alice has her hands on her hips.

Guy has no idea – he can't actually remember getting home. The last thing he remembers is drinking Pinot Grigio with Peter Stringfellow. He can also dimly recall tucking fifty pounds into a black girl's suspender belt and buying falafel from a kiosk in Leicester Square.

God, work can be so exhausting sometimes! This is the side of the job that it's hopeless trying to explain to Alice, the fact that sometimes it's necessary to get hog-wimperingly wankered in the line of duty. It's called networking.

The lager commercial has been cast and shot. A young Irish stand-up, twinkly green-eyed twenty-five-year-old Tommy O'Reilly, has been plucked from the obscurity of the pub circuit and launched Johnny Vegas-style on to the television public as the new face of Hetheringtons lager. The three-year contract drawn up by his brand-new management won't make him Ferrari-rich but it'll be enough to buy him a small flat somewhere unfashionable, like Lewisham.

That's if he doesn't piss it up against the wall, thinks Guy, vaguely recollecting a distinctly tanked-up Tommy, cross-eyed and rambling, slumped in a corner of Stringfellow's with a pint of Guinness in one hand, a whiskey chaser in the other and a redhead on his knee. Very bad form. The least he could have done was stick to Hetheringtons.

Still, Guy muses, you can't really blame him. It's not every day some little bog-trotter gets taken to the best Japanese restaurant in town followed by a trip to London's premier lap-dancing club, all courtesy of a bunch of middle-aged suits with fat expense accounts. The boy from Kilkenny had probably been a bit out of his depth – Guy smirks as he recalls the lad struggling with his chopsticks.

He lifts his head off the pillow. This is a mistake – he has obviously broken his neck. Instantly he has a vision of Peanut in a saucy nurse's outfit and his penis stiffens. At least that's not broken.

'Come on,' Alice bellows, pulling the duvet off the bed. Fortunately she is in too much of a hurry to notice his priapic state. Guy was too pissed to put his pyjamas on when he finally managed to crawl up the stairs in the early hours, and his erection looks like a small purple soldier listing dramatically to one side.

'At ease, old chap,' mutters Guy, rolling over. He missed Peanut last night. It was very much a boys' do and if she'd turned up there would have been talk. He'd phoned her, obviously: twice from the restaurant and three times from Stringfellow's, which on reflection might have been a mistake. The last time he'd called she'd sounded a bit pissed off. 'Guy, I'm, like, trying to have an early night.' Peanut shares a flat with two other girls in a house in Finsbury Park.

Guy has never been there, but he can imagine them, the three girls: playful as puppies, fiddling with each other's hair and walking around in their pants. For some reason this scenario makes him hornier than any number of last night's surgically enhanced lovelies shimmering up and down poles in their high heels. That's because I'm not a sleazebag, Guy concludes smugly, before despairing at the prospect of a whole weekend without the chance of a shag with his girlfriend.

Alice is frying eggs. 'You're on guess-how-many-jelly-beans-in-the-jar duty.'

'I beg your pardon,' Guy replies. He'd nearly been sick in the shower; saki is a terrible thing, especially when it's mixed with champagne, white wine, lager and tequila.

'I'm on bric-à-brac with Di.' Alice is wearing a large green T-shirt with 'St John's Primary School – Preparing Children for the Future' emblazoned on the back.

'Oh God, the school fête.'

Rain spits against the French windows. Alice bites into a fried egg sandwich and yellow goo dribbles down her chins. Guy burps, wasabi-flavoured with an aftertaste of falafel.

Only Max has managed to wriggle out of the annual summer fête. He's got a party: six of them are being taken to the Trocadero and then back to some boy's house for a sleepover. A toothpaste-white limousine picks him up at eleven; he's out of the house quicker than a bolt from a crossbow.

'Quite ridiculous,' Alice huffs, 'but what can you expect? Parents are divorced and they think that lavishing the poor child with daft treats is going to make it better. I feel sorry for him, I really do.'

The child in question hadn't seemed too traumatised to Guy. On the contrary, sitting in the back of a stretch limo, swigging a can of Coke with a big bag of cheesy Wotsits on his knee, he'd looked in his element. It was all Guy could do to stop himself diving in with them – anything rather than suffer the indignity of the summer fayre.

I have never been more miserable in my life.

This isn't true. Guy has forgotten for a second that his parents were killed in a car crash, and the gut-wrenching, sour-tasting feeling that he is currently experiencing is nothing compared to how he felt then.

Guy refuses to remember that time – it's over, it was ghastly. One day it was Wednesday and everything was normal, the next, a Thursday, he was an orphan. He went to his parents' funeral on crutches, having dislocated his knee playing rugby a couple of weeks earlier. His whole life was in ruins, he couldn't eat, he couldn't speak, his parents were dead and he couldn't even walk properly. He just hopped to the off-licence twice a day and watched television with the curtains drawn. Occasionally he ate a Pot Noodle.

His older sister asked him if he wanted to go and stay with her and her young family in Aberdeen, but Guy figured if he was miserable in London, Aberdeen would be worse. He didn't wash and he didn't go to work. He could afford not to: his share of his parents' estate came to £20,000. You can live on that for years if you just drink cider and eat kettle meals. In the end it had been Alice, turning up on the doorstep with a freshly roasted (albeit slightly burnt) chicken, who had coaxed him back to normality.

Guy couldn't remember her name at first – it was two o'clock in the afternoon and he was already on his second bottle of Woodpecker.

He was drowning and Alice had certificates for life-saving; she was a Queen's Guide, and a Duke of Edinburgh gold medallist. She bathed him and fed him and took him to the barber. 'Messed-up Guy' was the best project she ever had. So he'd lost his mum and dad? Well, now he had her. She grew on him, like mould on bread, offered him a replacement family, something to live for: 'I'm pregnant, Guy, and it's yours.'

He owed her.

Well, he's paying now. 'How many beans in the jar?' he chants half-heartedly. He's been at the fête for twenty minutes but it seems like a fortnight. Out of the corner of his eye he can see Michael Clements demonstrating tai chi at the far end of the playground. The man looks insane. Children are sniggering and a dog keeps running between Michael's legs, jumping at his testicles. 'Good dog, good boy,' mutters Guy.

Alice has set up stall around the corner, next to the bouncy castle and the cake stand, which is doing fantastic business, thanks mostly to Alice. So far she's had two flapjacks and a large slice of lemon sponge.

Occasionally Guy hears her voice carried by the wind: 'Bric-à-brac bargains, something lovely for everyone.' This is not strictly true. Alice's wares consist mostly of broken toys, unidentifiable knitted objects and a rusty fondu set.

Sam sidles up to him. For a second Guy doesn't recognise his youngest son. He's had his face painted. It's meant to be Spiderman but the black web has smeared into the red background and he looks like he fell face down on to a barbecue.

'Can I have fifty pee to have a go at Mr Carmichael, Dad?'

Mr Carmichael is the deputy head of the junior school. He is sitting in hand-made stocks while children line up to throw wet sponges at him. His 'good sport' demeanour seems to have worn dangerously thin – Mr Carmichael is radiating fury. Guy gives Sam three pounds in the hope that Mr Carmichael will crack, punch a child and the whole afternoon will have to be called off.

'Thanks, Dad.' Sam skips off, but Guy calls him back.

'Listen, Sam, can you just hang on for a bit, keep an eye on the jelly beans,' he instructs. 'I'll be back in a minute.' And with the change purse Alice supplied him with safely tied around his waist, he canters round the back of what used to be the bike sheds. His mobile is in his pocket.

'Hi, it's me, where are you?'

Peanut is in Covent Garden with her friend Abigail, who is just trying on a pair of shoes in LK Bennett. 'I like the suede ones better,' she says.

'Listen, sorry about last night.'

Peanut tells him he'd sounded really pissed.

'I was a bit,' admits Guy. 'Sorry.'

Peanut is silent.

'Peanut, are you still there?'

She is.

'So,' says Guy, forcing a Mr Carmichael degree of jollity into his voice, 'what are you up to tonight?'

Peanut replies that she is going to a party with Abigail in Wimbledon.

(NOOOOOooooooooo.)

'Oh well, have fun.'

Peanut assures him that she will.

'Dad!' Guy can hear Sam shouting. 'Daaaad!'

'Got to go.' He is about to tell her that he loves her but her phone's gone dead.

Guy sprints back to the jelly-bean stand. Sam is jumping up and down. 'Dad, they took the jelly-bean jar.'

Suddenly Alice is there, furious as a female Hulk. 'What the hell's going on, Guy, where were you?' she demands.

'He went behind the bike sheds,' sobs Sam.

'I needed a wee,' hisses Guy simultaneously.

Alice is appalled. 'I hope you didn't wee behind the bike sheds. There are lavatories available, Guy!'

'He went behind the bike sheds,' reiterates Sam, 'and some big boys ran off with the jelly-bean jar.'

'Teenagers from the estate, no doubt,' mutters Alice, 'with nothing better to do than steal jelly beans.' Joyriding, mugging old ladies, robbing jelly beans – it's all the same to Alice. 'Probably high on glue,' she adds.

Guy feels dreadful. The hangover, instead of getting better, has got worse. He really needs to lie down. He sinks to the ground. He literally can't stand up any longer.

Alice, mistaking his physical collapse for remorse, instantly softens. 'It's all right, Guy, stay there. I'll get you a nice cup of tea.'

I should have been a nurse, thinks Alice as she bustles over to the tea and cake stall. I'm good in an emergency, practical and calm. While everyone else around me falls to pieces, who keeps it all together? Me! 'Cup of weak tea with two sugars, please, oh, and one of those little cherry buns.'

The story of the jelly-bean theft courses around the playground. Everyone is very understanding.

'You poor old thing, what a shame I didn't see the blighters.' Michael Clements has wandered over. 'I'd have seen them off,' and very slowly and deliberately he demonstrates a couple of martial arts moves.

Guy feels hysteria rising in his throat. 'I think I'll just go home.'

'Yes,' says Alice, 'I'll be back in about an hour. You really do look quite dreadful.'

Guy unties his change belt and gives it to Alice. His hands are shaking, she notices; he's obviously been quite traumatised by the whole incident.

'See you later.'

Guy limps home. It's only five minutes round the corner but he could do with a cab. Once safely in the house, shivery and nauseous, he lies on the sofa and shuts his eyes, just for a second.

'Cooey, it's only us.' Alice bursts through the door. 'Well, Guy, I'm afraid you only took four pounds and the jelly beans actually cost five, but I've sorted out the shortfall. We did rather well on the bric-à-brac, I'm very glad to say.' Thunder cracks in the distance. 'Look who's come back for supper.' Standing behind Alice, Guy can see what looks like a small band of travelling circus folk: it's the Clementses.

'Yes,' crows Di, 'Alice and I beat our own record.'

'One hundred and thirty pounds,' they chorus, giving each other a clumsy high five.

'Who'd have thought that box of Guy's old Clash records would have fetched so much?' burbles Di. 'I didn't think anyone bothered with vinyl any more.'

'I know,' screeches Alice gleefully. 'Twenty pounds for the lot.'

Let me die, thinks Guy.

14

Grannie Maxine

Nina is taking Freya to see her grandmother. Maxine still lives around the back of the Elephant and Castle in the same two-bedroom Peabody flat where Nina grew up.

Lawrence House, despite its unfashionable SE1 postcode, has always enjoyed a reputation for clean nets and no trouble. Nina remembers how, compared to most of the multistorey scrapheaps locally, the low-rise redbrick was considered just one step down from a maisonette in Maida Vale.

I was lucky, reckons Nina, even though she was bullied for being 'posh'.

The 171 bus lumbers towards south London, slower than a double-decker hearse. Nina and Freya sit upstairs. Nina holds on to Freya's legs as the toddler gabbles away to an old man who sits behind them, slurping Tennent's Super from a purple can.

The old man is telling Freya (in between belches) about how once upon a time he had a little girl (burp) but he hasn't seen her for years and that she won't be a little girl any more, she'll be a big girl now (burp) with babies of her own.

Oh Christ, thinks Nina, what if I turn round and it's my dad?

She pivots her head slyly and instinctively she knows he's not. This one looks like Father Christmas after a big fight. His knuckles are split, blood oozes through grime and the blue ink of home-made tattoos, and there is dandruff on his collar, thick as snow.

My father was a small, dark, curly-haired man, Nina reminds herself.

According to her mother he looked like a cut-price David Essex with bad teeth. 'They'll have fallen out by now,' her mother says. 'Green they were, worse than the Queen Mum's – with any luck he'll have lost his hair and all.' Sometimes, when Nina conjures up her father, all she can see is a toothless bald dwarf. He's probably in panto somewhere.

Over the river – 'Boats, Freya, boats' – and past the Hayward, where Joe had an exhibition back in the eighties. He's frustrated, realises Nina: he thinks he should be famous and he isn't and now he's probably too old. Anyway, you don't get famous doing pack shots of oven-ready chips and girls in cheap nylon bras.

Everyone thinks they're going to be famous, she muses, remembering old boyfriends travelling the motorways in transit vans with their electric guitars, existing on Ginster's sausage rolls and lager, all wasted arms and bloated bellies, living in bedsits. She'd caught crabs off one of them. Bastard.

A massive billboard catches her eye, just past Waterloo. It's whatsisname, the one Shelley fancies? Apparently she met him once, before he was a stand-up. He was working in a pub in Dalston. He was just a no one back then, and now look at him. All over the place all of a sudden. What's his name? Tommy something, Irish, he was on Graham Norton the other night.

One of the lucky ones, maybe, who knows? 'Here today, gone tomorrow' – that's what Joe says, his voice as bitter as an unripe plum.

Past the adventure playground with the three bronze bears sitting primly in a circle: 'Bears, Freya, bears!' Hannibal-like in its slowness, the 171 lumbers into SE1. Freya is sad to leave the old man. Before they get off the bus she wants to kiss him goodbye. Nina has to physically drag her away. 'Come on, Freya,' she demands, uncurling her fingers from the handrail one by one. The whites of the tramp's eyes are the colour of hepatitis, yellow as yolk.

Nina unfolds the buggy and lifts her daughter into it. As she does so, she realises Freya is wearing just one of her brand-new shoes. 'Stop!' she yelps at the bus, but the doors hiss shut and almost sarcastically it winks away from the kerb. I could sit on the pavement and cry, thinks Nina, when suddenly a small pink object lands by the bus stop.

Pissed Santa has chucked Freya's shoe out of the window. He is waving a bloody hand from the top deck. You can't catch hepatitis off a shoe, thinks Nina, and buckles it back on to Freya's wide little foot.

'Thank you,' she yells.

'My grandad,' beams Freya.

Nina doesn't bother to correct her. After all, Freya's real grandfathers haven't proved much use. One disappeared over twenty years ago in a puff of Embassy Regal, and the other? Well! Nina feels an itch of discomfort, just as she had a second ago when she'd remembered the crabs incident. Joe's dad is a really nice man, but . . . 'They'll love you,' Joe had said, referring to his parents, but they don't. They love Hils. As for Freya, it's as if they are ever so slightly allergic to her.

Joe laughs it off. 'They're getting old, toddlers are hard work. You wait, when she's older they'll want to see her more, it'll be just like it is with Tabitha and Saul.' Nina isn't so sure.

Joe has told her how his father used to paint elaborate watercolours of dinosaurs for Saul and penguins for Tabitha when they were little. Freya will get paintings, he promises, of polar bears and gingerbread men, and hand-knitted hats with pom-poms on the top. But Freya doesn't, she gets premium bonds. The truth of it is, Joe's parents are dutiful but distant. Freya is kept at arm's length; it's as if they don't want to get too involved.

So why do *I* feel so guilty? puzzles Nina. You know why, replies her subconscious.

Sometimes Joe's mother looks at Freya and then at Nina and there is something in her eyes, a sadness, that makes Nina wither inside.

She doesn't trust me, and why should she? She will be the first to say, 'I told you so.'

Nina wheels the buggy away from the junky blood-red

mausoleum that constitutes the Elephant and Castle complex. Her mother lives a mere mugger's sprint away. On the pavement a man is selling rugs featuring the faces of Elvis and James Dean. Joe would rather die, she thinks, than have one of those in the house. Will I ever have anywhere that reflects my personality? she wonders. Joe is so rigid when it comes to decorating. It's like living with a style Nazi.

How will I ever know what I like if I'm never allowed to choose?

Maxine has a new rug covering the entrance to the flat. Nina steps on to Marilyn Monroe's nose.

'Fab, isn't it?' states Maxine, who is a vision in leopardskin and sky-blue Capri pants. Nina looks around her. If anything, the flat is fuller than it was the last time she visited. On Sundays her mother trawls the car-boot sales of south London and the spoils of her lootings are crammed into every available square inch.

Maxine is a fiend for kitsch. The knee-high china poodle is new, but the Hawaiian-style bar in the corner complete with cocktail shaker, pineapple ice bucket and jars of maraschino cherries is an old favourite. Vintage Barbies line the windowsills and the walls are covered in posters for Hitchcock movies. Fairy lights twinkle everywhere and plastic flowers gather dust.

'Hi, Mum.' They kiss awkwardly. She's too thin, thinks Nina. She doesn't eat properly.

'And how's my little poppet?' coos Maxine, unstrapping Freya and sitting her on her bony lap. She doesn't look like a grandmother, thinks Nina. Grandmothers should be plump and smell of gravy. Maxine smells of menthol cigarettes and Silvikrin stronghold hairspray. Her hair is electric-rollered and backcombed into a beehive, the grey obliterated with a mahogany dye.

Joe's mum makes pies, stewed apple steaming through sugary crusts, smothered in hot yellow Bird's Eye custard. Maxine lives on biscuits and Slimfast diet drinks. Nina has never seen her finish a meal. As for cooking, Maxine can barely fry a fish finger.

As a girl Nina lived on toast toppers and spaghetti hoops. Maybe that's why my dad left, maybe he lives with a big fat woman who cooks him bacon and egg . . .

'Mum, what was my dad like?'

'An arsehole, darling.'

Maxine has got a present for Freya. It's an evening bag, black satin with a diamanté trim and an old-fashioned clip fastening. Inside it are strings of coloured plastic beads. Freya is delighted. She chews the bag and allows Maxine to festoon her neck with the beads.

'I've got cakes,' says Maxine, with as much pride as if she'd stuffed a swan with hummingbirds, and she opens a packet of Mr Kipling's Bakewell Tarts.

'How's that Joe?'

Maxine is nervous of Joe. She's only at ease in the company of homosexuals. Since the day Ray wandered off she's never bothered with the opposite sex, not the heterosexual ones anyway. When Maxine has friends round it looks like the cast of *Queer As Folk* have dropped by.

'Fine. We're going away in a couple of weeks, Italy,' Nina tells her mother. 'With Joe's other children,' she adds.

She wants her mother to sympathise, to latch on to the doubt in her voice, to actually have a proper adult conversation with her. Over the years Nina has struggled to come to terms with the fact that her mother can only deal with the upper epidermis of emotion. Anything below the surface, anything messy, is avoided.

'Ooh, *La Dolce Vita*, lovely bums, Italian boys, there's one works behind the bar in the club, like two snooker balls in a Lycra bag. Here we go, sweetie,' and she picks all the cherries off the tarts to give to Freya.

Nina gives up. On the bookcase in the corner is a heart-shaped box covered in quilted pink velvet. Fifty years ago it contained chocolates. Nowadays, in place of the violet cremes is a bundle of photos. Nina on her first day at secondary school, Nina tap-dancing, various Freddie Mercury lookalike 'uncles', and right at the bottom a photo of Nina on her father's knee.

'Do you mind if I take this?' she asks.

'Help yourself,' her mother replies.

'Mum, do you think Freya looks like me?'

'No, not really, in fact, not one bit. We've never had a copper-knob in the family as far as I can recall.'

'Auburn,' corrects Nina, 'and only in a certain light.'

'I suppose she takes after Joe's side.' Maxine pauses for a second. 'Mind, Joe's like a big, blond shaggy camel really, isn't he? Hairy with big feet.' She shudders. 'Ooh, that's something I never liked, a man's foot touching mine under the duvet, like a fidgety guinea pig.' Maxine slides a CD into an incongruously modern-looking portable stereo and she and Freya dance to 'It's Raining Men'.

Later, when Nina puts Freya to bed, she is still clutching the diamanté handbag. 'Now, if you were a boy and you were doing that, your granny really would be proud,' mutters Nina, stroking her daughter's nose, staring at her face, searching for clues.

15

Hils Requests the Pleasure

Time is a great healer, they say, and it is, sort of, only it's a bit like having a leg amputated. The stump forms a shiny new skin, but the leg doesn't grow back and you have to learn how to hop.

When I was very small I went to ballet classes. They were held at the local institute: a red-and-yellow brick building built during a time of Victorian optimism. Down in the basement where the hot water pipes gurgled, a very thin lady shouted at six-year-olds and a very fat man played the piano.

'Skip,' the skinny lady yelled, 'skip!' But I couldn't skip, I could only hop. Until one day the hopping turned into skipping and I thought my heart would fly through the window.

When my husband left I felt as though I'd lost the power to skip and I was back to square one, just hopping hopelessly.

Diary of a Divorcee

The summer holidays have crept up on Hils. Tabitha and Saul have broken up ludicrously early – it's only the middle of July! The state schools still have another week or so to go. Mad, she thinks, the more you spend, the less they're there.

Still, at least it gives her time to get organised for Italy. She's promised to take them shopping tomorrow. Hils isn't sure she can face the West End again – her credit card's taken enough of a battering this week. Guilt makes her heart palpitate, while the mere thought of tonight is like an enema. What does a first-time author wear?

She could go for the whole Dorothy Parker number and wrap herself in purple velvet complete with turban, pearls and peacock feathers. She could smudge her eyes with dark grey shadow, paint her lips the colour of blood and smoke a cheroot from an ivory holder, but then the kids really would refuse to come with her. These days they prefer it if she blends in with the wallpaper. A nice roll of beige-painted woodchip would have sufficed.

Hils unwraps the dress from its nest of pink tissue paper. The Visa receipt lies at the bottom of the bag, her shaky signature testament to just how much this outfit cost. She shouldn't have done it – is she mad? She could have worn her denim skirt. What if no one else bothers to dress up? It's only a Thursday night. A few glasses of sparkling wine – that's what it says on the invitation.

'Redback Publications request the pleasure of your company to celebrate the launch of Hils Morgan's touching debut novel. On 17 July 2004, drinks 7.30 pm at the Groucho Club.'

Hils blushes at the 'touching' bit. Is it a euphemism for over-sentimental piffle? As for the Groucho Club, she's not even a member. Maybe they won't let her in and she'll have to say, 'Do you know who I am?' and they'll reply, 'No, never heard of you, get out.'

Making sure her nail varnish is totally dry, she picks up the dress by its skinny spaghetti straps. A sheath of cream satin overlaid with a web of intricate black-beaded netting tumbles down like hair from a bun.

Three hundred pounds, thank you very much. Who does she think she is? Elizabeth blinking Hurley?

Then there are the shoes. Oh God, the shoes, another two hundred quid. Little Emma Hope cream and black velvet embroidered mules with a kitten heel, shoes that are too beautiful to wear. Ideally they should be put in a glass box on the mantelpiece, a work of art entitled 'Forty-one-year-old woman goes mad in shoe shop'.

Once when Hils was little she was given a spun-sugar Easter

egg studded with violet and pink rosebuds, too gorgeous to eat, so she kept it on her dressing table until it was inedible, thick with grey dust.

Maybe she should just take the whole lot back, plead insanity, tell them she needs the money for her sister's eye operation. But Hils knows they'll only give her a credit note, and anyway the woman in the shop had been so nice. So nice that Hils had ended up inviting her to the launch, a last-minute attempt to inject some glamour into her party. The woman was very tall and thin with black hair. Hils imagined her looking sophisticated in a doorway and people thinking, 'Blimey, hasn't Hils got some interesting friends?'

She hasn't invited many people. She had gone all shy about it, leaving it too late for friends to find babysitters, embarrassed by the whole thing. She hadn't even asked her mother, not until it was too late, then when she had she'd underplayed the event so much that her mother had said, 'Actually, darling, the Chamberlains are having a barbecue and I've already said I'll be there. I'm on salad duty. Anyway, we're all off to the Lakes Friday morning.'

Oh well, Janey's coming, and all the school-gate mums and the poofs from number six, then there's Henry and Jane, Alex and Sylvie, all the usual gang apart from Sally and Nick, who are spending their wedding anniversary in Venice. Sally had wanted to cancel the trip, but Hils wouldn't hear of it. 'Don't be daft, it's not a big deal.' Oh yes, and her brother, of course, James, and her sister-in-law Midge, and Tabitha's piano teacher, Miss, er, thingy.

Maybe she should have a gin and tonic. Hils looks at her Timex, its big cheerful cheap face reminding her she has neither time nor a tiny diamond-encrusted lady girl Tiffany watch. Get dressed, woman.

It's only when she stands in front of the big chipped gold mirror in the hall that she realises you can see right through the dress and her big pants are clearly visible. She's read about nude-coloured thongs but she hasn't got one. Hils whips her knickers off and instantly feels horny and vulnerable. 'Please God, don't let me fall over, don't let anyone see my vagina.'

At least there seems to be enough carefully placed beading to render her pubes invisible. She wouldn't like to get busy with a razor, not now, not when her hands are shaking so much she could do herself a mischief.

Right: purse, fags, keys, phone, kids.

A taxi toots outside. 'Tabitha, Saul, cab's here.' Tabitha emerges from her room, all pink lip gloss and glitter nail varnish, a skinny My Little Pony with her long legs and enormous feet. She's nearly as tall as me, thinks Hils, and for a second she feels like crying, beautiful Tabitha making an effort, silver diamanté stars glinting on her cheek, a tiny Miffy T-shirt and yards of denim flares. Saul appears behind her.

I mustn't laugh, gulps Hils.

Her son has decided to mix and match. He is wearing his white school shirt, a waistcoat Hils had made out of an old curtain (gold brocade for a Christmas 2001 production of *Bugsy Malone*), a bow tie, his combats and trainers. He has also decided to experiment with hair gel. There is a tidemark of pale green grease around the back of his collar. 'You look fantastic,' his mother lies.

'I know,' says Saul. 'I look like James Bond.'

'A great fat pie-eating James Bond,' sniggers Tabitha, and then, 'What are your pants doing in the hall, Mum?'

For some reason Hils picks them up and stuffs them in her handbag. She locks the front door behind her and shouts, 'Bye, see you later, Mike!' This is to ward off burglars. Mike is actually a very old cat, a she cat at that, with lesbian tendencies and the breath of rotting garbage. Mike might not be able to savage an intruder, but one whiff of her breath would at least render them unconscious.

It would have been nice if the minicab had been something smarter. To be honest, it would have been nice if it had possessed a gearbox and hadn't stunk of ganja and fart with semitones of synthetic Alpine forest. Oh well.

Tabitha, who is very sensitive to smell and can throw up just by sniffing slightly off milk, winds down the window and the diarrhoea-coloured Nissan shuffles and crunches its way to the West End.

I'd rather be watching *EastEnders*, thinks Hils.

Forty-five minutes later the car grinds to a halt outside the

Groucho Club. Smoke is pouring from under the bonnet. 'Cool,' mutters Saul.

'Just get out,' snaps Hils. There's no way she wants to be in this car when it blows up, not when she's wearing five hundred quid's worth of clobber. She throws a twenty-pound note at the driver and they scramble out.

Joseph Fiennes has just exited the club's revolving doors.

'I thought you were great in *The English Patient*,' gushes Hils.

'That was my brother, actually,' he replies.

'Ha ha ha ha,' laughs Hils.

'Hasn't that man got a narrow face?' bellows Saul.

Hils puts her head down and makes for the door. Behind her she hears the cab driver ask Joseph Fiennes if he's 'any good with gearboxes, mate'.

The girl behind the reception desk raises the most beautifully plucked eyebrow Hils has ever seen. 'Can I help?' she enquires. Hils is tempted to ask directions to the nearest Aberdeen Angus steak house. She has never felt more suburban in her life.

'This is the authoress Hils Morgan,' announces Saul, 'and we are here to celebrate the publication of her latest work.'

The receptionist grins. 'I think you're up in the Gennaro Room. May I just remind you that we operate a no-mobile-phone policy here in the club, so if you'd just like to make sure your phones are turned off that would be great.'

Hils burrows in her bag and pulls out her mobile. A pair of purple Asda 'three pairs for six quid' knickers flies on to the desk as she does so. 'Whoops, my hankie,' says Hils, and to demonstrate that she is not lying, blows her nose theatrically on her pants.

Fortunately at this moment there is a commotion at the door. A fat woman has got her sari caught in the revolving doors and is banging on the glass panels, shouting in Hindi.

'I didn't know you'd invited Mrs Gupta, Mum,' says Tabitha.

Neither did Hils. Oh God, now she remembers. Mrs Gupta is the lollipop lady outside Saul's school. They'd got talking, you know how it is, and now here she is trapped by reams of billowing turquoise silk, knocking and shouting and holding something that looks like a small mountain covered in tin foil. Mrs Gupta finally frees herself and, huffing like the Hogwarts Express, she thrusts herself into the foyer, proudly announcing that she has brought along some 'home-made onion bhajis'.

'Still warm.' She smirks, lifting a corner of silver foil to release a pungent whiff of deep-fried onion.

A couple of bhajis have rolled on to the floor. The girl on reception is trying to make out that bringing your own food to the Groucho is quite normal. However, Hils notices that her perfectly plucked eyebrow has disappeared into her hairline.

'Ha ha ha ha,' laughs Hils.

'Can I also remind you that we do not tolerate any drug-taking on the premises,' warns the girl, and then adds, 'Through the doors, up the stairs, down the corridor, second room on your left.'

Tabitha intones the instructions like a mantra. Hils clenches her buttocks and her skirt gathers in the cleft.

Without gawping, it's difficult to see exactly what's going on in the room they enter. There's a bar on the left and a cluster of butterflies who turn out to be ridiculously pretty girls giggling on a sofa to the right. Saul manages to grab a handful of peanuts from a passing tray, ice chinks in long glasses and a fat man smokes a cigar in the corner.

'Ooh, look, Mum,' whispers Tabitha, 'there's that bloke who does the lager advert.' Hils looks. Tommy O'Reilly is dropping coins by the cigarette machine. His shirt is unbuttoned and he seems to be having trouble standing upright.

Bending down to retrieve his change, Tommy staggers and careers headlong into Mrs Gupta. The onion-bhaji mountain explodes, volcano-style, and spicy missiles fly through the air like hefty, brown ping-pong balls. One lands on Tommy's head; another drops – horribly turd-like – into Anthony Minghella's gin and tonic. Up until this moment Hils had been promising to make every other drink a glass of mineral water.

The day the estate agent came round to value what had once been 'our house', I felt premenstrual with fury. There I was, facing forty, my husband had left me for a younger woman who was pregnant with his child, my dad was dead, and now I had this no-arse, bum-

fluff of a boy sneering round my house, saying things like, 'Well it's only got one bathroom and the kitchen could do with a facelift.'

Right then I made up my mind that, despite the fact that I was on the brink of divorce and too depressed to get dressed in the morning, I was not going to lose my home.

Diary of a Divorcee

16

Alice vs the World

Alice is going to school to talk about 'the unpleasantness'. In a nutshell, she doesn't want the bullying of Sam to continue next term. Alice is determined. She has jotted down phrases such as 'zero tolerance' on the back of an envelope to remind herself not to accept any excuses.

Not that she's expecting to be fobbed off, not after the triumph of the bric-à-brac stall last weekend. Apparently, with the funds raised, the school is going to buy new sports equipment, which is a shame, really – Sam hates games.

Maybe she'll suggest to the headmistress that a percentage of the money should be redirected towards some of the more academic children in the school? I mean, really, the sporty ones don't need much. If they're that desperate they can kick a can around like they do in the slums of Mexico.

No one ever takes the needs of the brighter children into consideration. Alice saw some super interactive globes in Peter Jones recently, or what about a nice microscope? She practises the phrase 'the science-curious are very poorly catered for' out loud.

Sometimes Alice despairs over her sons' education. It's bad enough at primary level, but Max's secondary – well, maybe that was a mistake. As far as Alice can tell, it seems to be less of a school and more of a holding bay for the pustulent (the girls) and pestilent (the boys). Guy's offered to pay but Alice insists that she will not, as the *Guardian* puts it, 'perpetuate a two-tier system', and anyway, if she does opt out of the state system, Di will never speak to her again.

Alice is buzzed into the school. At least they've prioritised their security. After all, you can't have any old stranger wandering in unannounced.

'Actually, it's to stop *them* getting out,' the school secretary explains.

Alice sits on a red plastic chair. Behind her on the wall is a collage depicting all the different religions around the world. Celebrating Diwali is lovely, thinks Alice, but it's a shame that Harvest Festival has been done away with. She used to enjoy filling a shoebox with imaginative yet practical tinned goods. Once she included a tin of shoe polish, which she thought was a novel touch.

Anyway, she's not here to discuss the practising of different creeds, she's here to talk about Sam – clever, sensitive, small for his age – and his daily torment at the hands of bullies, one in particular. Alice isn't afraid to name names, the truth will out, justice will be done, the ring-leader will have to be expelled. It's very sad, but Alice is determined that exclusion is the only solution.

'Ms Kabir is ready to see you now.'

The school secretary opens a door into the headmistress's inner sanctum, and Alice arranges her face into an expression of steely concern.

Ms Kabir is new to the school. The common consensus is that she's 'really very good'. Alice extends her hand and Ms Kabir shakes it warmly. 'Mrs Jamieson, so good of you to take the time.'

'Well,' replies Alice, 'it is rather important.'

'Yes,' sighs Ms Kabir. 'Tell me, has your son ever been seen by an educational psychologist? Only I suspect that a lot of his problems stem from ADD, which is of course compounded by his chronic dyslexia.'

'Hold on a minute, Sam has a reading age of thirteen.'

Ms Kabir looks confused. 'Sam?'

'Yes, Sam Jamieson,' snaps Alice, and it dawns on her that this new headmistress hasn't a clue who she, Alice Jamieson, pillar of the PTA, is! 'My son,' she adds.

'Sorry, wrong Jamieson. Let's have a look, should we?' Ms Kabir manoeuvres a beige plastic mouse around a frankly tatty mat. 'Ah, here we are, Sam Jamieson, year five.' She squints at the screen in front of her.

'I don't think you'll find there's any problem with his school-work,' Alice states, rather more belligerently than she intended. 'Sam is a very gifted boy.' She smiles fondly. 'My son has a thing for numbers, square roots are his speciality, it's really quite amusing, ha ha.'

'Really,' replies Ms Kabir, failing to be amused and putting on a pair of half-moon glasses. 'Yes,' she finally agrees, 'his SATS are very encouraging, but' – long pause – 'no one likes him.'

Alice swallows hard. 'We're not here to talk about his popularity, Ms Kabir. It's not as if Sam is eligible for some cheerleading squad (oh, good point). We're here to discuss the fact that he is being bullied.'

Ms Kabir leans forward sympathetically. 'Maybe he's being bullied because . . . no one likes him?'

'That's not the point,' argues Alice, 'and anyway he's been to lots of parties this term.' (Well, two of the Clements' children's anyway.)

'Well,' responds Ms Kabir, 'maybe it is the point? Maybe we should look at the problem from the bully's point of view. What is Sam doing that provokes them?'

Alice cannot believe the guff she is hearing.

Ms Kabir consults the screen again and reads the contents out loud. 'He's superior, condescending, uses his intelligence as a weapon, oh, and he hides things.'

'Hold on,' interrupts Alice. 'Someone threw a plimsoll at his head, someone chucked his lunch over the wall, someone flushed his Harry Potter torch down the lavatory.' (As for the 'hiding things' accusation, Alice refuses to waste her breath on such nonsense.)

Ms Kabir nods. She seems to be thinking very seriously. 'Hmmm, well, maybe *someone* doesn't have a pair of plimsolls? Perhaps *someone's* mother hasn't enough food in the house to pack a lunch.

And perhaps he flaunted his Harry Potter torch in front of *someone* who can only dream of owning such a fancy toy?'

Alice is standing up now. 'So it's all Sam's fault!' Saliva is spraying from her lips. She is rabid in her fury.

'Not just Sam's fault.' Ms Kabir gives Alice a penetrating stare.

Alice, dander up, begins to pace. 'Oh I get it. Because I buy him plimsolls, pack nutritionally balanced lunches and spend £3.99 in Woolworths, it's all my fault?'

The headmistress sighs and shrugs. 'Hopefully the holidays will give both you and Sam time to think. Let's start the new term afresh. Children have a habit of sorting their own problems out. Sometimes parental interference makes things worse. I'm prepared to wipe the slate clean. I can't say fairer than that.'

Alice is hyperventilating. The door opens behind her. Ms Kabir barely looks up. 'Goodbye, Mrs Jamieson,' and the next thing Alice knows she is out of the office and the door is shut.

Unless her ears are very much mistaken, Ms Kabir is sniggering on the other side of the frosted panel. Alice has to summon every last drop of self-restraint to stop herself putting her fist through the glass. It's twenty past three. Just another ten minutes before Sam comes out; she'll wait by the gates. Dumbfounded, she reels away from the office. Buddha smirks serenely at her from the collage. 'And you can fuck off as well,' steams Alice.

She still cannot believe what just happened. The woman is insane, all that fudging round the issue, turning the problem on its head. As for accusing the victim of being the perpetrator – ha! We all know who the real guilty party is: Aaron Gibb, that's who. A swaggering eight-year-old with a shaved head and a pierced ear.

Alice is still shaking as she crosses the playground. Suddenly, standing just beyond the gate, she catches sight of Aaron's infamous mother, Mrs Gibb.

Well, if that fool Ms Kabir isn't prepared to sort the problem out, then, as a mother, surely it's her duty to tackle the predicament head on. 'I shall be polite, I shall be reasonable, but I shall be firm,' determines Alice. 'I shall seize the bull by the horns.'

Considering the size and demeanour of Mrs Gibb, this is an unfortunate turn of phrase. Mrs Gibb takes a dress size twenty –

she makes Alice look like Calista Flockhart. Undaunted, Alice approaches her.

'Mrs Gibb. We appear to have a problem in so much as your son is making life difficult for my son.' She smiles pleasantly. This is a much more effective way of sorting things out.

Mrs Gibb takes a cigarette out of her mouth, throws it on to the pavement, smiles back at Alice and says, 'Go fuck yourself, you snooty cow.'

Several other parents, smelling blood, gather closer.

Mrs Gibb has obviously watched a lot of Jerry Springer shows. She jabs her finger in Alice's face. 'Did you hear what I said, toffee nose? If I was you, Mrs Hoity-toity, I'd be careful what I say when I open my big fat mouth, so shut it.'

Alice backs away. There's no reasoning with people like Mrs Gibb. She's the sort who dumps her rubbish in other people's skips. She's the sort who keeps milk bottles on the table. She's the sort who will punch Alice's lights out if she says one more thing.

Alice's face burns. Fortunately Sam comes running out and she calls him over in a quivering falsetto. 'Hello, darling, Mummy's here.'

Sam slides his hand into his mother's. 'I got a Chinese burn today,' he tells her.

'Aaron Gibb?' she hazards.

'No, me and Aaron are friends now, it was Ashley.'

'Aaron and I,' corrects Alice, 'and why is this Ashley boy being mean to you?'

'It's not a boy, Mum, she's a girl. Ashley McKenna.'

Suddenly Alice feels rather sick. Ashley McKenna's mother is a very nice woman who lives in a rather large Georgian house in one of the area's better roads. Rumour has it she's a BBC radio producer. Alice was very much hoping to invite her along to one of her book club soirées. Her heart plummets even further when she realises that she might just owe Mrs Gibb an apology.

Suddenly she is furious at Sam. This is his fault. 'Oh for Christ's sake, don't be so wet.'

Sam's face crumples. 'You don't love me any more.' Alice has to buy him an ice cream to shut him up. Thank goodness they break up next week.

She doesn't tell Guy about the day's events. She might have done, but as soon as he walks through the door they're not speaking. All she'd asked him to do was pop into the chemist to pick up something for the holiday during his lunch break, but had he? No!

'Why, Guy, why? What else did you have to do that was so vitally important?'

'I had to fuck my girlfriend,' he could reply, but of course he doesn't. Not yet, but soon. After the holiday. Guy has fallen in love, he is besotted, infatuated; every second that he is not with Peanut his heart and his balls ache for her.

'I just forgot.'

Alice stomps up the stairs. What a bloody day, and on top of it all Sam has casually informed her that he's lost his swimming trunks, but she knows he hasn't, he just hates swimming. Well, you can't avoid swimming on holiday. It's all part of the lovely family fun.

Alice charges into her youngest son's bedroom and rifles through his IKEA chest of drawers. As she rummages, she knocks the lid off a tin box in which Sam used to store his Pokemon cards. The cards are gone. At the bottom of the tin is an inhaler, one of Guy's special cufflinks, a Game Boy Super Mario game, Max's signed photo of Cat Deeley and a small white plastic wand. Alice recognises the wand immediately. It's a pregnancy predictor kit. Two fading blue dots are still faintly visible in the little window aperture halfway down the stick.

Alice sits heavily on the bed, shaking the inhaler. She hasn't a clue how to use it. Di is the only person she knows who is a proper diagnosed asthmatic, but her breathing has gone funny and just maybe it might help. She sucks in a cold breath of chemical-flavoured gas. It reminds her of something, of being on her back with her feet in stirrups.

I have been in labour twice, she recalls, but I have been pregnant three times.

She takes the predictor kit and puts it back where it should be, under her knickers along with the book of baby names. Florence, Chloe, Abigail: those were the top three choices that once upon a time she'd ringed in blue biro, convinced her third child would be a girl. Afterwards she goes back into Sam's room and picks up everything that she threw on the floor. The words 'Oh, and he hides things' buzz around her head like trapped flies.

Eventually she finds the swimming trunks. Somehow they've accidentally got caught up inside the sleeve of an ancient Aran jumper.

The dream returns that night. She was so certain it would that before she went to bed she made herself a little stack of cheese and tomato sandwiches and left them in the fridge for later.

17

Mourning after the Night Before

Hils wakes up with her left cheek stuck to the pillow. She has been dribbling again. Sometimes it's a blessing to be single. Her skin feels as dry as choux pastry, the pillowcase is daubed with black smudges of mascara and smears of red lipstick, and her bladder is stretched to bouncy castle proportions.

Stumbling into the bathroom, she catches sight of herself in the mirror. Her face is lopsided, as if she might have had a small stroke in the night. She collapses backwards on to the toilet. Fortunately the lid is up and she wees long and hard like a horse. The cat brushes through her ankles, and when she bends down to say hello, she reels back.

Jesus, even Mike thinks I've got bad breath!

Hils hauls herself up and cleans her teeth with an electric toothbrush that for the last six months she's been meaning to buy new batteries for. Her handbag is lying unzipped on the landing, a packet of machine-bought Silk Cut gaping open, one left. Oh fuck. The dress lies in a puddle by the bed and suddenly Hils realises that she is in the fiendish grip of a hellish hangover. Who was it that said 'the devil is just God after a few drinks'? Tom Waits?

Bugger fuck.

Downstairs the kids are watching telly. She can hear the chirrup of the Powerpuff Girls.

'Help me,' she wails. They can't hear. 'Tabitha, Saul, help.' For all they care she could have choked on her own vomit in the night, and whose fault would that be? Hers, she supposes.

Hils lies down on the bed. She can only see out of one eye. The vision in her right eye is blurred. Oh great – she's drunk her retinas off. Then she remembers: contact lens. She blinks and pushes her eyelid this way and that and eventually a folded silicone disc falls into her hand. She either managed to get the other one out last night or it has worked its way round the back of her eye and is probably stuck somewhere in the withered recesses of her poorly brain. How much damage did she do to her grey matter last night? Hils pictures her brain like a large pickled walnut swimming around in a jar of discoloured alcohol, complete with floating fag butts.

She checks her watch, only to find that telling the time requires enormous concentration. If the big hand is on . . . and the little hand is on . . . Fuck, it's quarter to eleven. Hils closes her eyes. The next thing she knows it's midday and Tabitha is standing at the end of her bed with her arms folded.

'Well, young lady, what time do you call this?'

Saul is wobbling behind her with a tray. 'We thought you could do with some solids, Mum.'

'Tea, just tea,' she whimpers, and Tabitha hands her a mug of something that looks like sprout juice but fortunately turns out to be a peppermint infusion. There are two white pills in an eggcup.

'Nurofen,' instructs Tabitha.

'And lots of Marmite on toast,' adds Saul. 'We'll soon have you right as rain.'

Tabitha flings open the curtains and Hils has a Norma Desmond moment. If there'd been a pair of sunglasses to hand, she'd have put them on.

'Bath, I need a bath,' she croaks.

'You're not kidding,' retorts Saul, wrinkling his nose and disappearing off to the bathroom.

Tabitha sits on the edge of the bed. 'So what happened to you last night? We tried waiting up but when it got to gone one, we gave up. Janey stayed.'

'Oh God, Janey!' Bits of the night before are slowly flooding back. The initial awkwardness of the occasion, the flutes of champagne, her publisher making a speech, Hils making a speech, Mrs Gupta making a speech. A hot dog bought from a stand on the corner of Cambridge Circus – no, that was later, after she'd had a nice little sleep on the floor of the ladies' toilets.

And before that? A table all set with a pile of her books, her friends smiling and telling her how clever she was, the nice waiter with the shiny black hair filling her glass again and again. What was his name? Stanley from Clerkenwell, that was it, half Chinese, half Scottish. The non-existent food. She'd thought it was a tray of Liquorice Allsorts but it was sushi – all that raw fish and a belly full of champagne, no wonder she felt rubbish.

What a crap mother I am, thinks Hils, as she gathers fleeting images and patchworks them together. Thank Christ for Janey!

Janey had been the kids' nanny when they were small. 'Nanny' made her sound like she wore a grey uniform with a starched white pinafore on top and pushed the children round in a big Silver Cross pram. The reality had been a girl with a northern accent thicker than George Formby's, a ruby stud in her nose and a tattoo of a tiger crouched on her shoulder. Big, loud, laughing Janey with her hennaed TinTin crop, purple dungarees and skinny little roll-ups.

Janey had pitched up last night, paint-splattered and five months pregnant, and taken the kids home when it became apparent that their mother had no intention of leaving the party.

'We got the bus,' Tabitha informs her mother.

'And we had pizza when we got in,' adds Saul. 'I've put smelly stuff in your bath, cos I tell you something, Mum, you don't half pong.'

Yes, of course, Janey had let her in last night, helped her up the stairs and told her to drink at least a pint of water. A glass sits beside Hils's bed, the water undrunk. 'Where Janey now?' she burbles. Jesus, I can't even speak.

'She slept in the spare room, but she had an antenatal appointment really early this morning,' Tabitha tells her.

Hils attempts to text Janey to say thanks but the little letters dance around the keypad.

'Here,' sighs Tabitha, taking the phone off her mother, 'let me do it. Really, Mum, it's a good job you're only a part-time alcoholic.'

Two hours later, more fragrant but still fragile, Hils makes it into Covent Garden with Tabitha and Saul. The bus journey was dreadful; she could smell the alcohol oozing from her pores. I'm all right as long as I don't make any sudden moves, she thinks, sitting on the floor in Gap while Saul tries on swimming trunks.

'I like these, Mum.'

'Yes, they're great,' enthuses Hils, even though the vivid orange hibiscus pattern hurts her eyes.

Tabitha finds a couple of T-shirts on the sale rail in H&M. 'Are you sure, Mum?'

Hils laughs. 'They're four quid each, Tabitha.'

She hasn't told them how much she got for the book. She can hardly believe it herself. It was only when she saw the physical evidence last night that she could finally believe she'd done it. So the fee might be chicken feed to the likes of J.K. Rowling-in-it, but it means she keeps the house; it means she doesn't have to go running to Joe for shoe money and housekeeping.

Catching sight of her corpse-like features in a mirror, Hils swerves into the chemist on Long Acre and buys a Chanel lipstick, matching nail varnish and the smallest pot of the most expensive antiwrinkle cream she can find. Jackie Collins, eat your heart out!

Almost immediately she is overwhelmed by guilt. What if no one buys the bloody thing? What if the publishers ask for the money back? With horror she remembers picking up her party dress this morning and noticing a great big fag burn on the bum, the material all puckered, brown and singed. Oh well, it had been a great night. What she can remember of it.

She is in a daze. If only she could lie down on the ground like an old lady tramp, but Tabitha is dragging her into Books Etc.

'Tabs, we bought books last week,' protests Hils feebly. Maybe what she really needs is more food. Something to settle her stomach. For some reason she reckons a big suet pudding might help.

'I just want to see something,' her daughter insists. And there on a table along with other 'summer holiday recommended reading' is a big pile of copies of *Diary of a Divorcee*. Before she can stop him, Saul has gathered up a large bundle and is redistributing them in the window.

Hils blushes. He's going to get told off, then there'll be a scene. Already Saul is causing a small commotion. Outside the shop, people are turning their backs on a fire-eating contortionist to watch the chubby blond boy on the other side of the glass. Saul, fuelled by the attention, has started mucking around. The hibiscus trunks are on his head and he is doing a rather clumsy dance that involves waggling his ample bottom and putting his thumbs up. People have started clapping, and when the branch manager finally taps him on the shoulder and manages to haul him out, Hils can hear boos from the pavement.

The three of them exit, fast. I'm too old to run, thinks Hils, dodging people-statues, tarot readers and jugglers.

Safe on the other side of the piazza, weak and giggly, Saul remembers that he hasn't had any lunch. 'Well, I just might faint,' he gasps.

Suddenly Hils is struck by the symmetry of the situation: she is standing just yards away from where she first set eyes on their father.

I am twenty-two years old and I am leaning up against a wall with my friend Philippa. We are wearing aprons and smoking. I have a bad perm and Philippa has a wedge cut. Above our heads is a wooden sign with the word 'Bewleys' in gold paint against a burgundy background.

Bewleys was a wine bar in Covent Garden. It isn't there any more so I can say what I like about it without getting sued. Suffice to say the manager was an arsehole and the standards of hygiene were questionable to say the least.

Down in the basement Bewleys served bottles of nouveau Beaujolais and a selection of pies to media types in red braces. I'm not talking your Fray Bentos pies here. I'm talking earthenware brown bowls brimming with gravy bubbling out of thick crusts that were artfully manufactured to look home-made.

Upstairs and outside, under the colonnades, Bewleys served bowls of prawns, cheese platters and ham salads to tourists. It was right on the edge of the piazza. Café culture was new to London – I'm going back nearly twenty years – and people were happy to be ripped off just to sit outside and watch out-of-work ex-drama students doing dreadful mime shows, or listen to Peruvian pan pipers in stripy shawls sitting on the floor. It seemed quite exotic at the time.

I was waitressing, filling in time between jobs. I wasn't hoping to meet a husband – I had a boyfriend; it was the last thing on my mind.

I think a lot about fate. What if he'd fancied a baked potato from the stall opposite, or a pizza from Luigi's three doors down, or a pint and a packet of crisps in any number of pubs? But he didn't. One day a hungry man took a seat at the last empty table in the sun and it was as if the next fifteen years of my life had been mapped out for me.

Life is like some elaborate board game. You move backwards and forwards, you get flu and miss a go, you land on the 'get your hair bleached and buy a red lipstick' square. You inherit £500 so you Go to Greece, you miss a period, and 300 squares later you spend twelve hours in labour! And you keep throwing the dice, on and on, until one day you find yourself on the big snake that has divorce at the top and a big fat question mark at the bottom.

Oh, Joe.

Had I known the end result, would I have married him? Oh yes. I fell in love with him. I looked at him and immediately felt like throwing up. It was either love or a massive allergic reaction. Love, I decided. This was exactly how I'd felt when I'd first seen Donny Osmond on the telly.

'Table six – he's mine.'

I know exactly what I served him: a glass of house white and a selection of French cheese and biscuits. It was 1985; this was what people ate back then. Sushi, sun-dried tomatoes and rocket came later. The bill came to £4.50 including coffee – black, no sugar. I know this for a fact. I've still got the receipt.

He only had four pounds. When he stood up and started digging in his denim pockets for spare coins, the bottom two buttons of his

'Mum, Mum.'

Hils reroutes her hijacked brain and lands it back in the present. Tabitha is hopping. 'Can we go to Wagamama, please?'

Hils hasn't the strength to say no and she allows herself to be led down a flight of steps into a large airy basement. They've missed the lunchtime rush and within seconds they're sitting at a long wooden table and a very beautiful Oriental girl with soy sauce-coloured hair is waiting to take their order. She reminds me of someone, thinks Hils, her brain still foggy, and then she realises. Of course – that Stan man! Stan, Stan the champagne man. And something that feels like a beetle dances deep inside her and her knees feel like mercury.

'Do you do chips?' asks Saul.

18

Never Apologise, Never Explain

Guy is having a bad day. It doesn't start badly, it just disintegrates around his ears.

Breakfast is fine. He avoids his family by oversleeping and having to order a minicab into work. At Leicester Square he buys himself a skinny latte and a tub of papaya and yoghurt from Pret à Manger. These days his waistbands are feeling deliciously loose; his stomach, if not washboard, is firm, especially if he breathes in. For a moment he enjoys being himself, a mature, successful man with a glamorous job and an expensive pair of this season's Persol sunglasses perched on his fine nose.

Guy catches sight of his reflection in a shop window. Go me! I've a good head of mahogany hair, a smashing goatee and a spring in my step, he notes. I would fancy me if I were a woman.

His father had thick hair too, he suddenly remembers – not that he lived long enough to go bald. Fifty-five is no age for a man these days: 'middle youth' they call it in the trade, the ideal time to buy a Porsche. Guy has an image of himself in his fifties, tanned, in a crumpled cream linen suit, driving a gleaming red Boxter with Peanut at his side.

Ah yes, there is plenty to look forward to. I should be able to afford to take early retirement, he calculates, even if there is a divorce to take into consideration. He won't have to fork out for

Alice and the boys for ever, and who knows, Peanut might want a baby of her own.

At this moment, Guy trips over a tramp's outstretched leg and coffee spurts like a birthmark down his pristine shirt. Dreams of Porsches evaporate and he tuts his way through the glass doors of Shelby, Jamieson and Mott. In the old days he'd have taken the lift up to his office on the third floor. Now he bounds up the stairs, two at a time. I'm in my prime, he reminds himself. Fuck the coffee stain, I might treat myself to a new shirt at lunchtime. I can do what I like, I'm in love.

Penny is in situ. She always is. Guy sometimes thinks she sleeps under her desk like an enormous moth-eaten cat. 'Good morning, Penny.'

'Well, it isn't really,' she replies, with an element of gloating.

She is waving a newspaper at Guy. It's one of the red tops, the *Daily Mirror*. Licking her fingers in a manner that makes Guy feel slightly queasy, she turns to the gossip section in the middle and lays the paper out flat in front of her. 'Maybe you should have a look at this?'

Guy removes his Persols and edges closer. Splashed across the left-hand page is a large colour photograph of what looks like a homeless person fighting with a black man who may or may not have been Lennox Lewis. The caption reads 'The new off-his-face of Hetheringtons'. The smaller print swims before his eyes but he makes out phrases such as 'bust-up at celebrity hangout', '*EastEnders* star punched in face' and 'Tommy O'Reilly, famous for one minute'.

Guy checks the photo again. It is Tommy, with blood streaming out of his nostrils, arms flailing, one foot up as if about to kick the bouncer in the testicles.

It's bad, but to make matters worse, Tommy is wearing one of the brand-new Hetheringtons promotional T-shirts. Albeit heavily stained and crumpled, the words are still clearly decipherable: 'Hetheringtons. Neck the nectar! Like licking the tummy buttons of angels'.

This is Tommy's catchphrase. On the television advert he sits in a deckchair on an allotment. To either side, old men drink from flasks of tea surrounded by withered sweet peas and drooping sunflowers. By stark contrast, everything on Tommy's patch is coming up roses, literally. Butterflies dance around his head while ten-foot hollyhocks and football-sized honeysuckle bloom in the background. Bees buzz and hummingbirds hum while Tommy sips from his can of Hetheringtons, smiles his twinkly-eyed smile and delivers the line 'Like licking the tummy buttons of angels' in his treacle-and-fags brogue.

'The stupid cunt,' expletes Guy.

Takes one to know one, smirks Penny silently. Out loud she says, 'Damage limitation meeting in thirty minutes in your office.'

'Shit,' replies Guy.

Tommy's rise to fame has been meteoric. Within weeks of the advert going to air he'd been a panellist on *Have I Got News For You* (a last-minute replacement for an under-the-weather Will Self), sat on Richard and Judy's hallowed sofa, and according to this week's *Broadcast* was currently the hot ticket to host a new Saturday-evening game show.

Some people haven't got the brains they're born with, seethes Guy.

The meeting is uncomfortable, to say the least. The senior accounts director of Hetheringtons turns up – in a chauffeur-driven Mercedes, even though their offices are a three-minute walk around the corner – along with the head of Hetheringtons promotions, a lawyer, Tommy's manager and his press agent. His press agent! Six months ago, the lad couldn't get a booking at the Comedy Store.

Suddenly Guy's office seems rather small and he wishes his partner Toby Mott were here to offer some moral support. Unfortunately, Toby is in hospital having his sinuses drained. Lucky bastard, thinks Guy, who, given the choice, would opt for a general anaesthetic over his present predicament any day.

Penny comes in with some coffee and Jaffa Cakes. Guy could kill her. No one eats Jaffa Cakes. She's a big, fat, ugly embarrassment. Jesus, it's like having two crap wives.

For ninety minutes they talk in circles. Words like 'loose cannon' and 'negative marketing' are bandied about. For a second Guy wants to shout, 'Oh come on, everyone knows drinking beer turns you into an arsehole,' but of course he doesn't. In ad land

111

everything must have a positive spin, unless you've been commissioned to do the Christmas anti-drink–driving campaign.

It's the press guy and the manager that come up with the best solution. They can work this round. Tommy should go into the Priory to be treated for depression. It's very important that the papers should know that he isn't an alcoholic, merely a man driven to excess on the anniversary of his mother's death.

'I didn't know Tommy's mother was dead,' ventures Guy.

'She isn't,' snaps the press agent, 'but for our purposes, she has to be.'

'Are you going to tell her?' asks Guy.

'Don't worry about that.' Tommy's manager grins. 'We'll square it with her – nice bunch of flowers, basket of fruit, she'll love being dead.' Tommy's manager is a well-fed shark with a blond quiff and a theatrical dress sense.

The meeting draws to a close. As the men stand up and shake hands, the head honcho of Hetheringtons says, 'Whose idea was bloody Tommy O'Reilly in the first place?'

Everyone looks at Guy.

Bunch of fucking hypocrites, he thinks, as they file out and the door shuts. It's not as if they weren't all steaming the night they went to Stringfellow's. He has a vague recollection of the accounts manager being yanked out of the girls' toilets, cocaine crumbs suspended in the snot dribbling from his nose.

Guy is so depressed that he eats four Jaffa Cakes and seriously considers sticking his fingers down his throat. Oh well, the day can't get any worse. It's just a blip. As for the Jaffa Cakes, he'll skip lunch. Ah, lunch. He and Peanut have taken to meeting on an almost daily basis in the little wine bar round the back of St Martin's Lane.

Café Koha reminds Guy of Paris. He went once, a long time ago, before his parents were killed, before Alice. They went up the Eiffel Tower and his father bought his mother a silver duplicate to hang off her charm bracelet. Every significant event in his parents' married life was celebrated in silver charms: a tiny rattle symbolised Guy's birth, his sister's penchant for ballet immortalised in a minute slipper.

The walls of Café Koha are nicotine yellow, the lighting discreet, wine comes in carafes and the olives taste of chilli and garlic. Not that they eat much. Maybe a shared Mediterranean platter or a simple dish of kalamari. Instead they gaze into each other's eyes and hold hands under the table, the one at the back, or 'our table', as they call it.

Guy sits at 'our table' and orders a carafe of Rioja. He wouldn't normally drink red wine in the middle of the day, not with the diet and everything. Guy has opted for a low-fat, high-fibre regime; everyone else is on the Atkins, but it's a well-known fact that the side effects include having the breath of a chihuahua, and what with so much snogging to do, it's not an option he can afford to take. He crunches an extra-strong mint. She should be here soon. He pours himself a glass of red wine and waves away the offer of fresh rolls and butter.

Well, that was a shit morning, he reckons, almost glad that he's off on holiday at the weekend. Not that he wants to spend a week away from Peanut, but a change of scene will do him good. Guy imagines himself diving into a pool wearing his new Paul Smith trunks.

Come on, Peanut. He tries to resist phoning her mobile – she'd call him if she was going to be late. Oh God, what if she's had an accident? They happen every day – men go berserk with knives, scaffolding collapses, parents collide with oil tankers. Guy dials her Nokia but it's switched off. Peanut never switches her phone off. He tries her work number and a voice he doesn't recognise answers. Guy tries to sound casual. 'Hi, is Peanut around?'

She isn't. Apparently she rang in sick this morning.

'Thanks, cheers.'

Guy phones her flat with sweaty fingers, but no one answers. He doesn't know what to do, so he finishes the carafe of red wine. He's too miserable to eat and the sight and sound of other people chewing makes him feel sick.

At two o'clock he stumbles back to the office, ignores Penny, who by the sound of it is talking to her mother – 'You have taken your insulin?' – and heads straight for the sanctuary of his office. Loosening his tie and kicking off his shoes, he lies down on the black leather sofa and falls asleep quicker than if he'd been anaesthetised.

On the dot of three Penny phones him. Guy hurls himself off

the sofa and reaches for the phone. Peanut, it could be Peanut, poor period-pain or migraine or food-poisoned Peanut!

'Hello, Guy,' intones his PA. 'As you're no doubt aware, it's three o'clock and the people from Barnardos have arrived. I've—'

'Fucking hell, Penny, you fucking imbecile, why didn't you remind me? Jesus Christ.'

'I've sent them in,' continues Penny, but Guy isn't listening. He's mid-rant and oblivious to the fact that two people have entered his private office and are standing, blinking, on the threshold.

'You fucking moron! That's all I need after this shitty morning, to listen to a couple of wankers from fucking Barnardos.'

Guy turns round. Is it his imagination or has the room suddenly gone very chilly? He blinks: two people he has never seen before in his life are standing in the doorway, their jaws at carpet level.

At this point Michaela Evans and Sandy Romsgrove walk out of Guy's office. Michaela is a born-again Christian and will not tolerate 'language', and as Sandy is her junior, he has no choice but to follow.

It is possibly the shortest business meeting in the world. In under thirty seconds, half a million quid's worth of advertising campaign has gone up in smoke. Guy has a Basil Fawlty moment. 'Bang goes my early retirement,' he despairs, 'bang goes my Porsche Boxter with Peanut in the passenger seat.' And shoeless and tieless, he lies face down on the carpet and doesn't get up until it's going-home time.

By the time he leaves, Penny has already disappeared, which isn't like her at all. For some reason Guy feels abandoned. For once it will be quite nice to get home.

Only it isn't. Alice wants to discuss the boys' reports, and there's another thing she wants to discuss. Guy feels a momentary panic.

'What?' he stutters feebly.

'I found them,' she replies.

Found what? The Photo-Me! booth photos of Peanut with her top off, taken in Covent Garden tube station last week, the lipstick-stained underpants, the Tiffany receipt, what?

Alice is chewing her lips. 'The bloody Paul Smith swimming trunks, eighty-five pounds. Are you completely mad, Guy?'

'Probably.' It's the only remotely truthful thing he can think of saying.

19

Bon Voyage and All That

Hils is feeling ever so slightly sick. Tomorrow has turned into today, and today she has to drop the kids off at Joe's because tomorrow they fly to Italy.

I don't want them to go – they have earthquakes in Italy, they drive too fast on the wrong side of the road, and tides turn in the blink of a lifeguard's eye.

She tries to get her breathing right, but all she can do is take shallow little breaths. Stop it, she tells herself. I'm not going through all that nonsense again. Gradually she allows the natural mechanics of her heart and lungs to maintain their steady rhythm, and she tries not to think about how hard it is to swallow.

In the immediate aftermath of my husband's departure, there were days when I could barely get out of bed. I'd wake up, forgetting for a few fleeting seconds what had happened, then remember and immediately I'd get that sick feeling, just like you do when you're flying and you hit really bad turbulence.

I had trouble with my breathing and found it difficult to swallow. There seemed to be something the size of a quail's egg stuck in my throat. I went to the doctor and he gave me some little white pills. I have to admit they helped – as did the cigarettes and bottles and bottles of cheap white wine.

115

There were mornings when I'd make it down to the sitting room and there, by the sofa, was another empty bottle and another brimming ashtray. I knew I'd stayed up late but I couldn't remember what I'd watched on television. I had to check in Time Out.

On bad nights I would listen to CDs, snivelling, and small things like making the kids a packed lunch were beyond me. So they ate jam sandwiches and I'm surprised they didn't get rickets; the fruit bowl remained empty. I ran out of milk, clothes piled up in the laundry basket and I pulled on the same sour-smelling jeans day after day. On days like these I couldn't remember how to be 'normal'.

Diary of a Divorcee

Hils burps to relieve the ball of tension in her stomach.

I should be used to this process by now, she puffs, piling rucksacks, holdalls and sleeping bags into the boot of the car. Ooh the car, her brand spanking new car. She'd ordered it months ago but it was only delivered last week. Fourteen-and-a-half grand's worth of silver and chrome Chrysler and it's all hers – well, five grand's worth is. The rest is on a lease. She might have come into some money but she's not going to go mental with it. Oh, but look at it, smell it – so shiny, so sleek, so lickable. Bloody hell, thinks Hils, it's been so long since I've had a man that I'm reduced to being weird about cars. She dimly recalls an old tabloid story, something about a bloke fucking a Vauxhall Vectra.

How?

Takes all sorts, she supposes. At least her ex was unfaithful in the conventional sense; at least she lost out to a younger, prettier woman. There's comfort in a cliché. So much more embarrassing for the wife if he's doing the dirty with . . . a pensioner, or a goat, she decides.

Actually, Hils doesn't think Nina is all that pretty. She is young and nubile but she is shorter and more bow-legged than Hils had imagined. The first time she'd set eyes on the girl, she'd been hiding beneath a big coat, and inexplicably Hils had imagined something more exotic underneath. A cocktail of mango and lychee, perhaps, but in the end Nina had turned out to be a little tinned peach of

116

a thing, juicy enough but ordinary. Hils shuts the car boot with slightly more force than she'd intended.

When Joe left he took the family Saab with him. Hils was glad to see the back of it. Considering what had gone on in that car, she never wanted to see it again! Even to this day, the sight of a white Saab convertible with a black roof causes rage to rise in her throat. After all, the car played a part in that 'last straw' scenario. OK, so it wasn't the car's fault; it was what was going on inside the car that was to blame. But somehow the car became inextricably mixed up in the situation, an accessory to the crime, so she could never sit in it again without imagining puddles of semen on the seat.

Since it went, Hils has been driving her brother's old Fiat Panda, or the 'eggbox' as it came to be known. Janey has the eggbox now, Joe has the Saab, and Hils is the winner with the shiny new Chrysler.

Joe won't like it. He'll think it's a silly, faky kind of car, but then it's not up to Joe any more; she can drive what she likes.

'Come on,' she yells, as if she's in a hurry to get rid of them, and Tabitha and Saul climb into the back. They've given up arguing about who gets to ride in the front. Feeling like a Clyde-less Bonnie, Hils squeals off. She's actually not a very good driver.

I should have given them their tea, she realises too late. Oh for fuck's sake, why does she always have to accommodate bloody Nina? Surely the child is capable of boiling pasta. The sleeping bags are enough of a concession. Tabitha and Saul don't have a bedroom at their father's new place. They are always temporary, always sleeping on the floor, always able to be rolled away in the morning. Well, it's crap, that's what it is.

Hils has read enough books to know that, psychologically speaking, it's best for the children of divorced parents to have an identifiable 'space' at their estranged parent's new accommodation, not just a couple of square feet of bare floorboard in front of the telly. Bloody Joe, bloody Nina. If Tabitha goes on a shoplifting bender in Italy and Saul starts nicking his dad's fags, it will be Joe and Nina's fault.

Hils hasn't actually gone beyond the front door of her ex-husband's new apartment. She doesn't want to give him the satisfaction of actually liking it. It's best she imagines the place in her head – sterile, cold and uncomfortable. After all, Tabitha once said it was like an operating theatre with sofas. Everything about it annoys her. The fact that it's in a 'gated community', that you have to be buzzed in, that if you are a visitor you have to park in one of the specially designated bays.

She slides a Johnny Cash CD into the stereo and they all sing 'Ring of Fire'. When Tabitha and Saul were toddlers they were as familiar with Johnny Cash as any nursery rhyme. Hils is a fiend for Country and Western. The only thing she and Joe had argued about when he was packing his things was who actually owned the Willie Nelson collection.

The music fills the silence. Tabitha and Saul are subdued – they always are when it's handover time. It's as if they have learnt to put a lid on their excitement, in case it upsets her. She knows that they can't wait. She has heard them whispering to each other on the landing, Saul in the bathroom gargling 'Just One Cornetto'. It's the same when they come back from a weekend spent with their father. They are noncommittal about what they have done.

'Did you have a nice time?'

'Yeah, it was fine.'

Once, when Saul had an open evening at school and his work was put out on his desk for her to have a look at, she'd flicked through his written English book and found herself reading a 'what I did at the weekend' story.

'At the weekend me and my sister went to my dad's and we went to the zoo and I like the big lizzuds best and baby Freya cride because the top of her ice cream fell off so my sister Tabitha gave her the one she had. I wood of given her the one I was eating but I had all reddy eaten it all up. It was choclat. Then we went back to Dad and Nina's flat and we watched spie kids which is reely good and the next day we went back to mums and she had buyed us spie kids so we watcht it all over agen which was good.'

Hils remembers sitting on a very small chair wondering why they hadn't told her about the zoo, and realising how they'd pretended to be so pleased that she'd bought them *Spy Kids*. She was so caught up in these thoughts that she forgot to worry about

Saul's appalling spelling. Joe wasn't there; he was going to try and make it but at the last minute some work had come up.

My children lead two lives, she thinks. Over the past couple of years they have learnt to split their loyalties, transferring affection from one parent to the other as easily as if changing shoes. Nina rarely gets mentioned, but for some reason they talk freely of Freya. Freya is the one thing they have been enthusiastic about from the start. After all, everyone loves a baby. You can't blame the baby, it's not her fault – or is it?

Sometimes Hils can't help feeling that actually it *is* Freya's fault. Without Freya, the affair would have eventually petered out, just another one of those mid-life crisis flings. Surely Nina isn't special enough to have bagsied Joe just for herself. When you think about it, it was the baby that clinched the deal. Hils once found a picture of Freya when she was just a black-and-white fuzzy scan, tucked in the back of Tabitha's homework diary. Tabitha had covered the Polaroid in sellotape to save it from harm, protecting her baby sister before she was even born.

Hils tenses at the wheel. Glancing in the rear-view mirror she imagines Joe and Nina in a tangle of bare legs and underwear. A horn blares and Tabitha squeals, 'Fucking hell, Mum.'

I must concentrate, decides Hils. Looking again in the rear-view mirror she sees a man miming 'wanker' at her from a BMW. For the rest of the journey she drives at ten miles an hour.

Joe buzzes them in. They talk over each other on the intercom.

'Where have you been?'

'Sorry I'm late.'

Immediately Hils feels livid. Why do I always end up apologising?

Joe comes out to greet them and inevitably Hils loses the ability to park.

Thank God the Chrysler is automatic. Even so, it's terribly hard work – fuck it, she's put the handbrake on. She releases it and the car leaps over the kerb and flattens a small bush. Joe smirks from behind his hand.

'Do you want to come in?' he asks casually.

'No, actually, I'm going out,' lies Hils, thinking, I bought him that belt. She tries to hug her children but it's difficult to get her arms around them when they're struggling with their luggage and jittery with excitement.

'Goodbye, I love you, take care, don't forget your suntan lotion and remember that cars drive on the other side of the road and send me a postcard and give your dad your passports and don't swim straight after your lunch and I love you, I love you.'

Twenty minutes later she is back home, and once the front door is shut she can't think of anything to do but cry. Crying can be quite cathartic, but it's also very tiring, so after ten minutes of howling she decides to stop, and rather than drink neat gin from the bottle in the kitchen she phones her brother. His wife Midge answers.

'Hey, Mrs Lady-novelist, how are you?'

'I'm fine,' sighs Hils. 'I've just dropped the kids off. I won't see them for over a week.'

'Lucky you, Caspar and Lulu are driving me up the wall.'

Caspar is five and refuses to wear anything but his Virgil Tracy outfit; Lulu is three and as bossy as an entire women's institute.

'I'll hand you over to James. Just shut up for a second, Lulu, and put your pants back on, we're bored of that bottom.'

James takes over. 'Got over your hangover yet?'

'I wasn't that pissed.'

'Hils, you goosed Stephen Fry and flicked a peanut at Keith Allen. To be honest we were a bit worried about leaving you, but you were being well looked after.' James sniggers.

Hils blushes. Out of the corner of her eye she can see an empty fag packet, covered in a drunken biro scrawl. Why hadn't she thrown it away?

'Listen, do you want to come over? We're having an Indian in front of the telly. Kids are still up, as you can hear.'

She can, and even though she loves James, Midge and the kids, she doesn't want to sit on the edge of someone else's family. A family that still has all its pieces. Sometimes Hils feels that with Joe gone they are like a car-boot jigsaw puzzle: a quarter of the picture is missing.

'No thanks.'

'OK, but come and see us soon. Lulu says it's a' order.'

Hils promises she will, and maybe she will and maybe she won't. Vaguely she starts tidying up. Last night she'd given Tabitha a pedicure and there are toenail clippings all over the carpet.

I should get out the hoover. But instead she tries to make out the scribbled digits on the side of an empty cigarette packet. The numbers are smudged and what looks like an eight could just as easily be a three. Written above the numbers in colliding capital letters is the name 'STAN'.

I'm over forty. I can't go running round after a waiter. But she doesn't throw the packet away; she fills it with Tabitha's toenail clippings and puts it in the seashell box, along with the chocolate pig, the gold ring and the receipt.

20

The Dobsons Get Ready

Nina and Joe are having one of those arguments that couples have when they pretend they're not actually arguing. Both are talking in quietly determined voices.

'I'm not being negative,' says Nina, 'I'm just saying I don't think it's going to be easy.' Even as she says the words she wonders why she is bothering. Because I've drunk three-quarters of a bottle of red wine, because I'm sick of being treated like a schoolgirl, because Hils is so bloody superior, driving round in that bloody new car.

'Well, what's that if it's not being negative?' replies Joe. 'Why can't you just look forward to it? It's a holiday, for Christ's sake!'

'Yes, I re-al-ise' – Nina splits the word into three, as if she is talking to a person with a severe learning difficulty – 'it's a holiday, but it's not going to be a holiday holiday with your kids!' Nina's voice has become rather high-pitched. If she were a child she'd be told off for whining.

'Oh, Nina,' pleads Joe. 'We've been through this. It's important, for me and you and baby Freya, but even more so for Tabby and Saul. Now for Christ's sake, keep your voice down.'

'Why?' Nina's vocal cords are fighting a losing battle with hysteria; her words have an edge now, sharp as metal. 'Why should I keep my voice down? Why is it more important for bloody Tabitha and Saul? This is the first foreign holiday we've had with Freya and you've lumped us with those two!'

Too late, Nina realises she has overstepped the mark. She knows the rules: never criticise a man's driving, his sense of direction, his hair, his tie, his DIY, his ability to perform cunnilingus, his football team, or his children. She backpedals madly. 'It's not that I don't think they're great kids, it's just, well . . . I don't know what to do with them,' she trails off lamely.

'Well, you've got seven days to learn then, haven't you?' hisses Joe. 'I need to see my kids, Nina, and not just for a couple of week-ends a month. I want to spend—'

'Don't you dare say "quality time" with them,' interrupts a reignited Nina. 'Don't give me that bollocks!'

Jesus, thinks Joe, momentarily taken aback. Nina is normally so docile. It's Hils that was always the temperamental one. Nina is pissed and premenstrual, he decides. Experience can be very useful. When you've lived with one woman, you've lived with them all. He presses on. 'It isn't bollocks. They're growing up. I want to be part of their lives, and if Hils is prepared to be grown-up about this holiday then I expect the same of you.'

Oof, that strikes home. Nina reels back. Deep down she reckons Hils orchestrated this whole disaster. She can hear Joe's ex in her head. 'Oh, going on holiday with your girlfriend and baby? How lovely. I know, why don't you take your other kids? Make it one big, happy family. Don't you worry about me, I'll be fine. Course I'll miss them, but they're your children too – oh, and just for old times' sake, would you like me to suck your cock?'

Manipulative cow! Flat-chested bitch! Just because Joe left her, just because he walked out on his wife and two kids, she's got him on some crappy guilt trip. That's what this whole week in Italy's going to be, seethes Nina, one long frigging guilt trip, with me minding the baby while Joe plays Superdad to Hils's kids.

Hils's kids are asleep on the sitting-room floor; their mother dropped them off earlier. It was 7.30 pm but they hadn't eaten! They never have. The first thing they do when they come over is tip the contents of the fridge down their necks. They're worse than Shelley and Carmen.

Nina had watched Hils leave from the sitting-room window, spying on her as she tooted, waved one last time and pulled out, narrowly missing a motorbike. As the front door opened the decibel level had increased, like a radio pitched at full volume. They were here, Tabitha and Saul, the space invaders.

This apartment wasn't designed for rapidly growing step-children. Ideally they should have a soundproofed attic room, preferably with en suite so that Nina doesn't have to queue for the bathroom every morning. As it is, as soon as they arrive she is tripping over them.

Nina had stepped into the hall to 'welcome' them. 'Hi, kids,' she meant to say, sounding light and casual, but she opened her mouth and 'How long has your mother had that car?' dropped out.

Nina knows she shouldn't have greeted her stepchildren with what sounded like an accusation of automobile theft, but she couldn't help it. This is what talking to Tabitha and Saul is like. She always says the wrong thing, like a conjuror pulling frogs instead of rabbits out of a hat.

They ignored her anyway, competing with each other to get their father's attention. 'Dad, Dad, Dad.'

They woke the baby – 'Waagh, waagh, waagh' – so Nina went and sat in Freya's tiny bedroom and kissed her daughter back to sleep. She was teething, the left-hand side of her face the dark red of a poisoned apple.

By the time she got back downstairs, Joe had made chicken fajitas and a Nelly Furtado CD was spinning on the stereo. Nina turned it down. She'd hovered, not sure whether to join them. Saul was sitting in her chair and Tabitha had thrown her denim jacket over Freya's highchair; the kitchen was full of them.

They were nice-looking kids. Tabitha's hair had been cut and streaked. It suited her: she looked like Gwyneth Paltrow's funkier younger sister. Nina viewed Tabitha's figure slightly enviously. Whippet-lean, she was wearing a pair of those stupid jeans, the ones that sweep the street, all filthy and torn at the bottom. God knows what she'd brought into the house, dog shit and fag ends. Joe turned round; he had a piece of chicken fajita hanging out of his mouth. Instantly he looked as guilty as a fox chewing a rabbit.

'Sorry, darling, these gannets have eaten the lot.'

'It's all right,' said Nina in a tense little voice, and she poured herself a large glass of red wine.

'Saul's been learning how to play the drums, haven't you?'

Joe was doing the proud Dad thing, throwing mock punches at his son, ruffling his hair.

'Yeah,' grinned the boy.

He'll need a brace, Nina thought, and how much will that cost? Saul grabbed a couple of knives and beat a rhythm on the kitchen table.

'I've just got the baby to sleep,' Nina snapped.

'Sorry.' Saul put the knives down.

Was she mistaken or did Saul and his father look at her and roll their eyes to the ceiling? She was getting paranoid.

'I'll, um, put the stuff in the dishwasher.' Tabitha was trying to be good. Was she wearing mascara? 'How's Freya?'

'Oh she's fine, Tabitha, thank you. A bit grizzly because of her teeth, but lovely, really lovely. She's talking – Mummy this and Daddy that.'

Tabitha's face clouded over. Christ, thought Nina, of course, she's thirteen, she's sensitive, what a fucking nightmare. I'm going to be walking on eggshells for over a week.

Joe defused the situation by turning the CD player back up and dancing with Tabitha. He overexaggerated his moves, John-Travolta-in-*Pulp-Fiction* style, to make her laugh. 'Get lost, Dad,' said Tabitha in that way teenagers do, but she was giggling through her train tracks. Suddenly they were all dancing, Tabitha, Saul and Joe, dancing like basket cases.

'I'm just going to make sure I've got everything ready,' mumbled Nina, and she left the room carrying her glass and the bottle of red wine. Nobody wanted to dance with her.

That was two hours ago. It is midnight now and they are in bed, Joe and Nina, back to back, as comfortable as metal coat-hangers. Nina has the beginnings of a red wine hangover; she hasn't even bothered to clean her teeth. All she needs to do to make this better is burrow under the duvet and take his penis in her mouth, glide her tongue from tip to root, but she can't be bothered. She feels defeated. Hils has won this round.

I'm too young for all this, thinks Nina. I'm twenty-five, I should be out taking E with boyfriends who live in rented accommodation and are still young enough to go skateboarding. He is seventeen years older than me. When he is seventy, I will only be fifty-three. I will never catch up and I don't want to. If he goes bald and gaga I will leave him.

Joe falls asleep. She hears his breathing change, a gentle whistling coming from his left nostril. If she had a knitting needle, she would shove it right up his nose and into his skull. It's the car that's got to her. If bloody Hils is doing well enough to splash out on a new car then she can bloody well start helping out with the school fees. Tabitha and Saul go to some knob school up in Hampstead. Eighteen grand a year, thank you very much. Just think of the shoes you could buy for eighteen grand. Nina imagines a wardrobe full of Jimmy Choo fuck-me spikes and soft-as-butter Gina suede boots. When she finally falls asleep, she dreams that Hils has crashed the silver Chrysler and there are shoes and teeth scattered over the road.

She feels so bad about this that in the morning she attempts to make pancakes for breakfast. Unfortunately, she gets the measurements wrong; frying glue would be easier. In the end Tabitha and Saul take bowls of cereal into the living room, which smells of adolescent feet and farts, and watch television in their cuckoo's nest sleeping bags.

'Don't worry,' Tabitha says, 'Mum can't cook either.'

'No,' adds Saul, 'though even she can make pancakes.'

The flight isn't until 2.30, there's plenty of time. Joe is finishing off some invoices. The past couple of years haven't been great. Joe blames September 11, but Nina can't see the connection. They met through work. Nina was a stylist on one of his shoots. She knows all the tricks. She knows that if you put a tampon in boiling water and shove it under a plate of spaghetti the resulting plume of steam will look most appetising.

Nina forces a pancake down her throat and tries to trick Freya into eating one by spreading it with jam. Freya reacts as if Nina is force-feeding her cyanide. Nina boils her an egg.

'Ooh, can I have one?' asks Saul.

'No,' snaps Nina, 'I'm not doing a running buffet.'

Freya will not eat the egg, she will not eat toast, she will not eat yoghurt, she will not eat a cheese triangle or a rice cake or a lovely apple or nice raisins. She sits in her highchair and pulls at her left ear. Her beady squirrel-brown eyes are dull today. Nina spoons some Calpol into the child's mouth. She tips it into the left-hand side of her daughter's mouth and watches it slide out of the right. Saul gathers up the leftover egg, toast, yoghurt, Dairylea triangle, rice cake, apple and raisins and does his impression of a human waste-disposal unit. For the first time this morning Freya laughs.

Nina turns her back. She's run out of Nurofen and her head is killing her. Surreptitiously she lifts the bottle of Calpol to her mouth and drains it.

21

crying over Spilt coco-pops

Guy is packing. Alice is on the stairs, yelling at their sons, 'Max, Sam, I want you to get all the stuff you think you might need in your rucksacks – now!'

Max and Sam are sitting in front of the television. Sam wants to put the television in his rucksack. They are watching a Japanese cartoon. Sam, squatting on the floor, looks like he belongs on the screen, a red-haired nine-year-old Manga character. Max, three years older, lies proprietorially on the sofa, his massive jeans looped round his skinny waist with a metal chain. He has wrapped his skateboard in a black bin-liner; his packing is done.

Guy rolls his Muji T-shirts, black and grey, into sausages, and tucks his new Birkenstocks into the empty corner of the canvas bag. He's not sure about these sandals, they're a bit lesbian. Oh well, Alice can always wear them. For a woman, she has the most enormous feet. Peanut is a dainty size four. He knows this for a fact – last week he bought her a pair of violet satin Manolo Blahníks.

Alice is thundering about the house, a pink towel tucked tightly under her armpits. She has just had a bath – it was too hot and now she is sweating. She stomps into the bedroom and furiously pulls on a pair of knickers. Carroty pubes escape on all sides. 'Buggeration, I've forgotten to shave,' she expletes. Alice rarely blasphemes; she believes that swearing is a sign of a limited vocabulary.

128

Guy looks at his wife. Don't most women wax their bits? Peanut does. Peanut has a neat dark triangle, edible as caviar. Lovely Peanut, all blonde on top and chocolate underneath.

Guy realises, as he places his black nylon toilet bag neatly on top of his cellophane-wrapped 'good shirts', that the next time he packs it will be to leave his wife for ever. Alice bought him this toilet bag last year when he had to have an ingrowing toenail removed and it went nasty. Two days in King's, another lifetime ago, before he met Peanut. He could really do with a nice new leather one.

Alice is wearing big pants with a rip in the grubby lace trim. She pulls yesterday's bra over her head and fights to get her arms through the requisite holes. She looks like a small ginger pig trapped in an elastic fence. The scar of Sam's emergency caesarean reminds him that the struggling pig is the mother of his children and he experiences a mild pang of guilt.

Fifteen years of marriage. Alice has freckles all over her back and a couple of scars where ugly moles were dug out. Non-malignant, but she is careful in the sun, slathering herself with factor thirty. The holiday mantra: 'Sam, if you don't cream up you can go indoors.' Sam has the skin of a nineteenth-century female aristocrat, white as melamine. Max, on the other hand, is like his father, honey-coloured in comparison with the jellyfish blue of his wife and youngest son.

Alice has a big bruise on the back of her leg; her calves are as wide as Peanut's thighs. She is fighting to zip up a pair of combat trousers. They pull tight across the pouch of her stomach. When she bends down, the outline of her vast pants is clearly visible.

Guy's bag is locked. Alice is folding beach towels, ancient frayed matted rags.

'We won't need them, Alice. The brochure says "beach towels provided".'

'Thank goodness for that,' says Alice. There are small grapefruit-sized sweat marks already forming under the armpits of her khaki T-shirt.

Why is my wife dressed for battle? Guy ponders.

He checks his Mulberry mock-croc briefcase. Tucked inside are the travel documents, tickets, passports, driving licence, a new Jake Arnott, a couple of hundred quid's worth of euros and a packet of Migralieve. Should he bother with condoms? No, he isn't having sex with Alice at the moment. She doesn't seem to mind, she's never been that keen. Resigned rather than enthusiastic, Alice has always been a strictly lights-off, missionary-position kind of girl. Peanut, on the other hand . . . Guy's stomach growls. He's not hungry, he just wants Peanut. It's Saturday; he hasn't seen her since Wednesday.

At least he managed to get through to her yesterday. She had been ill. 'Some virus,' she muttered weakly. He'd wanted to go and see her, take a cab over to Kilburn at lunchtime, but she said she was spending the day at her mother's in Crawley. Guy didn't know she came from Crawley; it's the sort of place people make jokes about. Peanut should come from somewhere more credible, like Camden or Notting Hill.

'I'll be going back to the flat tonight,' she told him, and then her battery had died. He'd left a couple of messages on her answer machine, but she'd either got back really late or had stayed another night at her mother's.

Alice is throwing disposable razors and reels of film into her overflowing wicker beach bag, a souvenir from Corsica, or was it Sardinia? Guy can't remember. All he knows is that he won't be going on holiday with his family again. He tries to recall the times when it was just himself and Alice, before the kids – where did they go?

Greece mostly, and Alice trod on one of those spiky things and he'd weed on her foot to stop it getting infected. Alice with prickly heat, shivering and nauseous. Alice burning her leg on the exhaust of that moped, a weeping open sore that took months to heal. No wonder the woman favoured combat trousers – she was always in the wars. Life is a constant battle for Alice. In the past she dealt with these emergencies coolly and stoically; these days life seems to be wearing her out, hysteria bubbling in her veins. The control freak is losing control.

'Please, Guy,' she is saying, 'go and tell the boys to get a move on. I know for a fact Max hasn't cleaned his teeth, and make sure

130

they've packed enough books.' Alice is a reader. Literature is to Alice what insulin is to a diabetic: she would rather miss a train than get on without a book. The fact that she never has time to finish a chapter isn't the point. According to Alice, only very stupid people don't read.

Once upon a time Alice used to work in publishing, but when Max came along she went part-time, and then with Sam it got difficult, and anyway by then Guy was earning good money, an obscene amount really when you think what he does. Alice sighs. Her husband is a success, but she is disappointed in him. Once upon a time, after his parents' death, when his heart was hanging by a thread and she was slowly nursing him back to sanity, she'd encouraged him to bare his soul on paper. He had promise, he was young, he was angry and hurt, he was everything a young novelist needed to be. She'd retyped his tatty manuscripts, adding semi-colons where necessary. She had the connections, she was willing to help; he had the talent but he squandered it. When Guy's first book (about a man who lost his girlfriend, his parents and the use of his legs) had been rejected by the very publishing company that Alice worked for, he just gave up; decided that what he needed was a career rather than a vocation. Shame. Alice would rather be poor and married to a writer than . . .

Deep down Alice despises Guy's job. After all, at the end of the day, what does he do? He sells lies for a living. Even if you don't want it, Guy will make sure you buy it. Shiny cars capable of going faster than the law allows, bowel-cancer-beating breakfast cereals, and magical shampoos that are capable of turning straw into silk. In Guy's world, yoghurts talk, women salsa their way through the housework, and even students on Pot Noodle incomes have Smeg fridges. Guy is good at his job – he has the salary to prove it.

There's plenty of money to go round, for trainers and PlayStations and cars and cereal and lager. Not that Alice is extravagant. On the contrary, she has a morbid fear of debt. She takes her shoes to be mended and boils chicken bones to make soup. Alice is low-maintenance and proud of it; proud of the fact that she has never had a manicure or a facial. Alice washes her face with soap and water. Alice keeps her nails blunt by nibbling them with her teeth. Alice has no time for vanity, but when she catches sight of herself she realises it was a mistake to have attacked her fringe with the bacon scissors last night – she looks a bit remedial.

Guy takes his bag downstairs. The combination of the lock is easy to remember: 3, the number of their house; 9, Sam's age; 1, January, the month Guy was born; 4, the four of them. Not for long.

The hallway could do with painting. On the wall next to the cupboard under the stairs are the pencil marks where they used to measure the boys. Guy realises that in six months' time he will be forty and he won't be here to celebrate it, not in this house, which is a shame in some respects. He will miss the boys jumping on to the bed to wish him happy birthday, their gifts of ties and hankies that he never uses because Alice gets them from Peter Jones. On the other hand, he won't miss Alice's bone-dry coffee and walnut cake, and her resigned bedtime leg-spreading as if she was doing him a great big birthday favour. No, he will have a chocolate cake from Patisserie Valerie, which he will smear all over Peanut's tits, and then he'll—

'Earth to Guy, come in, Guy.'

Guy extricates himself from a fantasy which involves rubber sheets and whipped cream and Peanut begging for anal sex. Back in Dad mode he bellows, 'All right, you snotty oiks, telly off, your mother's going berko, so upstairs now, we're off in ten minutes and we're not coming back for anything either of you have forgotten.'

Suddenly he remembers going on holiday as a child to the Lake District, and his older sister making his father turn round because she'd forgotten her make-up bag. The bright red of his father's neck as he U-turned in the middle of the road. 'Now then, Bernard' – his mother's voice. They would have loved being grandparents; they would have been so proud. Oh well, at least they're not here to watch him pull the can from the bottom of the pile, so to speak.

Sam's rucksack is leaking Lego; there is nothing else in it. Max's hangs limply round the newel post.

'For Christ's sake, Max' – Max is still prostrate on the sofa, a rubbery skeleton, naked to the waist – 'you're not even properly dressed. Put some clothes on, get that bag filled and clean your teeth.'

'I'm just taking the skateboard,' his son mumbles, not taking his eyes off the screen.

Guy spies the bin-liner. 'Oh no you're not. It's one thing splitting your head open here, but I'm not having you getting brain damage in Italy and spoiling our holiday.' God, you're such a hypocrite, whispers Guy's conscience. Talk about spoiling things – you're the one who's planning to dump your wife and kids.

'Bloody hell, I never wanted to go on this spasticated holiday in the first place,' Max snaps, but he doesn't mean it. He's heard that women go topless in Italy, and he wriggles into a stale-smelling Nirvana T-shirt.

Sam wants to take Cow. Cow is a stuffed dog, but because he was white with black spots, the toddler Sam insisted he was a cow. Cow is now bald and grey. Guy thinks it's time Sam grew out of him. Sam thinks his father is being stupid – you can grow out of shoes and shorts but not out of a stuffed toy. Cow is coming, the skateboard is not.

'Not pissing fair,' bellows Max, who has just learnt to swear, slam doors and stamp up the stairs.

'Jesus, Max,' yells Alice, 'what is your problem?'

Suddenly Alice flies down the stairs, grabs Max's rucksack and starts shovelling Game Boys and Philip Pullman books into it. 'Crayons, take some crayons,' she twitters, and in a fit of lunacy she delves under the sofa, grabs the Scrabble set and crams it into the bag. An X, an A and a V fall out in the process.

Alice is spinning now and she falls backwards over Sam's cereal bowl. Brown Coco Pop milk splatters everywhere. Alice is so hot her glasses have slid off her face and are dangling from one ear. She looks better with her contact lenses in, thinks Guy, before running to the kitchen to fetch a cloth. When he comes back, Alice is rocking over the stained carpet, literally crying over spilt milk. She looks up at him, smudged and shiny as a honey-glazed ham.

'Sorry, darling, I really need this holiday.'

Guy kneels next to her and tries to put his arm around her shoulders, but it feels wrong, like a teacher comforting a pupil. It's too personal, so he pats her back, feeling the bulges where her bra cuts in, and says, 'It's OK, don't worry.'

You cunt, hisses the voice in his head.

22

Are We Nearly There Yet?

Lydia Sinclair swallows a yawn. At least she's got the latest palazzo mob on the coach without anyone going AWOL or whingeing about lost luggage. So far the trip from the airport has been fairly uneventful, just one quick wee stop for a chubby boy and his dad. Course, as soon as they'd got off another dad and his son followed them. It's all right for men, they can wee anywhere.

Lydia is desperate for a vodka and tonic. This job would be fine if it weren't for the people. She used to be a nursery school teacher but she got sick of kids crying and taking a dump in the Wendy House.

The trick to being a good holiday rep, she reckons, is hiding. Lydia spends most of her time at the palazzo lurking in the bushes avoiding the clients. If they catch her, they only complain about stupid things like the weather being too hot or not having enough teaspoons. The blokes who arrive with laptops are the worst: businessmen who like to appear far too important to take time off for a holiday. These are the ones who inevitably lose the family passports and return airline tickets.

This is Lydia's second season at the palazzo, and experience has taught her that first impressions really do count. As far as she can tell, among this latest bunch of new arrivals there is one potential wanker, a woman with fake tits, a really posh family with nice luggage (Louis Vuitton), a pair of hideous-looking twin babies, a screechy toddler, two quite good-looking older blokes, a kid that might have something wrong with it, a handful of adolescents, a girl not much older than herself and a bossy cow.

Lydia tucks her straw-coloured bob behind her ears and surreptitiously nibbles a cheese and tomato roll. The journey always takes longer than people are expecting. That's because it says ninety minutes in the brochure when the reality is never less than a couple of hours. After the initial buzz of excitement back in Naples, the group have settled down and there is a general air of grumpiness on board.

Lydia pretends to be doing some paperwork. There's no point looking out of the window, she's seen it all before. Vines and olive trees, vines and olive trees, oh look, a farm! Big bloody deal. She misses Sheffield, she misses Marks and Spencer and a decent curry, and as one sky-blue day melts into yet another sky-blue day she yearns for proper northern rain.

On the back seat the toddler throws her bottle on the floor for the sixteenth time. 'No, Freya.'

I'm sick of this fucking coach, thinks Nina, bending down to pick up her daughter's juice. Her left ankle is still smarting; she managed to trip over Freya's buggy getting off the Gatwick Express and blood is seeping through the plaster. Today has gone on too long. Ideally she'd like to be punched unconscious and wake up on the beach, preferably alone.

Freya's maiden flight has not been easy. For starters, she threw up all over Nina as soon as they arrived at the airport. Somehow tiny Freya managed to produce as much puke as a grown man after fifteen pints and a lamb pasanda.

Nina tried to wash the sick out of her clothes in the ladies', stripping down to her knickers, before vainly attempting to dry them under the hand-drier. When that hadn't worked, Joe had offered to buy her a new outfit. Unfortunately, Next had been closed for refurbishment and she'd ended up in Hargreaves, the sports outfitters. Emerging in a navy nylon tracksuit, Nina looked like she'd come third in a Sporty Spice lookalike competition.

For over six hours now her vomit-sodden clothes have been in a plastic bag on her knee, and every so often she can hear someone mutter, 'Can you smell sick?'

As if that wasn't enough, she'd caught sight of Hils's book in Gatwick's WH Smith – people were actually buying the bloody thing. She counted three people reading it on the plane, and a frizzy-haired middle-aged woman halfway down the coach has had her nose in it for the last hour.

Alice licks her finger to turn a page. She doesn't normally buy 'women's popular fiction', she has a horror of novels about thin women in kitten heels endlessly obsessing about men, but this, *Diary of a Divorcee*, is quite absorbing.

Shame it's getting too dark to read now, and if she puts her over-head light on she'll wake Sam. Sleepy Sam; his forest-fire head is heavy on her lap. He'd had a bit of a tantrum a while ago, something about a lost piece of Lego, and he'd upturned his rucksack in the aisle.

Guy had overreacted. 'Just put it away, Sam,' he'd said in a really horrible voice, and obviously Sam had become hysterical.

Guy is too impatient. He'd snapped at her, too, when she thought she'd lost the Scrabble set. 'But I know I packed it.'

'Just sit down, Alice.'

In the end she remembered it was in Max's bag. She does need to relax. Things keep getting on top of her. Well, they're here now . . . nearly. Alice contemplates her holiday. She's going to swim every morning. Before anyone else gets up, she will do twenty minutes of breast stroke and backstroke and then she'll probably wander down to the local *panetteria*. Buy some authentic bread from a nice friendly peasant who won't speak a word of English but will greet her every day with a toothless grin.

And even if the English papers are available (and Alice sincerely hopes they're not), she certainly won't buy one, not even the *Guardian*. The world and its wars can wait – this is her lovely family holiday and they're going to have such fun. She puts her book away and glances around the coach. There are even other children for the boys to play with, that tubby lad and his sister look friendly,

137

though the young girl who's with their father can't be their mother, not unless she was pregnant when she was twelve.

On second thoughts, maybe she shouldn't encourage the boys to socialise too much. One never knows with whom they might be mixing.

The little girl is sweet, though. 'Freya' they call her. Pretty name. Alice's eyes inexplicably fill with tears.

Across the aisle, next to Max, Guy sits in silence, his jaw still clenched. Sam's outburst had been humiliating. He's nine years old, for heaven's sake! When Guy had been nine, he'd been out on the streets playing football in the dark, only coming in when he was hungry, mucking about on the out-of-bounds construction site where they were building the new houses. Him and Jimmy Atkins smoking dog-ends.

Sam is molly-coddled. It's all right for girls to behave like that but Sam is a boy and it's embarrassing. Alice encourages him, cutting his food up, sewing Cow's back leg back on, pretending there was still such a thing as Father Christmas right up until last year. The situation is getting out of hand. Guy wonders if leaving will make a proper boy of his son, or will Alice cling to her youngest even more and turn him into a freaky eunuch? Already she gives him the day off school if he so much as sneezes. 'He's got a weak chest, Guy, and I don't want him having antibiotics.'

Bollocks. The only thing that's unhealthy about that child is his relationship with his mother. Max had ignored his brother's outburst, but the back of his neck went very red. He knew, and Guy knew, that everyone was staring, all the other parents thinking maybe he's emotionally disturbed, autistic perhaps? How sad.

I wonder if that ginger kid's got one of those funny syndromes, thinks Tabitha, like Kelly Hambling's brother, the one with the wobbly head. For a moment, she feels lucky to have Saul for a brother, even though he's eaten all the wine gums that Hils packed for them.

'I'm starving,' moans Saul. Saul is always starving; food is his

138

favourite thing in the whole wide world. Even when Gramps died and he'd had to be all serious and grown-up at the funeral, the only thing he can really remember was the buffet afterwards. Saul drools at the memory. What a feast, better than Christmas dinner, because you could help yourself and keep going back for more. Poached salmon, ham, chicken legs, rice salad, pasta salad, vol-au-vents . . . On the train going home he'd said, 'Wow, that cheese-cake!' and Tabitha had hit him, but his mum had laughed, just laughed till she cried. He'll never understand women.

He and his dad are outnumbered now. Before his parents had split up it had been more even, his mum and Tabitha, him and Joe. Four is a good number; it splits neatly into two. Him and his dad going to see *The Phantom Menace*, Tabitha and Mum going to Claire's Accessories. Then there were the grandparents, two on each side, Nanna and Poppa and Grannie and Gramps, another set of four, a good number for playing Cluedo or Monopoly.

Now it's all messy, pieces are missing, everything's got scattered. There's his mum, Hils, and her mum, Brenda, who used to have husbands that lived with them and don't any more because Mum's divorced and Grannie's a widow. They're on their own now and Grannie can't just pop by because she lives in a place called Norfuck, which is funny because it's got the word 'fuck' in it, and anyway she can't drive – Gramps did the driving, because he said he couldn't 'trust that woman'.

Then there's Nina who lives with Dad now, and Nina's mum, who's not really a relative at all, not even an auntie, and this baby half-sister. Saul likes Freya, but it would have been better if she had been a boy. He doesn't really get the 'half-sister' thing – it makes her sound like she's got no legs.

Nina's OK, but she's a bit like one of those student teachers that come into school to train to be a proper teacher and get headaches because they can't shut anyone up. So they try and eat paracetamol without anyone noticing and look like they're going to burst into tears 'if anyone else does anything silly'. Which means someone has to do something silly because even though you feel sorry for them, when their voices go really high you can't help wanting to push them over the edge so that they cry and wet their pants.

Freya wets her pants, but that's OK because she's a baby, and once Tabitha wet her pants because she had to be Mary in the Nativity. She was only six and she was so nervous the wee came out when she was on stage and, according to Hils, the hem of her dress went really dark.

Saul laughs.

'What's so funny?'

'You wetting your pants when you were the Virgin Mary.' The word 'virgin' makes Saul laugh some more, and Tabitha smacks him on the head with her hairbrush.

What are they doing *now*? Why can't they just sit still? When they start mucking around, Freya gets all overexcited and wriggles like a puppy with really bad worms. Nina wants Joe to tell them off, but he's doing his staring-into-the-distance thing. It drives her mad the way he does that. When Nina was at school there was a girl in her class who had epilepsy. Now and again she'd zone out, just like Joe is doing now.

'Joe, Joe?'

He's not listening. Joe is thinking. There is something familiar about one of the women on the coach, the one with the massive knockers, sitting next to a bloke who keeps giving the breast nearest to him a quick squeeze, as if he were tooting a car horn. Who the hell is she?

Joe shuts his eyes. Sometimes he feels so tired; he is forty-two and here he is doing it all over again, back to buggies and teething gel. He feels like a chameleon, changing skins and getting confused. Who is he? Nina's partner, Hils's ex, son of Marjory and Bill and father of three? Joe feels a pang of guilt when he thinks about his parents. They haven't really forgiven him for leaving Hils. It's not as if they don't like Nina, but they are vaguely dismissive of her, patronising even.

Joe's parents don't think Nina is as clever or as funny as Hils. It's as if they are slightly disappointed in Joe for living a cliché, for leaving the wife for the dolly bird. 'Dolly bird'? For heaven's sake, no one says dolly bird any more. Anyway, Nina isn't a dolly bird.

140

She might be seventeen years younger than him but she's not a simpering child, despite the fact that she occasionally sulks like one. That's why he had to 'accidentally on purpose' lose his newspaper at the airport. Nina is in a bad enough temper without catching sight of the *Independent*'s glowing review of *Diary of a Divorcee*. No doubt his mother will have cut out the clipping. She'll think it's wonderful, conveniently forgetting the fact that it's a thinly disguised autopsy of her golden boy's failed marriage. He can hear her in his head, preening at her Friday coffee mornings: 'My son's first wife, you know, the writer.' Meanwhile he has to phone to remind her to send Nina a birthday card.

Hils still sees his parents. She takes Tabitha and Saul up north on the train. Joe's dad takes photos of his ex-daughter-in-law and his grandchildren and pastes them into family albums. Joe is the only one missing and he is their son.

Occasionally he makes the trip up the M6 himself with Nina and Freya, but all his parents do is talk about Tabitha and Saul; they don't seem to be very interested in Freya, who in turn isn't very interested in them. It's not right.

Joe feels he is competing for his parents' affection with his ex-wife. Ridiculous.

They've only visited his new place once, just after Freya was born and Nina was still in hospital, shocked to the teeth. Joe had wanted their approval of his new pad with the shiny wooden floors and open-plan living space. 'It's very different from the old house,' was his mother's only comment. 'That's the whole point,' he'd wanted to snap. He'd done the Victorian terrace with the dark red walls and memorabilia all over the place. He'd done the crammed mantelpieces, the tongue and groove and the roll-topped bath, the fat cat curled up on a junk-shop sofa; now he wanted clean lines, white paint and stainless steel.

'I think we might have to put the central heating on,' his father had added, 'unless you want your mother to sit here with her coat on.'

They'd brought some tomatoes from his father's greenhouse, but Joe had got in some sushi. 'What are the little black bits?' his mother had enquired.

'Eel,' Joe replied, and she'd put her chopsticks to one side.

In the morning his mother got up early and fried the tomatoes for his father's breakfast, and for a while his designer loft smelt like their Derbyshire bungalow and it confused him.

Hils had been very good about Freya. She'd sent a present to the hospital with Tabitha and Saul, a small felt rabbit with the saddest eyes you've ever seen. Rabbit is Freya's favourite toy. However much Nina tries to tempt her with fluffy pink poodles sporting jaunty bows in their topknots, Freya clings to the little brown rabbit.

How do other men cope? Some of them do it over and over again, starting new families when they're well into their sixties, turning family trees into complex webs: half-brothers, stepsisters, forgotten nieces, cousins by third marriages. How do they find the time and energy to keep caring, never mind buying all those birthday cards? It's all so complicated. If people knew how tiring divorce was, how many of them would bother?

'Joe, Joe.' Nina's voice is like a mosquito in his ear. Freya has dropped her bottle again. 'Oh for God's sake, Joe, do I have to do everything?' The bottle rolls down the central aisle and veers under a seat further down the coach. Nina scrambles after it. 'Excuse me,' she flaps, bending over and reaching between a stranger's legs. Suddenly the bus lurches round a steep bend and Nina, finding herself momentarily thrown off balance, accidentally grabs the man's knee to prevent herself from falling. 'Sorry.' The man looks at her, a semi smirk hovering around his lips, and instantly Nina feels dizzy and nauseous. Maybe it's motion sickness, maybe it's the same bug that Freya had, or maybe it's something else.

Outside the coach, the sky is streaked deep turquoise and orange and the scenery turns suddenly to silhouette.

I wonder what Peanut's doing, thinks Guy. He'd managed to call her from the airport, huddled in a cubicle in the men's toilets with his trousers round his ankles. She sounded breathless. For a second panic made his knees tremble. What if she was shagging someone else?

'Guy, I'm in a bloody yoga class.'

Of course she was, it's Saturday. On Saturdays, Tuesdays and Thursdays, she salutes the sun and bends and folds her lovely little body into camels and fish and crabs. Clever Peanut, she can stand on her head and suck her toes.

'So you're better?'

'What? Yes, I'm fine. I thought you were going on holiday.'

'I am. I just wanted to say goodbye. I'm going to miss you. What are you wearing?'

'Oh for Christ's sake, Guy, what do you think? I'm at my yoga class, doh. I've got to get back in.'

'I love you, Peanut.'

But she'd gone.

'How many more kilometres, Mum?' Sam has woken up, a child of the metric generation.

'Not long now, sweetie,' smiles Alice in her best 'and isn't the journey fun' way. To be honest, this leg of the trip is rather longer than she had anticipated. She would really like to go to the lavatory.

'Mum, have you just farted?'

Sam again. His shrill tones coincide with the driver turning the radio off. There is a massive guffaw from the back of the coach and a few stifled sniggers.

Fortunately Lydia seizes the moment to take the microphone and announce: 'Ladies and gentlemen, we will be arriving at Palazzo Gardenia in two minutes. Please don't worry about your luggage. Staff at the palazzo will bring it directly to your rooms.'

The coach pulls through a pair of green-painted wrought-iron gates, slowly crunching its way down the fig-lined gravel drive and stopping in front of a great stone arch. Beyond the arch, strings of white bulbs illuminate a honey-coloured flagstoned courtyard, in the centre of which a lichen-covered fountain spits water through the fat lips of a copper fish.

Huge green-painted doors surround the perimeter of the court-yard. Behind them lie laundry rooms where massive wooden drying racks on rope pulleys groan with thick white cotton sheets. This is where small fat Italian women in pale blue nylon overalls fetch mops and buckets, all of them uniformly bandy-legged from lifting and carrying.

143

Diagonally to the right across the courtyard is the wide staircase that leads up to the apartments. Tucked into its broad sweep is an antique horses' cart, its leather upholstery gone brittle in the sun.

Palazzo Gardenia has sixteen apartments in the old quarter, ranging from small double-bedroom, one-bathroom and a kitchenette affairs at the back, to the grander two- and three-bedroom deluxe options with sea views and en suites at the front. Set apart from the original palazzo, discreetly screened by pine trees, is the modern block of eight new holiday suites.

Lydia opens the coach doors, pulls herself up to her full five foot two inches and puts on her 'now listen to me' voice. 'Hart Jones party, and Mr and Mrs Gaudi, if you could follow Lorenzo,' she bellows. 'Dobsons, Mario will show you to your suite, and the Jamiesons, if you would like to follow me?'

In roughly half an hour, thinks Lydia, I shall be drinking vodka.

23

First-night Nerves

Mario's buttocks are the size of quail's eggs. The Dobsons follow them as they sashay up two flights of stairs.

'And here we have Apartment Marguerita.' Mario (who once appeared on the Italian version of *Blind Date*) turns a key theatrically in a heavy wooden door and stands back.

'Ooh, ah, wow.' Tabitha and Saul are impressed, and even Nina is pleasantly surprised. It's more upmarket than, well, than she's used to. Her last holiday (pre-Joe) had been to some godforsaken dirt track of a resort in Turkey with a load of mates, five of them sharing two cockroach-infested rooms with no air-conditioning and a dodgy flush, which, considering they'd all had dramatic diarrhoea, had made for a rather unpleasant ambience. Nina remembers going out to buy joss sticks, and when she couldn't find any they'd resorted to removing the odour-eaters from Carmen's trainers, setting them on fire and wafting them around the flat.

Still, they'd had a laugh, drinking and sunbathing and swatting off hairy-bellied men in tiny primary-coloured Speedos, pretending to be lesbians in an attempt to put them off. Young, free and single. Mind you, it hadn't been that great. She'd burnt her lip on a glass of flaming sambuca and a donkey had trodden on her foot.

Growing up, Nina has realised, is about discovering that everything good has something bad about it. Like having a baby. There was something very special about being pregnant. Once she'd got past the puking stage, she'd felt so important. Nina had sported her bump celebrity-style in skinny vests, adoring the attention her new cleavage demanded. But on the day, when push came to shove, it had been horrendous, the most embarrassing, undignified experience of her life. Even the midwife had got cross with her. 'Anyone would think you didn't want to have this baby.' After two failed epidurals, she'd ended up with an episiotomy, a clumsy forceps delivery, and to top it all off, an emergency blood transfusion.

Hils, of course, had no problems delivering her two; she even had Tabitha at home! When Joe had imparted this information he'd added that Hils was 'quietly determined, with a very high pain threshold', and Nina had muttered, 'And not just a naturally baggy fanny then.' He hadn't heard. Sometimes she thinks Joe might be going deaf; he is forty-two, after all.

Shelley and Carmen are going to Ibiza this year. A week doing Ashtanga and then a week clubbing. Nina imagines them, water bottles held high, E'd off their yoga-toned tits, dancing in foam. Oh well, this is better. This is a grown-up holiday with a complimentary fruit bowl, a fire extinguisher and everything.

The alabaster walls are painted with broad yellow and white stripes, and a heavy gilt mirror hangs above a mahogany sideboard. It's nice, no, it's lovely, a sweet kitchen, electric kettle, fridge . . . 'Oh look, Joe, a cafetière.'

Tabitha and Saul have gone mad, running all over the place, dropping bags, switching lights on and off, jumping on beds.

'Dad, can we go swimming?' asks Saul, stripping off to his too-tight Pikachu underpants.

Tabitha is unpacking her Kipling bag, peeling off her socks. 'Hey, Saul, we've got our own bathroom.'

Saul immediately pees into the bidet. He has to, he's a boy.

Joe opens a door on to a balcony and Nina's optimism dissolves. 'Christ, what if Freya falls over the balcony? What if she squeezes through the railings? How high up are they? Where is the nearest hospital?' Saul slides across the hallway on the bath mat. The floors are polished marble, veined blue and grey like an old woman's hands. Skiddy as an ice rink. Freya will fall, she will fall on this floor and crack her head wide open and blood will pour out of it. The child needs a crash helmet. This is dreadful, this place is a deathtrap. I want to go home.

Nina chews the skin around her fingers. What is wrong with her? When did she turn into such a wuss? What happened to the girl who hopped on the back of motorbikes, smoked dope with strangers and gave blow jobs down alleyways? I got scared, she thinks. I want to sit on a sofa with Freya for the rest of my life.

Joe is grinning. The bags have arrived. Saul has broken into his holdall and is now wearing just his underpants and a pair of goggles.

It's only half past nine. If she was in Ibiza with Shelley and Carmen, they'd be getting ready to go out, drinking beer and putting on eyeliner, swapping clothes and doing each other's hair.

'I could do with a cup of tea,' says Nina, as weakly as if she'd just donated blood.

Joe is not listening. Freya is sitting on the floor hiccupping.

'Food, I need food,' yells Saul. Joe joins in – the two of them are shouting their heads off, 'FOOD, I NEED FOOD.' Nina realises she has a headache and her ankle is throbbing. Even more blood has seeped through the plaster and her baby-blue Converse sneaker is stained dark purple. Maybe she should have bought a bandage.

'OK,' says Tabitha, 'what's the plan?' She is applying lipgloss. Already Saul's side of the bedroom looks like it's been ransacked. Tabitha's side is an oasis of calm. A very old bear sits primly on the pillow of her bed and all her jewellery is neatly laid out on the dressing table. The bear is called Bill after Joe's dad, who bought it for her on her first birthday. This pisses Nina off. When Freya was one she didn't get a teddy bear, she got £50 worth of premium bonds, and you can't cuddle premium bonds.

'FOOD,' chorus Joe and Saul. Saul puts his jeans and T-shirt back on and they head for the door.

'But we haven't unpacked.' Nina knows she is being miserable. She knows it would be easier to go with the flow – they are on holiday, there doesn't have to be a timetable. But she can't. Something inside her has got twisted and she can't just relax and let it go. It's as if her heart is caught on barbed wire. Something is wrong. Ever since they were on the coach, she's had this nagging doubt, a feeling that coming here was the wrong thing to do.

'I'm tired, Joe.'

Joe looks bored, just for a moment. 'We're all tired, Nina, we're all tired and we're all hungry.'

Saul and Tabitha have disappeared out of the apartment. She can hear them running down the stone steps.

'I'll stay here. Freya needs to be in bed. I don't want to mess about with her routine.' As soon as she says this she knows she doesn't mean it. She just needs to be humoured; she wants to go, really.

'Fine.'

Joe walks out. She can't believe it! Joe has abandoned them. Another round to Tabitha and Saul. Nina is incensed. For a couple of seconds she stands still, and then she races to the top of the stairs and shouts, 'You fucker!'

Fucker, fucker, ucker, ker, ker – the words echo off the ancient stone walls and bounce back into her face. An elderly couple are walking up the stairs. The woman clutches at the pearls around her throat. Joe doesn't look back.

Mortified, Nina ducks back into the apartment. The balcony door is still open – where is Freya?

Freya has toddled into Tabitha and Saul's room; she is pulling at a tablecloth that covers a small round table between the two beds. Nina throws herself across Saul's bed and manages to catch hold of a heavy ceramic-based reading lamp before it topples on to Freya's cranium. Something else clatters to the floor. Freya grabs it and holds it up to Nina. It's a little wooden picture frame containing a photograph of Hils, Joe and the kids. Hils is grinning, even though the glass is splintered sharply across her face. She is grinning that lopsided red-lipstick grin. Shit!

'WAAaaaaagh,' screams Freya. A shard of glass has pricked her finger. Jesus, fuck, fuck, fuck and fuck. Nina kneels by her daughter and sucks the child's bleeding digit. She could cry, she really could – so she does. Mother and daughter sit on the floor and bawl.

Meanwhile, the other Dobsons, the Dobsons proper, are sitting in the restaurant, overlooking the floodlit pool. Joe orders a bottle of red wine. He intends to drink half and take the rest back to Nina, but he's already drunk his share before the waiter's taken their order. Saul wants chips with his spaghetti bolognese. He is ravenous, alternately shovelling down breadsticks and spitting olive stones at his sister. Tabitha wants a tricolore salad and pasta arrabiata, and Joe, Joe will have spaghetti carbonara. It reminds him of when he was a student, making his own version with a tin of mushroom soup and some chopped-up ham. I had a Baby Belling, he remembers, realising with shock that those days were twenty years ago, when life was a simple matter of Vesta curries and student-union-priced lager, and girls rolled in and out of his bed with no thoughts of babies or mortgages. It seems like yesterday, but he feels like a different person.

When I was twenty-two, Nina was just five years old.

He might have passed her on the street. After all, she'd grown up just half a mile away from his high-rise flat. And then I met Hils and for a long time I thought we'd be together for ever. It's my fault, he admits silently. I started treating her like a sister. I was reckless with her love and in the end I wanted a new toy to play with. Suddenly, Joe is reminded of a time when he was about twelve and he'd left his new bike out in the rain, and how his father had been angry. 'You've to look after what you've got, Joe. If you're not careful that bike will go rusty and eventually it'll just fall to bits.'

'Dad.' Tabitha is prodding him – the food has arrived. Joe orders a beer; Saul knocked the bottle of wine over doing an impression of Ali G.

By the time Tabitha and Saul are eating tiramisu, Freya is asleep and Nina has had three cups of tea, four paracetamol, half a packet of rather dull biscuits and a handful of annoyingly large-pipped black grapes. She has unpacked her own and the baby's clothes and pointedly left Joe's in the bottom of the bag. 'Selfish cunt.' She reads page 33 of *Captain Corelli's Mandolin* again and spends half an hour rinsing her sick-impregnated clothes in the shower before going to bed.

At midnight Joe and the kids come crashing in but infuriatingly Freya refuses to wake up. Nina pretends to be asleep while Joe and Saul have a burping competition in the kitchen. She wonders if Tabitha has found the note she left her about the broken picture frame; it was an accident, for heaven's sake. Joe slides into bed next to her. As he rolls over, he releases the loudest, smelliest burp Nina has ever heard, right in her ear.

'Good one, Dad,' yells Saul from the next room. 'You win.'

We're not even married yet, thinks Nina, and eventually real sleep steals her from her bed and takes her to Ibiza where she dances in foam with Freya in a rucksack on her back. She is trying to dance, trying to have a good time, but all the time she has to jump higher and higher to keep the rising tide of soapy bubbles out of Freya's eyes.

24

Hurdling for a Tomato - the Jamiesons Arrive

Alice is sucking up to Lydia. 'Isn't it just gorgeous? Aren't you a lucky girl to work here? It's ever so old. Would you say eighteenth century?'

'Actually some of it's seventeenth.'

Lydia's no architectural expert (she did media studies at Sheffield Hallam), but it's what it says in the brochure.

Alice stands with her hands on her hefty hips and breathes in great lungfuls of Italian evening. 'Marvellous, so imposing and yet so welcoming. Hmm, heavenly aroma, can you smell it, boys?'

'I can smell chips,' says Max. He'd kill for a McDonald's, and he'd have to – his mother would rather die than allow him 'that muck'.

'Ha ha ha, boys, eh? Not a romantic bone in their bodies. Rosemary and eucalyptus, I'd say. Well, really, this is quite inspiring. I've a yen to start sketching.'

'Mum, it's dark.' Sam's voice is querulous; he doesn't like the dark.

'Not now, you silly billy, in the morning. Tell me, Lydia, do they have easels at reception?'

Jesus, thinks Lydia, this woman is barking. She decides to ignore Alice out of politeness.

Alice doesn't notice, she can't stop prattling. 'Well, Lydia, I'm sure you're a font of local knowledge. Are there any unusual birds we should watch out for?'

What the fuck is she on about? Lydia is getting confused. Birds, easels?

Guy cringes. Why can't his wife shut up? He can't stand it when she gets enthusiastic. He knows that at this moment Alice is having visions of herself, à la Hannah Gordon, painting with watercolours, a pair of binoculars round her thick neck.

'Why are we still walking?' Sam stops and suddenly sits on the ground. 'I'm not walking any more.'

'Well, then, you can sleep here.'

'I hate you, Dad.'

'Well, I hate you.'

Happy families, thinks Lydia.

'Come on, Sam, upsadaisy.' Alice's tone is overly jovial.

'No.'

'Come on, soldier. I'll give you a piggyback.' Alice pulls Sam up rather roughly.

'Ow, you're hurting my arm.'

'The path's quite steep,' warns Lydia. 'You do know you're in the modern annexe?' She didn't mean to sound spiteful but she does.

The word 'annexe' rings alarm bells in Guy's head. Occasionally when he goes away on business and there's no Hilton available, say, in Lowestoft, Penny will book him into a 'country-house hotel'. Guy has a horror of 'country-house hotels'; they are a euphemism for poor service and no porn channel. And the worst-case 'country-house hotel' scenario is arriving and being told you're in the 'annexe', which is invariably some hideous seventies monstrosity with plastic windows and double-glazing. In Guy's experience, 'the annexe' is deliberately tucked away from view, round the back, past the bins, down a never-ending corridor, miles from the bar. The mere word conjures up orange nylon carpets and crappy Teasmades. All UHT milk and triple packs of ginger biscuits.

'I didn't know we were in the annexe.'

'Yes, well, it was a lot cheaper, Guy,' and Alice strides ahead with Sam clinging to her back like an overlarge novelty backpack.

Why does she have to do this? Why does she have to scrimp on everything? The only belt Alice refuses to tighten is the one around her big fat gut, fumes Guy.

'La, la, la,' sings Alice tunelessly.

A long time ago Guy saw a film starring a young Kate Winslet, set in New Zealand – *Heavenly Creatures* – the one where Kate and her best friend kill the friend's mother. They are walking along a path when they suddenly set upon her with a rock in a sock. Remembering this makes Guy feel uncomfortable; Kate Winslet wore really big pants in that film, Alice pants.

'La li la li la li la.'

Why is Alice singing the *Archers* theme tune?

'Nearly there,' mutters Lydia grimly.

The pool glimmers below them to the right, a yellow inflatable ball drifting slowly and silently across the surface of the water.

All the apartments in the old block are named after flowers: Jasmine, Myrtle, Mimosa. In the new block the accommodation is numbered. The Jamiesons are in number 2. It's on the ground floor. 'Marvellous,' says Alice, who is puffing like a donkey with emphysema.

Lydia digs in her bag for a set of keys. 'Guido will bring your bags along shortly,' she says, opening a brightly painted yellow door and feeling for the light switch on the inside wall.

Sam has had enough. 'Hurry up.'

Lydia has to bite her lip so that the words 'fuck off' don't escape. She was right – that kid does have something wrong with him. He's a little cunt.

Bright white light fills the room. 'It's fine,' mutters Guy.

'Fine?' repeats Alice (only a complete octave higher). 'It's lovely, Guy. We are going to have such a super time here.' Something in Alice's voice makes this sound like a threat, and Lydia finds herself ducking. This Alice bird needs medication.

'Right.' Lydia dims the lights so that the apartment looks less like a pathologist's lab and goes into professional holiday rep autopilot, complete with hand gestures. 'Sitting-room, with French windows leading on to your own private sun terrace, kitchen and breakfast bar, though you may prefer to eat outside, fridge, cooker . . .'

'Washing machine?' asks Alice hopefully.

'Er, no. We do, however, provide a laundry service. You'll find the details in the file.' Lydia nods at a blue folder on a low glass coffee table. 'There is a cheaper launderette in town which is a two-minute walk away. Santa Helena is actually quite good for shopping, and during the season most things are open every day, even on Sundays, so you'll be able to stock up on anything you need tomorrow.

'Bedroom one, here on the left, and bedroom two is through that door there. Right, well, I'm sure you'd like to be left alone to settle in.'

Alice waddles over to the sofa and drops Sam on to its navy canvas cushions. By the time she turns round, Lydia has gone.

Alice rushes after her but she has disappeared, she can't see her anywhere. This is because, unbeknown to Alice, Lydia is hiding behind a tree. 'Well, how very odd,' she muses.

Guy is in the kitchen, the cupboards are bare and there is only a bottle of water and a small carton of milk in the fridge. Guy wants a beer, he wants a beer and some red wine, lots of red wine, and possibly a brandy or three. He wants to get very drunk indeed. It's the only way he's going to get through this. Guy has got to the point where he's started lying to his doctor about his alcohol consumption.

Alice, on the other hand, doesn't drink very much. It makes her feel out of control, it gives her migraines and she hates feeling what she calls 'woozy' in the mornings.

Guy has got used to feeling shit in the mornings. It happens more and more.

All of a sudden Sam realises no one is paying him any attention, so he lies face down on the sofa and starts to kick. 'I hate it here, I want to go home.'

Alice rushes over and pulls him on to her lap. 'Hush now, darling.'

'I'll be in the bar,' says Guy.

'Which bar?'

'Any bar.'

'Wait, you can't just go to the bar!'

'Watch me.'

Guy walks out of the door. Max follows him.

'Come back here this instant!' Alice is in the doorframe shouting. Neither of them does as they're told.

Sam weeps on the sofa. 'Boooohoooo.'

For a moment Alice doesn't know what to do. She is faint with hunger. Why hadn't she ticked the welcome hamper box? Because it had been forty-five pounds. FORTY-FIVE pounds for a couple of bottles of wine, some pasta, a jar of instant sauce, some cheese and a bit of ham and bread!

She rifles through the cupboards. Apart from a few sachets of tea and coffee there is nothing except a cruet set of salt, pepper and vinegar. The salt looks damp.

'I hate it,' moans Sam. 'Take me home.'

Alice doesn't know how it happens. One moment she is in the kitchen, the next she is standing over Sam slapping him! Her hand is raised to slap him again when a man arrives with the luggage. Alice immediately raises her other hand and does a rather clumsy arabesque. She wants the man to think she is merely dancing and not beating her child. He doesn't look convinced. He flings the bags on the floor and slams the door on the way out.

Guido has five children and has never hit any of them. He knows if he did, his wife Rosa would hack off his head.

Guy and Max have found the pool bar; it's almost deserted. Just an old Italian couple drinking cognac in a corner.

'Got any euros, Max?'

Max has twenty pounds' worth of notes that Aunty Judy, his dad's sister who lives in Aberdeen, sent him. He's supposed to share the money with Sam. He hands the notes over to his father, feeling like a grown-up. They never see Aunty Judy; she's a lot older than Dad, but she's very good at remembering to send money for Christmases, birthdays and holidays.

Guy goes to the bar and returns carrying a tray containing a bottle of beer, a bottle of red wine, a Coke and something that looks like cough medicine in a tiny little glass. He is clenching a large packet of crisps between his teeth, which he drops on the table.

155

'They don't do food here, son, just these, and there's ice cream in the freezer.' Guy drinks the bottle of beer in one go and pours himself a large glass of red wine.

'Cheers,' says Max through a mouthful of crisps. And then, 'Can I have the change, Dad?'

Back at the apartment, Sam has eaten a squashed KitKat that Alice found at the bottom of her bag and fallen asleep without brushing his teeth. Alice carries him through to the smaller bedroom and tucks him under the duvet. She can't be bothered to remove his shoes. She is tired, so very tired and so very hungry. She is tempted to find the restaurant and ask if she can borrow an egg, but she can't leave Sam. What if he woke up and found himself alone in the dark? There are lizards and all sorts, spiders and ants – no, she will stay and guard her child. She is the mother lion, protector from evil.

Tomorrow, first thing, she will do a big shop. That is, if she hasn't starved to death in the night.

She unpacks. A bottle of factor thirty suntan lotion has split in her toilet bag and everything is covered in thick white paste. Tears spring to her eyes. She can't be premenstrual, she's not even halfway through her cycle.

Alice likes to think she is in tune with her body. Sitting on the floor she imagines her ovaries releasing a plump egg. If Guy made love to her on this holiday, she could get pregnant. She's only thirty-nine. Didn't the Blairs conceive that little Leo on holiday in Italy? What a lovely idea. A child with a romantic conception, a happy-ever-after anecdote. If it was a girl her middle name could be Gardenia.

Alice tries to remember how and when the boys were conceived, but she can't. Back then they seemed to have a lot more sex, at least once a week. Oh well, everyone's libido takes a dive as they get older, it's natural. If it didn't, you'd have pensioners snogging on park benches and groping each other at bus stops – all very unnecessary.

Sex embarrasses Alice, it always has, but it's supposed to be important in a relationship, everyone says so, and it's still the cheapest and simplest way to make babies. She makes up her mind to fornicate with her husband this week. She mentally works out her dates: Wednesday or Thursday night would be best.

Alice takes the toilet bag into the bathroom and wipes and rinses the contents clean. Toothbrushes, plasters, tweezers, shampoo and soap. She might as well put her nightie on, try to sleep, start again in the morning. But all she can think about is food – cheese on toast with Branston pickle, jam sandwiches made with thick white bread, creamy mushroom risotto, lasagne and sponge pudding with treacle. She checks the fridge again, opens the salad tray – a tomato would do, with a drop of vinegar and a little black pepper. The fridge remains resolutely empty.

Alice is beside herself. Where the hell is Guy? She wanders over to the French windows and opens the doors on to the terrace. There is a switch on the outside wall. She clicks it on. A table and four chairs sit expectantly in front of her, as if they too are awaiting a meal. Over to the left, separating the terrace from its twin next door, is a low brick wall, and on the other side of the wall is . . .

For a second she thinks that she might be hallucinating, but no, on the table just a short jump over a wall away are two plates containing the remnants of an alfresco lunch: a sweaty lump of cheese, a few rinds of salami, and, yes, a tomato!

Alice, who was useless at the hurdles at school, is over the brick divide quicker than you can say 'Shergar' and shoving stale bread and cheese into her face before she can imagine what she looks like.

A fat woman stealing scraps from the plates of strangers.

The doors leading into the neighbouring apartment are slightly open. There will be more food in there, more salami, more cheese. Like a crack addict desperate for another rock, Alice tiptoes on her size sevens into the sitting room. A side light has been left on but there's no one at home. Before she can reason with herself, Alice is in the kitchen, the fridge is open and she has a salami sausage in one hand and a jar of pickled gherkins in the other. Out, get out now, but there is half a bar of dark chocolate on the draining board. She grabs at it, got it – out, out now. Alice is on the verge of nervous collapse. She turns to make her escape and as she flees through

157

the sitting room, something catches her eye, something big and black on the sofa. Just leave, get out, she commands herself, squeezing through the French windows, her mind racing as fast as her heart – that thing on the sofa, what was it, what had she just seen?

No, it couldn't have been, she's going mad. But as Alice hops over the wall her conscience argues that yes it was.

Lying on the sofa in the apartment next door was a huge black dildo.

Normally the sight of something so backstreet sex-shoppish would be enough to take the edge off Alice's appetite. But it doesn't, and it's only when she finishes her chocolate, gherkin and spicy pork feast that she wonders whether the sausage might have been purchased for something other than culinary purposes.

Alice cleans her teeth until they bleed.

25

Hils Home Alone

Hils watches the television. She alternates between Sky News and BBC News 24, the remote control in one hand and a cigarette in the other. It makes a change, smoking in the house. Usually the kids make her go outside. No planes have crashed so far today, no failed engines, no mid-air collisions, no terrorist hijackings, so that's a relief. Hils is a self-confessed rubbish flyer.

She spent her wedding night in a foetal ball of fear on a particularly turbulent flight to Thailand, utterly convinced they were going to die before their honeymoon began.

Two weeks later she spent the entire return trip holding a sympathetic air hostess's hand, not even daring to walk to the toilet in case it upturned the plane. 'I've married a nutcase,' her new husband had despaired.

They will be there by now, Tabitha and Saul, in Italy with Joe, Nina and Freya. Her mother larging it up in a caravan in the Lake District with bloody Basil and 'the gang', and Hils – home alone in Stoke Newington.

I'm bored, she realises. At least when I was writing the book I had something to do when the kids weren't here.

She wonders whether she'll ever have enough creative juice to write another. As hobbies go, it turned out to be a lot more lucrative than knitting, and she's saved a fortune on shrinks.

When the breathing problem had got bad enough to have to take little white pills, she'd been to see a woman her doctor had referred her to. It hadn't been a great success. Sitting in a room painted pale green (because it's meant to be calming) on dreary furniture (not too heavy in case it gets thrown) with a box of tissues at her side (extra sob proof), she'd felt phoney and self-indulgent. Other women have so much more to contend with, she'd concluded. So her husband had cheated on her and her father was dead. Well, that's what life is like, messy and painful. Happiness is fragile.

'Thank you for your time,' she'd said, wondering how she was ever meant to entrust her emotional baggage to a woman who, despite having letters after her name, was quite obviously incapable of dressing herself. Brown nylon tights and those hideous shoes that look like Cornish pasties! Anyway, it had been a no-smoking clinic and all Hils could think about throughout her fifty-minute session was the packet of cigarettes in her bag.

She'd never been back. That night, while the children slept, she'd started writing, on the backs of gas bills and envelopes, gradually building up the confidence to sit in front of the computer and start typing. She hadn't set out to get the thing published, not at first, but when Joe talked about having to sell the house, she thought, what the hell, and sent the manuscript off to six publishing houses. She didn't know what else to do and the scratchcards weren't working. It was only after she'd posted the envelopes that she realised she'd forgotten to spell-check the wretched thing.

Redback were the only company who bothered to get in touch, although several months later she did get a rejection slip from Virago. Strange how things happen. Her manuscript had ended up on the Redback slush pile to be read 'whenever' by a freelance 'reader'. Fortunately for Hils, this turned out to be a woman who had just gone through a similar marital meltdown. The book had touched a nerve and the woman insisted one of the chief editors take it home with him one weekend.

'To be honest,' he told Hils over a hastily arranged lunch meeting at Joe Allen, 'it's not really my cup of tea. I'm a murder mystery boy. But the wife loved it, kept on reading bits out loud.' He flipped his yellow tie over his shoulder and picked up his pork chop, nibbling it round the edges with newly bleached teeth. 'I reckon we could do business. Why don't you get your people to talk to my people?'

'I haven't got any people,' she'd almost admitted, taking his card with trembling fingers.

In the end she'd roped Nick in to help, and, posing as her literary agent, he'd clinched the deal at £90,000.

'How much?'

Even Nick, who was used to dealing with cubic money, was shocked by the transaction. 'I just kept pushing them up a bit,' he told Hils, his right eye twitching furiously. 'I told them there were three other publishers interested.'

Hils didn't know whether to laugh, cry or be sick.

'Do you want me to go and get some champagne?' Nick asked, but it was only 11.30 in the morning, so they had a cup of tea instead.

After she left Nick's office in Covent Garden she found herself wandering through the piazza, where 'once upon a time' the story first began.

It was a Monday, flea-market day. Hils meandered through the stalls. I could buy anything I like. I could buy molten honey amber beads, a mother-of-pearl-handled buttonhook, a stuffed toucan under a glass dome. A silver lighter caught her eye. In the corner were the elaborately engraved initials JD. I could get that for Joe . . . and she'd been about to get her purse out when she remembered. Ah, but he's not my husband any more. And she put her purse away

She didn't even get a cab home, she caught the bus. 'It's not my money anyway.' Forty thousand pounds needed to go to the bank to pay off the mortgage on Englestone Avenue, and just for a horrible minute Hils wished Nick had managed to get Redback up to a nice round hundred grand.

But she did buy the kids an Indian takeaway, and the next day a vast bouquet of stargazer lilies arrived from the Thorpes. 'Congratulations, clever, clever you' read the card.

She hadn't been clever really, just honest. At the end of the day it was a small book about love, loss and divorce. She's not alone

– very few people live happily ever after. Life has a habit of turning round and biting you in the face. Most people run out of luck somewhere down the line.

Hils remembers her brother being run over when he was six. It's a joke now, but it wasn't funny at the time. He ran out behind an ice cream van straight into a Ford Anglia. For a while there was talk about a hairline fracture of the skull and possible complications, and her parents shrank before her eyes.

'But will he be all right?' she asked her father, the man who could mend anything.

'I can't promise you anything, sweetheart,' he'd replied, and for what seemed like weeks, he didn't whistle once.

Even Sally and Nick haven't had it easy. Despite all their money and their great big house, Sally just couldn't get pregnant. 'I'd give it all away,' she told Hils, 'if I could have a baby. What's the point in having everything, if I can't have what I want?'

Contrarily, of course, it had been the money that solved the problem, Esme being the result of their fifth attempt at IVF.

Then there was that girl at school, Katherine Pike, the prettiest girl in the upper fourth. One afternoon she'd arrived home from school and while putting her bike away in the garage she'd found her father hanging dead from the rafters, his eyes bulging and his tongue black.

Everyone has had their heart broken at some time, and Hils is struck by a sudden memory of Joe's mother standing over a newborn Tabitha with tears streaming down her face. She'd watched from the door and backed away. The grief was too raw, too private to ask why. Moments later Marjory was back to normal, bossing Bill out of the kitchen. 'He's a picker, Hils, and I want that leftover chicken for an à la King.'

It had been years before Marjory had told her why the sight of Tabitha, a little scarlet prawn in scratch mitts, had made her break down, and when she'd told her she'd made Hils promise never to mention it ever again, to anyone. 'It was a long time ago, love.' So she hadn't, not even to Joe. She couldn't be sure if he even knew.

They are of a different generation, she realises, her mother, Joe's mother. Stuff happened and they were expected to get on with it.

Hils vividly recalls her brother regaining consciousness in the hospital as if it were last Tuesday. How his hazel eyes had flipped open and he'd demanded a Zoom ice-lolly, and how her father started whistling again.

I am going to have to get myself organised this week, she decides. I am going to see art exhibitions and phone Sally and Nick and paint the downstairs toilet. I cannot spend the next seven days waiting for my children to come back. So she runs a bath and removes swathes of hard yellow skin from the soles of her feet.

It's Saturday night. Young couples are cruising the high street, drinking lager in pub gardens. Later on they will fuck, limbs thrashing under sweaty duvets, telling each other they are in love, some of them meaning it, if only for the moment. And maybe babies will be born and wedding dresses bought and the whole cycle will start up again of teething rings and potties and pushchairs to the park, and millions more stale crusts will be thrown at ducks.

It's happening all over the world. First steps are being taken and new words spoken, while, at the other end of life, hips are snapping and hearts are winding slowly down.

Hils has been in the bath so long now that it's turned to school gravy. She climbs out and her knees click ominously. I am halfway through my life, she realises. I mustn't waste whatever I've got left. I mustn't get old and fat and wistful. Maybe I should buy a vibrator, or go online and enter a chat room. I could pretend to be a twenty-three-year-old au pair.

On the other hand, she could apply some fake tan and read a good book.

I'm not lonely, she reminds herself, settling naked on Tabitha's beanbag with a Maggie O'Farrell and waiting for the fake tan to dry. She eats some Boursin on crackers that crumble into her lap. Absent-mindedly she picks the crumbs out of her pubes. There are perks to being single. However, the sight of a grey pube shatters this delusion. Fucking hell! Instantly she imagines advertising herself in *Time Out*'s lonely hearts, forty-one-year-old divorcee, two kids, grey pubes, no s.o.h. – interested? No? Don't blame you.

I think I'd better go to bed, she decides, but before she falls asleep she spends five minutes with a pair of tweezers.

There is no dignity in death, that's what they say. Well, there is no dignity in divorce either. Come to think of it, life isn't very digni-fied. The day I married Joe, when I was supposed to be at my most radiant, I got a sudden attack of nerves and farted all the way to the church. Sitting in the back of a silver Bentley in a tiara and white satin I farted so badly my father had to open the window.

Diary of a Divorcee

26

Wild Boar and Rose-tinted Glasses

Saul is mulling something over. He's not sure but he thinks a girl, just a bit older than him, might have been rude to him at breakfast. She'd been watching him piling his plate with fruit and buns and boiled eggs and salami.

'I'm famished,' he'd told her, but she'd just tossed a brown pony-tail and snorted, 'Tell that to the Africans.'

'Tabitha, do you think I'm fat?'

Tabitha swigs her drink before responding.

'Am I? Am I a lard arse, a dough ball, a chubster freak?' They are sitting outside in the mid-morning sun; the aluminium café table is as warm as a radiator.

'Is that why you ordered a Diet Coke?' his sister replies.

Saul picks up his T-shirt and counts four rolls of flesh.

'It's puppy fat,' reassures Tabitha. 'Dad was like you when he was your age. I've seen the photos.'

'Oh good,' says Saul, and he wanders over to the counter and orders an ice cream. Tabitha oinks like a pig behind his back. 'It's not for me, it's for Freya,' he lies.

Tabitha and Saul are looking after Freya. It feels a bit like that time Saul got to take the guinea pig home from nursery, a vicious ginger and black creature with sharp yellow teeth and loose bowels. Freya should be a breeze by comparison.

Nina wasn't keen on the idea. 'What if she runs out into the road?'

'It's pedestrianised,' Joe had sighed, his patience worn perilously thin, as dangerous as a bald tyre on a motorway. Nina is getting on his nerves. 'She can't sit on your knee for ever.'

Why not? thinks Nina, trailing miserably after Joe. They're only going to the chemist up the road. Freya needs a new bottle – she threw her favourite Tweenies one over the balcony back at the apartment. Saul ran down to fetch it but it was cracked. Of course it was – everything on this holiday is cracking and breaking. Nina cannot rid herself of this feeling of impending doom.

Normally she'd be in her element. The temperature is already in the eighties and the shops are loads better than she was expecting. A few of them are shut because it's a Sunday, but most of the gift shops, the supermarket and a couple of little delis are open. If she didn't feel so paranoid she could be having a nice time.

I have felt sick ever since we arrived, Nina admits silently to herself. I feel sick because I saw something, correction, I saw *someone* yesterday, who reminded me of a night I have been trying to forget for over three years. It's guilt, she tells herself, it plays tricks with your eyes, it isn't the same person, it can't be. She's not ready for her luck to run out, not yet, not now. 'Joe, wait for me!' she yelps, but he just keeps on walking.

Freya is being very good. She is wearing a yellow dress with a matching sunhat. Tabitha and Saul let her eat brown sugarlumps out of a little stainless-steel bowl. They're only her first teeth; they'll fall out anyway. The toddler gets very excited when she sees a cat and wants to stroke it. 'Catty,' she crows, 'pretty catty.' The cat is not very pretty: she has no collar and a festering sore behind her ear. Tabitha doesn't want Freya to touch the cat. It might have fleas.

'No, Freya, dirty cat.'

Freya jettisons tears, her face crumples and turns purple, her shoulders heave and she starts screaming, her complexion darkening with every noisy exhalation. Freya is forgetting to breathe between shrieks.

Tabitha might just as well have pinched her. The toddler sounds like she's being tortured. People are staring. Tabitha lets her stroke the cat before she explodes and instantly the child stops crying. It's as if her tear ducts have been disconnected; her cheeks are still wet but she is smiling. For some reason, Tabitha half expects to see a rainbow around her.

They are writing postcards to Hils. They promised they would, just to let her know they got there safely.

Saul's handwriting is big and round. 'Hi Mum, we didn't crash, there is an excellent breakfast buffet, love Saul X.'

Tabitha's handwriting is small and neat. 'Dear Mum, landed safely, gorgeous apartment, weather blissful, don't worry, I won't get burnt! You'd love it here.' As soon as she has written this line, Tabitha wishes she hadn't, but she can't cross it out and she's already stuck a stamp in the corner. 'PS Give our love to Stoke Newington.' She adds three exclamation marks, lots of kisses and a PPS: 'Don't worry, I'm keeping an eye on Saul.'

Saul's ice cream arrives. It's what their grandmothers would call 'a knickerbocker glory'. The waiter brings three spoons and Freya gets chocolate sauce all down her clean yellow front. This makes her cry again. Freya is one of those children who can't abide being dirty. The merest speck on a T-shirt has her in hysterics. Tabitha tries to pull the dress off Freya's head but she forgets to undo the button at the back and it gets stuck. 'You're strangling her,' observes Saul. Freya is like a small tornado on Tabitha's knee. 'Where the hell is Nina?' This is all her fault: she and Freya are nothing but trouble.

'Maybe we should be getting back.' Nina tries to prevent the urgency that she feels from infecting her voice. Joe has stopped to look in a shop window glittering with shiny new cameras, like he hadn't got enough of the stupid things already. The woman in the chemist's had flirted with him. Nina is convinced that if she hadn't been there, the silly slag would have closed the shop and given him a blow job on the spot. She had that kind of mouth.

Joe is so handsome, so full of life. Sometimes Nina feels like his misshapen shadow, or worse, on ugly days, like his pet troll.

'Look, Nina, there's a shoe shop. Come on, let's buy you some shoes.' Nina is torn. On the one hand there is Freya, little baby Freya. On the other there are shoes, three-inch wicker wedges embroidered all over with strawberries, soft orange leather moccasins and sequinned flip-flops. She dithers for a moment.

'No, Joe, we must get back.'

Joe's nostrils flare. 'God you're a miserable cow.'

Before she knows what she is doing, Nina is kicking Joe. 'Fuck off.'

'Well that's grown-up,' sneers Joe. 'OK, Nina, let's go back to the other children, shall we?'

He strides ahead and Nina trots after him. She is in full troll mode now. 'Sorry, Joe, I'm sorry.'

A teenage couple are snogging up against a wall, tongues darting into each other's mouths like pink lizards. Joe's mouth is set in a thin hard line as if someone has drawn it on to his face with a sharp pencil. Why is she being like this?

Tabitha, Saul and Freya are exactly where they left them twenty minutes ago: same seats, same table. It's like one of those 'spot the difference' pictures. Everything looks the same, but a few of the details have changed.

Freya's buggy is upside down, the nappy bag is open, Tabitha's sunglasses are on the floor, there is a large empty glass on the table with three spoons sticking out, oh yes, and Freya is naked apart from her nappy. Where is her dress, where is her hat? Saul is wearing her hat. He put it on to cheer her up just after she ripped her dress; he looks ridiculous in it.

'Give Freya her hat back!' Nina squeezes past Saul to pick up the buggy, and as she snatches the frilly hat off his head she steps on Tabitha's sunglasses. Inevitably, there is a cracking sound.

'Everything cracks, everything breaks,' snivels Nina, and then she sees the dress with the big rip in it and she sits on the floor and weeps silently into the nappy bag.

'Right,' says Joe grimly. Today is not going very well. 'Nina, why don't you take Freya back to the apartment?' he instructs. 'I'll pay up and we'll be back in half an hour.' With that he plonks Freya into the buggy, chucks a wad of euros on the table and walks out, followed by his older children.

Nina dutifully wheels her daughter back to the palazzo. We could always go and live with my mum, she thinks.

168

An hour later, just as Nina is starting to intone 'selfish, selfish cunt' in her head, and 'it's fucking lunchtime, where is the bastard?', Joe and the kids return. Tabitha is wearing a new pair of pink sunglasses with a heart-shaped diamanté motif in the corner of one lens, while Saul is toting a very large plastic submachine-style water gun.

Before Nina can even form the words 'Is that a good idea?', Joe is handing her a box. Inside the box under crackles of scarlet tissue paper is a pair of shoes. The shoes are beautiful. The shoes are shiny black patent with a spike heel as long and as sharp as a Sabbatier knife, a cluster of glass cherries hanging off each ankle strap.

'Oh Joe,' says Nina, 'thank you.'

They really are lovely shoes. It's just that given a choice she'd have preferred the flat sequinned flip-flops. Nina puts the shoes on. They're porn star shoes and she must clench her calf muscles to remain upright in them. Joe looks ludicrously pleased with himself. Tottering only slightly, she moves to give him a kiss, a proper teenage, leaning-up-against-a-wall, lizard-tongue kiss, which is only interrupted by a jet of ice-cold water in her ear.

'Ha,' sniggers Saul, followed by, 'I'm starving, what are we having for lunch?'

Tabitha stands silently watching in the corner. She can't get used to her father kissing Nina. It doesn't look right, even through rose-tinted glasses.

They have lunch in the apartment. As well as the shoes and the sunglasses and the water gun, Joe has bought cracker biscuits, cheese, olives and tomatoes. If I work hard, if I pre-empt everything that everyone is feeling, if I jump through flaming hoops, this holiday will be a success, he promises himself. Relationships are like expensive racing bikes, he realises. You've got to look after them, make sure they're kept in good working order. He's got to keep his eye on Nina – occasionally her gears stick.

After lunch, Freya has a nap, so Joe, Tabitha and Saul take a stroll around the palazzo while Nina minds the baby. She lies on the bed in her new shoes. I'm not going to even think about it, she tells herself, but the pea-sized doubt is growing, and her brain plays games of prosecution and defence.

'You can't be sure?'

'No, m'lud.'

'But you can't be sure, you're not sure.'

'No, m'lud.'

All she does know is that there is a man staying here at the palazzo who reminds her of someone she once slept with. If only she *had* just slept with him – but they didn't just sleep together, they made love. No they didn't, they fucked. Oh, Nina, a stranger inserted his penis into your vagina and it's quite possible he has come here to haunt you.

'But he hasn't even looked at me!'

'Not yet, but what if he does? What if he looks at you and he knows and you know?'

'But he hasn't. Maybe he has forgotten all about it.'

'Maybe, and maybe if you're very lucky you will get away with it.'

While Nina twists and turns like a dying goldfish in the king-size bed, Tabitha reads out loud from a pamphlet entitled 'A Visitor's Guide to the Palazzo'.

'Originally built as a hunting lodge for the ancestors of the current Principe di Salvadore, the Kings of Spain and Italy once met at the palazzo to hunt wild boar and shoot quail on the surrounding estates. To this day the Prince keeps a private apartment at the palazzo and may often be sighted during the season surveying the five acres of mature gardens that are now shared with the discerning and grateful clientele.'

'Blimey, wild boar,' breathes Saul, making up his mind to hide behind a tree and charge Tabitha making ferocious boar noises when she's least expecting it . . . when it's dark. He chuckles secretly to himself, trying to resist the temptation to rub his hands together in glee.

'I wonder which is his bit?' Tabitha cranes her neck. The palazzo is built on three floors; their apartment is on the first.

'I reckon he'll be on the top floor, like a penthouse thingy.'

They are walking through the courtyard. Women in overalls cross this way and that carrying fresh laundry, cats weaving between their bow legs. They have already found the library and games room, the office and an outhouse stacked with bicycles for hire. The mid-afternoon sun is almost ultra-violet in its brightness. Joe takes arty shots of shadows and lizards. Beyond the courtyard is the pool and set amid pine trees on a slope to the left of it is the modern annexe.

Joe puts his camera away. It's become harder to make the effort. So many photographs over the years, the attic at the old house full of them. Sometimes it feels like he's on a permanent busman's holiday. At least now with digital you can edit out the ugly moments. If only the same was true of real life. There are pictures in his memory that he would like to get rid of for ever. Hils's face the moment the truth sank in, Sally's disdain, Nick's surprise, the children's hurt; his parents' looks of surprise and disappointment.

Sometimes Joe wonders what would have happened if Freya had never been born. Where would he be? But I love all my children equally, he reminds himself.

Two men are strolling through the gardens towards them, holding hands. Both have moustaches and are speaking German.

'I think they might be gay,' shouts Saul, cheerfully.

'Gay, yes – deaf, no,' the taller one responds, and Saul turns the colour of the inside of a fig, red but slightly green around the edges.

Joe grins sheepishly. 'Er, sorry about that, lovely day.' Tabitha marches ahead, silently repeating: I'm not with them, I'm not with them, they are nothing to do with me. For want of anything better to do, Saul pretends to be a wild boar and charges her from behind. The gay Germans laugh and Joe, because he thinks it might be the right thing to do, offers his hand. 'Hi, I'm Joe.'

Dieter and Peter shake it, in a manner that suggests both frequent the gym. 'You stay here, *ja*?'

'*Ja*,' echoes Joe.

'We stay in modern block, not so nice as old place, and we have mouse problem.' For some reason they find this hilarious. 'Ha ha! Someone is eating our cheese.'

171

27

Sun, Sea and Spar

Alice has been shopping. She went very early this morning, before anyone else had woken up. Most things were open apart from the bakery, which was a shame. Alice looked longingly at its charmingly scarred wooden shutters. Catholicism is all very well, but some hot focaccia would have been just the ticket.

Originally she'd set off with the intention of trawling the delicatessens, buying a little cheese here, some pâté there, maybe an interesting bottle of olive oil, with scarlet chilli peppers suspended in the golden goo? But in the end the Spar had been so much easier. Sam does like Coco Pops for breakfast. Cereal, milk, bread, jam, a bag of peaches, yoghurts, eggs, cheese, tomatoes, coffee, juice, washing powder. Alice's arms were almost hanging out of their sockets by the time she got back.

Still, the morning has been quite successful so far, even though Guy had woken up with a headache, demanding to know why they couldn't have breakfast in the dining-room.

'Waste of money,' Alice had replied, unpacking sliced white bread and sweaty shrink-wrapped Edam.

'Alice, how many times do I have to tell you we're not skint. In fact, I'm rolling in it.'

'Don't be vulgar, Guy,' reprimanded Alice.

Fuck it. Save your money for Mauritius and Peanut. The voice in his head is back and as insistent as ever.

There had been one small-scale row over some stickers in the Coco Pops packet, which had landed in Max's bowl. 'Give them to Sam, Max' – and to give the boy his due, he had, only slightly marring the act of generosity by saying that the stickers were 'spasticated' anyway. Obviously Alice had deemed it necessary to have a little chat about the true meaning of the word 'spastic', and how the condition was caused by a lack of oxygen at birth.

'Is that what happened to Sam?' queried Max, and Alice had sent him to his room to 'think' for twenty minutes.

After Max's 'think', the boys (Guy looking remarkably paunch-free in his Paul Smith trunks) had gone down to the pool while Alice tidied up and made a picnic lunch. She didn't mind, really she didn't. As she said, there was nothing to it. All she had to do was 'tidy the breakfast things, hardboil a few eggs, rinse some underwear, fill some rolls and make the beds'.

'Alice, you don't have to make the beds, the maid does that,' Guy had interjected. But Alice knows she will make the beds regardless. It's like when she's at home and the cleaner comes on a Thursday and Alice gets a guilt rash on her chest because Glynis is older than she is with a bandage around her left leg and a son who's on dialysis every other day.

Alice overpays Glynis and Glynis repays Alice, not with unswerving devotion as one might expect, but with lethargy and premeditated corner cutting. Glynis never wipes under the toilet seat, the backs of the radiators are thick with dust, and she never changes the hoover attachment so that she can get in the corners.

'Why don't you just sack the fat cow?' Guy enquires.

'She's got a gland problem,' replies Alice.

The maid here is called Rosa and she isn't very friendly. She arrived just after the boys had gone swimming and proceeded to bang about the apartment, ignoring Alice's conversational overtures and offers of coffee.

She'd just barged in without knocking. I mean, they could have been doing anything! For all she knew they could have been making love – they are on holiday after all.

173

We'll just have a nice easy day today, thinks Alice. We can go exploring tomorrow. And she makes her way down to the pool, only to find that her family aren't in it. Her heart tosses like a pancake, but the panic subsides when she spots them over by the bar. 'Come on, chaps,' she bellows.

Guy was about to order a lager. He feels guilty and caught out. '*Achtung*, boys,' he mutters, stuffing money back into his wallet.

'But I thought we were going to have an ice cream,' whines Sam.

Alice is laden with bags full of food and bottles of water. (Alice doesn't like the boys having fizzy drinks, holiday or not.) She has a beach towel tucked under each arm and a third around her neck. 'To the beach,' she hollers, sounding uncannily like Captain Mainwaring. To save themselves any further embarrassment, they follow her.

'Round the corner and down the steps,' she commands. She has read the blue folder on the coffee table from cover to cover; Alice knows what's what and where to go. The steps are wooden and very steep. 'Hold on to the rail, Sam,' she instructs.

Fall and break your neck, Sam, thinks Max.

'Mum, can I have a super sub-machine-water gun?'

'No, Max, you know how I feel about guns.'

Alice feels 'very strongly' about guns. She has never let either of her two sons play with them. She believes in a fertile imagination and educational toys – preferably made out of wood. Little does Alice know that Max's imagination is so fertile that he quite often points two fingers at his mother's head and pretends to be shooting at it.

'Not fucking fair,' seethes Max, dragging his feet.

His mother spoils bloody everything, dragging them away from the pool when they'd only just got there, issuing orders like they were on a boot camp, not a bloody holiday. Max likes swearing, he swears almost constantly in his head. Fucking Mum, fucking Sam, the fucking arsehole, look at him, what a gimp.

Alice has insisted that Sam should wear his fluorescent armbands at all times, whenever he is anywhere near water. Max is surprised she doesn't make him wear them in the bath.

'Why can't he just learn to swim?'

Sam is crap at all sports. He can't ride a bike, he can't rollerblade, he can't climb a tree – all he can do is sums.

Max had wanted to stay at the pool. You could dive in the deep end, and there was a buzz about it. But Alice doesn't like group activities, not with people one can't be sure of. Anyway, the pool is a manufactured thing, beautifully landscaped perhaps, and all very tastefully done with the little thatched bar tucked in the corner and the bougainvillea, but who needs a pool when you've got a lovely sandy beach on your doorstep?

A square plot of beach has been marked out for the palazzo's clientele. Smart blue canvas sunloungers are crouched under coconut-matting shades. Most of the loungers are full. Damn, thinks Alice. We should have come down earlier. Not that she approves of staking 7 am claims on deckchairs like the 'you-know-who', but really.

Alice, who is all for the cancellation of third world debt and a more equal distribution of wealth, actually hates sharing. What she wants is a bit of beach just to themselves, with an uninterrupted view of the sea and preferably out of earshot of other people's children. Children who have been allowed to bring battery-operated beeping games on to the beach. Really, the parents should be lined up and shot.

'Let's walk this way,' she commands. It's rather hard going, what with the sand in her shoes and the towels under her arms and round her neck. If only Guy would offer to help. The wicker holdall digs into her shoulder, bulging with dry shorts and T-shirts for the boys, suntan lotion, her book, of course, and the plastic bags containing the picnic.

Actually Alice has forgotten her book, but she has yet to realise this. It's on the bedside table in the apartment. Rosa has spitefully closed it. Her husband told her about the child-beating so-called mother staying in this apartment.

It takes half an hour for Alice to find a suitable bit of beach that doesn't belong to another hotel, that doesn't have dogs (Sam is scared of dogs), or snogging teenagers (disgusting), or topless middle-aged women (ridiculous), or gay men (fine – but not in front of the children).

This bit of beach is slightly grubbier than where they started out from. There is a brimming litter bin overflowing with rubbish and buzzing with wasps; the sunloungers have no padding and the canvas shades are stuck in ugly bits of breeze block. They have to search to find a shade that isn't too rusty to get up or, once up, isn't too badly torn. Eventually they find one. It's right next to the litter bin.

Alice is trying not to feel too disgruntled. After all, isn't this what she wanted, away from the crowds, a bit of privacy, just the family? She arranges the towels on the loungers while the boys run into the sea. She didn't bring one for herself. Oh well, she's not sure she wants to swim, she might just have a paddle. She's got her costume on under her skirt and T-shirt, but for the moment she'll just have a little sit-down. Alice digs in the holdall for her book. It isn't there. I could spit, she thinks – not that she ever would. It's what common people and footballers (who are paid well enough to know better) do.

Max is throwing seaweed in Sam's face. Guy dives under the water, catches Max by the ankles and flips him over. Max is laughing and choking, his lungs full of seawater. Guy always goes too far, he pushes everything, he doesn't know his own strength.

Alice stands up. 'Come on, let's stop being silly, it's lunchtime.'

Max is still spluttering, his eyes streaming, and as he runs over to Alice he grabs a towel and blows his nose on it, long and hard. Alice has to use every last drop of self-control not to smack the boy. 'How dare you!'

'What, what have I done now?'

'You are a disgusting, vile child.'

Max is genuinely taken aback. 'But—'

'But nothing. Sit down. If you ever do that again . . .'

Guy and Sam have joined them now. 'What did Max do, Mummy?'

Sam is revelling in the drama, shivering. Alice holds out a snot-free towel and wraps her youngest son up tightly, like a baby.

Max sits down, reaches for a stick and writes the words 'fuck off' in the sand, but wipes them out before his mother notices.

The picnic is not a huge success. Alice is just getting everything out when what looks like a smelly tramp comes along and demands twenty euros for the use of the loungers.

Guy pays up. 'I'm not having any more crap,' he tells Alice.

They eat in silence until an insistent wasp refuses to leave Sam alone. It sits on his ear and then his nose and then his lip. 'Just stay calm, Sam,' says Alice, but Sam can't and he runs screaming into the sea. He can't swim, thinks Alice, and he took his armbands off to eat his lunch. She runs after him, trips over and falls flat on her face in two inches of water. No one dares laugh.

Alice decides it's time to go back to the palazzo. She's got a heat rash and her skirt is filthy. She can't wait to retire into the cool of the apartment; after all, now is the hottest part of the day, mad dogs and Englishmen and all that. They march back in single file. The pool is quiet. Max wants to swim.

'No, Max, you can't go in the pool. It's not been an hour since lunchtime. Anyway, we're all going to have a lovely siesta.'

'Look, Mum, that lady and that man were on our coach.' Sam is pointing, which is rude. Alice, chief constable of the manners police, tells him not to. But he's right, they were on the coach, more's the pity. Coarse, that had been her first impression, and look at them now, lolling around, smoking. The man is as hairy as a bear. What's their name again? The Gaudis, that's it. She can't imagine that they have any connection with the Spanish architect; he looks like a plumber, and she, well, she looks like a tart. Max is taking off his T-shirt, threatening to dive in. 'Don't you dare, Maxwell Thomas Jamieson, don't even think about it.'

Jonty Gaudi opens one eye. A boy is flicking V signs at his mother's fat back. His new wife Gayle rolls over. She has been lying on her front with her bikini top undone so that she doesn't get strap marks. As she manoeuvres herself on to her back, her breasts sway free of the tiny yellow triangles. The boy who wanted to swim stops flicking V signs at his mother and his mouth drops open.

'Come on, gormless,' the fat woman yells over her shoulder.

Gayle has remoored her breasts and Jonty remembers being twelve and having his first wank over a poster of Wonderwoman. He laughs and the boy scurries away.

The siesta idea is, if anything, more stressful than the picnic. The boys fight in their room for an hour and a half while Alice soaks her muddy skirt and Guy decides to go for a walk. 'Why on earth are you taking your mobile, Guy?' asks Alice as he casually picks his Nokia up from the dining table.

'I thought I might try and ring the office,' he replies.

'Oh, Guy, you silly old goose,' Alice chuckles. 'It's Sunday. Not even Penny will be in the office on a Sunday.'

So Guy trails around the palazzo gardens phoneless and miserable. This is a fucking nightmare. He hardly managed to speak to her yesterday. What had she been up to last night? Probably another party. Peanut is a popular girl. Peanut gets invited everywhere. After all, you've got to have Peanuts at parties.

What did she wear, who was she with?

Just a week, he reminds himself. I'll be back in a week. I'll call her tonight.

She won't call him, she knows not to do that. So far he has been very careful about this affair. Peanut's number is filed under 'Keith' in his phone.

Guy trudges back to the apartment. Bloody Alice didn't buy any booze this morning. But she did buy a bag of pasta and a jar of Napolitano sauce.

'I thought we'd have supper in the apartment tonight, Guy.'

'But we haven't got anything to drink, Alice.'

'We've plenty of juice, Guy, you don't need to have a drink just because you're on holiday.' And Guy eats boiled pasta with red sauce accompanied by a nice glass of apple juice.

Much later, when the boys are asleep and Guy has nipped down to the bar for a quick one – 'If you must, Guy. I'll just stick to a nice cup of tea' – Alice flicks through the diaries she bought for her sons. Sam's is full of numbers: those of their flight, the times of departure and arrival, kilometres from the airport to the palazzo, and at the bottom of the page how many times Max has been mean to him. So far, at the end of their first day, it totals forty-eight.

Alice's heart withers slightly and, with a sense of trepidation, she opens Max's jotter. She shouldn't have. Max hasn't written anything. He's drawn a scrappy biro picture of the layout of the palazzo. At the bottom of the page, by the side of the pool, is a picture of a woman with no top on. I might have to have a word with Lydia, thinks Alice.

Meanwhile, Guy reads yesterday's *Daily Mail* by the pool. He bought it at the airport yesterday but hid it from Alice. There's a small article about Tommy entitled 'Follow the Priory Road'. The photo of him kicking the bouncer is reproduced alongside another of a contrite Tommy being delivered to the clinic the next day. In the main, the piece is sympathetic. Much is made of the death of Tommy's mother and how fame cannot cushion the rich and famous from everyday mortality. Tommy comes across not so much as a drunken yob but a tender-hearted lost soul who misses his old mum. I'll drink to that, thinks Guy, and he weaves over to the bar for another 'quick one' before he calls Peanut.

28

Old Scars

Nina is feeling better. It isn't him, she's more or less positive now. Just after breakfast, as she wheeled Freya back to the apartment, Rabbit had fallen on the floor and the man had picked it up.

'I think this is yours, young lady,' he'd said, passing the rabbit to Freya as casually as a security guard handing over a dropped purse in a supermarket.

'Thanks,' Nina had muttered, but there was nothing in his eyes, no recognition, no 'Hey, you're that slag I picked up three years ago.'

Lots of people look a bit like other people. Men especially, because they don't have the disguise options that women do. They don't dye their hair so often or colour in their faces. He is just a man, here on holiday with his family. Just because she was unfaithful doesn't mean that everyone is. Anyway, this man has a goatee – she would have remembered that, definitely.

So she can relax. It's been a good morning. Joe took Tabitha and Saul snorkelling on the beach, while she played by the pool with Freya and her rubber ring. 'Oh, Joe, you should have seen her, she loved it!'

Joe is relieved. Nina seems to be enjoying herself at last. She is brimming with gossip. Ever since they met up for lunch she has been acting out various pool-side scenarios.

Apparently, Dieter and Peter, the German homosexuals, had

spent an hour doing pilates in their Speedos, and every time Dieter bent over one of his testicles fell out of his trunks. Nina's teutonic gay accent is hilarious.

This is why Dad likes her, thinks Tabitha, when she does impressions and is mean but funny. Tabitha feels a bit guilty laughing. Nina isn't usually this amusing. Turns out she's had two cocktails.

'Actually, Joe, I think I might be a bit pissed.'

'Good,' responds Joe.

'It's that Gayle woman, she made me. I asked for a Diet Coke but she said I had to try this cocktail. God, she's mad.'

'Which one is she again?' asks Saul. 'Miss Yellow Bikini?'

'That's the one. Turns out she used to be a page-three model. She's on her honeymoon, love bites all over. He's like a wolf, you know, hairy, like Sean Connery.'

'James Bond would never wear trainers and socks with shorts,' interjects Tabitha, and for once Nina agrees with her.

'So, anyway, she's got these acrylic nails and she's trying to light a fag and the lighter catches one of the nails and it's burning up, the nail's all melting, so Jonty, that's her husband, chucks her in the pool. "I hate you, Jonty Gaudi," she's shrieking, and because the bikini's like yellow knitted string, it goes all see-through and baggy and you can see everything!' Nina is snorting. 'And Freya made friends. You know those posh twins that were on our coach? Guess what they're called!'

'Snot and Pooh,' hazards Saul.

'Hyurk,' responds Nina, laughing hysterically. Joe wonders if maybe she should have worn a sunhat.

'Get this – they're called Bertie and Lettice! They sound like a music-hall double act, and they look like two little pigs – spam babies.'

'Are they the ones with the horrible sister?' Saul has just connected the fat baby twins with the sneery girl who was mean to him yesterday.

'Her name's Sofia. I think she's a bit bored. Maybe you two should make friends with her?'

'I'm not making friends with that witch,' mutters Saul darkly. 'She thinks I'm fat.'

'Loaded, I reckon. The mother's called Helena Hart Jones, they live in Chelsea, just off the King's Road, he's an accountant, Charles I think his name is, just sits there in that Panama hat reading the *Financial Times*. Guess what? They're IVF.'

'What's that?'

'Test-tube babies.'

'No way, those two couldn't fit in a test tube.' Saul is genuinely perplexed.

Joe laughs. This is more like it. So far, so good. This morning has been a success. He was right – a holiday was a good idea. He allows himself a moment of smug contentment. They've found a bar that serves lunches just a short walk from the palazzo's beach, a jaunty yellow-and-white-painted shack on rickety stilts. The waiters have made a fuss of Freya, Nina is happy, the beer is ice-cold, the chips crisp, and his children are beautiful.

If only his parents could see the five of them together like this – Saul drawing cartoon pigs for Freya on a paper napkin while Tabitha feeds her ice-cubes – maybe they'd relax about 'the situation'. Even Hils copes better than they do, and she is the one who must share her children with another woman. 'For now', he can imagine his mother tutting, 'but one day she might meet a nice man and then we'll see how you like it.'

'Ow!' Joe burns his tongue on an extra-hot chip. 'Bloody hell!'

'Did you talk to the nutty boy's family?' asks Tabitha.

'The one with the mum that goes, "But I know I packed the Scrabble"?' Nina's impersonation is uncanny. 'No, but apparently Gayle was saying that last night, she and Jonty, that's her hairy husband, were having a nightcap and the dad was drinking by himself, like loads. In the end, he got up, staggered a bit, dropped his mobile and started punching himself in the head. So if the kid is a bit nutty, we know who he gets it from. Apparently they're called the Jamiesons. Lydia told Gayle that the mum is really uptight.'

'Who's Lydia?' Joe can't keep up with all this information. Nina hasn't been this animated for a long time.

'She's the rep, the one in the red Aertex shirt.'

'I saw her hiding behind a wall,' says Saul. 'When me, Dad and

Tabitha were going to the beach, she was all crouched down.'

'Maybe she'd lost an earring.'

'Maybe she's a spy.'

Saul is in his element. This is fantastic – there are wild boar and gay men, topless models and spies. He wouldn't be at all surprised if something very peculiar happened on this holiday.

Later, when Joe, Nina and Freya are having a siesta, Tabitha and Saul are allowed down to the pool – 'As long as you stick together, and I mean that. Saul, are you listening?'

'Cross my heart,' utters Saul.

'You don't go down to the beach or into town without telling us. I trust you not to do anything stupid.'

Saul wishes his father hadn't said that. As soon as a grown-up says stuff about 'not being stupid', it makes him want to run round with his eyelids turned inside out pretending to be a chicken. He resists the temptation and, pausing only to reload his water uzi, he and Tabitha make their way to the pool. It's almost deserted. The gay couple are asleep on sunloungers, their possessions heaped into two neat piles: leather-tasselled deck shoes, Armani T-shirts, Oakley sunglasses and magazines. Saul wonders if they have gay dreams of poodles and Elton John.

The three o'clock sun blisters in a duck-egg-blue sky and there is a sign requesting that parents make sure their children 'respect the siesta period between 2 and 4 pm'.

Tabitha arranges herself under a parasol. She's wearing something she has told Saul is a 'tankini'. It's a stripy vest-and-pants thing, really. As she lies down her tankini bottoms slip and he can see the slice of her appendix scar. The sight of it bothers him. It's not as red as it used to be, but it's still part of the horrible night.

The horrible night happened when he was only seven and Tabitha was ten – not that she was at home to witness the incident. She was in the hospital; she didn't see what he saw. He didn't tell her, either. Nobody knew. They'd thought he was asleep.

Saul tries to put the events of that night in order. It's a long time ago now, when everyone was collecting Pokemon cards. It probably started with Tabitha being sick, puking her guts up while Mum stood over her in the bathroom saying, 'It's all right, darling, it's probably something you ate. You'll feel better in the morning.'

But in the morning Tabitha wasn't better: her tummy still hurt and she was all sweaty. So she didn't go to school and Saul didn't think he should go either, because if it was something she'd eaten then he would probably be sick too. After all, they'd had the same tea: chicken Kievs with peas and new potatoes.

But Mum said, 'No, Saul, you're going and that's that.' So off he went with his dad, moaning all the way. 'Not fair.'

But after lunch there had been a message for him sent via the school office. You didn't get messages often. Once, Saul's friend Ricardo had got one saying his Spanish grandma had died, but that was ages ago.

They were doing Christopher Columbus and the secretary had come in with a yellow slip, which she handed to his class teacher Miss March. Silently Miss March read the note while the whole of Red class held its breath. When she looked up, her eyes swivelled round the room and he'd known in that instant that his name would be called. 'Saul, may I have a word?' And everyone stared and whispered as he walked over to Miss March. She'd had a 'word' in the corridor.

'I'm afraid your sister has had to go to hospital, Saul. She needs to have her appendix out, but everything's going to be OK, and you're going home with Angelica.'

'Can't I go home with Barney?' he'd asked. Angelica was a bit annoying because all she did was play with Polly Pocket and watch soppy videos, and anyway everyone would laugh if he went home with a girl.

In the end it hadn't been too bad at Angelica's because her mum was really nice and bought a Wall's Viennetta specially, and Angelica let him watch *Home Alone* in case Tabitha died. But she didn't die, because otherwise she wouldn't be here in Italy reading *The Amber Spyglass*. But he had been a bit worried, so it was nice when his mum and dad had turned up and taken him home and said she was going to be fine, but that he would have to be very good and not jump on her. So that night had been a bit bad, but it wasn't the very bad night. It was the next night that it all went really bad.

Saul concentrates. Mum had spent the day at the hospital, but Dad was working so he went to see Tabitha in the evening. Saul had given his father a card he'd made for his sister at Angelica's house, with all ponies on because that's what she liked at the time, and Mum was very tired with the worry of it all. So he'd been especially good, even though all there was to eat in the house was tinned ravioli, and had gone to bed when he was told.

'Because really, Saul, I'm at the end of my tether' – and she did look tired, his mum, all hunched with no lipstick. So he'd even cleaned his teeth without being told and burrowed under the duvet.

It was very dark when the noises had woken him up, and even though his alarm clock said it was only just gone nine o'clock, it felt more like midnight, which is when all bad things happen. Saul had looked through the curtains into the night-time street and seen his mother kicking the car. She was shouting and all spit was coming out of her mouth, and his dad was trying to get out of the car, but his mother kept hitting him, punching his shoulders. There was someone else in the car, sitting in the passenger seat, but he didn't know who it was because they were on the other side. His mother was yelling the same thing over and over again – 'I only came out to get Saul's lunchbox' – at the top of her voice.

For a moment he remembers thinking it might have been his fault because he'd left his lunchbox in the car after his mum had picked him up from Angelica's. He was going to go out and get it, but as soon as they'd got home, his dad had been waiting to drive off to see Tabitha in the hospital, and now there was all this shouting.

Saul couldn't understand what all the fuss was about. He was always leaving his lunchbox in daft places. It was a *Phantom Menace* one. He felt sick and that made him really scared in case he might have caught appendicitis, so he lay down under the covers and stayed very still so that the sick didn't come out, and he squeezed his eyes shut.

Saul shuts his eyes now, and over three years on he again hears the slamming of the front door and the Saab driving away. He remembers waiting for the car to come back, but it didn't. For some reason, even if he tries very hard, he cannot remember the next day. It's no good asking Tabitha what happened the morning after the shouting because she was still in the hospital. But the one thing he can work out from all this is that the last time his dad spent the night at home was the night Tabitha had her appendix out.

That's enough thinking, he reckons, and he turns, only to find that Tabitha has got hold of his water gun and is firing it straight into his face. Saul stands up and pushes her into the pool, following up this most excellent move with a perfectly executed knees-to-chest dive bomb on to her head.

As they surface, Saul notices two boys are standing by the edge of the pool. The bigger one is taking off his sandals, but all the time he is staring at them. The smaller one, with the bright red hair, is wearing armbands. Armbands! Like doh! thinks Saul, pausing for a second before shoving Tabitha's head underwater. He's glad she didn't die when she had her appendix out. It's good to have a sister to push under the water on holiday. Maybe he will pull her tankini bottoms down too?

29

Distress and Dysentry

Alice cannot for the life of her understand what is wrong with Guy. For some reason he's in a dreadful paddy about his mobile phone being broken and he keeps delving into his toilet bag for Nurofen.

'Maybe if I charge it up,' he twitters. 'Alice, where's the charger?'

'I didn't pack it,' sings back Alice gaily. She's just rinsed some of the boys' smalls out. They could really do with a clothes-line on the balcony. Oh well, she'll have to drape the undies over the wall.

She opens the sliding doors and ventures out on to the terrace. Beneath her feet the sandstone slabs are as hot as freshly baked biscuits.

'*Morgen!*' booms a voice to the left of her. Alice jumps. A very tall man in what looks like a pair of drawstring cheesecloth pyjamas is smoking a cigarette on next door's balcony. Alice coughs pointedly in the direction of the cigarette smoke. As she splutters, a second man steps out and kisses the very tall man between the shoulder blades. It's now the tall man's turn to cough. 'Ahem!' The shorter man turns and notices Alice. '*Guten Tag,*' he grins, white teeth shining under a blond moustache.

'Hello, hello, lovely day for it,' burbles Alice. The Germans smirk as if she means 'lovely day for some rimming in the open air'. With cheeks the colour and temperature of grilled tomatoes, Alice backs into the apartment and closes the door.

Gays are super, they really are, but when one has impressionable young sons – well, you can't be too careful. Obviously not all queers are paedophiles, but some of them must be, stands to reason.

She really will have to track down that Lydia girl.

In the meantime, there is a fabulous day of family fun to be had. Exploring Santa Helena is on Alice's agenda today. With any luck they will find a lovely architecturally interesting church where the boys can light a candle. Not that they are Catholic, but when in Rome and all that. Hopefully she can get them to say a prayer for someone less fortunate than themselves, someone who hasn't got a PlayStation for example.

This will be Alice's second trip into town today. She went out earlier to get fresh bread. '*Buon giorno*,' she sang cheerily as she walked into a delicious fug of hot dough.

'Yes, yes,' replied the rather slatternly-looking pregnant woman behind the counter. Now Alice is very anti all those daft new European Union health and hygiene laws – 'bureaucracy gone mad' – but this girl was smoking! Smoking in a bakery, and furthermore (this is one of Alice's favourite words) she was pregnant! Did the girl know what she was doing to her unborn child, not to say her own lungs and heart? Alice had felt rather sad. 'I mean,' as she said later to Guy, 'one's used to such sights on the sink estates of south London' – but here in lovely Italy, it was a crying shame.

She'd forgotten her phrase book so she'd had to point. 'Four' – Alice held four fingers up – 'ciabatta rolls, *s'il vous plaît*.' Alice has a smattering of schoolgirl French. It may not have been the pregnant slut's native tongue but at least she'd made an effort not to speak English, and surely, thinks Alice, that's what counts.

There had been a bit of a débâcle (another word Alice uses a great deal) over money. Alice didn't have any coins and the girl had been very sulky about changing a twenty-euro bill. In the end Alice had had to go to the newsagents and buy a biro; she'd refused to buy a newspaper, especially as they only seemed to stock the *Daily Mail*. She'd toyed with buying *La Stampa*, but decided that would be silly.

After the bakery she'd popped into the Spar. Sam had requested peanut butter. The woman at the checkout used to live in Catford. 'It's a small world, innit,' she informed Alice.

'Come on, everyone.'

Guy is slumped on the sofa with his head in his hands. 'I can't believe you didn't pack the charger.'

Alice is suddenly exasperated. This place is riddled with topless tarts and homosexuals and all Guy can think about is his ridiculous mobile phone. Well, he can bloody well light a candle for it.

She marshals her troops, and what a sorry squadron they are. Sam has been bitten in the night and he cannot stop scratching the six screaming-red lumps on his left leg. Max is wearing his vile Nirvana T-shirt yet again, and Guy, his backbone seemingly filleted, is having trouble getting off the sofa.

'Come on, boys,' hollers Alice, sallying forth with gay determination. As they exit the apartment she thinks she catches a glimpse of Lydia. 'Oh Lyyyydia!' But she seems to have disappeared behind some bushes.

The Jamiesons troop down the gravel drive and follow their leader out of the palazzo. 'Hup, two, three, four,' sings Alice, trying to inject a little *Jungle Book* jollity into the proceedings.

The town of Santa Helena del Castellabate lies literally minutes away. It centres variously around a small harbour and an elevated town square in front of a surprisingly grand church. The main shopping drag is pedestrianised, although hordes of Italian teenage boys on bicycles weave with needle-like precision through tutting throngs of old women.

'Let's get some postcards,' Alice trills.

'Who for?' asks Sam.

'For whom?' corrects his mother. 'Well, the Clementses, and, Guy, you should send one to Penny, and Aunty Judy of course.'

Alice doesn't include her mother on the postcard list. They barely communicate these days. 'After all I did for you, Alice.'

'What is the point in sending a postcard to Penny when I know for a fact she's in Weston with her mother?' snaps Guy.

'Because she always sends us one and it would be rude not to.'

Alice prides herself on having exemplary manners. At Christmas she writes an inventory in her Filofax, neatly filling in gift, sender and recipient as they open their presents. Ideally she would like the boys to spend Boxing Day writing their thank-you letters. Gratitude is something that was drummed into Alice from a very early age, for a roof over her head, for food and clothing. 'Let us pray, Alice, let us thank the Lord.'

Guy is hungover and exhausted. Alice strides on determinedly, as if she is doing a sponsored walk. Silently her menfolk trudge behind her. As soon as they reach the town square, Guy suggests stopping for a coffee.

'But it's not even eleven o'clock. We haven't seen anything yet.'

Max spots an amusement arcade in the corner. Italian boys his age are hanging over pinball machines, calling out to passing girls, girls with dark hair and bare legs.

I'd like to come down here by myself, he thinks. I'd like to come down at night, when all the lights are on, and look at girls in shorts.

'Let's just pop into the church and then think about coffee,' wheedles Alice.

Max has an erection. It feels wrong to be following his family into a church with a boner, but he can hardly explain to his mother why he doesn't want to go in. As they stroll through the creaking wooden door, Alice starts to whisper, 'Looks like a service is going on. How splendid. Just sit in one of the pews at the back.'

As soon as they sit down, an organ swells, a priest appears, and to Alice's horror she spies a small white coffin on a raised dais at the far end of the aisle.

A dreadful moaning rises above the music, incense fills the air and a young woman dressed in black darts like a distressed bat from her front-row seat and throws herself, wailing, over the casket.

'Get out,' hisses Guy, 'just get out now.'

Max no longer has an erection. Silently, the Jamiesons creep out of the church.

'What's happening?' demands Sam, barely out of the doors.

Guy is grim-faced. 'Your mother decided it would be a good idea to gatecrash a child's funeral.'

Alice, for once, is silent, at least for a few seconds. 'But I didn't know,' she protests.

'Just shut up, Alice.' Guy strides ahead. Once they are a good few hundred yards down the high street, he stops. 'I need a drink.'

'But—' starts Alice. Guy looks at her.

'Yes,' she agrees, and they sit at a table on the pavement and wait for someone to take their order. Alice feels dreadful. She is embarrassed, she didn't do it on purpose. Guy is being mean.

'Boys, why don't you go and have a look at those lilos over the road?' she suggests. Immediately her sons disappear into a forest of novelty inflatables. Guy takes off his Persols and shuts his eyes.

'I'm sorry, Guy. But it's not as if I don't know how she—'

'Don't you dare try to bring that up, Alice. You have no idea what that woman is going through. Don't even try. It's her grief, not yours. You have no right, do you understand?'

Alice bites her lip. Guy's hands shake as he orders two Cokes, a coffee and a lager.

Lager before lunch! She chews her lip harder, surprised not to taste blood. Guy can sometimes be very cruel.

The boys come back full of orders for lilos in the shape of crocodiles and Superman, flippers and snorkels. Max also wants a harpoon.

'We'll pop back later,' says Alice. 'You don't want to be carrying stuff around all morning.' Alice is very cunning: the shops will be shut later. Guy pays for the drinks. He leaves a ludicrously large tip. Why does he do everything he can to spite me? thinks Alice, surreptitiously palming a few coins back.

After postcards have been bought and Alice has dithered over some pottery – 'I'm sure Di would like a lovely olive dish' – and the boys have got bored and hot, they walk back along the harbour. 'Look, boys, boats,' points Alice, as if they are toddlers.

Old men are fishing from the end of a jetty. Worms writhe in discoloured plastic boxes, while boys as young as Sam are diving off the harbour wall. One seems to be wearing his underpants. As they emerge from the sea with their black hair sleeked down, they look like seals.

My mum would never let me do that, thinks Max, she never lets me do anything. It's all he can do not to just run and jump.

Alice spies the rather smart family who are staying at the palazzo, the ones with the unfortunate-looking twins and the sulky-looking adolescent girl. They are sitting outside a restaurant under large cream-coloured canvas shades. The heavy white-clothed table is laid with finger bowls, and the dark green neck of a wine bottle pokes out of an ice bucket.

They seem to have dressed up for lunch. Their clothes are as crisp and laundered as the napkins. They look as though this is what they do when they come to Italy: they eat shellfish with cold white wine at lunchtime.

Alice feels hot and sticky. 'Coooee,' she chirrups.

The woman barely smiles. She lifts a hand half-heartedly, as if deciding to wave, but picks up a menu instead.

Guy looks at his watch. 'Lunch?'

'Not here,' replies Alice stridently. 'It says in the brochure that a lot of the harbourside restaurants are ludicrously overpriced tourist traps. I'm sure we'll find something a good deal more authentic just round the corner.'

Just round the corner a dog is feeding on a large and bloody bone and the air is thick with flies; men are carrying carcasses into the back of a butcher's. 'Oh Lord,' breathes Alice, 'so much death,' and she trots quickly down an adjacent back alley.

Forty minutes later, she finally finds something suitably authentic that doesn't offer pizza.

'Pizza is authentic,' argues Guy.

'You know what I mean,' retorts Alice.

Max couldn't see what was wrong with the bar they passed half an hour ago. Yellow Bikini was in there with her husband, Gorilla Man. They were eating cheese toasties and watching football on a big plasma screen. 'Hi boys!' She'd waved. She was wearing a lilac top, all lacy, and underneath it was a big black bra.

Alice had marched on. 'That woman is as common as muck.' A lot of people are as 'common as muck' according to Alice. Zack Fulton's mum is because she smokes on the street and dyes her hair. Mrs Gibb is because she has home-made tattoos and puts her baby's dummy in her own mouth to clean it. As for the people who live on the estate at the end of their road, not only are they as 'common as muck', they are also 'low-life'. Max sighs.

The restaurant Alice has chosen is so far off the beaten track as to be resolutely empty. In addition to having no customers, it has no air-conditioning, no chicken, no burgers, no salads, no omelettes – just fish.

'I don't like fish,' says Sam.

'Yes you do,' his mother tells him.

Alice orders mussels. Guy orders tuna steak and advises the boys to do the same. 'It comes with chips,' he urges them under his breath.

Lunch is served by a boy who is blind in one eye. Just like the Alsatian in the offy at home, recalls Guy, trying to avert his gaze. It's no good. He's lost his appetite; everything he puts in his mouth tastes of diseased eyeball.

Max and Sam pick at their chips. Alice drinks hungrily at her bowl of mussels, dabbing at the juices with a thick slice of stale bread. Some of the pesky shells are a bit tricky to prise open. 'Hmm, delicious,' she pronounces, licking her fingers, 'a real taste of the sea. You lads don't know what you're missing.'

Guy pays up. This time he doesn't leave a tip. 'It was filthy, Alice,' he mutters tersely, 'let's go.'

Halfway back to the palazzo, Alice's stomach contracts. Maybe I'm ovulating, she speculates. She isn't – she is in the first stage of food poisoning. By the time they reach the gates of the Gardenia, she is trotting.

If they'd been staying in the old building she might have made it, but before they reach the annexe Alice is sick three times behind three different trees. 'Quick, quick,' she moans as Guy fiddles to get the key into number 2. As soon as he opens the door Alice bolts for the bathroom. The noise that emanates from the lavatory is disturbing enough, but it's the smell that really has the rest of the Jamiesons reeling.

'I think I've got a bit of a gippy tummy,' bleats Alice from behind the locked door.

For the rest of the afternoon Alice reads Hils's book while sitting on the lavatory. There's no point getting up. At least while she sits on the toilet she can reach the sink if she needs to be sick.

Guy decides to take the boys down to the pool; it really isn't very pleasant for them to hang around in the apartment. The

Jamieson boys set up camp by the shallow end. Guy knows he must keep an eye on his youngest son. He has forgotten the sun cream. If Sam's shoulders go pink, Alice will be cross, but if he drowns she will be livid. Fortunately there is a set of armbands in one of the rolled-up towels that Guy grabbed as they vacated the stinking apartment. Armbands at his age! Hopefully anyone watching will jump to the conclusion that Sam is a very tall five-year-old and not just a soppy almost ten-year-old coward.

He allows himself to relax. It's easy with Alice out of the picture. This is what holidays in the future will be like, the only difference being that Peanut will be joining them. She will stretch out on a sunlounger like a little cat, her pierced belly button glinting in the sun.

Max is talking to the plump kid who had stopped the coach for a piss. He is showing Max his water gun, a massive lime-green plastic monstrosity. Max makes friends easily; if only Sam wasn't so . . . well, fucking weird, really.

The plump boy's older sister is asking Sam his name, but he turns on his heel and crouches in the bushes, lizard-watching. The girl shrugs and swims away. Give her a couple of years, thinks Guy, and she'll be jail-bait. He feels instantly embarrassed, as if he is wearing a filthy rain mac over his trunks. I need to cool off, he decides.

30

Aunty calls Hils

By late Monday afternoon Hils has painted the downstairs bathroom. It's a rather dubious pink. The label on the tin says 'petunia', but Hils can't help thinking it's more 'perineum'.

Oh well. Just as she is running the paint brushes under the cold water tap, a PR girl from the publishing company calls and informs her breathlessly that she's been 'booked on to Thursday's *Woman's Hour*, and isn't that marvellous?'

Hils gibbers at the prospect. 'You mean *Woman's Hour* as in Radio Four, as in Jenni Murray?'

The PR girl is in a hurry. 'Sorry, Hils. I've got A.S. Byatt on the other line.'

What on earth should I wear? thinks Hils, absentmindedly wiping the brushes on her jeans and automatically dialling Sally's number.

Esme answers sounding like a very efficient secretary. 'Hello, the Thorpe residence.' She is seven going on twenty-seven, the antidote to her mother's scattiness and her father's academic vagueness.

'Hello, darling, it's Hils. Is your mum around?'

Esme shouts for her mother and in the background Hils can hear the familiar clatter of heels on the stairs. Sally grasps the phone. 'Hello, my novelist chum, are you pining dreadfully?'

'Actually, I've completely forgotten about, er, whatever their names are,' lies Hils. 'I've got more important things to worry about!'

'Like?'

'I've got a date on Thursday.'

Sally guesses wildly: 'Orlando Bloom, Shane Ritchie, the bloke from the kebab shop?'

'Jenni Murray, actually. They want me on *Woman's Hour*.'

Sally whistles, as suitably impressed as a best friend should be.

'Thing is, I don't know what to wear.'

'Hils, it's radio!'

'I know, but . . .' Hils trails off hopelessly.

'Tell you what, come over for supper on Wednesday. You can raid my wardrobe and see our Venice photos. Say, seven-ish? Make it an early one and you can have a sniff of Esme, get your maternal juices running.'

Hils doesn't really need to reboot her maternal juices. She spent yesterday with her brother and his family over in East Dulwich. After a few hours with Lulu and Caspar she was almost grateful to get home. Her niece and nephew had been at their most demanding: a mini dictator double act with matching pudding-bowl haircuts. Hils had ended up spending a great deal of the afternoon sitting under the kitchen table playing tea parties with Lulu and a variety of stuffed toys.

Her three-year-old niece had been a formidable host, insisting that Hils should eat vast quantities of grubby raw pastry, while Caspar stamped around dressed as a fireman. Obviously, it had all ended in tears, and only when the children had screamed themselves to sleep did Hils manage to have a proper conversation with James and Midge.

'I'd forgotten what it was like,' she'd admitted, collapsing into a deckchair in the garden.

'Boring, you mean,' Midge had responded, passing Hils a large glass of something a lot more palatable than Lulu's jam water drink.

'Not boring, just relentless.'

Midge sat on James's knee, and suddenly Hils was overwhelmed by a terrible feeling of something she could only describe as homesickness. How long was it since she had been so at ease with a man?

They were a unit, Midge and James, sitting there together on the step. You couldn't really tell where James ended and Midge began. They were an amorphous mass of white T-shirts and denim, gardening-brown forearms entwined. Had she and Joe ever really been like that? Feeling gooseberry-ish, she'd made her excuses and left.

Twenty-four hours later and splattered in emulsion, Hils is suddenly struck by the memory of James's pre-Midge girlfriend. A ghastly ice-maiden of a blonde with an allergy to anything that wasn't real gold. Her brother had been smitten, buying the woman earrings that cost more than he could afford so that her ears didn't turn green.

Eventually there had been an engagement, the ice-maiden sporting her third-finger-left-hand sapphire with undisguised triumph, the rest of the family congratulating the couple through gritted teeth. Two months before the Big Day, the wedding was called off. James, due to the ice-maiden's fear of love handles, had been jogging through Dulwich Park and seen a girl falling off her bike into a large patch of mud.

'Lord Christ and Shitty McShit,' the girl had sobbed, laughing, crying and swearing all at the same time.

Later, James said it was like being hit by a thunderbolt in the neck, the sudden realisation that his fiancée was incapable of such emotion. How the nearest she ever got to showing her feelings was when she adopted a strange baby voice when she saw somfink in a shop window that she weally weally liked.

James had helped the girl up, and by the time he'd put the chain back on her bike, he'd fallen in love with Midge, a small, plump, freckle-faced brunette, and the ice-maiden was history.

Maybe that's what I should do, thinks Hils. Take Tabitha's bike out to the park and deliberately fall off it. I need a man, I miss my children, and I have a horrible feeling my mother might be getting more nookie than I am.

This unexpected and uninvited thought has Hils reeling. No!

Her mother and Basil? Surely not. Do pensioners really get off with each other? Just what exactly are the sleeping arrangements in that caravan? Should she be advising her mother on the use of condoms? Who knows where that Basil had been! Hils's head fills with images of a Terry Thomas lookalike seducing and discarding the ladies of the bridge club with a twirl of his cravat. If he does anything to hurt her, I will kill him, she swears.

When I first met Joe, he had a girlfriend and I had a boyfriend. Mark worked 'in computers'. He was nice enough but he had an odd smell, and his penis was rather sweaty from being tucked into leather trousers. I found sucking him off rather unpleasant. He tasted as if his genitals had been in a Tupperware box.

Joe was going out with a woman called Gloria. I said she sounded like an old woman. Joe showed me a Polaroid of Gloria: she was a beautiful black girl, topless, in white stockings and suspenders. She had an afro and silver false eyelashes and she looked like the kind of woman who could put a condom on with her tongue. Just the sight of her made me feel as dull as All-Bran.

Fortunately Gloria was a backing singer and she went off to America with the singer Joe Jackson and never came back. All she left behind was a lilac-coloured Persian cat. Persephone lived with Joe in his Camberwell council flat. She would only eat chopped-up freshly cooked chicken fillet and gave Joe a look as if to say, 'What's she doing here?' every time I went round.

Diary of a Divorcee

Some people just go together, thinks Hils, sitting by the window and watching an early evening Stoke Newington go by. Like Sally and Nick. Without Nick, Sally would be too loud. Nick supplies the lid to the pressure cooker of her personality. He stops her from spilling over and making too much mess. Without Nick, Sally would boil herself dry. Yet without Sally, Nick would retreat into a world of naval history, quietly turning battleship-grey in the process.

Her brother James needs Midge to make him laugh and forget about work, and Midge needs James to make sure there is oil and petrol in the car.

Her mother needed her father to waltz her round the kitchen singing 'Blue Spanish Eyes' off-key into her ear, to check the guttering for debris, and to bleed the radiators. Her father needed her mother to measure his arms for the jumper she was knitting him, to remind him when *Inspector Morse* was on, and turn the bedside light off last thing at night. Suddenly she senses her father, smelling of bonfire, coming in from the cold, her mother picking leaves off his navy-blue crew-neck jumper, catching his hands and warming them up with her own.

What do I miss most about being part of a couple? wonders Hils, watching a short, fat girl trot to keep up with her very tall boyfriend. I miss someone to finish off the bottle of wine before I do, having someone to talk about the kids with, to change light bulbs without having to get the ladder out, and to check if that noise really is a burglar. But what I miss most is having somebody next to me in bed when I am lonely.

When the kids are here, I don't notice it, but when they're not, I'm too aware of my own heartbeat. The short girl and the tall boy have stopped to kiss. She stretches, he bends. Hils watches, feeling fifteen again, when it seemed like everyone else in the world had a boyfriend but her, sitting on sofas at parties watching other people snogging. A quarter of a century on, it feels like nothing has changed.

'All right, Hils, stop it, go and get yourself something to eat and stop feeling so sorry for yourself, you drippy cow.' Oh Jesus, now I've started talking to myself – and she tells herself off all the way to the kitchen.

31

Picking Scabs and Salad Spoons

Joe sleeps, lying naked on the bed. He looks like a donkey that has been knocked out by an electric fence. He is a big man with big feet and a big penis that twitches as he dreams.

Nina watches him resentfully. Freya is teething. How come he never hears his daughter when she whimpers in the night? How come it's always her who must rock and soothe and smear gel on Freya's ravaged purple gums? When they get back to London she's going to insist he gets his ears syringed, the deaf old cunt!

Nina, her arms numb under Freya's weight, comes to the conclusion that holidays with babies are tiring and men are fucking useless. Unfortunately, her conscience won't let her get away with this sweeping generalisation. You're a nasty conniving bitch, she admonishes herself, and at once she is swamped by that familiar three o'clock in the morning sense of dread. The feeling creeps over her, of fear, guilt and sickness. The constant nag at the back of her mind. Stop it – you've already decided it's not him.

No, Nina, it might not be him, but it was *someone*. Remember that night? Remember what you did? How dare you criticise Joe! People in glass houses . . .

Just stop it, she begs her brain. Just let it go.

But it won't go away. There is something in Nina's head, like a scab that she cannot resist picking. What have I done, what have I done?

Deep down she knows what she has done, and the worst thing in the world is that she can't tell anyone. This 'thing' will kill me, she decides, laying the inert Freya back in her cot and getting into bed next to Joe. Joe is turning golden. Only his bottom is white – white and hairy. 'I do love you, Joe. I promise I will try my best.'

In the morning she has forgotten her promise. Her eyes are drylidded and scratchy from lack of sleep.

'What's wrong with you?' demands Joe, attempting to tickle her.

'Just fuck off,' she snaps. 'I'm so tired I could cry.'

'Well go back to bed then,' insists Joe. 'I don't want you crashing around in a filthy mood all day.'

Nina does as she is told. She should be grateful, she should stretch out on cool white sheets and sleep, but she feels like a naughty child who's been sent to bed early on a summer's day. Beyond the bedroom everyone else is playing in the sunshine.

I can't afford to keep getting this wrong, she decides. I'm not going to waste this holiday. And she gets up, hauling herself from the bed, making sure she has a bright smile plastered all over her face. 'What day is it, Joe?'

'Tuesday.'

Tuesday, according to the blue information file, is market day in Santa Helena. Joe looks up from the file, his chin full of salt and pepper stubble. 'Why don't you take Tabitha? Saul and I will look after Ms Plop Plop.'

Saul laughs heartily. 'Ms Plop Plop – good one, Dad.'

Nina and Tabitha eye each other warily. They don't normally spend much time together without Joe. Both of them feel slightly shy. Joe notices their hesitance. 'Just go, before I change my mind.'

'Buy me a present,' demands Saul, casually picking his toenails on the sofa.

'You can come too if you want,' offers Tabitha, slightly too eagerly.

Saul is a natural mood lightener. If Saul is around there is never an awkward silence.

There is an awkward silence. Saul breaks it by farting cheerily. 'Nah, I'll give it a miss.' In Saul's experience, markets abroad usually consist of lace tablecloths and not much else.

Tabitha and Nina set off for town. They're not the only ones:

201

down the drive a mini pilgrimage seems to be taking place from the palazzo.

A few yards ahead of Nina and Tabitha are Yellow Bikini and Gorilla Man, aka Gayle and Jonty Gaudi, and behind them are the posh family, the ones with the moody-looking daughter and the twin pigs. 'The Hart Joneses,' whispers Nina.

Gayle has to keep stopping to remove gravel from her slingbacks. A crimson thong is clearly visible above her shorts every time she bends down. Nina and Tabitha soon catch up.

'Hello, girls,' chirrups Mrs Gaudi. 'Where's that little baby?'

'Her dad's got her for the morning.'

Nina's not sure she really wants to get too friendly with Gayle. She's a laugh and all that, but you wouldn't want to get stuck in a lift with her. She's like a one-woman Ann Summers party.

'Listen, love, your old man, is he a photographer? Only it's been bugging me.'

'Yes, he is.'

Tabitha shoots Nina a look. She and Joe aren't married; has Nina been telling people that they are?

'I thought so. What did I say, Jonty? I done a job wiv him, couple of months back, Asda knickers. Does he do a lot of glamour?'

'Er, no, not really, mostly food.' Nina feels a little sick. Joe has seen this woman in her undies. Gayle obviously couldn't care less.

'I thought as much. He's, what you call it . . . a gent. Some of them can be right cunts, 'scuse my French.'

Tabitha is blushing, a habit she can't wait to grow out of.

'You must be Tabitha. I love that name, and how old are you, darlin'?'

'Thirteen,' mumbles Tabitha, feeling about nine.

'Ooh, teenager, eh, you'll have to keep an eye on her, Nina, she'll be off snogging the locals!' Gayle laughs like a parrot stuck in a spin-drier.

Tabitha is now plum-coloured.

'You're embarrassin' the kid,' notes Jonty, fiddling with a gold ring on his pinkie finger. Black hairs curl like a small ruff around the neck of his T-shirt.

'Oh fuck off, Jonty, you miserable lump. You're not embarrassed, are you, darling?'

'Only a bit,' admits Tabitha, noticing that Jonty is a good three inches shorter than Gayle.

The four of them exit the palazzo together. Tabitha is mortified yet fascinated at the same time. These people are dead common. Jonty picks at his ear with a credit card and proceeds to sniff the waxy deposit.

'Ooh, you pig, Jonty Gaudi.'

Jonty attempts to wipe the credit card on Gayle's denim derrière and she screams as if he is trying to strangle her on the street.

Fortunately, the Gaudis have to find a cash machine before they hit the market and Tabitha and Nina make their getaway. 'See you later.'

'They're quite loud, aren't they?' Tabitha suggests, as a truck containing a thousand watermelons trundles by, its tyres leaving zig-zag patterns in the melting tarmac.

And you're so middle class that it hurts, thinks Nina, but she just grins her best stepmum grin. The Gaudis come from the same place as me, she realises. I'm working class too. Where I grew up, kids sniffed glue and bunked off school to have sex. Tabitha is so clean, so nice, so unspoilt.

The girls at Nina's old school would have made mincemeat out of her. Tabitha would have had her head shoved down the toilet on a daily basis. That's because when you were her age, everyone you knew was a shoplifting slut. You've had to fight to get where you are, and you don't want to go back there, she reminds herself. So watch it.

The market stalls are set up in the town square in front of the church, a patchwork of multicoloured awnings, an open-air Aladdin's cave of plastic toys, tablecloths and cheap watches.

'Oh goodie,' says Tabitha.

She's pure fucking Enid Blyton, marvels Nina.

Actually Tabitha is forcing an unnatural jollity, which is affecting her speech pattern. Oh goodie? Jesus, I sound like I've spent my entire life at pony camp.

Fact is, Tabitha feels guilty just being with Nina: the very act is treachery to her mother. Hils would be in her element here. Tabitha can visualise her in her holiday straw hat, her beaky nose burnt scarlet, poking around the leather goods.

Suddenly Tabitha is aware of a shooting pain in her right buttock. 'Someone just pinched my arse!' she informs Nina.

Nina laughs, only slightly miffed that her arse has remained unpinched. I must smell of milk and motherhood, they must know, she reasons.

A good-looking boy of about fifteen is standing a couple of feet away, laughing. 'Bloody hell, he looks like Enrique Iglesias,' Nina says.

'And therefore he must be a twat,' replies her stepdaughter, striding on to the next stall. The boy follows her with his eyes.

I can't be invisible yet, seethes Nina, putting a little extra sauce into her walk. 'Bella, bella,' says a filthy old man sitting on the kerb. He has snot down his lapel and black toenails. Oh great, sulks Nina, I'm big with tramps.

Tabitha spends all her money on Hils. She buys sticks of incense, a clear perspex bangle, a jade seahorse dangling from a silver chain and a rope of dried red chillies. She only has a few euros left. Dithering over a basket of coloured glass rings, she is suddenly aware that the 'sulky witch', as Saul calls her, is standing opposite.

Tabitha hides behind her hair. The girl is called Sofia, Nina told them. Sofia reaches into the basket of rings, picks up three, puts two back and edges away.

Blimey, breathes Tabitha, she's nicked a ring! Stunned, she stays rooted to the spot. What should she do? Before she can decide she feels a hot, salami-flavoured breath in her ear: 'You like ring?' It's Enrique Iglesias.

'Um, yes, they're really pretty.'

The boy speaks swiftly in Italian to the girl in charge of the stall. 'She my cousin, you have ring two euros.'

They're meant to be five. Tabitha hands over the requisite coins. She chooses an orange one with a big purple splodge in the middle.

'Thank you,' she says to the boy. He smiles. One of his front teeth is badly chipped and his eyes are the colour of unwashed denim. All of a sudden, all Tabitha can feel is her brace in her mouth, as big as a radiator. I need to go before I dribble, she decides, sweat prickling her armpits. 'Nina!'

Nina has bought some wooden salad spoons. I'm getting old, she sighs. By the time she and Tabitha get back to the palazzo, she has persuaded herself that she bought them for her mother. Maxine will never use them; she will take them to a car-boot sale and swap them for something shiny.

Joe, Saul and Freya are waiting to go down to the beach bar. Freya has a new tooth: a sliver of enamel has finally wormed its way through the gum and she is all smiles. She is Daddy's girl today, clinging to Joe's knees, demanding to be carried. Nina feels she has to work to ingratiate herself back into Freya's affections. Children are so fickle. Just because she left her daughter for a couple of hours, she is being punished.

Down at the shack, waiting for their lunch order, Freya refuses to sit on Nina's knee. Instead, she clambers on to Joe. Nina feels panicky. What if it all goes wrong? Freya can't rely on Joe for ever. I never had a dad – I coped, she thinks. Freya would too. 'Come to Mummy.'

'Dadda,' smirks Freya. 'I love my Dadda.'

For the first time ever, Nina smacks Freya, and everyone looks at her, appalled. Apart from Freya, who turns her head away and refuses to look at her mother until bedtime.

'Don't you ever, *ever* do that again, do you understand?' hisses Joe, his whole body taut with disgust.

I am a bad person, thinks Nina. She refuses to cry, but for the rest of the day it feels like someone has ground a packet of salt and vinegar crisps into her eyeballs. I don't deserve to have what I've got, I cheated to get it and I will be punished. One day Joe will find out. One day Freya might need a kidney and Joe will find out that she isn't his.

The kidney scenario is something that rotates around her mind with horrific regularity. It combines two of her worst fears: Freya being ill and being found out. I am so tired of feeling like this, she admits. Every day I feel as if I'm bracing myself for the moment my world spins off its axis and crashes into a ball of flames. Remorse, she realises, chews like a rat at her heart.

32

'Dancing Amoeba'

Alice would love to go to the market. The mind is willing but unfortunately the bowels are still weak. 'You boys go,' she instructs feebly from the sofa.

'Alice,' replies Guy firmly, 'neither Max, Sam nor myself are in the least bit inclined to traipse around some godforsaken market, wasting good money on cheap tat.'

'But markets are so colourful and vibrant, it'll be full of fascinating local characters buying aubergines, artichokes and olives. I was hoping you could find me a really nice hunk of Parmesan cheese.'

'Alice, my office is in Soho. What do they have in Soho apart from fetish shops and more dildos than you can shake a stick at? Delicatessens! Soho is the capital of sun-bleeding-dried tomatoes, so for God's sake just let it go.'

She can't, it's not in her nature.

'But it's Tuesday, everyone will be going to the market.'

'More reason to hog the pool then. Come on, lads.'

Guy is a big fan of the pool – the bar is open from 11 am. 'Drinking stops you thinking' is his new motto. Not being able to talk to Peanut is driving him insane. Her number is safely stored in his comatose Nokia. All he can remember are the first three digits: 077.

Alice hasn't the strength to argue. It's all she can do to drag herself to the loo every five minutes. Last night, she'd slept on the bathroom floor, curled up between the toilet and the sink. 'I think my stools are a little less watery today,' she ventures.

'More information than necessary, thanks,' responds Guy, swallowing hard and stuffing towels into the beach bag. If I can just sneak off to a public phone, I could get her work number through directory enquiries . . .

Ten minutes later Alice is alone in the apartment. Neither of her sons has taken a sunhat. Gingerly she makes her way over to the dining table. Her rectum, if she's honest, feels like a white hot poker has been inserted into it several times with great force. This is what those gay men next door must feel like most of the time!

Anal sex has never appealed to Alice, who can hardly bear to have her nipples pinched. Bosoms are supposed to be sexual organs, she supposes, but really, since the children she can't see what all the fuss is about. Breasts are for feeding babies. They are bags of fat and tissue, coursing with blue veins; nipples are designed for the toothless mouths of babes, not for being slobbered over by grown men.

The media's obsession with sex makes Alice both bored and angry and she despises men who are suckered into the whole nonsense. Early on in their marriage Guy was forever forcing her head between his legs, but Alice, who has managed to acquire a taste for most things, and will happily chew on a pork pie that's three days past its sell-by date, could never swallow semen.

The postcards bought yesterday lie scattered on the table. Max has scribbled one to his friend Zack Fulton. His handwriting is appalling and he's forgotten to leave space for the address. In large loopy letters he has scribbled: 'Italy hot, pool mega, no telly, can you tape Simpsons for me' – no question mark.

I might have to get a tutor, despairs Alice, turning with dwindling optimism to Sam's effort. 'Dear Aunty Judy, We are in Italy, the flight took 2 and a half hours, the temperature is 35 degrees and the pool is three metres in the deep end. PS Mum has diarrhoea.'

Yes I have, thinks Alice, clenching her buttocks as she makes her twenty-seventh trip to the lavatory. There is one sheet of toilet paper left. If the worst comes to the worst I shall just have to use one of Guy's hankies, she decides.

Alice staggers back to bed. With any luck she might manage a crust of dry bread later – not that there's any in the apartment.

Guy couldn't be bothered to pop to the Spar this morning, despite the fact Alice had taken the trouble to write a list. Instead, the boys had sampled the breakfast buffet. Apparently the orange juice was freshly squeezed and Sam had eaten 'cake and meat'.

It's not fair, she seethes. You'd think someone would want to stay behind and look after me.

She tries to read but she keeps getting spots in front of her eyes. Oh great, she despairs, this is what it's going to be like when I'm eighty, blind and incontinent.

It's about three when Guy bothers to waltz back through the door. Alice has been alone for four hours. 'I managed a little boiled water,' she rasps.

'Really? We had hot dogs,' Guy retorts, rolling casually into the bedroom, reeking of lager. 'And crisps,' he adds. He peels off his trunks and throws them on the floor. His tan is the colour of crispy bacon.

'Where are the boys?' Alice is feeling very frail. The cramping is easing up, but just when she thinks she might have beaten what-ever amoeba is tangoing with her small intestine, she must ride another wave of nausea and her colon buckles. She doubles up.

'The boys?' says Guy vaguely, oblivious to the fact that Alice is clutching herself and moaning. 'Oh, they went into town with those other kids.'

Alice rears up from the bed. 'What?'

Guy repeats himself, as if Alice must be very old and very stupid.

Alice is incensed. 'You mean you let our sons go into town with complete strangers? Jesus, Guy!' Her husband is naked.

'Oh relax, Alice. There are four of them. The girl's thirteen, Max is twelve, he's not stupid, and it's about time you stopped treating Sam as an emotionally retarded four-year-old.' Guy walks into the bathroom for a shower. 'Jesus it stinks in here.' He backs out holding his nose.

'Right, that's it, I'm going to find them.' Alice is dressed in a big T-shirt and a pair of knickers circa 1994. She pulls on her 'It Ain't Half Hot Mum' shorts and almost makes it to the door. Unfortunately she is still a hostage to her rear end, and at the last minute she has to change direction and dart into the bathroom. By the time she has pulled down her shorts and pants, brown liquid is spraying out of her backside. A little bit misses the pan.

'I will never forgive him for this, I can't forgive him full stop.' And Alice weeps furiously, fat wet tears landing on her big bare knees.

Guy is wrong when he says that both Max and Sam have gone into town. Unbeknown to either parent, Sam had a strop halfway down the gravel drive, and like a small ginger mule he turned on his Adidas rubber hoof.

'D'you think we should make sure he goes back to your dad?' asks Tabitha, watching the flame-haired boy retreating back into the courtyard.

'No, just leave him, he does this all the time,' spits Max. He's had enough of Sam. Sam spoils everything. Well, he's not spoiling this. Max desperately wants to go into town. His dad gave him some euros and made him solemnly promise to be back by four. 'Let's go.'

Sam stops by the fountain in the middle of the courtyard and runs his hands under the cold water that spits from the fish's mouth. He wipes his wet fingers across his forehead. Max is a bastard and as soon as Sam gets a chemistry set he's going to poison him. He knows he should go back to his father. Guy is having a cold beer and talking to Tabitha and Saul's dad.

'Stick together,' both dads had said. Well, it's not his fault that Max made him break a promise. It's quite nice sitting here. If he goes back to the pool his dad will make him practise swimming with just one armband and he doesn't want to do that. Mum wouldn't make him do the one-armband swimming. He'd go back to the apartment and do some really hard sums but it smells of poo, even with all the windows open, so he's not going to do that either. Sam isn't quite sure what he's going to do.

A woman walks out from one of the big laundry rooms. She is carrying a bucket and a mop on a long handle. Sam knows the woman is called Rosa because she cleans their apartment.

'*Giorno*,' she says as she passes.

'Hello,' replies Sam.

Rosa feels sorry for Sam. He is the little boy with the violent mother, and look at him now, all by himself, sitting by the fountain. 'All alone, little boy?' Rosa is not a stupid woman. Sometimes it suits her to pretend she speaks no English when, in fact, a long time ago, she spent three years working in an Italian restaurant in St John's Wood and is as fluent as she chooses to be.

'My brother has been mean to me.'

Rosa has five children. They fall out every day but deep down they love each other; they have to, they are family, it's a blood thing.

'I've got nothing to do,' continues Sam. 'Everyone is horrible.'

Rosa's maternal heartstrings twang. 'You come with Rosa, you help me clean a special secret place where no one else allowed – just me and you.'

The idea appeals to Sam – not the cleaning angle, but the bit about the special secret place. He follows Rosa; she gives him the long-handled mop and he feels important. He'd quite like to skip, but then he remembers skipping is what girls do.

Behind the antique cart at the foot of the stairwell is a narrow silver door. Rosa presses a button and the door opens to reveal a small lift, barely big enough for the two of them. 'Shhh,' whispers Rosa, pressing a finger to her lips, 'private lift.'

Sam's heart beats fast. This is fantastic – he's in a private lift! Once the doors shut, Rosa presses another button and the metal box surges upwards. By the time Sam has counted to twelve, the lift has stopped and Rosa is stepping out of the door.

Sam follows, and together they walk down a wood-panelled hallway that smells of churches and the stuff his mum got for Christmas once. 'Ooh how lovely,' she'd said, 'Di's made her own po' pourri.' His mum had waved the box under his dad's nose and his dad had pretended to choke.

At the end of the corridor is another door with a metal rectangle set into the wall next to it. It's like the one at Dad's office, a combination lock. Sam's theory is correct. Rosa punches at a succession of numbers: 2 1 3 3 9. That's easy to remember, two plus one is three, three times three is nine; it's like a baby sum. Rosa pushes the door, it swings open and beyond it is . . .

Rosa catches sight of Sam's saucer-eyed gaze. 'The prince,' she explains, 'he stay here when he need holiday, only him and me allowed in these rooms. *Bella, si?'*

Sam knows nothing about antiques, but he does know posh when he sees it. Alice is a member of the National Trust and the Jamiesons often visit stately homes and places of historical interest. His dad hates these trips. 'All this way for a crappy bit of flap-jack,' he moans.

The prince's apartment has stuffed animals with long delicate faces and twisted horns mounted on the walls. Gold and silver glints in the sunlight and the curtains are as heavy as wedding dresses. Sam counts thirteen ornate mirrors and three glittering chandeliers. The prince sleeps in a four-poster bed, and when he gets out of the bed he must watch where he puts his feet, other-wise they will land on a tiger's head. The tiger has the same yellow teeth as the caretaker at his school. 'Smoker's teeth,' says Alice.

Rosa works while Sam stares. Coloured glass reflects from a cabinet, making rainbows on the dark polished floor, and there are matching Chinese vases the size of a small child on the mantel-piece. Rosa gives Sam a can of polish and a duster. 'You do the wardrobe,' she requests, and Sam reaches as high and as wide as he can, rubbing till his arms ache. It's as tiring as swimming, this cleaning lark.

Rosa mops the kitchen and the bathroom. The bathroom is all gold mosaic, tiny centimetre squares. Sam tries to calculate how many but he gets confused. The bath is round and the inside is dark blue enamel with towels to match.

Sam looks at his watch: it's ten to four. 'I have to go, Rosa.'

Rosa has a pair of pink rubber gloves on. She's loads better at cleaning than Fat Glynis who does their house, reckons Sam.

Rosa sees him to the lift. 'You want me come down with you?'

'No,' says Sam, but as soon as the coffin door closes he changes his mind. Just count to twelve, he reminds himself. As Sam exits the lift – it was quicker going down, but that's gravity for you – he hears Max shouting. Quickly he runs to the fountain and sits down on the stone ledge.

His brother strolls into view. He is carrying a huge orange plastic water gun. Sam's heart threatens to burst with the unfairness of it all. Just when he thought he'd managed to get one up on the bastard, Max gets a bloody water gun. It's not fair.

Max sees Sam. 'Have you been sitting there all afternoon?' he demands. 'You really are sad.'

Sam laughs. Max might have a water gun, but he's got a secret and secrets are better than stupid toys.

Max is slightly unnerved by Sam's superior snigger. He'd expected him to go mental at the sight of the gun, throw himself on the floor and scream and cry till he got a tummy ache like he normally did. But Sam just sits by the fountain, hugging himself and laughing silently.

'Listen, Sam,' says Max, 'does anyone know you didn't come with us?'

Sam shakes his red head.

'Well, I don't think it's worth telling them. We'll only get into a shitload of trouble.'

Sam raises one eyebrow. The other one comes up as well, but Max knows what he means.

'We'll share the gun, OK, if you keep your mouth shut. I'll have the gun for half an hour, then you can have the gun for half an hour, OK?'

Sam nods. This is brilliant. Now he has two secrets and a time-share on a water gun.

Max explains the situation to Tabitha and Saul. Tabitha looks a bit upset. 'We shouldn't have gone. I'm sorry, Sam.'

Sam almost swoons. Two secrets, a timeshare on a water gun and an apology from a big girl. This is possibly the best day of his life.

On their way back to the pool, the three older children explain in minute detail what they did in town, should anyone ask. It sounds pretty boring. They sat on the harbour wall, ate an ice cream, bought the gun and watched some Italians play pinball in the arcade.

Big deal, thinks Sam. I know where there's a hidden lift and I know where the prince lives and, most important of all, I know the numbers of the prince's combination lock. Sam starts to skip. 'One and two is three, three times three is nine,' he chants under his breath.

'Is he OK?' asks Tabitha.

33

Migraine and Memories

Tabitha is still feeling guilty about yesterday. They shouldn't have left that little boy; he's obviously not right in the head. What if he'd wandered off and a stranger had decided to kidnap him? Tabitha had had the 'stranger danger' talk when she was in primary school. She should have been more responsible.

There is a tension in the air today, as if the palazzo is suspended in the middle of a balloon that's been blown up to bursting point. Tabitha felt it as soon as she got up. It's too still, too hot. Nina has a migraine, so Joe has taken Freya into town to buy the Italian version of Migralieve.

Poor Nina. She lies in the bedroom with the curtains drawn and a cold flannel over her face. The light hurts her eyes, but every time she closes them, all she can see is the woman in the chemist with the dirty mouth unzipping Joe's flies and slipping a beautifully manicured hand into his pants.

Well who could blame him after what you did? The migraine rolls around in her head, dragging her back to a night just over three years ago, her birthday, twenty-two years old and in love with a married man, a man with a wife and two children, a man she wouldn't let go.

Joe was meant to meet her. After all, it was her birthday. She'd expected presents in gold paper and kisses and champagne – but what did she get? A mumbled telephone call and some feeble excuse about an emergency at home. She was livid. How dare he, on her birthday! What emergency? Some blocked drain, a dead hamster – so what?

'It's my birthday and I'll get pissed if I want to.' So she had, with Shelley and Carmen and some people they knew but she didn't in a pub in south London. Lager and red wine and vodka and whisky. They were all going on to a club but she'd already been sick once.

'Come with us.'

'I can't.'

She was miserable then, maudlin and weepy.

'Forget him, Nina, come with us.'

But she hadn't. She'd ordered a minicab and waited and waited, and even though that night is long ago, Nina is transported back to a damp April evening, somewhere between Brixton and Camberwell.

She wishes she'd gone with them now. The pub is closing. She calls the minicab office again and they assure her it's on its way. 'A red Nissan,' they say. So she waits on the side of the road, sitting on the pavement, too pissed to care. Maybe she will take the cab to whatever club the girls have gone to. She is lonely and cold now. The houses over the road are putting themselves to bed, lights are extinguished and behind her the pub door closes for the last time. She looks in her bag for her mobile and notices both her phone and her purse are missing.

On her knees, crying, she feels a man's hand on her shoulder. He gives her a ream of crumpled-up pink toilet paper and the next thing she knows she is walking with the man. 'What's your name?' she asks. He tells her but she instantly forgets. He is drunk, too. They bounce off each other's shoulders and into a brick wall. She stumbles, he offers his hand – what was his name again? She needs to wee, her bladder brimming with alcohol.

He says his house is round the corner, she can phone for a cab, he will lend her money, she is safe, he is married. She laughs and so does he.

215

Laughing into his house and up the stairs and crying now on the strange man's bed with another woman's scent on the pillow and she doesn't care about anything. He brings up coffee and whisky and wipes her tears and she catches only glimpses of his face, which is very close to hers, and they lose themselves in deep tongue kisses and it's the last thing that she wants but it's the only thing she can think of doing.

The bottle passes to and fro, his tie comes off and his shirt, she is naked, and the next thing she knows she is looking over his shoulder as they make love – not love, they fuck, with their eyes shut tightly, just fucking. The most unforgettable forgettable fuck.

Some 266 days later, Freya was born.

Work it out, Nina, do the maths. And she has, a hundred million trillion times. She has checked her diary, worked out dates and consulted 'average gestation' periods in countless pregnancy manuals. The equation is always the same, it's just that she can never be sure she has the right answer.

Joe has told Tabitha and Saul to 'leave Nina in peace', so they wander down to the pool, but it's closed for cleaning.

Lydia the rep is perched on a bar stool dealing with the pissed-off clientele. 'It's not my fault,' she announces before they even ask. 'Apparently some baby dropped a turd in the shallow end and they've decided that rather than risk bubonic plague they're going to refill the thing completely. Should be done in about an hour.'

I'd rather be up a tree than sat here doing this, thinks Lydia. Honestly, some people are so difficult. That Hart Jones cow is already bleating on about taking things further. It was probably one of her mini morons who crapped up in the first place.

'We could always go down to the beach,' suggests Saul.

'But we told Dad we'd be by the pool,' insists Tabitha, pulling her Philip Pullman paperback out of her bag. The air is thick with small dark flies.

'Ping-pong, then?' volunteers Saul. Tabitha puts her book down. A rickety old table and a few bats and balls are available in a stone outbuilding just beyond the pool bar. It's shaded, which would be a relief.

The table lists dramatically to one side and the net is ragged and limp. Saul smashes the balls with his red rubber bat as if he was playing on Centre Court at Wimbledon, and Tabitha scrabbles around on the dusty floor picking them up. In the corner of the barn is a dead mouse. Tabitha flinches, remembering her first dead hamster. Ferdie's lollystick-marked grave is still in the back garden at Englestone Avenue.

'Fifteen, nil,' crows Saul.

'Stop showing off,' she snaps. 'You're hitting the stupid things too hard.'

'Just because you've got no hand-to-ball coordination,' responds Saul. 'Just because you're a gimp.'

There is a snigger from the door. 'Ah, brotherly love,' speaks a voice dripping with sarcasm. Tabitha turns around. It's the sulky witch thief. A ball rolls towards Sofia's feet; she makes no attempt to pick it up.

'Are you as bored as I am?' she drawls. Occasionally Sofia adopts a mid-Atlantic twang, an accent borrowed from her best friend Jemmilla Soudopolis, whose mother lives mostly in New York.

'No,' the Dobsons chorus.

'Don't suppose you've ever been to Sandy Lane then. Now that's a proper hotel. This place is like fucking Fawlty Towers.' Sofia places a silver DKNY trainer on the egg-fragile ball and squashes it flat. 'Oops, sorry. Now, how can I apologise properly?' She reaches into her shorts and pulls out a crumpled packet of Benson and Hedges. 'Ciggy?'

'Actually, we don't smoke.' Tabitha would have liked to sound slightly less dorky, as if she used to smoke but she'd got bored of it. Unfortunately it doesn't come out like that. She sounds like a girl in her class who still refers to her mother as 'mummy'.

'Really,' Sofia smirks. She casts her eyes over Saul. 'You should try it. It's great for suppressing one's appetite.'

Saul's eyes bulge. If they popped any more, they'd fall out and he could bat them at the girl monster. Sofia picks a slightly bent cigarette out of the packet and lights it with a disposable purple lighter.

'My brother's not fat!' Tabitha gasps.

Sofia is puffing away. 'Oh forget it,' she exhales. 'Pax. My name's Sofia. Listen, would either of you care for a drink?' She smirks again. 'Or perhaps a nice big ice cream?'

There is something hideously fascinating about this girl. Neither Saul nor Tabitha have ever met anyone quite so hypnotically vile. They glance at each other. Neither of them has any euros in their pocket, and it's horribly hot.

'Um, OK.'

Sofia stubs the cigarette out on the wall, creating a mini shower of red sparks. 'Come on then.'

The three of them sit on bar stools while Sofia orders. 'A latte for me, and . . .'

'Er, Diet Coke, thanks,' mutters Saul.

'And me,' parrots Tabitha.

'Just charge it to the tab,' commands Sofia, pushing a pair of Dolce and Gabbana sunglasses to the top of her head.

She's actually not that pretty, thinks Tabitha. She's got a big greasy nose and a weak chin.

'So, is this your first time here?'

'Yes,' replies Saul, for once refraining from blowing down his straw.

'We normally do the Caribbean, but Daddy's gone mean this year, Mummy's absolutely livid, she says she's never been to somewhere quite so Butlins. There are some very peculiar people here, don't you think?'

'Like us,' challenges Tabitha.

'Well, not specifically. I mean, it's obvious that girl's not your mum, but I've seen her snogging your dad, so I hope she's not the au pair.' Sofia snorts gleefully.

'No, she's our dad's girlfriend,' explains Saul.

'Ah. Girlfriend. So the little baby is your bastard half-sister.'

Saul splutters. Surely Freya isn't old enough to be a bastard. 'Well, your baby brother and sister are medical freaks.'

'Yah,' agrees Sofia, reverting to her home-grown Kensington vowels, 'you could say that. Biggest mistake Mummy ever made, apart from coming on holiday without a nanny. She's not really used to looking after them by herself. I think she's rather wishing she could take them back to the Portland, swap them for liposuction.'

'Don't you like them?' asks Tabitha.

Sofia grimaces. 'They're useless, just like my dad. No wonder Mummy's having an affair with her tennis coach.'

Tabitha's and Saul's jaws drop. 'Do you think you should be telling us this?' asks Tabitha, rather primly.

'Oh, I'm meant to talk, my therapist says it's good for me. Is your mum dead?'

'No!' yelp Tabitha and Saul in unison. 'She's in London,' adds Tabitha. 'She's a writer.'

'Oh, are you rich?'

'No.'

'We are, only I don't think we're quite as rich as we used to be. My dad's behaving very oddly about money, and of course my boarding-school fees are astronomical.' Sofia looks directly at Tabitha. 'Are you going out with that boy?'

Tabitha instantly blushes.

'Oh you're blushing, then you are.'

'Which boy?' queries Tabitha. She'd seen Cracked Teeth in the distance as they were leaving town yesterday; he'd waved but she'd kept on walking.

'The one with the weird brother with the red hair.'

'You mean Max? No way. He's a year younger than me – he's twelve.'

'Oh, are you thirteen? You don't look it. I'm twelve, but I'm well developed for my age.' As if to prove the fact, Sofia pushes her chest out.

Tabitha blinks. She used to blink a lot when she was younger but she managed to stop.

'Have you got something wrong with your eyes?' observes Sofia meanly. 'Only there's a girl at school who started blinking when her mum and dad got divorced. Are your mum and dad divorced?'

'Yes,' whispers Tabitha, desperately trying not to blink.

'I think mine would like to but Daddy's too mean. He'd have to buy himself a flat, you see, there's no way Mummy would leave the house. We live just off the King's Road. Where do you live?'

'Stoke Newington,' replies Tabitha.

'Oh,' says Sofia. 'I've never heard of it – is that in London?'

'Of course it's in London,' grunts Saul. He's had enough of this devil girl now. She keeps upsetting Tabitha, which should be funny only somehow it's not.

Tabitha suddenly notices a glass ring on Sofia's middle finger. She stares at it. It's the same as hers, only instead of being orange with a purple splodge it's purple with an orange splodge.

'I saw you at the market yesterday,' she says evenly.

'Oh yeah,' responds Sofia, but she avoids Tabitha's eyes.

'I think we should go now, Saul.' Tabitha jumps down from the bar stool and Saul follows suit. Gruesome – that's the word. This girl is gruesome.

As they walk away Sofia gives Tabitha marks out of ten for hair, eyes, skin, figure and personality. This is what they do at school. Occasionally it gets nasty. Mylin Chong took an overdose of paracetamol after they gave her a zero for her figure, and her mother came to school and called them all 'bitches from hell'.

'But we gave her a seven for her hair,' Jemmilla Soudopolis had pointed out indignantly.

Sofia normally gets eights for everything apart from personality, which usually scores her a six. This is because, according to Atlanta Wymbourne and Cressida Carter, she can be 'two-faced and spiteful'.

'It's better than being a flat-chested ginger,' Sofia had retaliated (pronouncing the ginger with two hard Gs, which made Cressida cry).

That Tabitha girl then: eight for hair, the blonde streaks are a nice touch. Eight for skin; she'd get a nine but Sofia counted three blackheads. Seven for her figure, with two marks knocked off for not having any tits. As for her personality: three, she's a soppy drip.

'Saul, d'you think I'm a bit of a . . . ?'

'What?' presses Saul.

'A soppy drip,' his sister replies.

'Hmmm,' considers Saul. 'I'm fat and you're a drip. Fatty and drippy, that's us.'

Saul can be incredibly comforting sometimes, thinks Tabitha, but the girl has unnerved her.

As they walk back to the apartment, a man in a hat is approaching from the other direction. He seems distracted. Tabitha recognises him as Sofia's father. As he passes she hears him muttering over and over again: 'It's got to stop, I can't stand it any more. Oh God, oh Jesus God.'

'Just keep walking,' urges Tabitha. Living in London, they're used to making themselves invisible in the presence of gibbering lunatics and mad tramps. Only this man isn't a tramp. Tramps don't wear Panama hats – not in Stoke Newington anyway.

Once they have scurried on a few yards, Tabitha looks over her shoulder. Sofia's father is sitting on a bench rocking to and fro with his handkerchief over his face. If he wasn't a grown man she would have sworn he was crying.

'Dad!'

Saul has spotted Joe. He is standing by the fountain in the court-yard, lifting Freya, his two big hands round her waist as she reaches out to pat the head of the copper fish. Saul runs to meet his father.

Tabitha stands still. Her father looks golden in the sun, like something out of a Greek myth. Once upon a time I was my father's princess and he threw me in the air and I had a pink dress with cherries all over it and little red button-up shoes. For some reason she feels like crying. I want my mum, I don't want to grow up, life is messy and difficult and some people are really horrid and some are really unhappy and how does kissing really work?

221

34

Badly Drawn Day

Alice is much better. She is well enough to walk to the shops and gather bread, milk and toilet rolls, lots of toilet rolls. She also puts some children's colouring pencils and a pad of paper into her red plastic basket. Ideally she'd like to be purchasing a wooden box of quality watercolours, tiny palettes of exotic colours, cadmium, burnt sienna, prussian blue, complete with delicate hog's hair brushes and a pad of thick cartridge paper. Alas, the Spar art department is severely limited. The paper she has found is as thin and shiny as poor-quality ham, but it's better than nothing. As a child Alice drew on the back of wallpaper samples, lumpy as porridge. 'A poor workman blames his tools, Alice.'

Today, she has decided, the Jamiesons are going to sketch together, as a family, just like the Brontës or that Bloomsbury group, only without the sex and madness of course. Guy will enjoy it, he did art O level after all, and if Max isn't going to be academic, maybe it's time to encourage his creative side.

Before she can stop it, her older son's biro drawing of the topless woman floats across Alice's memory. She pushes it aside. After all, Rembrandt painted a lot of nudes. The galleries in London are positively bulging with bare breasts and tapioca-dimpled buttocks.

She remembers taking the boys to an exhibition at the Royal Academy, years ago when Sam had just learned to read. He must have been about four. Standing in front of a painting entitled *Rape of the Sabine Women*, her youngest son had asked out loud, 'What does rape mean, Mummy?' This is one of Alice's 'anecdotes'; she tells it at dinner parties. It's one of her favourites as it says a lot about her.

A. The fact that she is the type of mother who takes her children to places of cultural interest.

B. That at least one of her progeny is precociously intelligent.

C. That she has a wicked sense of humour.

'Imagine,' she crows, 'a four-year-old! Out of the mouths of babes!'

'You're not very brown,' says the girl on the till who used to live in Catford.

'I've been poorly,' responds Alice, digging for euros. 'Anyway, I tend to get bored just lying on a beach.'

'Do you now,' says Miss Catford, scanning the industrial-sized pack of toilet rolls. 'If you want bored, you want to try sitting where I'm sat all day. Oh, hiya Gayle.'

Alice looks over her shoulder. It's Max's muse, the strumpet from the palazzo in a turquoise bikini top and pink velour shorts. 'Orlright, Dawn,' she greets the girl on the till. 'Got any plasters? My heels are all blistered to fuck.'

Alice pays and scurries away, clutching her plastic bags. The last thing she wants to do is get trapped with the foul-mouthed Cockney tart. Gayle is very brown, Alice notes; she's probably the type that uses sunbeds.

Alice marches briskly back to the palazzo; on the steps leading to the town square feral cats with impossibly bony shoulders fight over a broken bin-liner of fish bones. She is wearing Guy's Birkenstocks – the slaggy stilettoed one will never catch up with her.

Already the sun is beating down, causing havoc with her sweat glands. The Mediterranean is all very well but a bit of cloud would be a welcome relief. She doesn't really like warm weather. In the winter you can cover your arms. Alice has bingo wings, despite the fact she doesn't play bingo.

What day is it, Wednesday? This holiday is going so fast. It would be nice to hire a car and see some ruins, but of course Guy hasn't organised anything. It's always Alice who has to take responsibility, carry the passports, read the guidebook, rinse the chlorine out of the children's costumes. Alice's bowels growl discontentedly. Maybe it's best not to be too far away from the lavatory for at least another day or so.

Oh but she is hungry. The only things that have passed her lips in the past forty-eight hours apart from water are the Imodium tablets she stole from Guy's washbag (as a rule Alice prefers to avoid over-the-counter pharmaceuticals). He didn't bring any condoms, she noticed.

She is looking forward to eating today. Last night the boys went out and ate pizzas, which according to Sam were the size of cheesy steering wheels. It would have been thoughtful if one of them had brought her a little slice home in a doggy bag, but they didn't. They hadn't got back till gone eleven, and even though Guy was obviously sloshed he'd insisted on going down to the pool bar for one last nightcap.

He really should cut down. Small red veins are bursting round his nose, and in the morning the whites of his eyes are the colour of blood oranges. It's a good job she's feeling so much stronger. Her family really need her to keep them in order. Without Alice in charge, things get out of hand. That wretched water gun for starters. Alice tried to confiscate it but there were tears from Sam and 'language' from Max. In the end Guy had intervened and said, 'Jesus, Alice, they're on holiday, it's a fucking water gun, leave it.' So she did, but she's not happy about it. A gun is a gun is a gun. 'What about Dunblane, Guy?'

Guy is so sloppy about everything. Sam's shoulders are pink because he forgot to cream the child up. 'Skin cancer can be triggered by a single incident in childhood,' she'd reprimanded him, checking to see if any of Sam's moles had changed shape in the last twenty-four hours.

At home Alice keeps a health file in which she stores leaflets she has picked up from the doctor's surgery. 'Ovarian Cancer – your risk', 'Seven Signs of Solvent Abuse', 'Meningitis: When is a Rash Just a Rash?'

224

'Melanomas are usually irregular in shape. They are often crusty and can bleed.' Life is so fraught. One must be vigilant at all times, especially when one is a mother. Danger lurks round every corner.

Yesterday, waiting for her children to return from their unaccompanied trip into town, Alice had been in purgatory, her mind buzzing with technicolor disaster scenarios. During the hour-long wait, she'd managed to convince herself that the streets of Santa Helena were awash with rabid dogs. She could hear them barking, see their slathering jaws. Her children would be bitten – it was inevitable. If they hadn't been raped and stabbed, her sons would return delirious and foaming from the mouth – if they returned at all.

Well, today she can relax, she's back in charge. Today they will be together as a family. After the sketching they might play Uno, Rummix or gin rummy for matchsticks. Alice's thighs chafe as she hikes up the path to the annexe. A sore patch has developed between her legs that requires daily Savlon treatment.

'Hi,' she hollers, walking into the apartment. Rosa the grumpy cleaning woman emerges from the bathroom.

'Where are my children?' asks Alice, a tad shrilly, kidnap being foremost on her mind.

Rosa looks at her with barely concealed contempt.

What is it with this woman, thinks Alice. Maybe she's menopausal. She smiles sympathetically. 'Rosa, do you know where my family are?'

In Rosa's hand is a torn towel. Alice colours; she had to cut a strip off it yesterday when she ran out of toilet paper and had finished the last of her cotton wool. 'They go breakfast,' the woman snaps.

Alice is livid. 'Not again – how dare they?' She dumps her shopping on the table and semi-jogs back to the main palazzo and into the dining-room, building up steam as she goes. The restaurant is a third full. She squints round the room: where are they, the traitors? Spying her errant family in the corner, Alice bustles over, knocking a buttery croissant off a table with her buttocks as she passes.

'What do you think you're doing?'

Guy is eating a golden omelette glistening with fat black mushrooms, Max has two *pain au chocolat* on his plate and a third hanging out of his mouth, while Sam has, at a rough estimate, about fifteen slices of salami in front of him.

'We are eating breakfast,' Guy answers. 'Yum, yum, yum,' he adds conversationally, waving a metaphorical red flag in front of a raging bull.

'But I went to the supermarket!'

'No one asked you to go, Alice. We like having breakfast here.'

Alice is spluttering. 'Have you any idea how much this is costing?'

Guy looks up. 'I don't know and I don't care. Now either sit down and join us, or bugger off.'

Alice buggers off, all the way back to the apartment. At least that bitch of a cleaning woman has gone. She pours herself a bowl of her least favourite breakfast cereal and tears into a stale ciabatta. What she really wants is the omelette Guy is eating.

By the time the boys get back Alice has arranged a still-life on the table. It consists of a slightly withered peach, an orange flower (possibly a hibiscus) in a wine glass, an interesting pebble, a box of matches and a candle.

'We are going to sketch,' she tells them as they troop into the apartment, and there is something in her voice that makes them sit in their designated chairs. Alice hums. She hands them each a piece of paper and something to rest on. The packet of coloured pencils lies open on the table. 'You may begin.'

Twenty minutes later, Alice has crumpled up six sheets of paper. (Having used both sides, of course. Waste not, want not.) She cannot get the peach right, or the pebble, or the flower for that matter. As for the matchbox and the candle, they're impossible.

The coloured pencils are very cheap. They keep breaking: first the yellow, then the orange, then the red. 'This is stupid,' mutters Max, and Alice, in a fit of temper, sweeps the still-life to the floor. The glass shatters, scattering twinkling shards all over the floor.

'Don't anyone move,' threatens Guy, and they all freeze as he fetches the dustpan and brush.

Alice is mortified. What have I done, why am I behaving so

badly? It's too hot, if only there was some breeze. 'I'm sorry,' she blurts, 'but . . .'

'Just say sorry, Alice.'

'I am, I'm sorry, what can I do to make it better?'

You could die, thinks Guy, before he can stop himself. It's ten o'clock; he could really do with a drink.

Alice's mood swings from guilt to fury. It's their fault, really, ganging up on her. When the children were little she was the centre of their universe. Now they look at her with contempt and impatience. Even Sam hasn't been as sympathetic as she'd expected, rushing off to be with his father and brother when she'd been so poorly.

If only I had a baby again. A baby would love me and need me.

Sam is still drawing. His red head is bent over a piece of paper he has folded in half – it looks like he is making a card. Alice's heart melts. He is making a card for his mummy. She edges round the table and plants a kiss on her son's fiery curls. Looking down she sees that he is writing: 'To Rosa, thank you, love Sam.'

Rosa!

'Who's Rosa, lambkin?' Maybe she is a nice girl in Sam's class or a kind classroom assistant?

'The lady who cleans,' Sam replies, 'and anyway it's private.'

Alice feels sick again. My family has gone wrong. My husband stares into the distance, as far away from me as he can see. My oldest boy is shutting me out: day by day he confides in me less and less. Even my beloved youngest has betrayed me for another woman.

Alice's heart feels as crumpled and twisted as the discarded balls of paper. She retreats into the bathroom and medicates her thighs.

35

Ex Sex

Hils is in bed reading *Marie Claire*. Halfway through the magazine, sandwiched between an advert for foot deodoriser and one for hair removal cream, is an article entitled 'Which couple has the most sex?'

Six men and six women gaze out at her from a glossy double-page spread. Steve (27) from Bournemouth is a dreadlocked vet currently dating Vinnie, a multi-tattooed nursery school teacher (25). Hils scans the other suspects: bald design technicians, ginger lab assistants and busty nurses. She can't be bothered to turn the page and find out who scores the highest number of 'bonks per week'. The nurse and the motorcycle courier probably, who cares? All of them have more sex than her.

I've got the sex life of a giant panda, reckons Hils. It's a wonder I'm not lying here chewing bamboo. I could have a wank, she contemplates, but masturbating has never really been her thing, and anyway the window cleaner might turn up.

Since Joe left, Hils has had four snogs and a bizarre one-night stand with an old boyfriend. She blushes when she remembers this incident. What on earth had possessed her? A bottle of wine and a couple of brandies probably. She'd been to the theatre with Sally (culture being the last refuge of the newly separated woman). Afterwards they'd found a little bar off St Martin's Lane. Sitting in a window seat with just half an inch of house red left between them, he'd walked in: Mr 'Blast from the Past' Mark Pettifer! Her last boyfriend before Joe – a coincidence that Sally had insisted merited another bottle of wine, and she'd waltzed off to the bar before Hils could stop her. Returning with a bottle of Rioja in one hand and her mobile in another, Sally had blathered madly about Esme and a fictional earache before melting into the night as surreptitiously as only she could: ie, winking and nudging and making obscene hand gestures.

An hour later Hils had found herself on a 176 bus going back to Mark's flat in Kennington. Halfway over Waterloo Bridge, she'd vaguely remembered what she didn't like about him. His meanness for starters: 'You have got a Travelcard, haven't you?'

Oh well, it was too late to go back now. She was middle-aged, free and single after all. An hour or so later, as his IKEA headboard beat a jerky rhythm against the wall, all Hils could think was: This is bad, this is bad, this is bad.

His long, thin, clammy penis had still smelt like he kept it in a Tupperware container, and in the morning the first thing he did was confess that he was engaged to a girl who worked on the Clinique counter in Selfridges. 'She's only twenty-four,' he'd added proudly. He hadn't cleaned his teeth and his breath reeked of singed egg.

As Hils had reached down to pick up yesterday's knickers, she'd caught sight of the Durex he'd worn the night before, lying on the floor beside the bed. It was shrivelled but empty – both of them had faked it, then! All those 'oohs' and 'ahs' and 'oh babys' had been a mutual code for 'get off, I've had quite enough of this dreadful bone grinding, thank you'.

'I hope you'll be very happy,' she'd said as she headed for the front door. He'd tried to kiss her but she'd turned her head. 'I don't think it would be very appropriate.'

'I was just trying to be polite,' he'd replied.

Hils rolls off the bed. Since the kids have been on holiday she has retreated more and more into the bedroom. When they have grown up and left me, I might as well get myself a bedsit, she acknowledges, and the thought of this eventuality depresses her even more. Saul's room no longer smelling of socks, Tabitha's dressing table empty . . . What will I do when there's only me left?

There are toast crumbs stuck to her bare bottom and three coffee mugs she's used as ashtrays on the bedside table. Making her way to the bathroom she sidesteps the remains of a Marks and Spencer chargrilled chicken risotto, eaten straight from its microwaveable tray. I'm a cross between a pig and a panda, she admits.

It's eleven o'clock on Wednesday morning. Tonight she is seeing Nick and Sally, which means in eight hours' time she really will have to get dressed.

I'll have a bath later, she decides. Forgetting the coffee mugs, she wanders downstairs to the kitchen. Waiting for the kettle to boil, she forces herself to consider the four post-Joe snogs. Embarrassingly enough, one was with an old schoolfriend of her brother's. At James and Midge's Christmas party last year she'd allowed herself to be pushed up against Caspar's bedroom door by a man who was even shorter than she was. Only when the door opened and Caspar's spaceship night-light shone on to the pocket-sized Lothario's face did she realise who it was. Andy Robson!

She'd closed the bedroom door before Caspar woke up. 'I always fancied you,' slurred Andy, reaching for the buttons on her shirt. She'd slapped his hands away. 'But you're only twelve!' Obviously he wasn't; he just hadn't grown since 1978. 'Suit yourself,' huffed Andy, pulling himself up to his full five foot three inches. 'I've seen them before anyway. I used to hide in your garden and wait for you to get undressed at night. You never closed your curtains. I reckon you're still a thirty-four AA.'

So that had been romantic. Who else?

Hils vaguely recollects a disastrous incident with a man who'd helped her change a tyre on the Fiat Panda – Colin someone. She'd offered to buy him a drink and somehow he'd got his wires crossed and jumped to the conclusion that she wanted to go out on a date. Before she knew it, he'd arranged to meet her in a pub in Holloway the next night. Out of a warped sense of sympathy for a man who was obviously very lonely, she'd turned up, only to find him wearing a cheap grey suit and carrying a single cellophane-wrapped red rose. Halfway through her lager and lime, he'd shoved his beard into her face, and such was her surprise he'd managed to poke his tongue into her gaping mouth.

'I thought that's what you wanted,' he'd repeated, following her out of the pub. 'I thought you were up for it.' Fortunately a black cab had gone by and she'd managed to flag it down.

'You frigid slag,' he'd yelled as she jumped in.

'Oxymoron,' she'd slung back in response.

So that had been creepy.

The third snog had taken her completely by surprise. She'd been in Topshop using Tabitha's forthcoming birthday as an excuse to spend the afternoon trying on unsuitable outfits and buying silver glittery eyeliner. As she'd exited the store, wearing her red coat and with her hair in pigtails, a man had grabbed her from behind, spun her round and proceeded to kiss her passionately. She was just starting to enjoy it when he pulled away, held her at arm's distance and gasped, 'But you're not Abi, you're an old woman!' Apparently from behind she'd looked like his twenty-two-year-old girlfriend. Face-on, she reminded him of his mother. Wiping his mouth in horror, he'd backed away.

So that had been scary – for both of them.

Hils tries to avoid confronting the memory of the fourth snog. After all, it hadn't been a proper snog, just a fleeting kiss, but it had left her lips burning. I kissed a waiter, she reminds herself, denying it the next second. I didn't really, it wasn't a proper kiss, no tongues. I'm not a bad woman. Yes, I was drunk, but I wasn't *that* drunk. You kissed a waiter? Yes I did.

Hils is mortified. I am forty-one, I have two children, I am a published author, I can't kiss waiters. Ah – but you did, and he tasted nice.

Too late, Hils remembers that she'd been meaning to listen to *Woman's Hour*. This time tomorrow she will have made her Radio 4 debut. She shudders, and practises answering imaginary questions into a banana microphone. 'Well, Jenni, I wrote the book because—' There is a knock on the kitchen window. Oh great, thinks Hils. Well done me. I am naked from the waist down talking to a banana.

On the other side of the glass, the window cleaner smirks.

Hils creeps back to bed. Picking up *Marie Claire* again she discovers that it's not busty nurse Nancy and her Jamaican motorcycle-courier boyfriend who have the most sex. In fact the winners are Mark, a systems analyst from south London, and his fiancée Karen, a cosmetic technician (25), who by all accounts are at it like rabbits.

'No one can satisfy me the way Karen does,' oozes Mark. 'She's the first woman who has ever really turned me on.' While according to Karen, 'Mark is a sex god, and the fact that we're engaged and I know he would never be unfaithful makes our love-making even more special.'

Hils sniggers, but there is something disturbingly familiar about the small photo next to the systems analyst's copy. Turning back to the main picture for confirmation, she realises that 'Sex God Mark' is her ex, penny-pinching Mark with the Tupperware penis. She can't wait to tell Sally.

At bang on eight o'clock, Hils, bathed and dressed and clutching a bottle of pink champagne in one hand and *Marie Claire* in the other, arrives at the Thorpes. It's good to get out of the house.

Sally opens the door. She is so sexy, realises Hils, that even her butcher's apron looks like it came from Agent Provocateur. By comparison she feels faded and smudged, like a watercolour left out in the rain.

Esme is hanging over the banister. 'Hi, Hils,' she calls.

Hils looks up. Esme is in her nightie. 'I can see your bum,' she shouts.

Esme squeals. 'No you can't! I've got Barbie knickers on. Anyway, I'm going to bed, I've had a long day. Try not to drink too much, Mum.'

'Goodnight, darling,' trills Sally, adding under her breath, 'Jesus, it's like living with Mary bleeding Whitehouse.'

Down in the kitchen a frosted glass vase sits on the table, bursting with heavy-headed peonies, and a mass of night-lights twinkle along the mantelpiece. Sally has pulled out all the stops. A heap of silver cutlery glints on the sideboard next to an oozing cheeseboard.

'Where's Nick?' asks Hils, pinching a glistening green olive from a crackle-glazed dish.

'He's up in the attic with the architect.' Sally looks guilty.

'You haven't set me up?' demands Hils. 'You know I can't stand blind dates.'

'It's an accident. You know Nick never listens to me. He's my husband – that's his job. I told him I'd invited you for supper and this morning he just casually informs me he's got this bloke coming over. We're having the attic converted. Apparently this man is the business – did the Robathams' place in Cornwall. Sorry.' Sally hands Hils a glass of pink fizz. 'Get that down you.'

Hils relaxes as the bubbles hit her bloodstream. 'Oh, it doesn't matter, as long as you lend me that Nicole Farhi suede jacket.'

'Done,' grins Sally. 'It's too small for me anyway and I'm not going back on the Atkins for anything.' She starts to clatter pans, ruby nails reaching for wooden spoons. 'You can set the table.'

Everything is so beautiful in this house, thinks Hils, laying Georgian knives and forks and breathing in something deep and meaty.

'Pheasant casserole,' explains Sally, smirking at her own expertise.

Hils's stomach rumbles like Vesuvius. 'Hey, Sal, look at this, recognise anyone?' She opens the *Marie Claire*, helps herself to another olive and waits for her friend to react. Sally speed-reads the article. 'Oh my God, it's that old shag of yours, the one you picked up in the wine bar. It's—'

'Mr Tupperware Penis!' screams Hils, and she laughs so hard that she accidentally inhales the olive stone, which wedges itself halfway down her windpipe. As she starts coughing, Nick appears with a man-shaped person behind him.

'Who's got a Tupperware penis?' asks Nick, genuinely interested.

'This bloke Hils picked up the night we went to the theatre, the filthy slag.'

Hils can barely speak. Her eyes are watering and her nose is running furiously – for some reason Sally and Nick have invited the waiter for supper.

'Hi, Nick,' she splutters, 'ha ha ha ha ha. Sally's just mucking around, I'm not really in the habit of picking up strangers in bars.'

'Shame,' mumbles the waiter.

'Oh, this is Stan, Hils,' announces Nick, 'he's an architect.'

Hils is choking, seriously choking. She is coughing so hard now she is in danger of wetting her pants. The only thing within reach is the bottle of pink champagne. She grabs it and pours the contents down her neck. The upshot of this action is that the olive stone dislodges itself and she can breathe again; the downside is that she suddenly feels extremely pissed.

'But you're a waiter,' she slurs.

Stan grins slyly. 'No, you thought I was a waiter.'

'But you were wearing black trousers and a white shirt.'

'Armani, and anyway, I could have been a conductor – orchestra, not bus.'

'But you were handing round the sushi.'

'Only because you told me to.'

'God, I'm sorry.'

'Really, don't apologise, you gave me a lovely tip.' Stan grins. 'It's really nice to see you again.'

There is something in his voice that turns the blood in her veins to hot whisky and honey. A deep flush surges through her body and her brain plummets to her gusset. She felt like this once, a long time ago. It's either love, an allergic reaction or the menopause.

She blushes to her waist. 'Ha ha ha ha.'

The demise of a marriage, like death, comes in many forms. Some just slowly wither away, others end more shockingly, as if the marriage has been driven at high speed into a brick wall, leaving such a mess that friends and family can hardly bear to look. Others break as cleanly as a snapped neck – no kids, no big deal – while some rot so poisonously you can almost smell the relationship going off. A bad marriage smells worse than putrid mushrooms.

Of course, marriages can be saved, pulled back from the brink, salvaged from the wreckage, given a new chassis and a lick of paint. Cracks can be papered over with promises and candlelit dinners and holidays in the sun.

Sometimes you think your marriage is going to make it, that it's just got 'a bit of a cold', nothing critical, then gradually you realise it's pneumonia with complications and even your Relate counsellor is shaking her head.

234

This is what happened to me and Joe. For years I refused to believe there was anything seriously wrong, but in the end our marriage was like a really sick dog with cataracts and bulging tumours. We had to put it out of its misery. There is a phrase I learnt in German once: genug ist genug – *'enough is enough'.*

Diary of a Divorcee

36

Low Pressure Rising

The day has changed before Nina even has a chance to open her eyes. As she stirs, she feels an unfamiliar chill, and she reaches for the bedspread that lies tangled at her feet. Something is not right. It makes her want to burrow back into sleep. If there's going to be a problem, she doesn't want to face it yet.

Freya cries, a heart-tugging lonely little wail, and Nina, feeling like a puppet with its strings all tangled, staggers over to her daughter, roots her out of the cot and tips her into the big double bed. Freya rolls piglet-style against her father, and, instantly comforted, she sleeps. Nina prises open one of the wooden shutters. The weather has broken, the sun smothered by a thick band of grey.

We could be anywhere – we could be in Norwich.

An hour later they are all awake. The dull skies subdue the mood in the apartment. No one really knows what to do. It's as if they are waiting until they are allowed to pack, but it's only Thursday – they still have two nights left.

'I want to go home,' Nina whispers quietly to herself in the bathroom. 'There is no point being here unless it's sunny.'

The palazzo feels like a cheap imitation of what the brochure promised. Suddenly there are too many ants, too many flies, and the apartment is so gloomy that they have to turn on the electric lights.

The Dobsons traipse down to breakfast. 'I wish I'd brought some socks,' complains Nina, and Joe snarls, 'Don't be so dramatic, Nina,' while in the distance thunder rolls.

The atmosphere in the dining room is equally tense. The staff are embarrassed; they shake their heads and shrug. Lipstick can be removed from coffee cups, steaks can be put back under the grill, but they cannot roll up the grey blankets of cloud and drag the sun from its hiding place. These things happen. It is an act of God and bad weather is not refundable.

Tabitha is trying not to feel cheated. She was going to work on her tan today. All she has to show for this week in the so-called sun are a few thousand extra freckles and a pair of rosy shoulders – not fair.

Outside by the pool, two of the bartenders are fastening down the umbrellas. The wind is gusting fitfully and a lilo scuds across the water, momentarily taking off and flying through the air before crashing into a wall.

'I don't think we'll be swimming today,' remarks Nina, unnecessarily.

Joe feels a buzz of impatience. 'Oh for heaven's sake, it's not like anyone died. What's the matter with you all? Cheer up, for fuck's sake.'

The 'for fuck's sake' part of his sentence seems to bounce off the empty plate in front of him and reverberate around the room. Eyes swivel in their direction and Tabitha's face burns to peeling point.

Fortunately, two seconds later a waiter drops a plate of scrambled egg, and in the ensuing mayhem the room relaxes. It's like a chemical reaction: people are pushing their chairs back and ordering more coffee. A Hart Jones twin crawls across the carpet and on to Nina's knee. The one in the blue dungarees, the boy, Nina guesses.

Saul wanders over to the breakfast buffet for yet another apricot Danish. On his way back he takes a detour over to where Max is sitting with his brother and his dad. His mum never comes down for breakfast. They give each other a clumsy high five and Saul raises his hand again to greet Sam, but Sam pretends to be engrossed in his Game Boy.

'Weather's gone a bit crap,' remarks Saul as a French door slams alarmingly, causing waitresses to run around the room sliding bolts and shutting windows. Max's dad is swallowing round white pills and drinking cup after cup of thick black coffee. He's wearing dark glasses, which is a bit naff, thinks Saul, and he's pushed a barely nibbled full English breakfast to one side. Saul eyes a sausage – what a waste.

'So what you going to do today?'

Max rolls his eyes dramatically. 'Mum's hired a car. We're going to see some ruins.' Such is the despair in Max's voice that he might as well have been saying, 'We're booked in for group colonic irrigation followed by family root canal treatment.'

Saul, for want of anything better to say, replies with, 'Why?'

Max's dad sniggers, then rubs his face with his hands as if trying to get the creases out of his skin. 'Good question,' he mutters. And Max just shrugs hopelessly.

'Well,' decides Saul, 'if you don't want to go, you could always spend the day with us. We're not doing anything, just mucking around really, there's a pool table in the games room.'

Max looks at his father imploringly.

'No chance, Max. It's one in, all in. Your mother's got a bee in her bonnet and we're going to have a jolly super time all together.' Max's dad speaks as if his bile duct has got caught up in his vocal cords. He sounds so bitter that it makes Saul wince; even the coffee cup in Guy Jamieson's hand seems to shudder.

'Cooee!' Alice is waving from the doorway. Mr Jamieson raises one arm stiffly in the air and puts the forefinger of his other hand under his nose. 'Und here she is: Mrs Hitler. Heil, Alice.'

Max's mum puffs over. 'Don't be offensive, Guy. Some of our German friends might be watching.' She spits on a tissue and wipes chocolate from around Sam's mouth. 'Okey dokey, let's be off. I've packed a picnic and I've got the map and the guidebook, so why don't you three run upstairs and clean your teeth? I'll be waiting in the car.' Alice then delivers what she assumes is a dazzling smile (somewhat marred by a raisin stuck between an incisor and a front tooth), turns on her Birkenstocks and waddles out of the dining-room.

'See ya, Maxy boy,' rallies Saul. 'Have fun.'

Bloody hell. Having that mum must be like living with the world's bossiest teacher. At least his mum is only a bit embarrassing, like when she sings or wears a hat, thinks Saul.

The Jamiesons exit as if walking to the gallows, and Saul, because he can't resist it, steals the cold sausage from Guy's discarded plate. By the time he gets back to his own family, the grubby dishcloth sky is wringing out fat drops of rain.

Nina is still bouncing the enormous squinting baby on her lap. Apparently Lydia has been over to inform them that English Disney videos will be shown in the games room from eleven till one, and Freya now has a date with the Hart Jones twins. Nina is rather unnerved by this turn of events. Helena isn't her type and she most definitely isn't Helena's. Yesterday's headache is already knocking its way back into her temples.

'Count me out,' says Joe, before she's even asked. 'I'll take Tabitha and Saul off somewhere. We'll see you back in the apartment for lunch.' He kisses Nina's concertinaed brow and whispers into her hairline, 'That is possibly the ugliest baby I've ever seen!'

Nina sniggers, but immediately feels guilty, as if in laughing at Bertie she is jinxing her own child. 'You cow,' whispers her conscience. 'Just for that, Freya will fall into a fire, she will catapult through a windscreen, a dog will bite her nose off.' Nina tenses, and Bertie looks up at her with such an expression of apology that Nina has to fight back tears. 'I'm sure your mummy loves you,' she murmurs into his cradle cap.

An hour later, she is not so sure. Within the first ten minutes of *Dumbo*, Helena has confessed to Nina that really, apart from a disastrous perm back in the eighties, the twins are probably the worst decision she has ever made. 'All that money,' she sighs. 'If I could turn back the clock, I think I might have gone for a conservatory.'

Nina is genuinely shocked. Never, not even for an instant, has she ever regretted Freya. She has been riddled with doubt, tortured with fear, exhausted to the point of collapse, but never has she wished she hadn't been born. Helena changes Lettice's nappy with abject distaste, shuddering as the sticky brown contents are exposed. 'I normally have a nanny,' she explains, 'but her grandfather died and she buggered off back to the Czech Republic two days before we came away.'

'Fuckin' hell.' Gayle has just walked in. Immediately she pulls a bottle of Rive Gauche out of her fake Louis Vuitton handbag and squirts it liberally around the room. 'It's worse than when Jonty has a crap.'

Nina shrivels inside. Helena and Gayle? What a combination.

'Budge up,' commands Gayle. 'I love *Dumbo*.'

Turns out 'that arsehole' Jonty has buggered off to a bar in town where they have Sky Sports on a widescreen TV and the beer is cheap.

Helena is now fighting a losing battle with Bertie and a wayward Pamper.

'Here, let me have a go,' offers Gayle, and, as if Norland-trained, she locks Bertie's ankles in one hand, removes the stinking nappy and slides a new one under his dimpled buttocks with the other. The job is completed in seconds.

'My mum had another kiddie when I was eight,' she explains, wiping a smear of shit off her wrist with a baby wipe. 'Michael, my half brother, got run over when he was eleven. My mum's never been the same since.'

'You mean he was killed?' breathes Nina.

'Yeah,' nods Gayle. 'He was on his bike and a lorry smashed into him.'

'How ghastly,' mutters Helena, and the three of them sit wedged on the sofa, surreptitiously sniffing while Dumbo's mother lies weeping in a cage.

Outside, the sky tears open like a ripped tarpaulin and water tips out endlessly. Jonty sips his second pint. He has been joined by the German homosexuals, Dieter and Peter, who for poofs know a great deal about football, especially Freddie Ljungberg.

Jonty slept with a German girl once. At least he hopes it was a girl – she did have the most enormous feet. 'I've slept with some rubbish,' acknowledges Jonty, making up his mind to buy Gayle a big fuck-off present.

'I love my wife,' he blurts. 'I fucking love her.' Oops, maybe it's time he started pacing himself. Drinking in the morning makes him sentimental. 'And I love Dieter,' confesses Peter. 'And I love Peter,' echoes Dieter.

The rain lashes down. Jonty isn't too fussed, it's cosy in this bar. Suddenly the door flies open and that photographer bloke, Joe, comes crashing in with two of his kids. 'Hello, Saul,' chorus the poofs, and the boy blushes even more than his sister. Jonty pulls his chair back, making space around the table. This is more like it, a proper lads' day out. 'Here you go, mate, take the weight off your slingbacks.'

Joe looks a bit taken aback but he drops down into a spare aluminium chair, shaking the rain out of his hair like a Great Dane. He's very good-looking, thinks Jonty, if you like that sort of thing. Which obviously he doesn't because he isn't gay.

Joe opens his wallet and gives Tabitha ten euros. 'Go on, bugger off to the amusement arcade. I'll have a quick pint while the rain stops and then we'll head back.' He lights a cigarette, his first of the day. It makes his head spin. There is something weird about today – he can't explain it, but it feels like Halloween. Something is going to happen. A black cat weaves her emaciated body through his legs. Good or bad luck? He can't remember.

37

Snakes in the Rain

Alice waits in the hire car. It's a metallic green Vauxhall Corsa, much newer and a good deal less smelly than the L-reg Passat she's used to driving at home. Guy is always wittering on about getting a 'new set of wheels', talking nonsense about convertible Mercedes and fancy four-wheel drives. He does it to wind her up. Guy knows that Alice feels guilty enough about having a car in the first place.

In theory, Alice is very pro the Green Party. If it was up to her she'd get rid of the damn car. Unfortunately, recycling Guy's empties would be impossible without it. It's a dilemma! Every Monday, Alice does her bit for the planet. She piles all the old newspapers (mostly the *Guardian*, plus the *Times* weekend supplements) along with the empty beer and wine bottles into the back of the estate and drives to the nearest recycling bins half a mile away. The last time she was offloading the empties, a man looked at her with some admiration and yelled, 'Must have been one hell of a party!'

Guy's drinking has been even worse here in Italy. When she gets home she might have to leave a pamphlet on his bedside table: 'Alcohol Abuse and You.'

Back in London he uses work as an excuse to drink. 'You've no idea how stressful my job is, Alice.' Rubbish, thinks Alice. Men know nothing about stress. Real stress is when your youngest suddenly realises at 9 pm that he has to have a Viking outfit, complete with helmet, ready by the morning, and your oldest has tried to streak his hair with toilet bleach. If anyone has an excuse to hit the bottle it's her.

Alice surveys the dashboard. Maybe she should let Guy drive? The gearstick is different from the one she is used to, and putting the Corsa into reverse could prove lethal. Not that she rates Guy very highly as a driver. He has a tendency to be rather cavalier round corners, and who is it that's been caught driving in the bus lane three times? Not Alice! That said, he's a better driver than map-reader. It's always the lesser of two evils with Guy.

Alice has a quick flick through the guidebook. Ideally she would like to drive to Pompeii – so educational for the children, seeing all those bodies fossilised in lava – but it's too far. They will just have to make do with the historically inferior ruins that lie approximately ninety minutes from the palazzo.

Apparently the site, excavated some thirty years ago, 'features the remains of a small town decimated and abandoned by a plague back in AD 820. The ruins include various dwellings, a bathhouse and a small but significant amphitheatre. In addition, many ancient artefacts can be seen in the museum conveniently situated next to the car park.' So that should be exciting.

Alice loves museums. You rarely encounter any riff-raff in a museum, and with any luck she'll be able to buy a souvenir, like a tea towel or some coasters. Alice is conducting a conversation in her head: 'Oh yes, these coasters, do you like them? We found them in Italy, such a lovely holiday.'

Was it really a lovely holiday? Of course it was. Obviously it hadn't all been plain sailing, what with the homosexuals next door and the food poisoning and Guy being so . . . distracted, and the daily stand-off over breakfast, and that bitch of a cleaning woman, and the boys bickering every second of every minute, but apart from that . . .

Alice heaves herself over into the passenger seat. Her fungal infection is very itchy, but at least it's not so hot today. In fact, if she's not very much mistaken, it looks like rain. She knew she should have brought the boys' cagoules. Impatience gallops through her veins. She'd got them out ready to pack but Guy had sneered at her. Guy always thinks he knows better, but he doesn't, he doesn't know anything, not half as much as she does. Guy doesn't know how much a pound of mince costs, what size his sons' feet are, the names of their teachers, the number for the doctor's surgery. What would he do without her?

I do everything, concludes Alice. I make sure that all the boring things get done. When Max comes home with his head crawling with lice, who is it that gets busy with the special shampoo, the nit comb and the newspaper? Me. Who is it that realises when Sam's got threadworms? Me. Who sews the nametapes in? Me. No wonder I'm so bloody exhausted.

Alice closes her eyes for a second and allows her mind to wander. She thinks about Penny on holiday in Weston-super-Mare with her mother. Poor Penny, old and ugly, single and childless, with only a half-blind diabetic for company. Before she can stop herself she drifts into memories of her own mother, or rather mothers. Both had let her down. The first gave her away and the second, once she'd got her, didn't really want her. To be rejected by two mothers! Alice is sure Oscar Wilde would have had something suitably pithy to say about that. What was it with those women, what was wrong with them? What is wrong with me?

Alice pictures herself as a child, quietly reading, trying to be good and still getting on her mother's nerves. Alice doesn't know why her adoptive mother had no children of her own. It was never discussed – all she ever said was that she had 'really wanted a boy'. Lately Alice has come to the conclusion that Avril Norris's total lack of maternal instinct might have affected her reproductive system – hormonally she wasn't cut out for it. She should never have been allowed to adopt, she would have been better off with a budgie.

It wasn't as if she'd been cruel, not really. It was just when she brushed Alice's hair and bound it into rubber band bunches, she always pulled them so tightly that Alice thought her scalp might split. And as for her adoptive father, the only lasting impression he ever made was a small grease stain on an antimacassar. Bullied into silence by her god-fearing mother, her father had moved through life as if permanently on tiptoe.

Alice's eyes smart at the memory. Some things don't bear thinking about. I've done well, considering, she reminds herself, and today is going to be perfect.

The back door opens and slams immediately. 'I hate him,' pipes her youngest. 'Bloody Max, I wish he would die.' An apple has rolled into the footwell. Alice picks it up. On one side it is perfect, shiny and red, but the other side is deeply bruised, soggy and brown.

Guy and Max climb into the car. 'Tell him to stop whining,' instructs Guy, turning the key in the ignition and putting the car into what he presumes is reverse.

It isn't. They are millimetres away from smashing into a stone wall when Guy finally stamps on the brake. Alice hasn't had time to put her seatbelt on and inevitably she smacks her head against the windscreen. Surprised and slightly disappointed not to see blood smeared across the glass like tomato purée, she ricochets dramatically back into her seat. Guy says precisely nothing.

Why can't he apologise? She could scream, she really could. Even if he does say sorry, he never really means it.

'Jesus, Guy, I could have been killed.'

Grim-faced, Guy silently puts the car into reverse properly, and with one hand on the steering wheel, drives Starsky and Hutch-style out of the palazzo.

'Right, right,' yells Alice, as the first dollops of rain splash on to the windscreen, heavy as mashed potato.

An hour later the rain is so torrential that Guy is driving as if he were in a car wash. At this rate they will reach their destination a week next Sunday.

Alice is feeling peevish. Not fair. This is her special day. The ruins have taken on a huge significance. Without seeing them this holiday will have been a complete and utter waste of time.

'What is the point in being in lovely Italy,' she seethes, 'if one can't soak up some of its lovely culture? I want broken stone, a bit of mosaic and fragments of cooking pot – is that too much to ask?'

'I'm scared,' whimpers Sam. 'What if we go off the edge?' The road has turned into a series of stomach-lurching hairpin bends: inches to the right of them lies oblivion.

Guy is clutching the steering wheel, his nose almost up against the windscreen. 'I can't see a fucking thing.'

'There's no need to swear, Guy.'

'Fuck off, Alice.'

Suddenly the headlights of a lorry coming in the opposite direction flood Guy's vision. There is a moment when he can't seem to decide which way to turn the wheel. A horn blares and he freezes. Is this what it was like for my father, the seconds before he died? Is this what he saw, white lights distorted by rain?

Only his sons' eyes in the rear-view mirror force him to take action. He pulls down hard on the wheel. The Corsa comes to a stop centimetres from the edge of the road. Guy opens the door and vomits on to sodden grass.

'It's all right, Guy, it's just shock,' insists Alice. But deep down Guy knows that he is hungover, that he shouldn't be driving, and that he is a danger to himself, his children and his future happiness with Peanut.

He spits yellow bile and wipes away the bitter flavour from his lips.

'We're going back, Alice. This is dangerous.'

Alice nods mutely and an hour later they are splashing their way back up the driveway of the palazzo. The return journey has been conducted in virtual silence. At one point Alice started singing 'Ten green bottles hanging on a wall' but no one joined in.

At least the rain has stopped and the sun is making a weedy attempt to push through the grey cloud. A faint stain of yellow seeps like ointment through a grubby bandage, but the pool is resolutely deserted and Lydia is sitting alone at the bar drinking something turquoise and reading the *Daily Mail*.

'Yoohoo, Lydia,' bellows Alice, and Lydia waves as feebly as if her wrist was badly fractured.

Back in the apartment, Alice produces her trump card. This morning she found a compendium of games in the library. The instructions might be in Italian, but Snakes and Ladders and Ludo are the same the world over.

'Let's play a game till lunchtime,' she suggests.

Guy groans inwardly. It's twelve o'clock – just ten more hours till bedtime.

Alice lays out a game of Snakes and Ladders. Sam will begin, as he is the youngest, then Max, then Alice. Guy goes last, he throws a six, which means he has another turn. This time he throws a four.

'Down the snake, Dad, down the snake.' Sam is repetitive in triumph.

The snake is green with red eyes and a red forked tongue. Guy pushes his blue counter down the S shape of its back. He says nothing, it's only a game, but the grey matter in his head insists on whispering, 'You can't win. You just can't win.'

'Oh dear, Guy, look, you're right back where you started,' says Alice.

Go on, hit her, you know you want to. Punch her hard in the mouth, the ugly fat cow.

38

Tales of the Unexpected

'Well, that was a bizarre morning, wasn't it, Freya?'

'Babies,' replies Freya. 'Bertie and Lettith.'

Freya pronounces 'Lettice' as in the salad, as had Gayle, until Helena had pointed out that 'the emphasis is actually on the second syllable', to which Gayle had merely responded, 'Oh, and what's her middle name – Radeeesh?'

For a moment, Nina thought Helena was going to be horribly insulted, but she'd thrown back her head like a well-groomed pony and 'haw-hawed', which was apparently 'posh' for laughing.

Sitting on that sofa while the rain slid out of the sky, the three women seemed to weave a conversation out of individually different-coloured wool. They had nothing in common and yet there were no silences, no awkwardnesses – random words threaded together, taking surprising twists, followed by revealing turns.

Women are like that, thinks Nina. We spill our guts, we're incapable of keeping anything but the most deadly of secrets.

She is slightly embarrassed about how much of herself she'd given away. How she'd found herself telling these strangers that she'd known Joe was married, that sometimes she felt he compared her to his first wife, and how hard it was to be a good mother, never mind stepmother. 'After all, I'm only twelve years older than Tabitha.'

In return, Helena had admitted that she didn't fuck her husband if she could possibly avoid it, that she was desperate to have the twins' squints repaired, and how she felt she was losing Sofia.

'We're not as close as I imagined we'd be. Funny, I always expected her to be blonde. I never thought she wouldn't look like me.'

Nina nearly said something at this point, but fortunately Gayle, not to be outdone, had launched into a step-by-step account of how she'd shagged Jonty the first time she met him.

'We never even got out the car park, girls – I had him up against the back wall!'

Gayle had followed this revelation with the fact that the one thing she didn't like about her new husband was his unhealthy obsession with giving her one up the arse, and that what she wanted more than anything was a baby of her own.

'Oh,' Helena had replied airily, 'anal sex isn't too bad. You've just got to relax and use plenty of KY jelly.'

This had been Gayle's cue to laugh. Nina had been too shocked. If Helena took it up the bum then maybe all those sugar-pink lipsticked women in navy loafers who hung around the electrical goods department of Peter Jones liked it up the Gary too?

'I've a young Australian lover,' Helena had smirked by means of explanation. 'My tennis coach. Of course, it won't last – he's twenty-eight and I'm forty-three with cellulite.'

'But do you love him?' asked Gayle, as if that would solve everything.

'Don't be silly. He might have an extraordinarily large willy but he can barely use a knife and fork. Anyway, I love Charles. I just don't like him much at the moment. He's been a miserable cunt for months.'

Gayle attempts to say 'cunt' with the same cut-glass accent as Helena, but still manages to sound like something out of *EastEnders*.

At that point the video finished and Nina, feeling the conversation was becoming something she might regret, used Freya's lunch as an excuse not to expose her emotional entrails any further. As she walked back to the apartment with her daughter burbling at her side, she realised she would never be able to watch *Dumbo* again without his waggly grey trunk reminding her of Helena's boyfriend's penis.

She and Joe haven't had sex since they arrived at the palazzo. Nina blushes at the realisation. It's not that she doesn't want to, it's just that having Tabitha and Saul around puts her off, her sexuality daunted by their presence.

As if to remind her poor old blunted libido of what it feels like to be sexy, Nina puts on the high-heeled stilettos that Joe bought for her and teeters round the kitchen mashing an avocado for Freya.

Immediately her groin feels more alert. I have to watch it, she warns herself. We're not even married and I've started wearing apple catchers rather than thongs. I mustn't let myself go. 'He's done it once, he can do it again.' Carmen and Shelley's stereo chorus of disapproval echoes in her head.

Nina hears a noise on the stone staircase. Looking out of the kitchen window she can see Joe with Saul and Tabitha. Watching him makes her nipples prickle. I want him, I want to fuck him. And as an afterthought: Jesus, these shoes really work.

'Sun's coming out,' bellows Saul, stripping off as he walks through the door. Tabitha follows him into their bedroom.

'We're going to put our swimming stuff on under our clothes, just in case,' she yells.

Joe sidles into the kitchen, and Nina, despite being too young to remember *Nine and a Half Weeks*, is seized by a sudden impulse to open the fridge. The door swings back and she bends over to retrieve something she didn't know she wanted – the milk will do.

Nina is wearing a denim skirt. It's very short, and she knows that if she doesn't relax her knees you can see her knickers. They aren't her best, but at least they're small, black and lacy. Come on, Joe! Had there been a convenient pole in the kitchen Nina would have unbuttoned her shirt and swung on it.

But Joe is distracted by Freya, wiping avocado off her face, kissing her head.

What about me, Joe? I need attention too. Remember me, the one you left your wife for?

Nina sways her hips and sighs and at last Joe looks over.

'That looks nice,' he says evenly, as if she were a particularly well-grilled steak with all the trimmings.

But she feels him approaching. His hand slides between her legs and cups the damp nylon strip of fabric. He circles his finger a couple of times over the hot wetness before suddenly pulling her knickers down. Shivering, Nina steps out of them. The Marks and Spencer label pokes out in defiance, as if to say, 'Excuse me, in the kitchen, with your daughter watching?'

He turns Freya's high chair to face the window and pushes Nina against the door, wedging it shut with their combined weight.

Both of them are breathing fast now. Joe kneels down and runs his tongue up the bare flesh of her legs, while his fingers dance around her clitoris. Nina spreads her legs trying not to moan out loud. Joe stands up behind her, his lips reaching for hers, his whole hand working her cunt into liquid. 'I am going to give you such a fucking,' he breathes into her ear, as if it had been his idea in the first place. His other hand is on her breast, squeezing her nipple. She wants him to bite it, she wants to come, the ache is like a delicious migraine. She can hardly bear it but she doesn't want it to stop.

'Oh, Joe.'

This is what it used to be like, when their fucking was desperate, when he always had to go, when she'd attempt to fuck his brains out so that one day he'd forget to leave, he'd forget to go home to Hils, he'd forget everything except her.

'Daddy.'

Freya is bored now. She's been sitting in the highchair long enough. She has mashed avocado up her nose and in her hair, and for good measure she has the upturned bowl on her head. She is confused. These are the things that normally work.

'Mummy, Daddy, wotchoo doin'?'

Nina tenses. Joe can feel the muscles of her vagina stiffen. Suddenly it's like poking his finger through a hole in a freshly plastered wall.

'Shit,' they both mutter, and Nina's vagina expels Joe's hand like a cork from a bottle.

'Later,' he leers, running his tongue lasciviously across her burning cheek.

Nina's knickers lie in a little heap on the floor. Absent-mindedly she uses them to wipe avocado off the lino. This is what motherhood is all about, but she feels better – from the ankles up anyway. The shoes are crippling.

Joe is grinning, his erection slowly but visibly subsiding. 'Let me take you for lunch, you saucy little minx.'

'Let me go and put some knickers on then,' she replies, unstrapping Freya and passing her to her father.

'I dare you not to.'

Nina laughs, and as she walks out of the kitchen she lifts her skirt and shakes her arse.

Freya thinks this is one of the funniest things she has ever seen. 'Mummy, botty, bum-bum.'

The yellow-and-white-striped bar and grill is quiet. The chalk on the board advertising today's specials has run, but the waiters wipe rain-spotted seats and offer hot chocolate on the house for the children.

The beach is deserted. A lone red flag flutters forlornly on a wooden pole while the sun struggles to dry the cement-coloured sand.

Joe orders a bottle of red wine and four lasagnes – comfort food, the Mediterranean equivalent of shepherd's pie. Nina puts a little on a saucer for Freya. This is turning out to be the best day so far.

Just as they finish eating, a voice says, 'Hi.'

Tabitha turns around. It's Sofia. 'Listen, you don't have to, but if you want, we could play Cluedo. It's in the games room and my mum just thought – it doesn't matter, though.'

Tabitha suddenly feels sorry for her. Sofia looks less threatening in a pale blue Gap fleece. 'What do you reckon, Saul?'

Saul's eyes narrow. On the one hand this girl is a monster, on the other hand he is a world-class Cluedo champ, a Cluedo black belt no less. 'Yeah,' he decides, 'let the Cluedo commence.'

'Oh, sorry, I nearly forgot,' adds Sofia, 'my mum says would Freya like to come to our apartment and play with the twins? It's Apartment Rosemary, the big one at the front.' Sofia doesn't mean to sound like she's showing off, she just does.

Nina isn't sure. 'What do you think, Joe?'

Joe thinks it's a great idea. He might get enough time alone with Nina to finish what they started an hour or so ago! He has an image of his girlfriend, naked apart from the shoes, spreadeagled on the bed. Obviously, because Joe is arty, this image is in black and white.

'Well,' he deliberates, 'as long as Tabitha and Saul go with her and make sure she's OK, I don't see why not.' Red wine is rolling through his veins, and his balls are as heavy as marble. 'Just for an hour or so.'

'I'll keep an eye on her,' promises Tabitha. 'The games room is near your apartment, isn't it?'

'Yeah,' nods Sofia, 'just down the corridor.'

Freya climbs down from the table and puts one sticky paw into Tabitha's hand and the other into Sofia's. 'My friendths,' she crows. 'Freya see fat babies.'

The four of them set off. Nina looks anxious. 'Don't worry,' says Joe, 'she's my daughter too. I wouldn't let her go if I thought anything might go wrong.' And, as if to prove a point, he orders coffee, a couple of brandies and a tiramisu. 'With two spoons,' he adds, winking at the waiter.

A sudden gust of wind sends an empty glass flying off the table, and the invalid sun disappears once more under her grey blanket. Nina picks up the bouncing glass from under the table. As she looks towards the steps of the palazzo she notices the children have already disappeared.

39

Scoring Points

Alice is keeping score. So far Sam has won three games of Snakes and Ladders and two of Ludo. She and Max have each won a game of Ludo, but poor Guy hasn't won anything at all.

'Looks like your luck has finally run out, Guy.'

Go on, punch her in the mouth.

Guy has never hit Alice, or any other woman for that matter. Peanut likes the occasional slap on the arse but it's consensual, she dresses up for it. Peanut and her flatmates have a timeshare on a rather heavily stained school uniform. It consists of a blue pleated skirt, white shirt, blue and grey striped tie, and a blazer with a portcullis embroidered on the breast pocket. When Peanut wears the uniform she customises it with a pair of white ankle socks, white knickers and a pristine bra.

Sometimes Guy feels slightly out of his depth with Peanut. The day she'd appeared in his office carrying a large plastic bag, he'd never have guessed what was inside. Had she been Alice he'd have reckoned on cheese and Branston pickle sandwiches.

'Close your eyes and count to a hundred,' she'd instructed, 'slowly,' and he had. 'One elephant, two elephants . . .' When he finally opened his eyes, she was standing in front of him wearing full fifth-form regalia. It had been a bit of a shock, what with the pigtails and one side of her cheek bulging dramatically – for a second he thought she might have an abscess on her tooth, but it turned out she was sucking a Chupa-Chup lollipop.

Alice doesn't approve of Chupa-Chups. She would never let the children have them when they were small in case the head of the lolly came away from the stick and they choked to death.

'I've been a very naughty girl, sir,' she'd said, or something like that. It was hard to make out the exact words (what with the lolly business going on), and she'd thrown herself over his knee to be spanked. If he were to be honest, it took him a little time to get into the swing of things. None the less, he'd ended up working very late in the office that night. For a second he wonders what Peanut would say if he suddenly turned up in full fifties schoolmaster garb, complete with mortar board and cane. She probably wouldn't flinch. Not until he pulled down her knickers and gave her six of the best.

'Dad, it's your go.'

Guy's penis is as stiff as a ruler. Oh, Peanut.

'Damn.' Alice doesn't normally swear but she's just realised she left a couple of towels hanging over the balcony to dry. Looking out on to the patio, it seems that one has gone missing – it must have blown over the side.

'Max, can you nip down and fetch it?'

Max is more than happy to escape. Board games, ha! More like bored games. Running down the steps, he transforms into a fugitive escaping a Cuban drugs cartel, a spy dodging enemy fire. Max is tempted to make machine-gun noises but it's all a bit stupid when you're twelve. He can see that the towel is caught up on the small rocky slope directly beneath the apartment. Can he reach it? A bullet whizzes past his ear, he ducks, but the next imaginary blast chips his shoulder. He staggers, clutching his wound.

'Hey, Max.' It's Saul. 'You all right?'

'Yo,' responds Max, slightly self-consciously. If his mother had heard she would have made some comment about him not being brought up in the back streets of Harlem.

'We're gonna play Cluedo,' yells Saul from the other side of the pool. 'In the games room.'

'Cool,' responds Max. 'I'll come down in a minute.' Grabbing the sodden towel he runs back to the apartment. 'MumcanIgoandplay Cluedowiththeothers?'

'Slow down, Max, what others?' demands Alice.

'Just Saul and his sister and that snobby girl.'

Alice is caught on the horns of a dilemma (she often is). On the one hand she really doesn't know these children. On the other, Cluedo is such good fun she wouldn't mind a game herself.

'Why don't we all go?' she suggests.

'Don't be mental, Alice,' sighs Guy. 'They're kids, they don't want us sticking our noses in. Go on, Max, have a good time.' He digs in his pocket. 'Here, you can treat them all to an ice cream.'

'Cheers, Dad.' Max is almost out of the door when Alice shouts, 'Wait, haven't you forgotten something?'

Max looks genuinely confused. Watch, hair gel, flies, what?

'Your brother. You didn't think I'd let you dash off without Sam?'

Yes, just for a second he had.

There was a boy in Max's primary school who was an only child. 'Poor thing,' Alice had said. 'Why don't you invite him for tea?' Max had, and Alice made a big spaghetti bolognese which the child had merely toyed with (probably never eaten anything that hadn't come out of a packet before).

The afternoon hadn't been particularly successful. According to Alice, the boy was 'socially rather autistic'. However, the following week a return invitation to Niles's house had duly been issued and Alice thought it polite that Max should accept.

Max will never forget seeing Niles's bedroom for the first time. It was on a par with seeing that Gayle woman's breasts the other day. He had everything: his own TV, PlayStation and DVD player. His Pokemon collection filled three large shoeboxes and he had a jelly-bean machine on his bedside table. When Niles fancied a snack he phoned his mother on his mobile and she brought up a tray of Coke and a tube of barbecue-flavoured Pringles. Tea consisted of chicken fajitas from Marks and Spencer followed by a choice of Häagen Dazs ice cream.

His mother was wrong – there was nothing 'poor' about Niles. Niles was the luckiest boy in the whole world, and Max would quite happily have swapped Sam just for the jelly-bean machine.

'They're not joined at the hip.' His father is speaking very quietly, and Max has a sudden fleeting image of a photograph he once saw in the *Guinness Book of Records*. It was a picture of two Chinese brothers who literally were joined at the hip. The fact that he and Sam aren't is something to be grateful for at least.

'Nonsense,' snaps Alice, who is secretly bored with Snakes and Ladders and would much rather lie on the bed reading.

Sam rolls his eyes. 'I don't want to go anyway. I hate those people, and I hate stupid Cluedo.'

But Alice is adamant, and her sons, once they've cleaned their teeth, been to the lavatory and brushed their hair, are allowed out.

'But I don't want you back any later than four.'

Alice and Guy are alone. It feels slightly embarrassing. What do they do when it's just the two of them?

'I'm tired.' Guy yawns theatrically. 'I think I might have a lie-down.'

Alice smiles in what she imagines might be a coquettish manner. 'Hmm, I might join you. I'll just clear the kitchen first.'

Guy lies on the double bed, fully dressed. At least at night, lying here next to Alice, he is too drunk to worry about what might be going on in her head. Anyway, with the boys next door and Max being such a light sleeper, sex is off the agenda.

Ah, but the boys are out and you are alone with your wife.

Guy's penis shrivels to the size of a small vole and nestles within his pubic hair as if hiding from a tractor.

Fortunately for Guy, Alice has found an ants' nest and spends half an hour boiling kettles and scalding them to death out on the patio. By the time she makes it into the bedroom he is genuinely asleep.

Alice views her husband dispassionately. He's not that good-looking, his mouth is hanging open and he looks gormless. 'He has never been as intelligent as me,' she concludes. Alice bends down to remove her Birkenstocks. They are covered in drowned ants. Very carefully she picks one off the strap of her left shoe and drops it into Guy's mouth. Then she lies on her side of the bed and reads. She's almost finished *Diary of a Divorcee* – just another chapter to go.

An hour later Guy wakes up to a dreadful groaning. For a moment he thinks Alice might be having a stroke, but it's only the wind. Suddenly he feels claustrophobic. 'I need to get some fresh air, Alice. I'm going to take a walk down to the beach.'

'I'll come with you.' Alice doesn't want to be home alone waiting for her sons to come back. It's three o'clock: she has an hour to waste before she's allowed to get hysterical. A nice bracing walk will be just the ticket.

Mr and Mrs Jamieson take the steps down to the beach on to gritty damp sand. It would be nice to walk hand in hand, thinks Alice, but Guy's hands are firmly rooted in his pockets. Alice swings her arms. She hasn't done as much swimming as she'd promised herself. She keeps meaning to get up early and take a dip before it gets too crowded, but what with the supermarket shop and the daily rinsing of the boys' smalls, she hasn't had the time.

A red flag is fluttering off a wooden pole, replacing the usual green one. It reminds Alice of the Labour Party and how thrilled she was when Tony Blair came to power. She'd had high hopes, she really had, but nothing seems to have changed. Max's secondary school is a disgrace, the druggies still deal on the corner of the road, and there is dog shit all over everywhere, including her hallway.

Suddenly Alice realises Guy has disappeared. He was here a second ago. Where the hell is he?

Guy is in the sea. The waves are big enough to surf on – not Australian-style maybe, but they would be pretty impressive for somewhere like Cornwall. He has waded too far out for her to call him back. She tries, but the wind takes her voice away and throws it back over her shoulder. Bloody idiot – doesn't he realise the red flag means danger, no swimming?

Alice hates it when people deliberately flaunt regulations. Rules, according to Alice, are not made to be broken, they are there to provide a safety net, like the age of consent (Alice would put it up to 22), seat belts and cycling helmets.

The beach at Santa Helena shelves very gradually. This is why it's so popular with families. You have to walk at least fifty yards before you're out of your depth. Guy is in up to his waist; his shoes, shorts and shirt lie Reggie Perrin-style a couple of feet away from where Alice is standing. Unless she's very much mistaken, he's gone in wearing just his underpants.

Alice rolls up her baggy linen trousers and steps into the sea. It's surprisingly warm. 'Guy,' she yells, 'come back.'

Suddenly she realises he is not alone. Dieter and Peter are out there too, up to their necks in white foam, further out than Guy. Typical, smarts Alice, forgetting her *Guardian*-reading politics for a second. Homosexuals are so selfish, wilfully insisting on living by their own moral code of conduct – no wonder AIDS spread like it did.

Furious now, Alice has waded in as far as her knees without realising. Suddenly a dragging sensation at her feet catches her off balance, and before she can redistribute her weight, she is sitting on her bottom and another wave is about to break over her head. Struggling to her feet, she manages to jump over it. It's like the wave machine at the Latchmere swimming pool, where she occasionally takes the boys. 'Hee heee ha.' Alice hears herself laughing; this is surprisingly good fun.

Dieter and Peter are waving. Another head pokes up behind Dieter: it's that common man, the one with the dreadful wife, Gayle. Oh Lord, she's there too, hanging off Jonty piggyback-style – well, she is until a massive wall of sea slams into her from behind and knocks them both flying.

This is dreadfully dangerous, thinks Alice. Tendrils of seaweed wrap themselves around her ankles and her clothes are completely waterlogged. Unbuttoning her denim shirt, she hurls it backwards on to the sand. It's a shame her bra is so ancient and grey.

'We must be mad!' yells a voice behind her. It's that Nina girl, stripped down to her underwear. Alice recognises the girl's matching bra and pants – she was wearing them in the ladies' toilets at Gatwick.

Nina is holding hands with the big blond bloke. Together they run past Alice, flying headfirst into the white foam. Even Sofia's father, the man who does nothing but read the *Financial Times*, is in the water somewhere – he must be, his Panama hat is spinning around in the surf.

40

In the Games Room with . . .

Up in the games room, Tabitha, Saul, Sofia and Max are on their third round of Cluedo. Sam isn't playing. 'I don't want to, leave me alone.'

So far Mrs Peacock and Professor Plum have been found guilty, in the dining-room with the lead piping and in the conservatory with the top hat. Some Monopoly pieces seem to have got mixed up with the contents of the Cluedo box.

They've been playing this latest game for half an hour now and it's getting boring. It's obvious that Miss Scarlet dunnit with the rope, they all know that, but where? Saul moves his foot. Stuck to the bottom of his trainer is the billiard-room card. 'Saul,' huffs Tabitha, 'you moron.' They've had enough sleuthing.

'What shall we do now?'

No one will remember whose idea it was, and it isn't important anyway, but someone says 'Hide and seek', and they all groan because it's a 'crap' idea, but they end up playing it all the same.

'We have to have some rules,' insists Tabitha. 'Sam is only little, he shouldn't be allowed to just wander off.'

Sam sulks on the sofa. Silly bitch girl – he knows this palazzo better than anyone else.

'Just this wing, not outside, just down to the courtyard and no further.'

Tabitha closes her eyes first. 'I'll count to a hundred.' While she counts she thinks of the boy with the cracked teeth. She'd seen him this morning, his hair wet from the rain. He'd been in the amusement arcade with his friends. She and Saul had hung around the door and he kept looking over. Tabitha hadn't known what to do. There were girls there, Italian girls in black eyeliner; one of them kept giving her filthy looks and whispering to her friend. Cracked Teeth was playing pinball, showing off, swearing in Italian, laughing too loudly.

'Coming, ready or not.'

Sam hasn't bothered to hide. He is still sitting on the sofa.

What's his bloody problem? thinks Tabitha.

Saul is behind the curtain and Max is in a broom cupboard halfway down the corridor. Together they discover Sofia, who's behind a chair in the library. Max jumps on her and tickles her. 'Stop it,' she says, but her face is pink. Max has accidentally touched her breasts.

Saul closes his eyes. It's his turn to seek and they scatter in different directions. Even Sam has decided to play. Sofia runs to her apartment – it's not really cheating.

Her mother is reading one of the twins' books to Freya. Freya looks bored. It's a baby book, just pictures of balls and cats. 'I think it's time this one went back to her mother,' says Helena. She is exhausted; the one thing she can say in the twins' favour is that at least they're not triplets. Bertie and Lettice are splayed out on the floor. 'They just dropped off,' explains Helena, looking as if she herself is on the point of collapse.

'I'll take her back to Tabitha,' promises Sofia, and Freya puts a little hand into Sofia's. 'Let's go and find your sister, shall we?' says Sofia. She means 'half-sister', but she's forgotten to put her bitch hat on today.

Only Sam is in the games room. 'Saul found me under the piano,' he explains, 'so it's my turn to seek when he finds everyone else.'

'Where's Tabitha?' asks Sofia. Sam nods towards the door. 'Behind the door,' he mouths.

'Tabitha,' says Sofia, addressing the door, 'Freya's here. My mum says can you take her back to your mum, I mean, her mum?' Tabitha doesn't reply. 'I know you're behind the door, Tab.' Freya is squatting on the Cluedo board, meddling with tiny instruments of death.

The game is not yet over, decides Sofia, darting out of the room and diving into a basket of laundry at the bottom of the stairs. Moments later, she hears Saul talking to Max: 'Right, we just need to find the girls and then I think we should all have that ice cream you were talking about.' Sofia sniggers in the basket as they pass her by.

Five minutes later they are back. Saul lifts the lid of the laundry basket. 'Found you,' he yells.

'Did I win?' demands Sofia.

'No,' says Saul, 'I still haven't found Tabitha.'

'She's in the games room behind the door.'

'There's no one in the games room,' corrects Max. 'We just looked.'

'Yes there is. Sam and Freya are in there.'

'They aren't.'

'Where are they then?'

'This is getting boring.' Saul is hungry. 'I bet they've gone for ice cream. Come on, I'm starving.'

'I've got some euros,' says Max, chinking the change in his pockets the way his father does. 'My treat.' And the three of them wander down the stairs, across the courtyard and through the gardens to the bar.

'Thanks, Max,' says Sofia, daintily licking a strawberry cornetto, and Max thinks, She's not that bad really. In fact, he wouldn't mind having another go at tickling her.

Saul has chosen a white chocolate Magnum. As they walk back across the courtyard, he hears someone calling 'Help!' It's Tabitha.

Tabitha has been hiding in one of the staff toilets and she is stuck. She's been turning the handle and turning the handle and it keeps turning but the door won't open. She is trying not to cry but she's starting to feel like she'll never get out. 'Help!' She bangs on the door and Saul trots over.

'Hold this,' he tells Max, passing him his Magnum. 'Stand back, Tab,' and Saul runs at the door with his shoulder like he's seen men do in the movies. He doesn't really expect it to work, but it's good when it does, because even Max, who is two years older, says, 'Well done, mate.'

Tabitha is really relieved and tries to hug him, which is a bit much. After all, a man's got to do what a man's got to do.

'I think we should do something else now,' says Tabitha, who is slightly embarrassed that she, the oldest of them all, managed to get stuck in a toilet.

'Yeah,' they agree, and as an afterthought someone mentions that they should tell Sam.

Sam is sitting in the games room with his eyes tightly shut.

'I thought I might try counting to a million,' he explains.

'Where's Freya?' asks Sofia casually, packing away the Cluedo paraphernalia.

'What do you mean, where's Freya?' demands Tabitha.

Saul is about to finish his Magnum. He looks up, and the last bite of ice cream falls away from the stick. There is a feeling in his stomach. It could be appendicitis but it could be something worse.

Somewhere Freya is hiding and everyone must seek.

41

Seeking Freya

They send Saul to tell Joe. 'Dad!' he screams. 'Dad!' And he runs into the sea in his trainers.

Joe knows. As soon as he sees his son's face he knows it's bad. He remembers seeing that face once before, in a window, sickly as the moon, a long time ago.

'We can't find her.'

Nina doesn't hear. She is still laughing, reaching for his hand, her underwear sodden, head back and laughing.

'It's Freya, we can't find Freya.' Saul's eyes are enormous and anxious. Joe tries to be calm, tries to fight back the panic, but the same sensation he felt when Hils told him Tabitha was in hospital courses round his body.

He looks at his watch. Four o'clock exactly.

'What do you mean, you can't find Freya?' Nina's voice is as urgent as a siren and she canters out of the sea and over the crumbling sand.

It is five o'clock now and everyone is searching. They have been through it over and over again. 'Where were you exactly, where was she last seen?'

'She can't have gone far, she's too small, she's only two, she will be frightened.'

Joe is frightened, Nina is hysterical. She runs in her bra and pants calling for her child. Her voice is ragged now, her face swollen from crying. She won't come near him – she searches alone, her bare feet bleeding. She blames herself. Joe tried to comfort her, tried to hold her, but she pulled away, her face twisted.

How long will this go on?

At first he expected to see her, his little wind-up doll with her clockwork walk. He'd even paused to pick up their clothes from the beach, put an arm around his son's shoulders.

'Calm down, Saul, she can't be far away. Tabitha has probably got her by now.'

But she hadn't. Tabitha was alone and ashen in the games room. 'I'm sorry,' she'd sobbed. All over the floor lay miniature daggers and tiny revolvers.

'Calm down,' Joe had said again, but now, sixty of the longest minutes of his life later, nothing is calm, and through the window he can see the red flag fluttering down on the beach. She couldn't have got down there, they would have seen her. What was she wearing? Pink shorts and a little floral shirt? She can't have got out, but what if someone got in? Nightmares are made of this. This is what people read about in newspapers, lost children with half-smiling 'you'll never find me' eyes staring from newsprint, someone else's tragedy, not mine, not mine.

Joe tries to be logical. The palazzo is on three floors, but there is no access to the top floor. It's private, and the steps of the stone staircase end abruptly at a massive wooden door which is heavily padlocked.

The games room, along with the apartments (apart from those in the annexe), is on the first floor, but at the end of the corridor are the steps leading down to the ground floor, and there is nothing to stop her from wandering into the gardens.

All the residents have been alerted. They are all looking, in wardrobes and under beds. Staff are running down corridors with pass keys. This is worse than bad weather. A little girl is missing. Did she climb on to a balcony and fall?

The grounds must be checked! The pool!

Oh Jesus, the pool, but already the bar staff have dived in, they have swum lengths backwards and forwards underwater with their eyes wide open. There is no child to be found in the pool. Momentary relief, consumed instantly by fear. Where is she?

'Yes, we are doing everything.' The manager of the palazzo is in his office issuing orders. 'Soon it will be a matter for the police.'

'When?'

'Now, I think now we must call the police.'

Joe is summoned to the office. He can't sit down, he can't keep still. He is telling a man in a blue uniform what his daughter is wearing; he is taking a photograph from his wallet, a little girl with dark copper hair in a yellow dress – today she is wearing pink.

Joe's chest is hurting. As he hands over the photograph of his youngest daughter, he realises that he has a pain deep inside that he has never felt before. So this is what it feels like, he realises, when your heart is breaking.

The policeman has children too. 'We will do everything we can,' he tells Joe.

Nina runs. She runs down stone steps and into laundry rooms, she checks inside the mouths of washing machines and tumble driers. She can hear a dreadful noise, a screaming, someone is screaming Freya's name, there is blood in the voice – her voice, she realises.

Somehow she seems to have been split in two. There is the screaming Nina, pulling at doors, and the other Nina who is calmly telling her: This is what you deserve. After all, it's your fault. You wanted everything, you took everything, and now it's time you were punished. You got greedy, my girl. You lied, you cheated and you stole, and this is how it feels to have the thing you love the best taken away from you. It's payback time, lady. Not nice, is it?

Her mouth is full of stolen sweets. Soon she will be sick.

This is the beginning of the end. The nightmare has begun. It started in the games room, questioning the children, trying to make sense of it: 'Who saw her last?' and someone said, 'Sam.'

'Sam.' Nina had grabbed the red-haired boy. 'You were the last one to see her.' On her knees, looking into his unblinking eyes, she had been reminded of something, a game she had played when she was small. The game was called Pick a Pair – Nina used to

266

play it with Aunty Lou, the lady who lived in the flat downstairs. Little square cards featuring pictures of everyday objects such as umbrellas and smiling cats were laid face down, and the aim of the game was to turn over the cards and eventually find the matching pairs. Why had she thought of this game now?

Because, just over three years ago, the morning after the night before, coming round in a stranger's bed, she had opened her eyes to find two small boys looking down at her. Brothers, obviously, in identical green V-necks. The younger of the two had bright red hair and his top teeth were missing; behind him an older boy with brown hair – how old, about nine or ten? The satin frame around them was studded with shimmering blue sequins.

Yelling into the boy's freckled face – 'You were the last one to see her. Where is she?' – it had suddenly struck her that she had found them, the matching pair. The boys in the photograph on that bedside table were here in this room. Sam's gummy six-year-old grin is cobbled now with crooked yellow teeth, but the give-away Dumbo ears are the same, the tips burning red as she yelled into his face: 'Just think!'

'That's enough,' his mother had said, pulling her child away. His brother stood nervously to one side, his dark grey eyes looking this way and that. Max and Sam, the boys in the photograph, the matching pair.

She ran then and she is still running. She is looking for her daughter but all she can see are pictures of the day that went on for ever, every last detail lying face up; there are no umbrellas or smiling cats, just her and what she did.

The photograph of the schoolboys sat in the midst of a heap of bedside-table clutter: a pot of Vick vapour rub, a broken silver chain, an empty glasses case. She can see herself sliding out of the bed, silent as a cat. The man was asleep, a gold ring glinting on his third finger left hand, the fingernails badly chewed. She'd picked up her clothes: jeans, knickers, T-shirt, boots. Where is her jacket? Creeping like a burglar, she'd found it on the stairs.

The house was untidy. Piles of books, a jumble of trainers by the front door. She'd tiptoed to the door but it was locked, the keyhole empty. Panicking silently, she'd darted through the house, pulling on her clothes, her mouth stale with whisky and sex. In the dirty lemon-coloured kitchen, a chimney breast was smothered in drawings of monsters and rainbows. Under one of the monsters, a child's hand had written 'Mummy' in crooked letters. The mother had green hair and a purple mouth.

Alice, of course. She had fucked Alice's husband.

His leather jacket was hanging over the back of a chair. The label pronounced it to be made by Kenzo, soft as kittens. She rooted in its silk-lined pockets and found a bunch of keys hanging from a heavy silver hoop. Turning to leave she'd noticed a plastic basket of dirty clothes perched on the draining board ready to be loaded into the washing machine. Little red Y-fronts sat on the top of a grubby grey bra. Next to the basket was a pile of loose change. She'd gathered up three pound coins and headed for the front door.

Thief, slut, thief.

Sorting through the keys she found a likely-looking Chubb and prodded it into the lock. It grated a little but turned full circle and she felt the door give. Quickly, she'd walked back into the kitchen and replaced the keys in his pocket. The fridge door was covered in magnetic letters: she hurriedly spelt out 'sorry' and left.

That was you, Nina. That is what you did. You have tried to forget it but it's true. A stranger inserted his penis into your vagina, Nina. These are the facts and nothing you can do will change that. It happened.

What did she do next? Another picture flips face-up into her memory and she recalls walking out on to an unfamiliar street, a dustbin lorry blocking the road, her nostrils filling with its maggoty stench. It was all she could do not to throw herself in with all the other rubbish.

She walked round the corner to a bus stop where people who hadn't spent the night before fucking strangers stood waiting for buses. Men in suits reading newspapers, school kids eating crisps, an old woman with a dog. She joined the queue. What else could she have done? When a number 45 trundled round the corner she'd almost laughed. Its destination was the Elephant and Castle – of course, she would go and see her mother.

Maxine was surprised to see her. She'd been working the late shift. Her beehive leant precariously to the left and she was still in her dressing gown. It was 8.30 am. Too early for questions. She ran her daughter a bath and while Nina lay in orange blossom bubbles rinsing her knickers, Maxine fell back into bed. A little while later, Nina slipped in next to her and wept into her mother's satin-wrapped bones. 'Hush now, hush.'

Nina cannot hush. Three years on she is wailing, dreadful animal noises that grow from her belly, like the noises she made when she was giving birth. Running blindly she careers into one of the cleaning women. The woman holds her; she can feel her soft belly and breasts, a mother's embrace, so different from her own mother's poky hardness. Maxine could never really cuddle. Nevertheless, 'I want my mum,' sobs Nina, and a cleaning woman whispers Italian words of comfort into her tangled hair.

Nina is in pieces. There are bits of her everywhere, but part of her is always stuck in that night. That night, and the events of the next day, events that will haunt her, it seems, for the rest of her life. She'd slept most of the day. Late in the afternoon, her mother had brought her some tinned chicken soup and a piece of charred toast.

'I've got to get ready for work, sweetheart.' And Maxine had sat at her kidney-shaped dressing table, doing her face.

The ritual was oddly comforting for Nina to watch. False eyelashes, electric curlers, black eyeliner, the smell of her mother's make-up bag, potent as a pharoah's tomb – her mother worked with her right hand and smoked with her left.

'Come with me to the club, Nina. It will do you good. There are dancing lady boys and karaoke. Gay men are an inspiration. You get knocked down, you get up again, never let it get you down. Simple.'

Nina dressed in the clothes that she suddenly despised and knew she would never wear again. 'I don't think so, Mum. I don't fancy it. I'm not in the mood.'

Like a zombie she had walked with her mother to the Elephant and Castle. Her skin smelt clean but she was ashamed to be inside it. Dull skies spat intermittently as they crossed the river on a 171, and the water below the bridge lapped thick and grey.

Maxine got off at the Strand. She patted Nina's knee and slipped her five pounds. 'Get home safely, chicken.' And somehow she had, although she might as well have been crossing roads with her eyes shut. 'You stupid bitch,' a driver had yelled, and she'd just shrugged meekly in agreement.

Shelley and Carmen were out – of course they were, it was a Thursday night, they went out every night apart from Sunday. Nina had wandered round the flat. Her birthday cards were still on parade along the mantelpiece and torn wrapping paper lay discarded on the floor. Carmen had bought her a Paul Frank T-shirt, and Shelley, 'Because you're knocking on now, Nina,' had presented her with some Elizabeth Arden eight-hour repair cream.

She did feel old, old and defeated. She should just go to bed, start again tomorrow. But she had slept all day, she needed to see Joe, needed to know if it was over. What if he had been calling her mobile all night? It wasn't his fault it had been stolen. 'Joe,' she howled at the wall. 'Oh, Joe.'

She knew where he lived. She had looked his road up on the A–Z countless times. It was only a twenty-minute bus ride away, near that park, the one with the funny name, Clissold Park, the one Joe called Clitoris Park. She could just knock on the door, pretend to be doing a survey, or looking for a lost cat, a black and white one, have you seen it?

She liked the cat idea more than the survey. The survey required a clipboard and a laminated badge, but all a lost cat needed was someone who looked a bit upset, and she reckoned she could pull that off. She looked like shit. Her roots needed doing and her face was so white it made her teeth look yellow.

Nina changed. Her new birthday T-shirt felt cool and unspoilt against her skin, and she zipped herself into a pair of Carmen's best Levi's. Throwing on a battered brown suede sheepskin for warmth, she headed for Stoke Newington.

You should have stayed at home, you made all this happen.

Joe's house lay in darkness. The only light visible shone through a crack in the wooden shutters downstairs. She couldn't see his car either and her nerve disintegrated. Hanging back in the shadows of a garage opposite, she shivered for half an hour before heading back to the main road. Her boots made clip-clopping noises along the pavement, but before she could make it back to the bus stop a car pulled up alongside and a foreign voice asked if she wanted business. Nina was genuinely shocked. 'No, thank you very much,' she replied, politely, as if refusing a third scone, and the car sped off, complete with baby seat strapped into the back.

Shaking now, she was furious with herself. You're fucking pathetic, Nina, but as she crossed the road a white Saab turned the corner and she stepped back on to the pavement.

'Joe!' she shouted, and he stopped. The passenger door swung open and she jumped in. She had undone his trousers before he had even parked.

He pushed his seat back and she climbed on top of him. 'I can't, Nina' – but he could, it was obvious. She had one leg out of Carmen's jeans before you could say who-said-you-could-borrow-those?, and with the sheepskin maintaining some (but not much) decorum, she fucked him. 'No, Nina, no.'

'Yes, Joe, yes.' She was winning, she could tell, his hips were rolling into hers and she stopped him speaking with her tongue. His body obeyed her commands, but she knew his mind was somewhere else.

Come back to me, Joe, come back.

But all he could say was, 'Oh, Nina,' followed by, 'Oh God, Oh Nina, Oh God, Oh Nina, Oh God, Oh Nina', as she rode him into a bucking climax.

He leant his head back, closing his eyes for a second. Nina, suddenly feeling her left hip cramping, lifted herself off his glistening penis and he opened his eyes at the sensation. 'We shouldn't have done that.'

Suddenly there was a sharp knocking on the rear window. Nina's first instinct was to giggle, but Joe didn't laugh; he was looking in the rear-view mirror and pushing her away. 'Get out,' he urged, 'it's Hils.' But she couldn't, she had one leg in and one leg out of the Levi's.

Then the shouting started.

You didn't think you'd get away with it for ever, did you, Nina? This is karma.

'Freya, Freya!' All around the palazzo people are calling her daughter's name, louder and louder. Nina joins in: 'Freya, Freya!' But it's no good, she can still hear Hils.

Underneath her own screaming, another woman is crying too.

42

Losers Weepers

Gayle and Jonty are looking. They've split up. 'Makes sense, darling. You take the main building, I'll do the outside bit. What's her name again?'

'Jesus, Jonty, it's Freya.'

'I'll find her, darlin'.'

Jonty really thinks he will. He's good at games like this. Sometimes him and his mates go paintballing – he always wins. No one can hide from Jonty Gaudi for long. Take that cunt Kev Borsley. He thought he could just disappear – bollocks to that. Jonty sniffed him out, gave him a good seeing-to.

Be nice to find this little baby. Gayle would like it. Course, what she really wants is one of her own.

Jonty's not too sure about that. He can't imagine Gayle all puffed up like a Space Hopper with varicose veins. Mind you, a little lad, another little Millwall supporter, a Jonty junior? Sweet. You can get them Nike trainers for babies these days. I'd be a good dad, thinks Jonty. I'd never let *my* kid out of my sight.

Gayle can't think where else to look. She doesn't want to bump into Nina again, it's frightening. She looks like she's gone a bit mental, running all over the place in her knickers, horrible noises coming out of her mouth.

It seems ages now since they'd first heard about Freya's

disappearance. The news had spread through the waves like an infection and everyone got out of the sea. Suddenly it didn't seem like fun any more. There was a foolishness about it, a bunch of grown-ups behaving like ten-year-olds.

It's a fine line, thinks Gayle, between everything being just lovely and everything turning to shit. It's like when you get your nails done and they're all shiny and perfect, and then you forget they're still wet, get your phone out of your bag and, bingo, they're smudged to bollocks.

That useless cow Lydia had been running round telling everyone to check their apartments. Well, she's not in the Gaudi suite, that's for sure. Gayle's even checked the blinking cutlery drawer.

Poor baby Freya, such a cute little kiddie, not even three. You read about such terrible things. There was that blond boy vanished off some Greek island years back, never seen again. Course, most kiddies get found. It's the waiting that must be doing Nina's head in.

She remembers her own mother the night her brother didn't come home, furious with him at first, banging pans in the kitchen, cauliflower gone to a soapy mush. 'I'll kill him.' Findus crispy pancakes they were having. What's the time, Mr Wolf? Five o'clock, six o'clock, then it was dark and they'd run out of fags. Kids didn't have mobiles in those days – wouldn't have done any good if he had. 'An accident,' they said. Two coppers at the front door, one of them a woman. They always send a woman if it's bad news. Soon as Gayle had seen her, WPC Karen Till, she'd sussed it. The second she'd answered the door, she just knew – they'd taken their hats off, it was obvious.

'Is Mrs Moran in?'

'Yeah, she's just inside.' As they'd stepped through into the hall, Gayle slipped out behind them, went to the corner shop, bought forty Bensons. She knew her mum would be needing them. By the time she got back, they'd told her. She could hear the wailing halfway up the street. Life can be a fucker.

Gayle wanders down the corridor, towards the apartments that overlook the sea. The toffs are down this end. The door of their apartment, Rosemary, is open. It's bigger than the Gaudis', all done out in pale green. I might get our sitting-room done green, thinks Gayle.

Helena is sitting on a sofa blowing her nose on one of the twins' muslins. She's obviously been crying. 'Have they found her?'

Gayle shakes her head.

'I feel so bloody guilty, it's all my fault.'

Gayle doesn't say anything. Where does blame start and finish? Whose fault was it that her brother got killed? Her stepdad's for buying him a bike that was too big, the kid who nicked his lights, the lorry driver for taking that particular route home, Michael's for not looking where the fuck he was going?

'I'll put the kettle on.'

Helena doesn't know what to do with herself. She feels so responsible. Why hadn't she taken the child back to her parents? Because the twins had passed out on the floor and she couldn't leave them – that's why she can't join the search party now. Someone has to keep an eye on Bertie and Lettice – what if they got lost too? Lost or stolen, whatever *has* happened to baby Freya?

Helena's eyes fill with tears. The twins may not be the most beautiful babies on the planet – they have squashed food gathered in the creases of their fat necks – but since getting to know them a little better on this holiday she has become awfully fond of them. They are so loyal, especially to each other. They may never set the world on fire, being neither ornamental nor particularly bright, but they are kind, comforting even. Seeing their mother weeping on the sofa, they had rushed to wrap their pudgy arms around her neck, covered her face in wet kisses, brought her toys to stop her crying, teddies, bottles and bibs. They had tried so hard to make her feel better that it had actually made her feel worse. They are nicer than she is, certainly.

Suddenly Helena decides she doesn't want the nanny back. If she is going to keep these babies safe, she is going to have to look after them herself. They may not like it, and no doubt at times it will be extremely tedious, but given that she isn't going to have any more, she might as well make the most of them.

Ryan will have to go, of course. She won't have time to look after the twins and give blow jobs to her lover. Something's got to give, and it will be a relief not to worry about him catching sight

275

of the dimples on the backs of her legs. It's been exhausting. Maybe, when the twins are in nursery, she could take up pottery instead.

Gayle brings her a cup of tea with milk in it. Helena only ever drinks tea black, but she doesn't say anything. This is her first step to becoming a nicer person. It tastes dreadful. Gayle has added two heaped spoonfuls of sugar, 'for the shock,' she says, and they sit on the sofa holding a baby each.

Meanwhile, Charles Hart Jones is searching the grounds. Being a fan of Sir Arthur Conan Doyle, he is meticulous in his methods. Starting at the gates of the palazzo, he works his way backwards, looking for clues. He scrutinises the flowerbeds for tiny imprints. Children can be remarkably quick on their feet. Once, a long time ago, he'd taken Sofia to the zoo. It was winter and they were looking at the seals. One moment he had her by the hand, the next he was holding an empty glove. As luck would have it, she hadn't gone far, but he can still remember the lurch in his stomach, the sudden realisation that she wasn't the only child with dark hair and a red anorak.

Which is worse, he ponders, losing your child or realising that your marriage is in shreds? He's known for weeks now about the affair. Helena has been careless – it's almost as if she wants him to know. The thought of divorce makes him feel weak. What is the point in it all? He's worked his backside off for over twenty years, and for what? For some Aussie bum to come along and take it all away? This afternoon, in the sea, he'd thought about drowning accidentally on purpose, only drowning isn't that easy when you can swim. Not that he is a particularly strong swimmer. He really thought the tide might do its bit, toss him far out into the ocean, smash his head against some rocky promontory – that with any luck once he'd lost consciousness the drowning bit would be easy, but it was useless. The only thing he'd lost was his hat.

And now I am about to lose my wife, my children and my house. She is the only woman I have ever loved, Charles admits silently, finding nothing but dog-ends (Sofia's, no doubt) in the gravel. 'So fight for her, you snivelling coward,' he responds, angrily and much louder than he expected.

This whole missing child thing has got to him. It's put his problems into perspective. So Helena is fornicating with her tennis coach? Well, she can just put a sock in it, and if she doesn't, then he'll drag her through the courts. He might even apply for custody – I will not lose my children. Real tragedy is unavoidable, reasons Charles, but Helena and I can get out of this mess if we try. We have a choice in the matter. And another thing, he decides, spying yet another bubblegum-pink-stained fag end, Sofia is not going back to that bloody boarding school. Twenty grand a year, and the only thing she seems to have learnt is how to inhale. From now on, things are going to be very different.

Charles feels better for the first time in months. Now, if he could just find this wretched child, they could all have a nice gin and tonic and get ready for supper. Where is she? He gets up from his crouching position and out of the corner of his eye sees the tail end of a lizard disappearing like green lightning into a minute crack in the stone wall.

Guy has been looking too. For a while he did his bit, taking on the area around the pool, the sunbathing terraces, the little thatched bar. To his disappointment there is no one on drinks duty. It's thirsty work, this sleuthing lark, but all the staff are off searching elsewhere, flapping round the palazzo like distracted penguins in their black trousers and white shirts.

Guy feels a bit guilty as he lifts the wooden counter flap and sidles around into the serving area. It might look as if he is trying to steal something. There is a crate of beer on the floor. He bends down as if trying to find Freya among the boxes of crisps and clean ashtrays, but in reality he finds himself reaching for a bottle of Bud. It isn't cold, but he opens it anyway and sits on his haunches, swigging.

The wind is still erratic, gusting fitfully, blowing debris into the pool. Suddenly the guts of the *Daily Mail* blow off a bar stool, over the counter, and more or less hit him in the face. Guy grabs the pages, ready to crumple them into the bin when something catches his eye. It's a picture of Tommy O'Reilly leaving the clinic and being greeted by his new girlfriend – a girl who looks remarkably like Peanut.

The print dances in front of Guy's eyes.

'23-year-old Dolores Pinner was waiting to meet the comic from his five-day stay at the clinic. In response to questions as to how long they had been together, Ms Pinner, who also goes by the name Peanut, blushed. Not so Tommy O'Reilly, who said they had been secret lovers for a number of weeks, but that now everything was out in the open he wanted to declare his love. With that, Mr O'Reilly got down on one knee and proposed to the edible Ms Pinner, slipping a Diet Coke ringpull on to the third finger of her left hand. The happy couple then left for an undisclosed location in a black Mercedes. A press statement released later said the comic was "sober but drunk on love".'

Guy howls, but shoves his fist in his mouth to muffle the noise. The last thing he wants is people crowding round, leaping to the conclusion that he has found the child in some ghastly state. Unable to silence himself, he runs down the steps to the beach. Everyone is shouting 'Freya'. Everyone except Guy. Guy is standing on the water's edge, screaming 'Peanut', tears streaming down his face.

Stumbling back up the stairs, he helps himself to another couple of Buds before taking refuge in the outbuilding where the ping-pong table is coated with a fine crust of white salt from the sea.

At some point the mother of the girl comes in. She starts when she sees him. 'Have you seen her?', and then, rather oddly, 'Do you care?'

He can only shake his head and shrug. 'I don't know you – of course I care, but she's not mine.' He's being honest. Isn't that what women want?

She spins and leaves. Guy finishes his third bottle of lager and alternates between punching himself in the face, chewing his finger-nails and crying.

43

Mother's Instinct

Alice has withdrawn from the search party. She would love to help – after all, her girl-guide training could come in handy – but her own child has been utterly traumatised by the whole event.

All that shouting and confusion in the games room – had it been strictly necessary? Of course Nina was upset, but then so was Sam. Poor little mite, it wasn't his fault. He was the youngest, apart from the little girl, of course, and there he was being given the third degree! Well, it just wasn't on.

If anyone was to blame it was the parents for letting the child wander off in the first place. One can't be too careful, not even in lovely Italy. At the end of the day the parents must take responsibility.

It's like school trips. Alice refuses to let her sons go unless she can sign up as a helper. It's a shame Max's secondary school doesn't seem to go on any excursions, but at least last term she'd had a lovely day out at Kew Gardens with St John's primary. All the other 'mum' helpers had sat at the front with the teachers, but she'd sat halfway down the coach with Sam. He hadn't wanted to sit next to anyone else – bless.

Sam is asleep now. She had to rock him like a baby. The child was trembling and yet rigid, his little fists clenched tight. She wouldn't be at all surprised if he wet the bed tonight.

Alice stands on the balcony. If the sun doesn't come out tomorrow, she's going to be left with a lot of damp things to pack. What a lot of drama for one holiday. She really must send those postcards. Dieter and Peter are scouring the wooded area behind the new annexe. She hears them calling Freya's name. Obviously the whole thing is utterly dreadful, but in some respects it's quite nice the way everyone has pulled together. It's that Dunkirk spirit – apart from Dieter and Peter, of course, who are 'on the other side'.

Alice sighs. Today seems to have gone on for ever. She'll be quite glad when it's bedtime. She has given Max permission to search until seven o'clock, as long as he doesn't go out of the grounds.

'We've already lost one child today, Max, I don't want you going missing too.' Ooh, you should have seen the look that Gayle woman had given her when she'd said that!

Deep down Alice has a gut feeling that the child will not be found within the walls of the palazzo. If she *is* on the estate, surely she would have been discovered by now. It's a dreadful thing to even think, but Alice fears the toddler must have been abducted. Delivery men come and go – who's to say the child hasn't been bundled into a laundry bag and thrown into the back of a van? There are weirdos and perverts everywhere, one can never be too careful. Please God she is found alive. Alice shivers with the drama of it all. But a small part of her can't wait to tell Di. 'Oh, Di, it was dreadful, quite dreadful.'

In the meantime, Alice is getting rather peckish. Obviously it would be disrespectful and callous to go out for a meal this evening, and what with all this fuss going on she can't imagine the palazzo serving supper tonight. Even if they do, no one will want to be seen guzzling in the restaurant when a child is probably lying stran- gled Lord knows where.

No, they will have a light meal here in the apartment, and maybe before bed they could each say a prayer for Freya, holding hands, as a family. That would be a nice thing to do.

She goes into the kitchen to see what she can throw together. There are eggs and some ham and tomatoes – if only Sam didn't loathe omelettes. She can hear him moaning from the bedroom.

Alice tiptoes over – where the hell is Guy? If he could put in an appearance, maybe she could run down to the shops and pick up some bread and a couple of tins of tuna. That's if the police haven't put incident tape up. That's what she'd do if she were in charge. She'd seal the place off. No one should be allowed in or out, not even the residents!

I'd happily go without a nice tuna niçoise if it would help, thinks Alice.

Sam has kicked off his covers. Alice creeps over to put them back on. He needs to be kept warm, her baby, warm and safe.

'I'd never let you wander off, sweetheart,' she whispers, bending over to kiss his cheek and noticing, as she does so, that Sam is holding something in his right hand. She pulls the blanket over him and he relaxes his grip. A small pink hairslide falls from his fingers.

Alice's heart races. She knows instinctively that it is Freya's, but she also knows that she must proceed with extreme caution. What is her son doing with the missing child's hairslide?

Alice crouches down. Gently she shakes Sam awake. 'Hello, poppet, look what I've found. It's that little girl's, isn't it?' She feels sick.

Sam shakes his head, but he is lying. Alice can always tell when someone is lying, always.

'It's all right, I can keep a secret.'

She certainly can. Alice has got lots of secrets. She stores them in her heart along with the half-truths, the silly excuses and the bare-faced lies.

'I just need to know where she is. Then I can give her back to her mummy and we can all have a nice tea.' Alice's stomach rumbles. Strange – even though she feels she might puke, she is still ravenous.

Sam has drawn his knees up to his chest and his eyes are squeezed tightly shut. 'It's Max's fault, and that fat boy and those horrible girls. They wouldn't play with me, they kept saying I was too young and that I didn't know any good games.'

'I know,' whispers Alice. 'Max is horrid, everyone is horrid, but the little girl isn't horrid, is she?'

Oh Jesus, what has he done with her?

281

Sam shakes his head again. Then he reaches under his pillow and pulls out a crumpled piece of paper. There are numbers on the paper: 2 1 3 3 9.

'We can do sums later, darling.'

'No!' he shouts. 'You need these numbers to find the baby.'

He *does* know where she is! Alice is very frightened, but deliberately keeps her voice low and calm. 'Whatever happens, Sam, this is between you and me, do you understand?'

He looks at her. His green eyes with the black pepper markings blink, just once.

'It's behind the cart thing, by the main steps, it's a lift. You have to press the button and after you count to twelve you get out and then there is this passage with a door like Dad's office and you have to do these numbers.'

She doesn't believe him. He's been reading too much Harry Potter. It's all nonsense – secret lifts and passageways – she could beat him, she really could.

'Listen, Sam, if you are telling me the truth, I can sort all this out, you won't even have to think about it ever again, we'll never mention it, but you must tell me the truth.'

He rolls his eyes this time. 'I just did, for fuck's sake.'

She slaps him hard across the cheek, grabs the hairslide, snatches up the paper with the numbers on it and leaves the apartment.

Sam rolls up under the covers like an armadillo. See, he can make up a good game. He invented the 'hiding the baby' game. It must be a good game because everyone in this stupid place is playing it.

Alice hurries, but in a nonchalant fashion. It's the same trot she assumes on Christmas Eve when she arrives at the supermarket and there is a danger they might be running low on organic turkeys. She doesn't want to appear desperate. The last thing she wants to do is attract attention. In the distance she can hear Dieter and Peter still searching for Freya: they are calling and whistling as if the child were a puppy – idiots.

If anyone asks her where she is going she'll tell them that she is taking the hire-car keys back to the office.

Please don't let me bump into Guy.

The courtyard is mercifully empty, although three of the cleaning staff are huddled in a gossiping knot at the entrance to one of the laundry rooms. The big one crosses herself and the other two shrug. As she passes the constantly dribbling copper fish, Alice veers to her left.

Why do I feel so guilty?

Because he's your son, and you were adopted. Bad blood runs through your veins. You have no idea where you are from. Who's your daddy, Alice? Drunkard, rapist, beggar man, thief?

Now I'm being ridiculous.

Alice puts her hand in her pocket and digs into her thigh with the sharp end of Freya's hairclip to remind herself not to be so silly. The cart is there, of course it is, it hasn't moved for a hundred years, Alice has trouble squeezing behind it. She feels foolish, as fat people always do when they are confronted by the physics of small spaces versus their own bulk.

Now what?

Alice can't believe she hasn't noticed it before. Tucked deep into the shadow of the wall and the stairwell is a small aluminium door, not much wider than a filing cabinet. To the right of it is a protruding silver disc. She presses the disc and after a couple of seconds she finds she can push the door open into an airless metal box.

Alice is terribly claustrophobic. What if she gets stuck? She steps in and the metal container gives a little under her feet. This is ghastly, but she forces herself to close the door, panicking for the couple of seconds it takes before the light flickers on.

There are only two buttons inside the lift. She pushes the top one and the box heaves itself upwards. Count to twelve, he'd said. She does, but at the same time she finds herself inexplicably reciting 'Our father, who art in heaven'. She's just got to the 'trespassers' bit when the lift lurches to a standstill. Alice pushes the door and it swings open.

For a moment it feels like she is back in the church where they'd stumbled on the child's funeral. God, that had been another appalling day!

The corridor is wood-panelled and wide enough to withstand

oversized ornate furniture. A set of baronial chairs with tapestry seats flank a sideboard, set up altar-style with candles and silverware. Above the panelling the plaster has been frescoed with images of celestial clouds and trumpeting angels. Religion seems to be everywhere. Hanging above the sideboard is a picture of a crucified Jesus. Blood-red paint trickles down his skinny white legs and his crown of thorns seems to penetrate Alice's own skull. She could do with a couple of paracetamol.

Thunder grumbles in the distance and she wouldn't be at all surprised if a lightning bolt struck her in the back of the neck. The air is bristling with electricity. Alice walks towards a heavy oak door at the far end of the corridor. There is something almost Scooby Doo-ish about the whole situation. Funny, really, Alice has always felt like Velma.

A steel panel of numbers is set into the wall to the left-hand side of the door. Checking the ball of paper in her pocket, she presses the corresponding digits firmly and carefully. The ruddy thing could be alarmed and that's all she needs; 2 1 3 3 9 and push.

The door creaks open and she's in. Alice holds her breath and slips off her Birkenstocks, carefully wedging them between the door and the frame. What if she got trapped – would they send out a search party for her? Squinting against the fading light, she ventures into one of the most beautiful rooms she has ever seen, and that includes that place up north where they filmed *Brideshead Revisited*.

Of course! It's the prince's apartment. It's mentioned in the guidebook. Well, no wonder he keeps it private. It's really rather splendid. Alice immediately adopts the pose she always does when visiting houses of historical interest – slightly quizzical but at the same time appreciative. The coloured glass in the display cabinet is rather vulgar. As for the butterflies, their wings tightly stretched and pinned, surely it's cruel, but then again, she reasons, they're probably Victorian, when that sort of thing was all the rage.

Stepping further into the room, the polished marble cool and smooth beneath her toes, she scans the doleful faces of the mounted elk, reflected into a huge multi-antlered herd by umpteen mirrors, before suddenly remembering what she is looking for: the child.

As her eyes become accustomed to the gloom, she sees her, lying on a moss-green velvet chaise longue, curled up next to an amber-eyed fox, stuffed obviously, but none-the-less startlingly lifelike.

Alice snorts. After all this fuss, finding Freya without duct tape over her mouth and with her hands not tightly bound is a bit of an anticlimax. The only mark on the child seems to be a small chocolate stain on her floral shirt.

Alice sits down on a leather armchair. Resting on a small round table at her elbow is a wooden tray inlaid with mother of pearl. The tray contains a glittering cut-glass decanter and six small emerald-coloured crystal glasses. She pours herself a measure of sticky red liquid, thick as medicine. Port, she guesses, filling one of the glasses right to the brim and staring at the sleeping child.

She is about the same age as her daughter would have been. Three next birthday. The celebration would have been sometime in mid-September, a little running, jumping, candle-blowing Virgoan. Alice takes a sip from the glass and a trickle of port spills on to her trousers, dark as menstruation. Guy never wanted a third, it was an accident, just one of Mother Nature's practical jokes. That's what she'd ended up telling Di anyway: that at thirty-six she'd found herself pregnant for the third time and that she'd suffered a miscarriage. It was a lie.

'I had an abortion,' says Alice, surprised to hear that she is talking out loud. 'I had an abortion because Guy made me, because he didn't want a baby that had something wrong with it, because he couldn't love a child that looked weird and that people would stare at. So I had an abortion, and when I came out of the hospital I found a condom wrapper under my bed and a long bleached-blonde hair, all black at the root. Not mine, Freya.

'And all this time I've kept my mouth shut because I believe in family life and two parents being better than one. Especially when one has sons. I've read the books, seen the documentaries. I know that it's important for boys to have a male role model, even if he is crap. These are the things I used to believe, Freya, because these things were important to me. I believed in keeping my promises, for better, for worse, for richer, for poorer, in sickness and in health, and you know what? I'm not certain I have done the right thing. There comes a time when you can't forgive someone just because you love him. It's not a good enough excuse, and once you stop forgiving him then the poison really takes hold and you start resenting him, and eventually resentment turns into despising, sour as vinegar, and one day you look at your husband and you realise he is an idiot. Your stupid, lying husband, with his ridiculous clothes and his daft goatee and his soppy girlfriend.

'And the funniest thing is, he hasn't got a clue. He looks at me as if I were a diseased fish in badly fitting dentures, and he thinks he is too good for me and that I know nothing. So who's the fool, Freya, him or me?

'Oh, but I did want a baby girl very badly indeed, a girl to buy a doll's house for, and she would have been a girl, because they told me.'

Freya stirs.

'It's all right, sweetie. Mummy's here.'

Alice goes to pick the child up. She looks slightly furious for a second, but she puts her thumb in her mouth and allows Alice to scoop her into her arms. Her little body smells of soap and milk. She barely weighs a thing, thinks Alice, clutching her tightly, breathing her in, wiping wet eyes against sprigs of pink cotton flowers.

'You're squashing me.'

'Sorry.'

Alice comes to her senses. Right, Birkenstocks, door, lift, then what, what will she say, how does she play this?

Instinct, she decides. Mother's instinct.

44

The Last Piece of the Puzzle

Nina leaves bloody footprints all over the palazzo. If they were trying to track *her* down it would be easy. The red splodges resemble a child's potato print, weaving their way backwards and forwards, in and out, round and round in circles.

He doesn't know – that's one thing at least. He'd looked at her with completely dead eyes; he didn't remember her. Course, she'd been blonde back then, she has changed, and so has he, he was clean-shaven when, when . . .

The drunken fuck is still her nasty little secret, the maggot that wriggles in her heart, the decaying albatross that hangs for ever around her neck, its carcass stinking of whisky and sweat. She hasn't touched whisky ever since that night, not since she fucked Guy . . .

His name is Guy, she remembers now, he told her down the alley. Just some Guy and he could be Freya's father. There, she has said it! After all, where else had Freya's red hair come from?

She corrects herself. It's not red, it has some auburn in it, a hint of a tint, a touch of chestnut. That Sam's hair is red like a fox – it doesn't mean anything. The other boy, the older one, has normal hair, brown as mud.

The doubt had grown like a tumour over the years. There had been a time when she first realised she was pregnant when she hadn't even considered that the baby might not be Joe's. It was only after he told Hils, when the full weight of what she had done suddenly hit her, that the suspicion had formed like a shadow on her brain. She is convinced that if she ever needed her head X-raying they would find it, a dark mass of confusion and guilt.

What if?

What if you made a man leave his family for a child that might not be his? Think about it. She has, God knows how many times.

Before the baby was born she'd managed to ignore the doubt. Her protective hormones had pushed it to one side as she prepared herself with womb-relaxing herbal teas and stretch-mark-busting coconut-butter belly rubs. The evidence would speak for itself, a little Nina or a little Joe.

But the truth of it was, when the child had finally been pulled, bent and blue like a folded bat, from that hellish cavity between her legs, Nina really didn't recognise her. 'A girl,' they said, 'you have a beautiful baby girl.'

Ha! A creature from the deep more like, a changeling. Where are my eyes, where is Joe's nose? What are these dark red wisps of hair doing on this baby's head?

The haemorrhage after giving birth had been ghastly, but in some respects a relief. It had meant that for another couple of days she didn't have to face the six-and-a-half-pound alien. When she was better, the baby seemed to have altered. She was at least bathed, pink and human, and although still a stranger, she was a stranger that Nina found herself falling in love with.

And now the love is so strong it feels like an avalanche on top of her heart. She can barely breathe. Winded, she stands still for a second. Where am I, what is happening?

You have lost your child, like a shoe or a bracelet. You are standing in the middle of a path that leads from the pool to the main courtyard. It is getting dark; soon they will be searching with torches. The thought is unbearable: her child will be cold.

'Nina.'

Her name reverberates around her. It bounces off bark and stone. 'Nina.'

It's Joe, Joe is calling you, run to Joe. She can't move, there is something in her mouth, a bitter thing that tastes of rancid shrimp.

She turns to where the voice is coming from and she can see him, on his knees by the fountain, all shadow now, the shape of Joe and something in his arms.

'I've got her.'

She is blind, and she is running. The tears feel like her eyes are bleeding. Her feet feel nothing. She is on top of the shadow and it turns to colour. There is pink, there are copper curls, there are two legs, there is Freya: her face, her ears, her neck, hands, all of her is here, breathing and warm.

The shape of Joe and Freya expands to let Nina in. She clings to them both. 'Alice found her, Nina.' A pair of Birkenstocks hovers by the fountain, a policeman blows a whistle, the search is over and the walls of the palazzo seem to heave a sigh of relief.

'I just had an inkling,' says Alice. The hairslide is still in her pocket, the courtyard is in commotion. Tabitha has flown at her, wrapping her skinny arms around her waist, while her chubby brother heaves sobs of relief by the fountain. Happy endings are so rare these days. Everyone is crowding around her – she feels like a child playing that party game, 'we all pat the dog'.

I am the most popular person here, I am the hero, I found the needle in the haystack, I am a good person – so why do I feel utterly shit?

Alice detaches herself from the heaving mass of gratitude and slips away, back to the modern annexe. Normality has been resumed as if at the flick of a switch. The bulbs around the pool are shining and music is playing from a cheap sound system behind the bar. 'Oops upside your head.' She should have given the slide back but it is too late now. She will keep it. Sometimes it's good to be reminded of things you'd rather forget.

Sam is still in the bedroom. He barely looks up from his Game Boy as she enters the room, and there are biscuit crumbs all over the bedclothes.

'I found her,' she tells him. 'She's back with her parents. Sam, look at me.' Alice sits heavily on the bed. Her son stares at her shoulder as if counting the stitches on the collar of her denim shirt.

289

'You must never do anything like that ever again. It could end up being even more serious. They called the police. Sam, why did you do it?'

He shrugs, what can he say? That hiding things is funny because people go crazy searching for the lost thing, and only you know where it is and that is a good feeling, like knowing the answer to a really hard sum.

'You won't ever do it again, will you, Sam?'

He buries his head in her lap, shaking it. 'Are you going to tell Dad?'

'No.'

'Do you promise?'

'Yes, I promise' – and another secret falls into the boggy mass of things never to be mentioned that lies rotting at the bottom of her heart.

Sam really wants to go back to playing with his GameBoy. He's on level five of The Legend of Zelda. But he stays still. He's not stupid – he knows that being like this, with his head like a turnip in the basket of his mother's lap, is all part of pretending to be sorry. It's boring, but it has to be done. His mother strokes his hair. She always does. Sam stifles a yawn.

There is a knock on the door. Alice slides herself gently away from Sam and opens it. Lydia stands on the threshold with a bottle of champagne. 'Courtesy of the palazzo management,' she smiles breezily. 'Just a token thank you for finding the baby. We're hosting a barbecue down by the pool in an hour, a sort of celebration thingy. It's free,' she adds.

Guy and Max have appeared behind her. Guy takes the champagne out of Lydia's hands. He looks dreadful, as if he's coming down with the flu.

'I hope you can make it,' says Lydia, backing away. This family are just too weird.

Alice closes the door. Max is buzzing with the events of the afternoon, using the drama as an excuse to use 'language'. 'Jesus, Mum, like, fucking hell, well done.'

Guy has opened the champagne and is guzzling from the bottle, like an alcoholic toddler. Alice is suddenly too tired to say anything, so for want of anything better to do, she pretends to faint.

While Alice stages her clumsy slide to the floor, Nina and Joe stand over Freya, watching her as if she were made of meringue. Oblivious to their concern, Freya squats on the floor, alternating between chatting to Rabbit and shoving breadsticks into her face.

The local doctor, summoned from the village, has pronounced the child unscathed. He seemed more concerned by Nina's torn and filthy feet, which are now bathed and bandaged and feeling like they have been minced.

Tabitha and Saul are showering. Saul is singing tunelessly, 'I believe I can fly.'

'She's so like Susannah,' says Joe.

Nina wants to go to the toilet. It's as if for all the time Freya was missing, her normal bodily functions just stopped, but now she needs to wee. Both bathrooms are occupied, so she sits on the bed, her legs tightly crossed and her feet stinging madly.

'Susannah who?'

'My sister Susannah.'

Joe is dressing Freya in her Winnie the Pooh pyjamas. Freya lifts her arms, surrendering to the fact that it's time to get ready for bed. Normally she would fight and run and hide, but it's been a long day for a two-and-a-half-year-old girl.

'Hold on, Joe, you haven't got a sister.'

Joe looks round. 'I know, I never knew her. She died before I was born, back in the fifties. I've only ever seen one black-and-white photo of her; she was only two.'

'How?'

'I think it was meningitis; my mother never talked about it, they didn't in those days. It was a long time ago, Nina. You coped differently back then. All I know is that her name was Susannah Louise and she had red hair.'

Nina's feet stop stinging. 'Red hair,' she breathes, 'how odd.'

'Not really. Apparently I had a grannie who, when she was very young, had a long red plait that reached down to her backside. When she cut it off, she put it in one of those reel to reel canisters you keep cine film in. It's somewhere in the attic at Englestone Avenue.'

'Can I have it?' asks Nina.

Joe laughs, and Nina realises that there has never been any question in his mind as to who Freya's father is.

Tabitha steps into the bedroom wrapped in a towel. Nina hobbles into the bathroom and locks the door. No wonder Joe's parents are so weird with Freya. It must be dreadful looking at a child who, by all accounts, is the spitting image of the daughter you lost.

Nina sits on the toilet. She wees long and hard while her mind whirrs and her feet gently bleed. Thank Christ she went round to Joe's that night, thank Christ she fucked him. Otherwise there wouldn't have been Freya, she is convinced of that now. They'd always used condoms before, of course they had, and why hadn't they this time? Because she didn't have one in her bag! Why not? Because she'd used it the night before, of course she did. In some respects Guy did her a favour – he wore the last condom in the pack.

I have punished myself enough, she decides. There are things I should never have done, but at least I've got a chance to make up for them. Guilt can drive you mad, she realises. She looks at her massively swollen feet – shame she won't be able to squeeze into her 'fuck me' shoes. Maybe it's time Freya had a little brother or sister.

292

45

A New Chapter
(To be continued . . .)

Hils sits on the back step with a cup of coffee. Usually she'd have a fag, but it's one of those days when even the most hardened smoker thinks about giving up. It is, she concedes, a perfect English summer evening, full of fat bees and cream roses.

'I'll be round at eight,' he'd said. It's almost quarter to.

Everything has been a blur since last night's dinner at the Thorpes'. Hils grins, salivating at the memory. Not that she can remember what they'd actually eaten. For once Sally's culinary expertise had been entirely wasted. She's sure the pheasant (or was it pork?) had been delicious, but as far as Hils is concerned she might as well have been eating J-cloths. All she can remember is the grazing of her knee against Stan's under the table, the accidental brushing of hands as he passed her the pepper grinder, the sly grins and prolonged eye contact.

'So you're an architect?'

'And you're an author.'

'Guess what, Hils?' Sally had interrupted. 'Stan's divorced too, so you've got lots in common. Potatoes anyone?'

In a break between the pudding (Sachertorte perhaps?) and the cheese (whatever), as Stan had sketched beautiful architectural line drawings for the Thorpes' loft conversion, he'd asked for her number. Resisting the temptation to pull her T-shirt over her head and run around screaming 'Yeeeess', like Saul did whenever he scored a goal, Hils scribbled it on the palm of his hand.

Meanwhile, in the background, Nick pulverised coffee beans and talked about his shelving needs, seemingly oblivious to the maelstrom of sexual tension emanating from the table, and Sally smirked like a cross between a triumphant fairy godmother and Cilla Black on *Blind Date*.

At the end of the evening they'd shared a cab, and even though his flat in Clerkenwell was closer to the Thorpes', he'd insisted on seeing her home first. We held hands, gloats Hils, and molten butterflies flit once more around her solar plexus.

'I'll call you tomorrow,' he'd said. As she got out of the cab her leg got caught up in the strap of her handbag and she'd had to hop inelegantly to the gate. He'd waited to see that she got in safely. She nearly asked if he wanted to come in for coffee, but the words coagulated in her throat, too cheesy to say out loud, so she just waved.

He'd phoned this morning, just as her cab had arrived.

'I figured you'd be leaving for the BBC soon,' he explained, and Hils swooned at the idea of him knowing what time *Woman's Hour* was on. Unless, of course – 'You're not gay, are you?'

'No, though I do like shopping.'

An urgent toot had reminded her that she had to leave. 'I have to go,' she told him, 'national radio awaits,' but he kept her on the line long enough to arrange to meet later. 'I'll come round at eight. Good luck. I'll be listening.'

'Oh God, don't do that,' she'd said. 'It'll make me nervous and I'll dribble.'

But she hadn't, not much anyway. Only at the end, when Jenni Murray asked if she could ever imagine being in a serious relationship again, did she splutter into her BBC coffee like a character in a seventies sitcom.

As soon as she got home, she'd checked her answerphone service and spent the next ten minutes replaying Stan's 'Well done, you were great. See you later. By the way, I'm really not gay' message.

All afternoon, she'd fluttered about, pulling things out of her wardrobe and trying to find a decent pair of knickers. She took a long bath, endlessly topping up the hot water with her toes, just like Tabitha.

'Oh God,' she remembered, 'my children' – and sinews deep in her chest tugged at their moorings. For a moment her heart felt like a small boat in a rough sea. Are they all right, are they safe?

She'd looked at her watch. It was four o'clock.

Pulling the plug, she'd Ajaxed the bath vigorously, horrified by her own tidemark and spent the next hour or so grooming herself, checking for whiskers and cleaning out her ears with cottonbuds. Then she'd run round the house hiding things that might make her look desperate and lonely, disguising piles of chicklit under Booker-nominated novels. She even changed the sheets, just in case, not because they might, but because, well . . . they were disgusting. She found a macaroon at the foot of the bed and the pillowcases were covered in jam.

At six her mother had phoned and chirruped about how they'd all listened to her on *Woman's Hour* as they drove back from the Lake District, and how wonderful Jenni Murray was.

'What about me?' demanded Hils.

'Oh you were super, dear. I read your book, by the way. I thought it was very good. Morag loved it too, though she thought it could have done with a happier ending. Now I must get off the phone, we've just got back and I'm giving Basil his tea. It's the least I can do after that long drive.'

I've got a new boyfriend too, Hils had been tempted to blurt, but she didn't, just in case she jinxed herself. Bloody Basil – he better not be sitting in her father's chair.

For a while she'd dithered over her CD collection. Maybe she should pretend to like classical music, like a proper adult, but in the end she'd opted for some background EmmyLou Harris and cleaned out the fridge in case he thought she was unhygienic.

Ten minutes to go. Hils's mouth is furred with coffee and the cigarette she wasn't going to smoke. Swiftly she runs up the stairs, cleans her teeth, sprays toothpaste all down her little black dress and, with seconds to go, throws on an ancient pair of Levi's and a floral Paul Smith shirt that Sally's bosoms had proved too big for.

It was only as she was opening the door that she realised she'd buttoned the shirt up wrongly.

'Hello.'

He is wearing a grey T-shirt and black linen trousers with just the right amount of crumple in them. Behind him, parked at the gate, is a cream 1960s Jaguar with a red leather interior that Joe would have killed for.

'I like your car.'

'I like your house.'

I like you, she nearly said, but she managed to swallow the words before they fell out of her mouth.

'Come in.' And he follows her down the honey-coloured hallway through to the kitchen. 'Beer?' she offers, proudly swinging wide the door of her freshly swabbed fridge.

'Thanks.'

And they stand grinning at each other. If I was a cartoon, thinks Hils, my tongue would fall out of my mouth and throbbing hearts would orbit my head.

'I wasn't sure what you wanted to do so I bought a copy of *Time Out*.'

Together they flick through the listings. Standing side by side, Hils breathes in a scent of fresh limes and notices that his ears lie flat against his head. They look pristine. Maybe he's been busy with a cottonbud too?

'We could go to the cinema?'

But there is nothing on that either of them fancy, and anyway it's too hot for the cinema. He isn't wearing socks. His ankles are smooth and biteable.

'Dinner then?'

Oh yes, food, that's what normal people do on dates, they eat food. Stop staring at his ankles, Hils.

They are sitting in the garden now, with cold Budweisers. It is nice not doing anything.

'We don't have to eat out. I can cook,' lies Hils.

Together they drive the Jag to the supermarket and buy salmon steaks, salad and wine.

On the way home, curiosity gets the better of Hils and she

presses Play on Stan's CD player. God, what if he likes Daniel Bedingfield?

David Bowie's 'Jean Genie' blares out – it's one of her favourites. Fortunately, just in the nick of time she remembers her solemn promise to her children never to sing out loud in public.

Back in the kitchen Stan takes over the food preparation while Hils sets the table outside. She fills a green jug with sweet peas and honeysuckle and claps like a six-year-old when Stan conjures up home-made mayonnaise.

'It's easy,' he grins, dipping a finger into the creamy mix and offering it to Hils to lick.

Leaning forward, she wonders if he has noticed that her nipples have gone mad.

Hils is what her mother would call 'all of a doodah'. For God's sake, calm down, don't laugh too much, don't say anything stupid, be cool, she reminds herself. But she can't. She tells him her tortoise joke, laughs till she farts (only a tiny one, just a squeak really), and they talk until it's dark enough to light candles.

Hils opens another bottle of wine.

'I'll get a cab home,' he offers, but both of them know that he won't.

Two hours later, Hils staggers downstairs to lock the kitchen door.

He's in my bed, my caramel-coloured boy, his T-shirt and trousers lie in a heap on the floor. She is glad he didn't fold them. She is glad about everything. There is nothing I regret, she reminds herself.

I am a grown-up woman and he is a man. We both have pasts. His involves an ex-wife and an eight-year-old daughter who live in New York; mine involves an ex-husband and two children who have a stepmother and a half-sister. We all just have to get on with it.

The phrase reminds her of her mother again. We have both lived without men for long enough, realises Hils, and if Basil makes Brenda happy then that's got to be good enough for me. She is sixty-eight years old; we all deserve a second chance.

Stan appears in the doorway of the kitchen. He is wearing Hils's ancient dressing gown, a frayed black satin kimono covered in orange chrysanthemums.

'Sorry. I've just realised I must look a bit Bangkok lady boy.'

Hils laughs. She has no idea how this is going to end, but as beginnings go, it's good, like the first chapter of a really interesting book.

She glances around her kitchen. Her children's faces grin back: a four-year-old Saul with a huge sticking plaster on his forehead, an eight-year-old Tabitha wobbling on ice-skates. They will be home in a couple of days. Her great big babies are coming home.

Stan's eyes follow hers. I do understand, you know. Let's just see how it goes. Let's just give ourselves a chance.

She moves towards him and he wraps her in the gown.

'Come on, gorgeous, back to bed.'

Moments later, as they roll around the mattress, Hils is seized by a sudden, unwanted but fortunately fleeting image of her mother and Basil doing something vaguely similar under her mother's flowery duvet.

46

Making Whoopee

By 10 pm Guy is very, very drunk. He is lurching and slurring and repeating himself. Earlier in the evening he seemed to be regurgitating part of a stand-up routine, something about a kettle and a helicopter, in a really bad Irish accent.

Alice can't keep her eye on him all the time. She only popped down to be polite. After all, in whose honour is this party being held? Her good self, of course, Alice Jamieson, Saviour of Lost Babies. She only intended to show her face for a couple of minutes, but she keeps getting sidetracked by people wanting to hear the 'finding Freya' story, 'from the horse's mouth', as it were.

'Well,' she shrugs modestly, this time to Gayle and Sofia, 'it's a funny thing, but I think I've always been a little bit psychic, and this morning, right from the word go, I just knew something odd was going to happen. I could almost sense it in the air.'

'You mean like danger,' interrupts Gayle, who adores anything to do with the supernatural and is forever consulting palm-readers who live in council houses just outside Croydon.

'Not exactly danger,' muses Alice, with a faraway look in her eye. 'More a feeling of expectation, but in some respects, yes, danger, although I'd call it a sense of trepidation.'

'Like before a French test?' ventures Sofia. This is a fantastic party – she's having a whale of a time drinking Bacardi and Coke and cadging Marlboro Lights off Gayle.

'Yes,' replies Alice, who despite wearing a calf-length khaki skirt and an XL rugby shirt is feeling slightly ethereal, as if her wrists may have shrunk and she has suddenly turned into something rather fragile.

'Anyway, late this afternoon I had this dreadful feeling of pressure in my head, just as the child went missing. I tried to ignore it, but by the time I got Sam, my youngest, off to sleep back at the apartment, I was in the grip of what I can only describe as a crippling migraine. I closed my eyes, and that's when I saw it – the lift behind the cart.'

'Fuckin' hell,' breathes Gayle, 'go on.'

'Well, it was strange, I felt compelled to go there – imagine! But with every step my head felt lighter and I knew someone was guiding me.' She chuckles at this point, at the sheer absurdity of her otherworldliness. 'Maybe Freya has a guardian angel. Anyway, I found the lift and, even though I am very phobic about confined spaces, I stepped in, and hey presto! Within seconds of pressing the button, there I was, walking down this magnificent hallway with a large wooden door at the end.'

'Then what?' Sofia and Gayle are bug-eyed with alcohol and intrigue.

'Well,' says Alice, trailing off a little. This is the bit where vagueness becomes paramount. 'It was open and I simply walked in and there was Freya, all snuggled up on the chaise next to a large stuffed fox, so you see I didn't really do very much at all.' She laughs mysteriously.

'Drink, madame?' Rosa is standing next to Alice holding a tray of champagne flutes. Alice allows herself just one more glass, she doesn't want to get too muddle-headed. After all, who knows when her special powers will next be required? How else might she be called upon to save the day? At a push she could perform a tracheotomy – she knows she has a number of biros in her handbag, should the need arise.

'So,' says Rosa, 'the door was open, yes?'

'Yes,' trills Alice, taking a sip of her drink. She doesn't like the way this woman is looking at her.

'How fortunate,' the woman mutters and, turning her back on

Alice, she heads over to Dieter and Peter, who are whooping it up in matching sarongs.

The Germans have already congratulated Alice, and in doing so informed her, with utter conviction, that they knew exactly how Joe and Nina were feeling this afternoon, because if anything ever happened to Herr Depp, their smooth-haired dachshund puppy, then they would jointly commit suicide.

'A dog is not a child,' Alice had remarked, smiling with benign condescension, thinking how ridiculous they look in their silly skirts.

Rosa knows that Alice's version of events smells fishy. She knows the prince's quarters were locked; she would stake her year's wages on it. She also knows that two-and-a-half-year-old Freya is not tall enough to reach either the buttons in the lift or the numbers on the combination panel. Alice is telling porky pastries. Rosa wouldn't put it past the woman not to have hidden the child herself. After all, she beats her own children. Who knows what she is capable of? No wonder her husband drinks like a trout.

But everyone else is happy with Alice's version of events, especially Alice, who, on this, her fourth glass of champagne, is revelling in her new 'third eye' status and has managed to convince even herself that she has always known, as far back as she can remember, that she was different.

'It wasn't just the adopted thing,' she is telling Lydia, 'there was something else, something special, but I didn't know what it was.'

Alice allows her eyes to well up at this point. It isn't hard. Thinking of her childhood is always like splashing her face with ammonia.

Lydia is looking for an escape route. Glancing over Alice's shoulder, she sees Guy putting his arm around Tabitha. The teenager immediately shrugs it off and Guy, left with no physical means of support, wobbles precariously before collapsing, his glass of champagne miraculously intact, to his knees.

There are mud stains on Guy's chinos. Fuck it, he can get some more. He shouldn't have touched the girl. He frightened her off. He was only flirting, just harmless stuff, silly girl – she'll learn one day. All the pretty ones turn into slags and all the ugly ones just get fatter and uglier and talk even more crap.

There will always be other more willing accomplices. He's realised that now. He's only been unfaithful to Alice with a couple of different women. Peanut, obviously – he made a mistake there, letting the little bitch get under his skin, he won't do that again. Fuck it, he'll stick to one-night stands, like that pissed blonde raver he picked up the night Alice had to go to hospital and she'd arranged for the boys to sleep over at the Clementses'.

From now on he's going to make up for lost opportunities. Guy feels omnipotent. Now that he has formulated a plan, he can get on with the rest of his life. I am reborn, he tells himself. I am the cuntmeister. If only his knees didn't feel like they'd slipped back to front – he's having a lot of trouble with his balance.

Helena and Charles are sitting on a wall. The twins are next to them, crashed out in the double buggy. Charles has never known Helena so contrite. He has had to be quite strict with her. 'You have to stop blaming yourself,' he told her, 'and you have to come down to the party, so put a nice frock on, wash your face, and I don't want any arguments.'

To his surprise, she'd done as she was told. 'I'm sorry, Charles,' she'd whispered as he'd zipped her into a raspberry-coloured dress.

Something has shifted in Helena. It's obvious in the way she is with the babies. We've got a chance, thinks Charles, and tentatively he reaches for his wife's hand and gives it a small squeeze. Helena clasps his hand as tightly as if it were a lifebelt. We can talk later, thinks Charles, and he clears his throat in relief. Looking up, he is suddenly aware that his eldest daughter is hovering a couple of feet away, staring intently at her parents. As their eyes meet, Sofia grins and winks.

We can be friends again, thinks Charles.

'Come on, you lot,' he says rather gruffly, 'let's get these kids to bed. Sofia, you can stay for another half an hour.' And Sofia astonishes everyone including herself by saying, 'OK.'

* * *

302

While Mr and Mrs Hart Jones push the double buggy back to the palazzo, Gayle and Jonty have sex over the ping-pong table in the tumbledown outbuilding.

'I've not been taking my pill,' admits Gayle, as her dearly beloved thrusts and grunts and the sea salt on the table crusts her sweaty backside as if her buttocks were precooked pork crackling.

'I know,' puffs Jonty. 'You want a kiddie, let's see if I can, ooooooh, well, let's just see, shall we, darling?'

Gayle is so thrilled she forgets to pick her knickers up. A size-twelve La Senza crimson thong lies like discarded bunting on the dusty floor.

'Listen, Jonty,' she says as they stagger out, 'if you really want, I'll take it up the bum for you.' She can't think of anything more romantic to offer him.

Hmm, thinks Jonty. He's not too sure. Bumming his Mrs has always been high on his Christmas wish list, but right now it doesn't feel quite right. 'Tell you what, make it a blow job in bed, first thing tomorrow morning.'

The party is winding down. Nina went up ages ago with Freya. 'Do you mind if she sleeps in our bed, Joe, just for tonight? I don't want to make a habit out of it, but . . .'

Joe understands. He doesn't mind. He wants her with them, they grow up so fast. He sits in a deckchair and watches Tabitha and Saul dancing with Dieter, Peter and Sofia. They are nice children. Freya is lucky to have them in her life. Hils has done a good job and he is grateful. Loving your children is easy, liking them is a bonus. Joe yawns, suddenly exhausted. With any luck they will all have a lie-in in the morning.

It's almost 11 pm. Alice has Sam over her shoulder in a fireman's lift. 'Max, Guy, we're going,' she trumpets, and as she turns to leave, Joe waves, but she pretends not to see him. There is something in her face. It could be embarrassment but it could be fury.

It's a combination of both. Alice has had enough. Guy has been showing her up all night, Sam has sat in a corner sulking, and as for Max, she's barely seen him. To add insult to injury, she's only managed a morsel of the barbecue. The least Guy could have done was arrange some supper for her while she held court. She'd seen Joe making sure Nina ate. Even that soppy Charles had organised a paper plate of chicken and salad for Helena, all nicely set out with a knife and fork wrapped up in a napkin. What had she had? An undercooked, overspiced sausage that Sam hadn't wanted.

She's not waiting any longer. There have been too many uncomfortable moments. The more wine people drank, the more they had started to wonder out loud how Freya had managed to operate the lift and how weird it was that the door had been left open. The evening had soured, as if the champagne had been switched from top of the range to something cheap and fake.

Checking to see that Max is following behind, Alice catches sight of Dieter and Peter, slow-dancing with their tongues down each other's throats. Yuk. Thank God there is only one more day of this ghastly holiday left to go.

Back in the apartment Alice insists that the boys clean their teeth. Both of them are like zombies and once they are in bed Alice finds herself picking up their discarded clothes. Out of habit she checks their pockets before chucking them in the 'to be washed when we get home' pile. She discovers a tiny crested silver sugar spoon in Sam's shorts. It's from the prince's apartment, obviously, and Alice immediately vows to bury it at the first available opportunity. In Max's jeans she finds a pile of chewing-gum wrappers (filthy habit) in one pocket and a size-twelve La Senza crimson thong in the other.

She knows it's a thong. She's read about them, and anyway she's seen one before: in the second drawer of Guy's desk, last half-term, when she'd taken the boys up to town and they'd decided to surprise Daddy by hiding in his office while he was at lunch.

Sam had a cold. 'Where are Guy's tissues, Penny?' Alice had shouted.

'Second drawer,' the old bat had replied, and then, after an ominous silence, by which time Alice had seen all she needed to see, 'Sorry. I meant top drawer.'

They'd left soon after. 'Are you not waiting?' Penny had asked, her head on one side in that irritating barn owl fashion of hers. 'Only he said he'd be back by two – though you know Guy!'

'Yes,' Alice had replied tersely, 'I know Guy.'

Alice has never worn a thong, but she is seized by a mad urge to try this one on. She's a size sixteen, but, damn it, it's elastic, it'll stretch.

She strips off in the bathroom. The lighting is cruel: her neck and chest are dark red but the rest of her is semolina-coloured. Her big ladies' pants balloon to the floor and she steps into the thong, yanking it over her thighs. She struggles to arrange the scrap of material over as much of her pubic hair as possible. She turns to peer over her shoulder. In the mirror she sees two matching dimpled pillows of flesh. So this is sexy, is it?

Alice's make-up bag is by the sink. Lying at the bottom is a ruby-red lipstick she bought when Sam played Rudolf in a religion-free Nativity play two years previously. Removing the lid she twists the lipstick out of its capsule and colours her nipples a deep scarlet. So this is sexy, is it?

Her hand is shaking as she draws the waxy stick across her mouth. Normally she wears a see-through gloss. That's if she can be bothered at all.

Now what? Hide!

Alice trots out of the bathroom and into the master bedroom. So what if she gets a bit of lipstick on the sheets? She's sure next door's are covered in much worse. Guy can't stay out much longer. She heard the metal shutter being pulled down over the bar five minutes ago, and all that she can hear now are the sounds of the staff clearing up: the sweeping of broken glass, the odd murmur of Italian. He'll be home soon, her idiot husband.

She must have fallen asleep, because when she wakes up, her mouth thick with champagne, she can feel him next to her, heavy as a sack of fertiliser, snoring like something out of a Hogarth print.

Alice slides down under the bedclothes. Fortunately Guy has forgotten to turn off the bathroom light, and even without her glasses she can just about see what she's doing. Guy is flat on his back, which makes finding his willy slightly easier. It's there between his legs, soft as margarine, all flopped over to one side.

Such a ridiculous object, that fleshy bit of plumbing. Women's bodies are so much more aesthetically pleasing. All one's bits are neatly tucked inside – unless one is wearing a thong, of course.

Alice positions herself halfway down the bed, sideways on, and buries her face in Guy's groin. It's as dry and hairy as Shredded Wheat, but as she slurps around, his penis involuntarily stiffens and he groans. Alice resists the temptation to snigger. It would have been nicer if he'd taken a shower. His cock tastes of soggy crisps, with a slight tang of the sea. Guy is stirring now, making little 'ung' noises. Alice brushes his belly with her rouged nipples, and he reaches for an uddery tit, the ung noises coming more rapidly and his penis now as erect as a dill pickle. Alice swiftly pulls the thong to one side and, with a hurdling action, she strad-dles her semi-comatose husband and inserts his penis into her vagina. She grips tight with her knees. It would never do to fall off, not now that she's got him.

Adopting a gentle bouncing motion, Alice allows herself a brief moment of pleasure. Ung, this is nice. Her breasts are swaying, the ruby nipples flying this way and that. 'Oh Peanut,' groans Guy, raising his hips to fit in with the rhythm. 'Oh Guy,' responds Alice, and even though she attempts a Mariella Frostrup-style huskiness, it still comes out sounding like a headmistress's admonishment.

Guy's eyes fly open. All he can see are two big red bull's eyes dancing in front of him. It takes him a while to work out that his wife is on top of him and her breasts are inches from his nose. He opens his mouth to say something, but Alice swiftly silences him with a 38 DD-cup. He can barely breathe. Locked in by flesh, he is ensnared in Alice's gargantuan human flytrap, and all the time she works his penis up and down with the full weight of her twelve-stone frame.

Guy is powerless. 'Fuck you, Alice,' he mumbles through his nipple and breast gag.

'No, fuck you, Guy,' she replies, and with one last bounce on his penis's head, hot cum spurts like a faulty water main into his wife's reproductive organs. Millions of sperm wriggle their way into Alice's nether regions and she wills them onwards and upwards. She has worked it out. Tonight is her baby-making night.

'You can call it a goodbye present if you like, Guy.'

What? Guy is repulsed. He is covered in Alice slobber. He feels like he's been sexually assaulted by an enormous golden Labrador.

My job is done, thinks Alice, and peeling off the thong she lies back in post-coital contentment. It's been an exhausting day, what with the weather and the abortive (don't even say that word, Alice) trip to the ruins, and all that crazy jumping in the sea. A child lost and a child found and at least five glasses of champagne followed by sexual intercourse – no wonder she's tired.

She shuts her eyes. It's important that she rests now. She positions a pillow under her feet, all the better to aid Sammy sperm on his journey to the fallopian tubes. Deep down she knows it will make no difference. She is pregnant, she's certain – cells will be dividing by morning. All she has to do is wait and get fatter and buy bigger bras and trousers with an expandable front panel and people will stand up for her on the bus and hold doors open.

How lovely it will be, muses Alice, imagining herself in the bath, a big pink island belly floating in front of her. She can feel it already, the wriggling and nudging inside. In approximately 266 days a child will be born. Florence, Chloe, Abigail? It will be a girl, of course it will.

Alice sleeps. She has no inkling that Guy is no longer by her side. She is alone again in the doll's house dream and the baby is crying. Only this time her porcelain legs have miniature joints and she can walk! Look at little doll Alice walking up the wooden stairs to the baby's nursery. Watch her pull back the blanket – what can she see?

Under the covers where once there was just a dried pea or a lost earring, there is a flesh-and-blood baby with a glittery pink hair-slide in her bright red hair.

47

At the End, In the Beginning

Guy crouches by the dimly illuminated pool. A ghostly yellow floodlight colours the water into apple juice – he is very thirsty. A bottle of beer left over from the party stands sentry on a nearby table. He reaches over and raises it to his lips. Too late, he realises that it is full of floating cigarette butts, filters swelling like tiny tampons. He spits out bitter black ash and wipes his mouth on his naked arm. He can smell Alice's saliva on his skin, taste its garlicky residue. She has covered him in her DNA.

Pulling himself to his feet, Guy is tempted to dive into the pool, but officially it's closed, and anyway Alice might hear and the thought of her marching out on to the balcony to tell him off makes his soul curl up. He'd be better off having a dip in the sea.

Weaving his way through the plastic bones of empty sunloungers, Guy blearily circumnavigates the pool before feeling his way barefoot down the rough wooden steps on to cold gritty sand. I'm very pissed, he realises, as the horizon tilts him off balance and his head spins.

Swaying, he pauses, looking into the enormous ink-pot sea. Above the black water, a heavy moon hangs bloated in the sky, a fat diva struggling to hold herself up while a thousand chorus-line stars dance around her. Tomorrow should be a nice day, he reckons, before remembering that tomorrow has probably already turned into today and Alice will be waiting for him.

Pug-faced Alice, with her horrible floppy tits, saggy belly and stale-milk thighs. Guy staggers slowly to the water's edge. Ideally he'd like to scrub himself down with a bucket of bleach and a wire brush.

He is tripping over seaweed now. The storm has churned up slimy green fronds. He needs to go further, beyond the seaweed and the rock pools, the detritus of plastic bags, out to where the water is deep enough to immerse himself fully.

He is utterly alone. Later this beach will be full again with nubile girls wobbling like tiramisu in rainbow-coloured bikinis, bossy fat-gutted toddlers and loud extended Italian families. Ha, families, and he thinks of his dead mother with her tinkling silver charm bracelet, her hair forever in a honey-coloured mid-eighties lacquered helmet. He pictures his father endlessly practising his golf swing in a neat back garden. For the first time in decades he remembers a rockery and an ornamental pond, orange fish, like giant tinned peach slices, slithering beneath the surface.

My father planted that rockery, he dug that pond.

The water is up to his waist now, rinsing away the goo of Alice. Guy relaxes his knees and allows himself to float on his back, his brain picking up signals of conversations he can barely remember having.

His sister Judy is telling him how her sons have finished university and are grown men now, making their own way in the world. One is a TV documentary producer and the other is a journalist. 'It happened so fast, Guy. They grow up so quickly. Blink and you'll miss it . . .'

But he can't hear her any more. Judy's voice has morphed into the flat vowel sounds of the girl he lost his virginity to. 'Is that it, 'ave yer finished?' Theresa Canning, a grubby girl with a salt and vinegar scent – her father owned the local chippy. It's like listening to a badly tuned radio: snatches of songs play and fade, Bowie and the Stones, his own clumsy attempts at acoustic guitar. Once upon a time I was going to be a rock star or a famous writer. Dreams just fell through my fingers. Whatever happened to the man I was going to be?

He is getting tired. He is becoming confused.

Stinky Patterson, his maths teacher, is telling him to turn over his exam paper. One moment he is sitting his A levels, struggling with Pythagoras, the next he is playing with Jimmy Atkins. They are mucking about on the bombsite where men in hard hats dig foundations for the new houses, and his mother is alive again and making spaghetti hoops on toast – 'Come on in before you catch your death' – and he is nine years old in front of the electric-bar fire watching *Crackerjack*, and so far nothing in his life has gone wrong.

Guy struggles to open his eyes. Above him is the galaxy and all around him is the sea. A minute star high above his head twinkles extra bright, as if fitted with new batteries, and he wonders where Peanut is and whether she is happy. After that he cannot remember anything, so he supposes he must have fallen asleep.

Peanut is in Manchester. Tommy has been called up to record the pilot for a new game show. They are staying at the Malmaison and everything including room service is courtesy of the production company. Suddenly Peanut wakes up. It's 1.30 am and she is lying in the damp patch. Tommy has hit the bottle again and he's pissed the bed.

While Peanut seethes in sodden sheets, a few miles down the M6 a woman with grey hair rolls away from her husband, gets out of her warm dry bed and creeps silently to the spare room. Breathing fast, she opens a drawer where a crocheted yellow cardigan lies buried in tissue and a little wooden box contains a single orange curl. Once a year she allows herself to do this, to stroke the silky lock and remember another middle-of-the-night moment, fifty years ago, when she gave birth to a baby, a beautiful red-haired baby girl. Oh Susannah. The grey-haired woman closes the drawer and sits for a while before making up her mind to get out her needles and buy new wool, in lilac or apple green. It's time she knitted something for her youngest granddaughter, for copper-headed Freya.

As she pads back to bed, another woman stirs. Hils can hear breathing from the pillow next to her head. For a moment she presumes it must be Mike, the cat, but there is no accompanying stench of minced tuna morsels. She opens one eye. Stan's black hair flops over his face, as soft as soot. She knows this for a fact, surprised it doesn't leave great smudges on her hands. His ears are perfect, flat against his head, but best of all, his penis, a perfect sushi roll between toffee-coloured thighs, has no whiff of Tupperware about it whatsoever. Hils grins, curls up closer to Stan and hopes that her breath won't smell in the morning.

In Los Angeles, a tiny tremor rumbles under the San Andreas fault, and in Sydney, hailstones the size of golf balls pound the Opera House. In Manchester, a wee-soaked Peanut gnashes. In Derbyshire, Marjory sifts through knitting patterns in her head, and in Stoke Newington, Hils secretly creeps to the bathroom and cleans her teeth.

But back in the deep black sea, Guy is oblivious to everything. To his wife Alice snoring contentedly, to his sons, Samuel William sucking on Cow's ear and Maxwell Thomas unknowingly growing his first pubic hair. Shhh, shhh, whispers the tide, and silently the earth spins on its ancient axis, weaving the night into day.

Epilogue

An early-morning jogger has found a body washed up on the beach at Santa Helena, limp and naked, hurled high on to the sand. Casually he lies alongside other storm debris: here a pant liner, a flipper, some cork and blue nylon string, there a drowned man.

Alice could have told Guy not to go swimming on a full stomach. In time, an autopsy will reveal his last meal to have consisted of sausages and chicken, bread and salad. As for the alcohol content in his blood, if he hadn't drowned he'd probably have died of alcohol poisoning.

A policeman called to the scene recognises the Englishman as a resident at the palazzo. He'd seen him yesterday when the little girl went missing, and now the man is dead and they must stop the local dogs sniffing at his corpse.

The palazzo is alerted and Lydia is instructed to break the news to Alice. 'Do I have to?' But the manager is insistent.

Lydia makes her way to the annexe. The weather is glorious again. The palazzo feels as though it has been spring-cleaned, waxed and polished, with air-fresheners plugged in at every corner, jasmine and pine.

Lydia knocks on the door of number 2, but nobody answers. Using her pass key, she enters the apartment. A discarded game of Snakes and Ladders lies on the table next to an unfinished glass of apple juice. There are towels on the bathroom floor, a blue toothbrush in the sink. None of the beds have been made and the sheets in the master bedroom are streaked red. Too bright for blood, thinks Lydia, relieved not to be finding any more bodies.

There was always something weird about this family.

The boys' room is a jumble of clothes, a pair of Digimon pyjamas and a water wing on the floor, a half-eaten biscuit on the bedside table. There is no one here.

Lydia exits and walks back along the path towards the main building, checking the swimming pool for a redhead, a skinny adolescent and a fat widow. Across the courtyard, where the fish refuses to stop dribbling, she decides to look in the restaurant. It's breakfast time, after all.

Hovering at the door, she surveys the tables. The pig twins are troughing in their highchairs, their parents talking earnestly over a pot of coffee. Dieter and Peter are at one of the side tables, dabbing at their moustaches with pristine linen napkins, and beyond them, at the back, in the corner, are the remaining Jamiesons, the newly bereaved Alice chewing contentedly.

Alice is eating breakfast with her two sons. In front of her is a pot of tea, a glass of freshly squeezed orange juice and a large mushroom omelette. Piled on to her side plate are several rounds of buttered toast, a brioche and a banana. After all, she is eating for two now.

'I wonder where Dad is?' ponders Max.

Alice says nothing, even though Max is talking with his mouth full. She is at peace now, her future is secure, her new best friend and ally is taking root in her womb. Everything will be put right with the birth of this child. It's a new beginning, that's what life is all about, beginnings and endings, they're happening all over the world. Alice hums, 'Hakuna matata.'

'Excuse me, Mrs Jamieson?'

Alice looks up and smiles.

To Antonia Hodgson for never giving up on me,
and to the Thompsons for *really* lovely times!